A Christmas Secret

Center Point
Large Print

Also by Katherine Spencer and available from Center Point Large Print:

The Way Home
All Is Bright
Together for Christmas
Because It's Christmas
Christmas Blessings

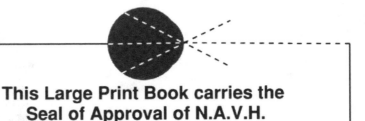

This Large Print Book carries the Seal of Approval of N.A.V.H.

Thomas Kinkade's Cape Light

A Christmas Secret

KATHERINE SPENCER

CENTER POINT LARGE PRINT
THORNDIKE, MAINE

This Center Point Large Print edition
is published in the year 2019 by arrangement with
Berkley, an imprint of Penguin Publishing Group,
a division of Penguin Random House LLC.

The text of this Large Print edition is unabridged.
In other aspects, this book may vary
from the original edition.
Printed in the United States of America
on permanent paper.
Set in 16-point Times New Roman type.

ISBN: 978-1-64358-092-0

Library of Congress Cataloging-in-Publication Data

Names: Spencer, Katherine, 1955- author.
Title: A Christmas secret : Thomas Kinkade's cape light /
    Katherine Spencer.
Description: Thorndike, Maine : Center Point Large Print, 2019.
Identifiers: LCCN 2018052809 | ISBN 9781643580920
    (hardcover : alk. paper)
Subjects: LCSH: Large type books. | GSAFD: Christian fiction.
Classification: LCC PS3553.A489115 C48 2019 | DDC 813/.54—dc23
LC record available at https://lccn.loc.gov/2018052809

To my nearest and dearest with all my love—
my husband, Spencer and my daughter, Kate.
And of course, sweet, silly Lily.

DEAR READER

AS A STORYTELLER, surprises are my stock-in-trade, an essential tool in my workbox. I can't imagine a truly good story without a few tossed in to befuddle and challenge my characters or delight them in some unexpected way. This book tells the story of a legacy and two generations during a Christmas past and a Christmas present. Martin Nightingale and his grandfather Walter each face their fair share of roadblocks and disappointments and are also delivered from their problems in astonishing ways.

But surprises don't always come in the form of a life-changing event, or even a beautifully wrapped gift. Sometimes, and far more important to me, surprises are invisible and happen deep inside a character's heart and spirit. My first job as a storyteller is to show ordinary people on their journey through our everyday world who arrive at unexpected insights, even revelations, deep within. People who come to see their life, and everyone in it, in a new light. People who are transformed, improved, and far wiser at the end of their travels because of the surprises they've encountered along the way.

Is there any better metaphor for Christmas morning? The world seemed little changed by the arrival of a tiny baby born in a stable to poor, obscure parents. But to those who truly saw and understood it, the moment was life altering. A quiet, almost invisible "plot twist" in the pages of history.

I hope the Christmas season, and every day after, brings only the kind of surprises that help you see the world through a lens of wisdom, gratitude, and joy.

Katherine Spencer

CHAPTER ONE

Thanksgiving Day, Thursday, November 22, 2018

Martin heard the siren coming up behind his car well before he saw the flashing lights. He was rounding a curve on the Beach Road, looking for the turn to the old house where his grandparents had once lived, the house that would soon be his. Right after the orchard, he recalled. Had he missed it? Maybe the orchard wasn't there anymore; he hadn't thought of that.

The scenery was distracting: woodsy stretches that opened to sweeping salt meadows, golden waves of tall, reedy grass that shimmered in the fading light of the November day.

He hadn't been to this place in over ten years—not for a real visit—and he recognized the views like old photographs discovered in the bottom of a drawer.

He had set the GPS on his phone for the route into town, but the cell service was iffy here and the signal kept drifting. Now he was lost and wondered if he should turn around.

The siren drew closer, commanding his full

attention, and a police car filled the rearview mirror. He pulled over to let it pass, but instead of flying by, the cruiser slowed and then parked behind Martin's SUV, the red light on top still flashing.

"Was I speeding, Milo? I don't think so." Martin turned to his traveling companion, who sat in the back seat.

The shaggy border collie mix leaned forward and nudged Martin's shoulder with his nose. The dog was pleased about the stop and eager to stretch his legs. The drive from Boston to Cape Light was at least two hours, and Martin could tell poor Milo was losing his patience.

"We'll be there soon, buddy. Let's see what this policeman has to say." It was almost dark out now and Martin watched the silhouette approach, backlit by the cruiser's bright headlights.

Milo stood up and wagged his tail. Martin glanced at him. "Let me do the talking, okay?"

The officer tapped on the window, and Martin quickly rolled it down. "License and registration, please."

"Sure . . . no problem." Martin looked up into a pair of startling blue eyes. A woman's eyes. He tried but couldn't hide his surprise.

He had a feeling she was amused by his response, though her stern expression did not alter. "Your license, sir?" she repeated.

"Absolutely. I have it right here . . ." Martin

fumbled with his wallet as his library and credit cards, gym membership, and other plastic rectangles spilled into his lap. He fished out the documents she wanted and handed them over. "I'm sorry. Did I do something wrong?"

"The radar showed you driving over sixty in a fifty-mile zone." She didn't sound as if she were accusing him; she was merely stating a fact.

"That fast? Really? I never saw a sign for the speed limit."

"I guess not." She checked his license, front and back, and glanced at him and then back at his photo, which had been taken a while ago, before he'd grown a beard. He noticed a nameplate on her jacket: OFFICER L. TULLEY. He wondered what the *L.* stood for but didn't think it was a good time to ask.

Though she was all business, he still couldn't help noticing that she was pretty. Very pretty, despite the bulky uniform—a heavy blue jacket, dark pants, and a peaked blue cap. Her hair was gathered at the back of her neck, under the hat, but the severe style brought her fair skin and fine features into even sharper focus. Like a portrait of a Victorian beauty.

She met his gaze again but didn't return the ID. A bad sign; she needed that to write a ticket. Some guys could talk their way out of a situation like this, especially with a pretty girl, but Martin knew he was not that sort and never would be. Efforts to disguise his innate shyness only made him seem reserved, even aloof. He wasn't really like that but knew it was the impression he made at times, and he couldn't quite help it.

"What brings you to Cape Light, Mr. Nightingale? Visiting for Thanksgiving?"

"I'm here on business. A few days or so." He kept his explanation brief. He didn't want to get into the details. He actually wasn't allowed to. "If you need to give me a ticket, Officer, I understand. But I really didn't see a speed-limit sign. I must have been distracted. I was looking for a turn."

She leaned closer to the window, about to reply, when Milo pushed his furry head out the window. He licked the police officer's chin and knocked off her hat. The officer jumped back with a shocked expression that made Martin bite back a smile.

"Milo, get down!" Martin turned and tried to grab the dog's collar.

The officer turned to pick up her hat, and Martin saw that her hair was clipped in a large knot. Loose strands curled around her face. Dark red hair, an unusual and striking shade.

"I'm so sorry." Martin turned to the dog. "Calm down, Milo. Sit back in your spot." He looked at the officer. "He's just too friendly sometimes."

"No harm done. I like dogs. My dog is even

more rambunctious." She adjusted her hat and didn't look quite so intimidating now.

"He's just restless. He's had enough of the car and wants to get out."

"Was he complaining a lot? Is that why you were speeding?"

He couldn't tell if she was joking. "I was wondering about directions. Isn't there a big inn around here somewhere? A friend told me about it," he added quickly.

"The Inn at Angel Island, you mean?"

"Yes, that's it." He remembered the place and had looked it up online. The website said they took dogs, too.

"It's not too far. Is that where you're staying?"

"I hope so."

"No reservation?"

"I didn't get a chance to call." Martin was usually much more organized when he traveled and rarely took a trip without knowing exactly where he would stay and how long he'd be there. But he had put this trip off a thousand times, dreading it. Until finally, it was just time to get up and go. He'd never expected rooms would be rare in this out-of-the-way place.

"I doubt the inn has any rooms tonight," she said. "They're always booked solid on a holiday. The Spoon Harbor Inn will be filled, too. There's a motel on the highway, before the exit."

He'd noticed that place, but it looked so dreary.

13

He had come all this way and had expected to stay in the village.

As if reading his thoughts, or maybe his disappointed expression, she said, "There's a guesthouse in town that might work out for you. It's very nice. A woman named Vera Plante runs it. She might even take a dog."

"That would be great." Maybe it was worth getting a ticket if it solved his hotel problem. Before Martin could ask for Vera Plante's phone number, Officer Tulley jotted a note on a pad. She handed the slip through the window.

Her small hand was very much at odds with her uniform. No wedding band or engagement ring. Though he wasn't sure why he noticed.

"Vera Plante, on Meadowlark Lane. Need directions?"

"I'll set the GPS. Did I miss the turn to Cape Light? I thought it was on this road somewhere."

"About two miles more. You'll see Potter Orchard on the left. It comes up after that."

"The orchard. Right. It's still there. That's good." He was talking to himself, but she heard him.

"The sign says 'Potter,' but new owners took over the business. Sophie Potter still lives on the property. Have you visited this area much?"

"Not at all. My first time." A bald-faced lie. But he had to remain anonymous. That was important. His attorney had warned him. Just his luck

14

that he hadn't even reached town and had to give out his real name. But it was unlikely that he and the attractive Officer L. Tulley would meet again. He was determined to be done with his business as fast as possible. A few days was all it would take, he hoped.

"My client mentioned the orchard." Another lie. If anything, he was the only "client" in this assignment.

She kept her eyes on him, studying him carefully. He wasn't sure she believed him, but she didn't ask more questions.

"Maybe I'll do some sightseeing while I'm here. I've heard it's a pretty place." He wasn't sure what else to say.

"I hope you do, Mr. Nightingale." She handed back his ID. "And while you're at it, watch your driving."

"I will, Officer." Was she letting him go? Just like that? "No ticket?"

Good going, Martin. Does she really need to be reminded? Maybe you should write one out for yourself.

Her blue eyes flashed with amusement. The start of a smile tugged the corner of her mouth. "I'll let you off with a warning this time. In the future, slow down."

He nodded respectfully. "Absolutely. Thank you very much."

He waited for her police car to pull away

before he steered his own car back onto the road, heading for the village.

"We wiggled out of that one." Martin glanced at Milo, who watched the road from his window. "Maybe knocking off her hat helped our case. In general, I doubt you should do that again."

Police officers were much friendlier here than they were in the city, he reflected. That was the way he remembered the place, though he wondered if it was just the lens of childhood coloring his memories in such a positive light.

His last visit to the town had been over ten years ago, for his grandfather's funeral. He had come down for the day from his boarding school in New Hampshire. His grandmother had died two years prior, and by that time, he had outgrown the long summer visits with his parents. His mother was gone by then, too.

But before those losses, he would travel on this road all summer long in the back seat of his grandfather's big, stuffy station wagon, the trunk loaded with beach chairs, umbrellas, and a huge cooler that took two to carry over the sand.

His grandfather drove so slowly, Martin could count the passing trees on the road side. The Red Sox were always on the radio. Martin recalled sticking his face out the window to catch the passing breeze until, finally, the ride ended, and the reward was worth all the bother—a long, golden day at Crane's Beach, sandy sandwiches,

16

naps in the shade of a huge umbrella, and, on the way home, an ice-cream cone that melted faster than he could lick the drips.

Other days were passed picking peaches or strawberries at Potter's and hunting for butterflies, hermit crabs, frogs, and salamanders in the boggy places behind his grandparents' house, which was set in a secluded spot on a large pond. At night he chased fireflies and kept them in a jar; in other containers, bright ladybugs and lazy caterpillars. His grandmother had an endless supply of jars and shoeboxes; she saved them all year for him. His mother was always excited to see the creatures he found, examining them curiously and never once flinching or even making a face. "That's a beauty, Martin," she would say. Though she did urge a "catch, observe, and release" philosophy.

Some days started in the cool dawn, sitting in a rowboat, rubbing sleep from his eyes while his grandfather carefully baited their fishing lines. At night, there were clambakes and bonfires, toasted marshmallows and stories whispered in the dark. Stories that started with goose bumps and ended with laughter.

He wondered what kind of shape the house was in now; if it was as roomy and interesting as he remembered. He would find out soon. He wondered what had become of his old room, the one his grandparents had kept especially for him. A cozy space with eaves in the ceiling and a big window over the bed where the fresh, salt-scented breezes blew in. Shelves filled with toys lined one wall—special toys his grandfather had made by hand. Martin spent rainy days in his grandfather's workshop, though he had never learned to be handy. At night, the toys seemed to come alive in the dark, but in a friendly, enchanted way.

As Martin got older, he realized how much his mother had loved that house and the long summer visits with her in-laws—maybe even more than his father had. Or maybe his father just took it all for granted because he had grown up there. His mother had no family of her own. Martin's grandparents had loved her like a daughter and had felt as if they had lost their own child when she died so suddenly. He could see now how the event had fractured the entire family and abruptly ended his childhood.

Once Martin's mother died, his father rarely returned to Cape Light. Martin was never sure why; they had never spoken about it. He guessed the memories were too painful for him. His own connection to the place had ended then, too.

Soon after his mother's death, his father sent him away to prep school, and his summers were spent at sleepaway camp or on teen trips. His father remarried quickly, settled in Arizona, and soon had a new family. Martin barely knew his stepmother and much younger stepsiblings. Visiting their home was like landing on another planet, a hot, sandy terrain dotted by cacti where he was a stranger with no hope of ever fitting in.

Of course, his father had invited him out West for Thanksgiving, as he always did on a holiday. An offhand, pro forma invitation he and Martin both knew rarely amounted to much.

Just as well. Martin needed to start his special project, one he could only take care of here, in Cape Light. Thanksgiving was a family day. Despite the good intentions and invitations of friends and coworkers, he was not comfortable joining a family gathering. He rarely celebrated holidays and barely noticed this one's passing—though he did enjoy roast turkey with stuffing and all the trimmings, and wouldn't mind such a dinner even if it wasn't homemade. Maybe after he found a decent place to sleep, he could find a restaurant that was still serving.

He hoped the guesthouse the officer had recommended would pan out, even for a night or two. He usually planned trips with little left to chance. This one had been put off for months. Martin had tried hard to avoid it altogether, but last week he'd learned that his legal attempts to maneuver around the terms of his grandfather's will had failed. His attorney had advised him to give up the fight. There was no choice other than to fulfill his grandfather's strange request—or

19

Martin's entire inheritance, a sizable sum, would go to charity. Finally, he had taken an extended leave from his job and forced himself to make a start.

His grandfather had been a charming, whimsical man. But the terms of his will pushed a joke too far. Martin simmered every time he considered the hoops his grandfather had set for him to jump through.

The speed of the car edged up again, and he made sure to slow down—just in time to spot the sign for Potter Orchard, a comforting sight. Moments later, he turned toward the village, and he was soon driving down Main Street. The quaint streetlights glowed in the early-evening light, and from what he could see, the storefronts looked unchanged from when he was a boy.

Village landmarks came into view—a movie theater, a bank, and a post office. The Clam Box Diner, still there but unfortunately closed. He looked for another place to eat or at least get a cup of coffee. A little café called The Beanery looked promising but that, too, was closed.

He gave up and headed for the harbor and the village green. He had to take care of Milo first anyway, before anything else. He parked alongside the deserted green. Soon Milo was tugging him along the well lit paths, past the old stone church. His grandparents had belonged to that church and had often taken him there for the

Sunday service, the only churchgoing he'd known. It looked exactly the same, he thought, the big gray stones untouched by the years or even the harsh winds that blew off the harbor.

Milo marched farther, dragging Martin along, sniffing in every direction, as if he had never been outside before. He scattered a pile of leaves with his muzzle before they rounded the gazebo.

Martin managed to dial the number Officer Tulley had given him. It rang and rang. Finally someone answered—a woman's voice, obviously that of an older person, but clear and strong. "Yes, this is Vera," she said.

Martin explained his situation and how he had found out about her guesthouse. "Officer Tulley gave me your name." *After she stopped me for speeding,* he could have added.

He was happy to hear that Vera did have rooms available and might accept the dog. "If he's a nice dog. Can you come in half an hour? My guests are just leaving."

Martin heard voices in the background and realized that he must have interrupted a Thanksgiving dinner. "I'm sorry for bothering you. I can come later if you like."

"Half an hour will be plenty of time for me."

Martin agreed to the time. He wasn't sure how Vera Plante was going to decide if Milo was indeed "a nice dog" but hoped his hound would do well on the interview.

Vera Plante's house was a short drive from the village. A good walk for Milo if it worked out. The house was nicer than he had expected, a large, well maintained Victorian set on a sloping lawn, slate-blue clapboard with white trim and black shutters. He wondered if he should leave Milo in the car, then snapped on the leash and let him jump out. It was best to find out straight off if the dog was unacceptable. That would save time for everyone.

"Be a gentleman, Milo. It's important," Martin whispered as they walked up the front steps. Martin was about to ring the bell, but the front door opened. A slim woman with a coil of silver hair on her head greeted him.

"You must be Mr. Hanson. Come in, come in."

Martin was about to correct her, then remembered he had given her a fake last name. "Please, call me Martin."

Mainly so I won't get confused, he wanted to add. But he had to carry out his task anonymously, as per the terms of the will, and the surname "Nightingale" was distinctive. It was certainly possible that someone would connect him with his family, especially someone older, though he guessed Vera to be at least ten years younger than his grandparents would have been by now. Either way, it was a risk he couldn't afford to take.

Martin led Milo inside, then stood by the front

door. "Thanks for letting me come by. I'm sorry to bother you on the holiday."

"No bother. My daughter and her family came up from Connecticut, but they needed to get an early start back. It all worked out." She turned her attention to Milo. "This is the dog?"

"Yes, this is Milo. I know he's big, but he's very gentle and friendly. And well trained," he added, though the point was debatable.

Vera looked down at Milo. Martin could see she was making up her own mind, despite his recommendations. She leaned forward and met the dog's questioning gaze. "Are you a nice dog, Milo?"

Milo panted and gave her a doggy smile. Then he lifted his chin and raised his paw. Martin was surprised. Where had he learned that?

Vera didn't seem surprised at all. She took the paw in her hand and shook. "How do you do?"

Martin smiled, feeling relieved. She was certainly eccentric, but his grandparents had been, too. Maybe it was something in the water around here. He would have to be careful.

Vera looked up at Martin. "I don't care for small dogs—usually too yappy. I like a more substantial dog that won't get underfoot."

"He never gets underfoot. And he rarely barks."

Finally, Vera gave Milo's head a pat. "All right, Milo. Let's see how it goes." She looked back at

Martin. "If you'd like to follow me, I'll show you the rest of the house."

"I would like that very much."

"You're welcome to use all the rooms." Martin saw a large, formal parlor to the left of the foyer and a small sitting room to the right. "There's a television in there, but I don't get many stations."

"That's all right. I don't watch much TV."

"Good for you. Mostly junk, in my opinion. Though I do enjoy those cozy British mysteries."

Martin could have guessed. "Yes, those shows are fun."

"The kitchen, of course." She led the way into a spacious kitchen with a black-and-white tile floor and old-fashioned wooden cabinets, painted white, many with glass doors. He remembered the same type in his grandparents' house and wondered if the room there had been changed.

"You can have a shelf in the fridge and store dry goods in this cupboard. The room comes with breakfast and dinner. But please let me know if you won't be taking a meal here."

"I certainly will." Breakfast and dinner? That would be convenient. Depending on Vera's cooking, he amended. He expected to stay here only a night. But maybe this place would make a comfortable landing spot until he was done with his task.

He followed Vera up a back staircase that led

from the kitchen to the second floor. She opened the first room on the long corridor, and he walked in, Milo softly padding behind them.

The doorway faced long windows covered with wooden shutters, closed now to the night. A small lamp on a bedside table cast a soft, warm light. He smelled lemon oil and fresh linen. There were a large bed, a night table, and an oak dresser. There was also a simple desk and chair set in front of the windows. The furniture was not new but gleamed with care. The fluffy pillows and dark blue quilt looked inviting.

"This looks very comfortable."

"I hope so. But if you need anything, I'm usually here. There's a private bath, right through there. You're the only guest right now, so it will be quiet."

He was pleased to hear that. The less small talk with strangers, the better. He asked Vera the rate and was surprised by the reasonable fee.

"That sounds fine. I'm happy to pay you in advance, Mrs. Plante. Extra for the dog, too. Or a security deposit of some kind?"

He doubted Milo would harm anything, but it might make his hostess feel more secure about taking them in.

"That won't be necessary. How long do you plan on staying, Mr. Hanson?"

Martin had to smile, hearing himself called by that name. "I'm not exactly sure. I'm visiting

25

town on business. It depends on how the project goes. I expect to be here a few days, possibly a week. And please, call me Martin."

"You can stay as long as you like. I was just curious. I'll leave a set of keys on the mail table near the front door. Is there anything I can get for you, or help you with?"

"I was wondering if you know of any place nearby where I can get something to eat. Even fast food would do. I saw one or two spots on the turnpike, but I'd rather not drive that far."

Vera looked shocked. "That awful stuff? Through a window? On Thanksgiving?"

Martin shrugged.

"I have plenty of leftovers. I'll warm a plate for you. If you'd like a turkey dinner, that is."

"I'd love a turkey dinner. But I hate for you to go to any trouble."

"No trouble. I wouldn't be able to live with myself, knowing you were eating fast food tonight when my refrigerator is bursting."

A dramatic reaction, Martin thought. And one that made him smile. "Well, thank you, Mrs. Plante. Really."

"Don't mention it. I have some scraps for my new friend, too. You bring in your bags. I'll let you know when the food is ready. And please call me Vera. Everyone does."

"Okay, Vera. I will." Martin thanked her again, and silently thanked Officer Tulley for directing him to such a comfortable place and such an accommodating hostess.

By the time he returned from his car, the house was filled with the mouthwatering scent of roast turkey and all the trimmings. Milo had waited for Martin by the front door as he came in and out, and now eagerly followed when Martin walked back to the kitchen. Vera stood at the stove, wearing an apron over her dress and a big hot mitt on one hand.

"Can I help?" Martin offered.

"You just sit down; everything is ready." Martin turned and saw the table set for one. He sat down, and Milo sat under the table, at his feet, his head on his paws.

Vera brought a platter of turkey and several delicious-looking side dishes to the table, including Martin's favorites: stuffing and cranberry sauce that looked homemade.

She glanced down at the dog. "Don't look so sad, Milo. I have something for you. Is that all right? Can he have some turkey?"

Martin nearly laughed at the question. "Sure, if you want a friend for life."

Vera returned to the counter and Milo followed. She set down a dish of turkey scraps, and the dog quickly cleaned it.

Martin started on his own dinner at a much more mannerly pace. "Everything is delicious," he said after a few bites. The compliment was sincere. Vera was a very good cook. He dipped his fork into the pile of tasty stuffing heaped on his dish. If he ate two meals a day here, he would have to find someplace to work out.

"Very kind of you to say. There's pie, too. When you're ready."

The teakettle whistled, and she poured the hot water into a waiting teapot. "Before I forget, I'm leaving the house early tomorrow. I'll put out breakfast for you before I go."

"That won't be necessary. I'll get something in town. I won't be hungry after this supper."

Vera looked satisfied to hear that. She took his dish and carried it to the sink.

"All right. But you'll find a pot of coffee. You can help yourself to anything else." She had fixed her tea and brought the cup to the table, along with Martin's favorite, a dish of pumpkin pie. "I don't normally go out early, but I'm on the decorating committee at church. We have a lot to do. Christmas will be here before you know it." She sliced a piece of pie and held it out to him. "Pumpkin? I baked it myself."

"I'd like some, thanks." He took a bite, savoring the pie's spicy custard. He knew pumpkin pie could be made year-round, but it seemed wrong to eat it anytime but the fall.

Vera had served herself a slice, too. "We're a small congregation but everyone does their part. There's so much going on this time of year. I don't know how we get it all done, but somehow—with a little help from above—we do."

"Is there a special service or something for Christmas?" He wasn't that interested; he asked only to be polite.

"That's just the sprinkles on the whipped cream. First, there's the Advent party, and then the Christmas Fair. Quite a production and a big fund-raiser. The whole town shows up. Most of the money we raise goes to families who don't have the means for Christmas gifts or even necessities. You'd be surprised to learn how some are struggling," she added. "There's also a pageant on Christmas Eve, and the Christmas Day service, of course."

"That is a full schedule. Do you work on all those projects?"

Vera waved at him. "Of course not. I'd be run ragged. I help where I can. Some years more than others."

Martin wasn't listening that closely to the laundry list of church events, but the mention of families that needed financial help snagged his attention. Wouldn't a minister be able to help him fulfill the terms of the will? And be happy to do it, too?

"Is your church in the village, Vera?"

"The old stone church on the green. You can't miss it. It's a real landmark, built in the seventeen hundreds when the area was first settled. You should take a look inside sometime. The stained glass windows are real works of art."

"I know that church." The words slipped out before he could catch himself. Martin avoided her surprised expression, wondering how to cover up.

"Do you? So, you've been to Cape Light before. I didn't realize."

He shrugged. "I drove around the village before I came here. I took Milo for a walk around the village green."

"Oh, I see." She didn't seem suspicious of his clumsy cover-up. "I grew up in the village, so I'm not going to tell you how long I've been a member there. My husband, Lester, did, too. Detweiller was my maiden name. My husband's father ran a print shop in town, and Lester took over the business soon after we got married. That was quite a while before Reverend Ben came. He was called to the church about nineteen seventy-eight, I think."

Martin took the last bite of his pie. "That is a long time. I bet you know the whole congregation."

Vera shrugged. "I suppose I do. Though there are always young families coming in. That's nice to see. And some who move away, of course. Or some who just grow old and fade away," she added with a sadder tone. She sighed and smiled again. "I'm not in that category yet, thank the Lord."

Martin had to smile at her plucky spirit. "Not at all. Not even close."

Vera must have known his grandparents, he realized. If not personally, she would certainly remember them by name. They had been very well-known in town and very active in the church. So many had attended his grandfather's memorial service; every seat had been filled.

He wondered if Vera had been there. He wondered if he had met her at church when he was a boy. But the chances that she would recognize him after all this time were slim to none, he reasoned. Especially since she didn't know his real last name.

"Reverend Ben talks about retiring," she continued, "but he never makes any plans. I would miss him very much. He's not all preachy like some ministers, but his sermons always leave you with something worth thinking about."

"He must be a good minister if your congregation has kept him around that long."

Vera laughed. "Very true. Would you like to come to the service on Sunday? You might enjoy it."

The invitation caught Martin by surprise. Vera was so welcoming and generous, it was hard to refuse. But the idea of going to church seemed so foreign and out of his routine. She may as well have asked him to the North Pole.

31

"Thanks. I appreciate that . . . Let's see how it goes?"

She didn't seem put off. He was glad of that. He didn't want to insult her. He could see she had a good heart and meant well.

"More pie, Martin? Maybe some tea?"

Martin smiled and shook his head. "I've had plenty of everything. It was all delicious." He rose and picked up their plates. "I can clean up. I bet you didn't expect to serve another Thanksgiving guest today."

"I did not. But that's what the holiday is about. To be full of thanks and be giving, right?"

Martin liked the way she phrased it. "Very true. That's why I should help you now."

Vera smiled and picked up her cup. "If you like. I'll take my tea into the sitting room and read awhile. If you need anything, let me know."

Martin assured her he would be fine and said good night. He put the dirty plates and silverware in the dishwasher and wiped the counters and sink. Then he took Milo out for a short "nightcap" walk.

Up in their room, he closed the door and unpacked his bag. He hadn't brought much. Some casual clothes and his notebook computer and some books. A sports jacket and tie, just in case. In case of what, he wasn't sure.

He set his laptop on the desk and arranged the pile of books on the nightstand: one or two new titles he had just started and a few long-standing favorites he read over and over again.

He rarely traveled without books. Real books that he could hold in his hand and jot a note in the margin or quickly page through to find a favorite passage. He had tried e-readers, but he liked the feeling and even the smell of a real book. There had been hundreds of books in his grandfather's house, lining specially made shelves that stretched from the floor to the ceiling. His grandfather never had the chance to go to college but had always loved to read and was more literate and widely read than anyone Martin had ever met.

Martin mostly read at night before he went to sleep. The truth was, he could easily get lost in a book any time of day and sometimes thought all he would do was read if given the choice. Books had always been his most trusted and reliable companions. They had never let him down.

Tonight, the good food and long drive left him drowsy. He stretched out on the bed, and as if mirroring his movements, Milo stretched out on the rug and gave a deep sigh.

"It's been a long day, Milo," Martin said.

And an emotional one, he silently added. Just thinking of the job that lay ahead made him feel drained and daunted. How would he manage it? He would never collect his inheritance. It would all go to charity. But he had to try.

The terms of the will said he had to make anonymous gifts to residents of Cape Light, totaling $150,000. Donations could be made to charities or schools, but no more than 20 percent, or $30,000. The rest of the funds, $120,000, had to be gifted to individuals or families by Christmas Day and totally anonymously.

Martin had no qualms about donating the money, even such a large sum. He was not materialistic and had simple needs. He did want to gain his inheritance, but had no interest in buying fancy cars or even investing. He saw his grandfather's gift as a ticket to his freedom, a path to a new life. He was only twenty-five, or would be in January. But sometimes he felt fifty-five, like a man who had reached a midlife crisis. He had only been practicing as a tax attorney for a few years, but already knew the field was not for him. He felt as if he was drifting, with no good reason to get up in the morning, except to take care of Milo. He needed to hit some hidden reset button and get his life going in a more positive, fulfilling direction. He wasn't sure yet what he wanted to do but felt sure his inheritance would give him the breathing room and resources to figure it out.

But first, he had to give a chunk of it away by Christmas. Martin had looked at the question from many different angles but had little notion of how to find people who needed his help.

Finally, his conversation with Vera had sparked

an idea. He could start at the church and speak to the minister.

Reverend Ben would have been at the church when Martin was a boy. Martin could vaguely recall him—his beard, glasses, and friendly blue eyes. He could also recall daydreaming through the whole service, wishing he was already on the playground or gobbling up a burger and fries in the Clam Box, where his grandparents would take him for lunch.

He felt encouraged. He had mulled over this problem for weeks and had never thought about walking into a church and speaking to a minister.

He grinned at the dog. "This idea could solve everything, Milo. If all goes well tomorrow, you'll be back in the dog park on Commonwealth in no time."

CHAPTER TWO

Friday, November 23, 2018

T HE TRICKY PART OF HIS PLAN WOULD BE avoiding Vera. Martin considered the problem as he walked into town with Milo on Friday morning. He wondered how long Vera's committee would be working at the church. If she caught sight of him there, he was sure she'd be delighted. But then she would wonder why he was requesting a private meeting with the minister.

From what he knew so far of his landlady, she'd ask a lot of questions and he would be in the position of making up a story. Another story. Vera was a nice person, and he didn't feel comfortable misleading her. Even giving her a false last name didn't rest easily on his conscience. It was better to avoid Vera altogether this morning. Not just better; imperative.

That was another thing about fulfilling the terms of the will. Martin was a naturally private person. But traveling under an alias and misleading people about his purpose here seemed much more to him than simply being private. It seemed duplicitous. And he had never been good at keeping secrets. For one thing, there was so little about his life that was interesting enough to hide. For another, he hoped this problem would be resolved quickly.

They reached the village green, and Milo tugged him down a path along the harbor, delighted to be back in his new "happy place." As Milo intently sniffed the ground and scanned the area for geese and squirrels, Martin checked the parking lot behind the church. He saw several cars, Vera's dark green sedan among them, with its unmistakable bumper sticker: I'D RATHER BE KNITTING.

Now he had to wait until the coast was clear. Luckily, he had brought a book. He found a bench a safe distance away, looped Milo's leash around a wooden slat, then settled down to read. Milo sat at his feet and watched the gulls swooping over the bay. The weather was mild for late November, and they had found a sunny spot; Martin thought they could sit there all day if necessary.

A few moments later, it was apparent that Milo did not share the thought. He jumped up, barking, then charged off. The leash slipped from the bench with barely a tug. Martin looked up, unsure of what was happening, and saw his dog already halfway across the green. Milo's prey, a large squirrel, scampered just a few feet ahead.

Martin shouted for the dog as he dropped his book and chased after them.

LOUISA DIDN'T TAKE MANY BREAKS DURING her shift; she was usually too busy. But this morning, instead of eating a snack in the police car, she parked at the green to stretch her legs and get a breath of air.

She soon heard shouting. "Milo, come! Come back, Milo . . . Bad dog . . ."

The voice sounded familiar and she immediately recognized the dog bounding in her direction, the trailing leash a telltale sign of an unauthorized adventure.

"Milo . . . here, boy. I have a treat for you." Louisa reached into her pocket and took out a sandwich bag, then crouched down and held out a cracker.

The dog looked at her, gazed back a moment at its target—a fat, gray squirrel that darted under a bush—then changed course and ran toward her.

She nearly fell over as Milo gobbled up the offering then quickly licked her cheek. She grabbed the leash and stood up, immediately face-to-face with the dog's owner, Martin Nightingale. Dark brown eyes peered out from his bearded face. His cheeks were red and he was out of breath. He looked surprised to see her, but pleased and also embarrassed.

She handed over the leash before he could

speak. "No loose dogs on the green, Mr. Nightingale. Did you miss another sign?"

His eyes grew wide with surprise. Then he realized she was teasing. "He's wearing a leash. I just wasn't holding it. I'm going to blame it all on the squirrel. How much willpower is a dog supposed to have?"

The question made her smile. "All right, I'll let him off with a warning this time." She deliberately echoed their conversation of the night before and could see that Martin remembered.

"Thanks. He'd have to pay the fine in dog biscuits, and he hates that."

She laughed and he looked pleased. She liked a guy with a sense of humor, especially the dry, offbeat kind.

"By the way, thanks for recommending Vera Plante. The room is very comfortable, she likes Milo, and she even gave me a turkey dinner."

Louisa was glad to hear that her suggestion had worked out.

Martin Nightingale seemed very intelligent but a little lost in some way that was hard to put a finger on. And why was he eating a Thanksgiving dinner at a guesthouse? Didn't he have a family?

Slow down with the questions, Louisa. I know it's your business to be curious about people, but sometimes it gets out of hand.

"I'm glad it worked out. Will you be in town very long?"

Martin shrugged. She noticed his glance slide away, as if the question made him anxious. "Hard to say. Only for a few days, if things fall into place."

His vague reply only made her more curious. "What sort of work do you do?"

"I'm a tax attorney."

"That sounds interesting." It probably was, to some people, though it was not a job she would ever want. She had just said that to be polite.

He seemed to guess her true feelings. "Oh, sure. But funny how you don't notice any TV shows about tax attorneys. Though there must be a million about police officers."

She laughed. "The TV crews haven't landed in Cape Light yet. On the other hand, you never know what the day will bring."

"Very true," he said, but seemed to be saying, *Who would guess I'd meet up with you?*

He met her glance and held it, and she felt something in her heart flip. She could not deny that yesterday, she'd found him attractive, but she had learned to shut down her personal side while carrying out her job. Today, in the broad sunlight, and mostly off duty, she found him genuinely handsome.

The radio clipped to her belt crackled and snapped her brain to attention. She picked it up, listened to the dispatcher, then replied, "Got that. I'm on my way."

"I've got to go. There's a fender bender on Highland Street." She glanced at him over her shoulder as she headed back to the police car. "See you around, Martin."

"Sure, see you." He smiled, with Milo sitting beside him, panting and offering a doggy smile. They made an appealing pair, she decided.

Louisa hoped she would see Martin around town again. But if he was only staying a few days, maybe not. That wasn't much time, which was a shame. More than his looks, there was something about him that got to her. Maybe because he was a little shy, and seemed a bit unsure of himself, unlike the alpha types she worked with and sometimes dated. Martin Nightingale wasn't anything like that, which suddenly seemed to Louisa a good thing.

MARTIN WATCHED OFFICER TULLEY DRIVE away and suddenly realized he didn't even know her first name. She must think he was such a dolt for not asking, but she had caught him by surprise. He felt fortunate that he had been able to carry on a somewhat coherent conversation. She was clever and fun to talk to and even prettier than he remembered. But another voice warned him to avoid her. Hiding his real purpose for being in town would be harder with a cop than someone like Vera. Much harder.

He wound Milo's leash around his hand and

walked back to their waiting spot. Just as he reached the bench, he spotted Vera's decorating group, working outside. Three women and two men were fastening a huge wreath to the big wooden doors at the front of the church. He recognized Vera, and one of the men wore a clerical collar under his coat. That had to be Reverend Ben. The other man was dressed in a plaid wool jacket and light gray pants. Martin figured he was probably a church sexton or a handyman. He stood on a ladder, adjusting the position of the wreath while the women directed him. He looked a little old for climbing ladders, Martin thought. But, with the minister's help, the task was soon done.

Martin waited, wondering what would happen next. Maybe decorating took all day and he needed to return tomorrow? But a few moments later, he saw the women saying good-bye to the minister and then heading off to the parking lot.

The handyman folded up the ladder and carried it back into the church while the minister, finally alone, stepped back to admire the wreath. Martin saw his chance and quickly approached, tugging Milo along. "Excuse me . . . are you Reverend Ben?"

The minister turned. "Yes, I am. Reverend Ben Lewis."

"My name is Martin . . ." Martin wondered if he should give his real last name or his fake last name. Finally, he offered no last name at all. "Could I possibly have a word, sir? It won't take very long. I think you might be able to help me. And maybe I can help you," he added.

The minister looked surprised—and curious, Martin thought.

"Come inside, Martin. We can speak in my office. I'd be happy to help, if I can." He pulled open the door then glanced at Milo. "Your dog is welcome, too."

Martin was grateful. He had been expecting to have to bring Milo back to Vera's and arrange to come back later. But now the minister led them into an office where a secretary was typing on a computer. A bulletin board covered one wall, and below that, a copy machine hummed along. A poster behind the secretary's desk showed a photograph of the ocean. The caption read, *Do not fear, for I am with you. Isaiah 41:10.*

The secretary looked up as they walked in. "You have a meeting with Emily Warwick at two, Reverend. About the fair. You asked me to remind you."

"Thank you, Mrs. Honeyfield. Please hold my calls for a while."

He opened the door to his office and stepped aside to allow Martin and Milo to walk in first. A desk sat on one side of the room, next to large windows. There were a couch and two chairs closer to the door. Reverend Ben sat on the couch and Martin chose an armchair. Milo settled at his feet.

"So, how can I help you, Martin?" Reverend Ben met Martin's gaze with a look that was open and relaxed, though definitely curious.

Martin hesitated. "Thank you for seeing me. I'm not sure where to begin. I assume whatever I tell you will be held in the strictest confidence?"

"Of course. That goes without saying."

Martin took a breath. "Let me start with my last name. My real last name. It's Nightingale. But I've been using the name 'Hanson' in Cape Light."

"And why is that?" The minister's tone was not disapproving or judgmental. Just interested to know the reason.

"Because of my grandfather's will. Walter Nightingale. He lived in this town all his life. My grandparents belonged to this church. Maybe you remember them?"

At the mention of his grandfather's name, Reverend Ben sat up sharply. "Of course I do. Your grandparents were wonderful folks. Everyone loved them. Big benefactors to the church, and very generous to everyone," he added. "They owned a toy store on Main Street. It was closed by the time I arrived, but people still talk about it. It was very well-known."

"Yes, he was a generous man," Martin agreed. "The very definition of it."

"The Nightingales had a son, Thomas," Reverend Ben recalled. "Is that your father?"

Martin nodded. "Yes."

The minister's expression grew bright with recognition. "I remember you now. You used to come to visit in the summer with your parents, when you were a little boy."

"That's right. You have a good memory," Martin added, surprised to be remembered. "I haven't been back for a real visit in about ten years."

The reverend shrugged. "This congregation is my family, you might say. You don't forget family members, even over time and distance. I must have seen you when your grandparents passed away?"

Martin knew that Reverend Ben had presided over both memorial services, first for his grandmother, and soon after for his grandfather. Both services had been held at this church, his grandparents buried side by side in the church cemetery nearby.

"Yes, I came back both times. My grandmother passed away when I was thirteen, and my grandfather not long after that. Almost ten years now."

"I'm sorry I didn't recognize you," Reverend Ben said sincerely.

"I didn't think you would. I've changed a lot since I was a teenager. Thank goodness," he

45

added with a self-deprecating grin. "The thing is, according to the terms of my grandfather's will, I can collect my inheritance next month, on my twenty-fifth birthday. But only if I fulfill some very strange and ironclad terms."

"What sort of terms? Can you tell me?"

"Happy to. This is where I think you can help, Reverend. You already mentioned my grandfather's legendary generosity. According to his will, I need to give away one hundred and fifty thousand dollars. I can give some of the money to charities and worthy causes. But most of it must go to residents of Cape Light, to families or individuals"—Martin paused, trying to recall the exact words—"'who face a pressing financial burden and are not likely to find help through other sources. The money must be dispersed, without too large a sum going to any single person.' And I need to do this all anonymously. By Christmas."

Reverend Ben sat back. "That is a unique request. Your grandfather was very creative. I'm remembering that now."

"Yes, he was," Martin agreed, though in this situation, he didn't find any charm at all in his grandfather's whimsy.

"So basically, he's asking you to be a Secret Santa, on a very large scale. An interesting quest. One that could be very gratifying."

"It could be," Martin agreed. "Though I have

to be honest, Reverend. To have the job forced on me this way, well . . . I don't see it as interesting or even gratifying. More like I've been commanded to jump through a lot of hoops to earn what should be rightfully mine."

The minister's expression softened. "I understand that you might feel that way. The gift from your grandfather, held out like a carrot on a string. Is that it?"

"Something like that. Please don't misunderstand. I'm grateful that he's left me anything. He didn't have to. It could have all gone to my father. And I'm not materialistic, honestly. I really don't mind giving some of it away. I just don't know how," he admitted. "Granddad was so friendly and open. He loved talking to strangers. It came naturally to him. He could find out a person's entire life story waiting on line at the grocery store."

Reverend Ben laughed and nodded, remembering. "Walter was like that. Exactly."

"But I didn't inherit that trait. Not at all. Maybe Granddad thought this would be an easy assignment. But I have no idea how to identify people who need these gifts. It seems impossible to me. That's how I thought you could help. Vera Plante mentioned that your church finds families who need support at Christmas to buy gifts for their children, or even to cover basic necessities. If you could let me know which families in town need that kind of help, I'd happily give them gifts from my inheritance . . . and, with any luck, be done with the job quickly."

"I see." Reverend Ben met his gaze. "I wasn't sure before how you thought I could get involved. Yes, there are families in the congregation and throughout the town whom we help at Christmastime. I suppose I could do some research and give you a list."

Martin's heart jumped with joy. And relief. "That would be wonderful. That would be perfect, Reverend."

"Would it, Martin?" The minister's serious expression dampened Martin's hopes. "Do you think this is how your grandfather wanted you to carry out his wishes? If I simply hand you a list of names, do you think that's in keeping with the spirit of his request?"

Martin could tell by the minister's expression that he certainly did not—though he didn't understand the objection.

"The will doesn't specify how to find the people or families," he explained. "There's an executor, one of my grandfather's lawyers. I can call him and find out if this would be an acceptable way for me to distribute the money. If he gives his approval, will you help me then?"

"I'm not sure." Reverend Ben looked like he wanted to help but still had reservations. "I understand your challenge. I really do. It is an extraordinary request, and there's nothing I can think of in the typical person's life that would prepare one for the task. But I must be honest with you, Martin. Having known your grandfather and the way he lived his life—and hearing what you've told me about yourself—I don't think I should get involved. I'm sorry, but I don't feel I should help you. Not in the way that you're asking."

"I don't understand. I could help so many people in your congregation. In your community. Why would you knowingly pass on a chance to do so much good?"

"I don't see it that way, Martin. I hope you will still help many in this town, as your grandfather asked you to do. But I don't think having a minister—or a social worker or our mayor or anyone—hand you a list of names is what your grandfather wanted to happen when he wrote his will. I think this task is hard because he didn't want it to be easily accomplished."

Martin felt so frustrated, he couldn't reply.

Reverend Ben met his gaze, then continued, "I'm sure it feels as if I'm making it even harder. The thing is, it's not important who *I* think needs the help. *You're* the one who has to decide. Who has to be inspired to help. You're the one who has to feel sympathy, even empathy, for someone else's plight and feel moved to ease their burden. Once you find someone with 'a real and pressing need,' won't it be satisfying to know that you can help them? That you can make a difference in their life?"

Martin tried to put his frustration aside. He could see the minister's point, though he didn't agree with it.

"I guess so, when you put it that way. But as I just told you, I'm not what you'd call a people person. I'm afraid I won't be able to find the people who need help."

"I understand. I was not always a 'people person,' as you say. In fact, I was horribly shy. Terrified to put myself forward or be the center of attention. To meet new people or speak in front of a group paralyzed me with anxiety."

Martin could not believe this description. Especially since Vera had praised Reverend Ben so highly. "If it was as bad as all that, I find it strange that you chose to be a minister."

"That's the point, Martin. I didn't choose to be a minister. It chose me. I was called. Just like you have been called, by the terms of this will. That's the way it goes with my job—and many jobs we have to do in life. I had to figure out how to make it work. How to face a church full of congregants, waiting every Sunday morning for pearls of wisdom to drop."

Reverend Ben smiled, and Martin did, too, though he still didn't believe Reverend Ben had been as shy as all that. "Vera says you give excellent sermons. 'Not preachy like some ministers,' she told me. But you always offer something interesting to think about."

"What a nice compliment. Thanks for passing that along. I will tell you my secret. How I overcame my shyness, my tendency to keep a comfortable distance from people, though I like people well enough. Isn't that what you're talking about?"

Martin nodded. "That's it exactly."

"First of all, what is shyness? Are some people just born that way? It's their temperament, personality, in their DNA like indelible ink? I think that's partly true. But only partly. Eleanor Roosevelt was a naturally shy person but overcame it. 'You must do the thing you think you cannot do,' she said. I'd heard that often, as I'm sure you have, too."

"I have. It didn't help much."

"Point taken. Easy to say, hard to do. I think my shyness was partly a safety mechanism," Reverend Ben confessed. "Something, somewhere had taught me it was safer to avoid attention. To avoid being judged. To keep my opinions and ideas to myself. If you know what I mean."

"I do." Martin could think back and find reasons why he'd learned to keep his opinions to himself. To avoid criticism and being judged. He felt his heartbeat quicken just talking about it.

"You don't need to tell me where or why you learned to be shy. But perhaps it happened that way for you, too," Reverend Ben said. "That strategy has probably served you well. But at this point in your life, it's not helping. It's like a heavy overcoat in the middle of the summer. You don't need it anymore. You can take it off and put it aside. You'll be perfectly fine," he promised.

"Perhaps," Martin agreed, though he didn't really think so. He could see the reverend's point. But he wasn't sure the simple advice would work for him.

"It's something to think about. To try, little by little. But another thing I discovered is probably even more important."

"What was that?" Martin asked, curious despite his pessimism.

"Very simple. I learned that my shyness and private nature were not very much in the big picture. God had called me for truly important work. How much did my shyness matter in comparison to that? Not much at all. I learned to put myself aside and focus on the job I had to do. On the mission and message I promised to deliver. That's when it got easier. A lot easier."

"I'm thinking about myself too much? Is that what you mean?" It was an uncomfortable truth to face, but Martin felt the minister would give him an honest answer.

"We've only just met and I don't mean to

presume. But you don't strike me as a selfish or vain person. I think you truly want to carry out your grandfather's wishes, but you're scared. You don't feel equipped to do the job. You focus on what you lack, instead of on the resources you do have. Abundant resources that only need to be strengthened, like unused muscles."

"That might be true," Martin allowed. "But you're saying to just bite the bullet. March on?"

"More or less. I'm not a big sailor, but living in this town, I find myself on a boat from time to time. They say when you're seasick to look out at the horizon and stop thinking about your queasy stomach. Get the big picture, Martin. Try not to think about yourself or even about what other people might think of you. Your grandfather entrusted you to fulfill his final wish. Focus on how much that meant to him and how proud he would be to see you carrying out this assignment. Focus on all the good it will do, lifting so many problems and worries, and bringing so much unexpected joy to people that you don't even know."

Martin sighed, unconvinced but knowing that the minister made good sense.

"I know you see it as an onerous task," Reverend Ben continued. "I understand why. But it's a task your grandfather planned with love in his heart; love for you and all the people you can help."

Martin considered Reverend Ben's words. There was a lot of truth and insight there. "I do have a dread of it, I have to admit. The stipulation seems very strange to me. Even arbitrary. But the way you frame it, I see it differently. I think I can understand why he asked me to do this."

Reverend Ben's face lit with a smile. "That's good, Martin. That's the first step, isn't it?"

"I guess so." He did feel more confident that he could do it. Or, at least try. "But I'm still not sure where to start."

"Get to know the people in our community. Live with your eyes open. And your heart. Watch and listen. I think you'll soon discover that there are so many people who can use your help, who are dealing with problems that will touch your heart."

"You make it sound easy, Reverend. I'm not sure it will be all that simple."

"I don't mean to dismiss your concerns, honestly. But I do believe that once you try, once you take a step or two in that direction, it will get easier every day if you stick with it."

"You sound like a fitness trainer. No offense," he added quickly. Martin didn't mean to be sarcastic and was glad to see the minister smile.

"No offense taken. The comparison is apt. You're just working on a different set of muscles. Your spiritual muscles. If you haven't used them lately, it will feel uncomfortable at first. But if you work out every day, you'll reach your goal. I guarantee it."

Would he ever be comfortable talking to complete strangers? Martin wondered. Getting to know the personal concerns in their lives? The minister seemed to think so.

"Thank you for your time, Reverend Ben. Thank you for hearing me out. I'm going to think about all you said. Not just think," he added, correcting himself. "I do enough of that. I'm going to take your advice."

"That's the spirit, Martin. You're on your way. I'll be very interested to see how this all turns out. I'm always here if you want to talk again. Anytime."

"Thanks. I'll keep that in mind."

The minister offered his hand and Martin shook it, feeling grateful and encouraged. The minister had not fallen in line with his plan. Not in any way. But talking things over so honestly, and expressing his fears and doubts with someone who listened without judging him, had been a great and very unexpected relief. Reverend Ben had helped him see the situation from a whole new perspective, and that made a huge difference.

Milo had been very well behaved during the meeting, lying quietly at Martin's feet. But once they were outside, walking along the harbor, Martin could see that the big dog was relieved to be in the fresh air and sunshine. It felt good to Martin, too. He cleared his head with deep breaths as they walked into the breeze that blew off the choppy waves.

"I need to get myself out of the way, Milo, and focus on the job I have to do. It's as simple as that."

Milo barked, pulling on his leash, then lunged at the seagulls who were battling in midair for a bit of fish that one held in its beak. Martin had to laugh at the dog's optimism.

I could use some of that optimistic energy, Martin thought.

As he'd told Reverend Ben, the next step was to stop thinking about it so much and just get to work.

REVEREND BEN TOOK A SEAT BEHIND HIS desk and stared down at the work he needed to do. There was the rough draft of a sermon to polish, an agenda for the Christmas Fair committee meeting, and so many letters and emails to answer. The paperwork, he corrected himself. His real work was helping people, like his unexpected visitor, Martin Nightingale. He hoped he had given the young man good counsel.

He might guess, but never really knew, what a person might say when they sought him out for a private conversation. Most confidences fell into a few categories—family, marriage, ethical, and spiritual issues, of course.

Once in a while, he was surprised by the problem presented. Martin had brought him a truly unique challenge, and Ben hoped he had done the right thing by sidetracking the young man's simple solution. What if Martin gave up and did nothing? It would be a great loss to so many who could have otherwise been helped.

But Ben believed he had made the right choice. In his heart, he truly did believe that Walter Nightingale would not have wanted his grandson to find an easy, quick fix to his request. Martin had been sent on a quest, a hero's journey, and in the process of satisfying the terms of the will, Ben believed the young man would learn some valuable truths, about the world and about himself, and would come out the other side a better person.

Outside, in Mrs. Honeyfield's office, he heard Carl Tulley's deep, raspy tones and the rattle of his ever-present toolbox. "Is the reverend in there? I need to fix the doorknob on his closet."

Before Mrs. Honeyfield could answer, Ben called out through the partially closed door. "Please come in, Carl. I don't mind."

Carl pushed the door all the way open and peeked inside. "I don't mean to bother you, Reverend. I can come back later."

"No bother. I'm not working on anything special."

"In that case," Carl said as he nodded and

entered, heading for the closet, "I'll have this done in a minute or two." He opened the toolbox and selected a screwdriver from a large array and began to loosen the screws in the knob. Ben noticed him squint, then crouch to get a better look. A few moments in that position and the handyman was overcome by a coughing spasm. He stood up and covered his mouth with his hand, then turned his back, the screwdriver dropping from his hand.

Ben rose from his seat and ran over to help. He lightly rested a hand on Carl's shoulder and picked up the tool. "Are you all right, Carl? Come sit down . . ."

Carl shook his head, a silent but adamant decline of the offer. As usual, the man would not give an inch to his infirmities, perhaps out of fear that any bit of ground surrendered could never be reclaimed. Or maybe out of fear that once his dwindling strength was exposed, he might be asked to leave his job at the church, which had been a lifeline for him.

Years back, when Carl had been released from prison after serving a sentence for manslaughter, he had wandered New England homeless and without hope. One morning Ben had found him sleeping in the church and quite ill, his life at a great low. His job as sexton had restored his dignity and purpose, and given him good reason to turn his back on old habits. With no wife or children of his own, Carl gave his whole heart to keeping the old church in good repair. A formidable offering, though many might not guess it if they judged him on his gruff and often ill-tempered manner.

Carl had stopped coughing but still stood with his back turned. He took a hanky from his pocket and wiped his face.

"Should I get the oxygen?" Ben asked quietly. He knew Carl kept a small tank on his desk in the choir room.

Carl shook his head and finally turned to face Ben. "No thanks, Reverend. It's passed. I'll be okay."

"Can I help with that repair?"

"I just noticed I don't have the right screws to fix it. I'll take care of it later, when you're out."

"No rush. I barely noticed it was loose. I appreciate how conscientious you are, Carl. I think this old church would fall down without you," Ben added.

Carl nodded, his mouth fixed in a tight line, but Ben could see he was moved by the compliment. "Thank you, Reverend. I try my best. Sorry again to interrupt your work."

"No apology necessary. See you later."

Ben watched him go, moving in slow, heavy steps, his big shoulders hunched to one side by the weight of his tools.

Someday, Carl would need to retire, either by

choice or because of his health. Ben didn't know when that day would be or how that difficult passage would be navigated. But he sensed it would be soon and sent up a prayer for strength and guidance, and some fair warning.

Alone in his office again, he saw the screwdriver Carl had dropped sitting on a book on the end table next to the armchair. He picked it up, noticing the book underneath. It had been written by members of the congregation and covered the church's history, from its founding in the 1700s up to the present day.

I should have shown this to Martin when he was here. Why didn't I think of it? Distracted by the conversation, he guessed. *Next time,* he thought. He had a feeling he would be seeing more of Martin, and soon. He opened the cover and sifted through the pages, which were filled with photographs. He searched for the faces of Walter and Frances Nightingale and soon found them in a section that covered the 1950s.

A large photo showed the couple standing side by side, in front of their shop in the middle of Main Street: Nightingale's Magical Toy Shop. The store was decorated and stocked to the rafters for Christmas, the shop window filled with toys, most handmade by Walter and his wife, Frances, the caption explained. In the middle of it all, Ben saw Santa's sleigh, ready to take off for its annual flight around the world.

By the time Ben had met the couple, they were middle-aged. But in the photo, they were quite young—late twenties, early thirties, he guessed. It looked as if they had been in the midst of a busy workday when someone had pulled them outside to snap the picture.

Frances wore a flowered dress with a velvet collar and a sweater on top. A very pretty woman, petite with soft brown hair and bright eyes. Walter wore a tan canvas workshop apron, a starched white shirt, and a tie under that. His dark, thick hair was combed back straight from his forehead, and he had warm brown eyes and a wide, relaxed, infectious smile.

Ben was surprised at Martin's striking resemblance to his grandfather. They could have passed for brothers, except for Martin's beard and Walter's wide smile. But perhaps those qualities of warmth and openness would come to Martin with time. Ben hoped so. As Martin already knew, Walter Nightingale was a very different man than his grandson. Had Walter set the bar too high for Martin with this final request?

Ben wondered again if he had offered Martin the best advice and direction to help him meet his challenge. Ben studied the photo a moment, hoping he had done the right thing.

CHAPTER THREE

Friday, November 25, 1955

WALTER NIGHTINGALE SLIPPED OUT OF bed and dressed quietly in the dark. He stopped in the kitchen to make a pot of coffee and poured himself a large mug of it, then crept down the single flight of steps, careful to avoid the squeaky ones. Frances didn't need to be up this early. She could sleep at least an hour or more before the alarm clock went off.

He was too eager and restless to stay in bed. Eager to get to work, though it was barely six o'clock, the day after Thanksgiving, and most people in town had the day off. But he didn't begrudge them. He was happy about that; all the more time for a stroll down Main Street to admire the decorations and window displays. To be inspired by the Christmas mood and start their shopping.

Down in the store, he flipped on the lights, though it was far too early to flip the sign on the door to open. His gaze skimmed the shelves and displays. He wanted everything to look perfect. A group of dolls seated around a small table were in the midst of a tea party, and he lifted the arm of the ballerina, just so. She sat with a princess, a nurse, and a cowgirl, who was wearing jeans and a red and white checked shirt, long braids, and a mischievous grin.

Walter smiled, admiring the unique outfits and personalities that Frances had created for each of them, carefully painting their faces and fixing their hairdos, designing and stitching their clothes. Many people admired the craftsmanship of his handmade toys, but Frances was an artist in her own right, too.

The model train display was his favorite. They had worked on that together and set it up at the very heart of the shop, the tracks winding in and out all around the store, eventually leading the long line of colorful cars back to the tiny village and countryside they had made.

There was no reason to turn it on so early, but he loved the sound of the wheels spinning along the tracks and the soft steam whistle as it flew through the crossroads. He loved to watch the engine tug the cars up a hill then down again. Along the straight stretches and around tight curves, then winding through the tiny village and open fields, complete with houses and cars, a school and yellow buses, a church with a tall steeple, and a farm with a big red barn, where tiny animals grazed on green meadows.

It was all there, a miniature and perfect world.

The only thing Walter loved more was watching the faces of the children who stood at the edge of the display, their eyes as wide as saucers, lit with amazement.

If he had his way, he would give a train set to each of them. But of course, he could not. "You're not Santa Claus, dear," his wife often reminded him. "Not yet, anyway."

He set his prices low enough, Frances would remind him. But Walter believed toys shouldn't be too expensive and out of reach for average families in Cape Light. Everyone should be able to buy toys—interesting, original, one-of-a-kind playthings that would spark the imagination and transport a child to a magical world. A special toy would find a forever home in a child's heart, to be cherished and treasured for a lifetime. Which was why, one day each Christmas season, Walter opened the doors to Nightingale's Magical Toy Shop to parents facing hard times and let them pick out gifts for their children, for free.

Walter didn't think the gesture was so much; just a kindness he could extend. But the families he helped were deeply grateful, and many said it was his generosity that made the store truly magical.

The store also sold the popular, mass-produced products made by big companies and advertised on TV. Every year, another fad. Pogo sticks and pop-up trampolines. Baby dolls that wet or cried—molded from hard plastic, Walter noticed. Not what he would want for his little girl, when and if he ever had a child of his own.

Mostly, they sold playthings made by hand. One of Walter's favorites was a small wooden stage, complete with red velvet curtains trimmed with gold brocade, which Frances had made. Walter had fashioned puppets for it and arranged the charming set in lifelike poses, eager to spring into action.

He turned next to a dollhouse, constructed from his own sketches, with intricate trim inside and out, the rooms filled with tiny pieces of furniture that mirrored the Victorian homes all around the village. He was carefully adding a Christmas tree, complete with ornaments and a star on top, when he heard his wife's light footsteps on the staircase.

"Walter? Are you down here already? Only the milkman will be out shopping at this hour. And he probably doesn't have time to stop."

"Is that why he didn't come in? I heard the bottles rattling. I did wonder."

She knew he was teasing and waved her hand, the other clutching the top of her plaid robe. "Breakfast is ready. Oatmeal with apples and cinnamon. You have time for a bite, I hope."

"Hard to start the day without it."

He rarely did, he might have added. Oatmeal

was inexpensive but nutritious and filling, and his clever wife found ways to sneak it into breakfast, lunch, and supper. Walter knew he was a lucky man to have married such an excellent cook, one who could make delicious meals from the most modest ingredients.

"Will you bring the milk up?"

Walter nodded, and Frances disappeared up the steps.

Walter went outside and found the metal box near the front door coated with a thin layer of frost. He pulled out a glass bottle of milk and one of cream, then flipped the box shut.

It was a chilly day and he wore only a sweater, but he walked out onto the sidewalk anyway, his breath leaving a trail of white puffs. He was eager to check the window display they had set up the night before Thanksgiving. They wanted to make their window especially eye-catching this year, and Walter thought they had done a very good job.

A life-size, stuffed Santa sat on a large red wooden sleigh that Walter had borrowed from Gus Potter, who owned the orchard outside town. The back of the sleigh was filled with gift-wrapped boxes and a huge pile of toys—from baby dolls in strollers to roller skates and rocket ships. Everywhere you looked, there was some intriguing sight to tantalize a child's eye.

He went back inside and ran up the steps, a

bottle in each hand. The table was set for two and Frances stood at the stove, stirring the oatmeal. Walter set the bottles on the table and took his seat.

"The window looks swell. I don't know how you made that Santa so quickly. I had to look twice, he looks so real."

Frances laughed. She brought over two bowls and sat down across from him. "Mrs. Bauer found a water stain on a bolt of red felt and she gave it to me for free. A few pillows and some cotton fleece did the rest. Oh, he's wearing your galoshes. I hope it doesn't snow."

"I thought I recognized those boots. It better not snow, or we'll have the only barefoot Santa in town." Walter sprinkled a spoonful of sugar over his bowl and dug in.

Frances often took in sewing for a dressmaker who had a shop down the street, Lydia Bauer. The pay wasn't much, but it helped. Walter didn't like to see his wife sewing late into the night. If she had to miss sleep, he would much rather see her up late taking care of a baby.

So far, they had not been blessed with children. Most couples their age were already raising several, but Walter tried not to dwell on that. Dr. Elliot had assured them that women in their thirties often had babies and there was no physical reason Frances could not. Every year, every month, it seemed more doubtful, but Walter had faith that their prayers would be answered.

"I think you did a great job setting up the toys, Walter. I bet every kid in town comes to a full stop in front of our shop and makes their parents look in our window, too."

"Exactly what I had in mind. Maybe I should add a stop sign out there, to make sure. There's probably room to squeeze in a dollhouse, too. I have one in the workshop that's nearly finished. Maybe I can get it out there tomorrow."

"I can watch the shop in the afternoon if you want to work on it. I just need to finish a hem for Lydia and bring her the dress by noon."

"All right, honey. If you're not tired after sewing all morning." It was important that Frances get enough rest. It would help her get pregnant, Dr. Elliot had told them. Ezra Elliot was about his own age, in his early thirties. Walter knew Dr. Elliot wasn't all that experienced, but both he and Frances trusted Ezra. What he lacked in years, he more than made up for with keen intelligence and a caring manner.

Besides, if Walter was in the shop in the morning and Frances stayed upstairs, he would collect the mail, including any serious-looking letters from the bank, the kind he had been receiving lately. Walter had opened one weeks ago but hadn't had the nerve to open any of the ones that followed. He just stashed them away in the bottom drawer of his desk.

Though he rarely kept anything from Frances, he felt it was best that she didn't see those letters. Dr. Elliot had told them that worry and stress could also hinder pregnancy. Walter knew it was his job to protect his wife, to take care of her. He could handle and solve the bank situation. After the holidays, when they had plenty extra in their savings account, he would sort it all out.

But he also said a little prayer, asking God to help them do the best they could this Christmas. He knew he wasn't a very good businessman. Although he loved the shop and put in long hours, and he thought a lot about how to improve the displays and stock, he still didn't have the knack for turning a profit, like some of his friends in town.

As long as he and Frances had enough to live comfortably and, with God's grace, support a family someday, that was all he asked. Lately, he worried that even those modest standards might not be met.

"Walter? Didn't you hear me?"

He looked up. Frances stood at the stove, the coffeepot in hand. "Sorry, dear. Just thinking about something."

"As usual." She smiled and shook her head. Walter knew that she was used to him drifting off, lost in his imagination. "Would you like more coffee?"

"No, thanks. I'm fine." He glanced at his watch

and rose from his seat. Half past eight. They usually opened the shop at nine, but he would make an exception today. "I'd better open up. There might be some early shoppers out there."

"Always a few early birds," she agreed. Mostly to humor him, he suspected.

He leaned over and kissed her. "See you later, sweetheart."

She touched his cheek and smiled. "Good luck, Walter. Let me know if the crowd gets too big to handle."

He knew she was teasing him a bit, but he replied in a serious tone. "Stand by for action, honey."

A few minutes later, Walter found that he did have early customers: Adele Morgan and her boys, Joe and Kevin. Adele was browsing the games—Chinese checkers and dominoes, Parcheesi and Monopoly—but the boys were drawn to the train display, as if a giant magnet pulled them there. Walter walked over to their mother. "Can I help you, Adele? Looking for something in particular?"

"The boys wrote their letters to Santa last night," she whispered. She glanced at her sons to see if they were listening. "I know Joe wants a two-wheeler, but we might get one secondhand from a friend. Clean it up and put on a new seat and such."

"Good idea. I'm sure he'll love it. We have

streamers for the handles and bike horns. A few new touches can dress it up nicely." Walter understood. Money was tight for the Morgans right now, and they had to make Christmas for two children. No wonder she was looking at board games and the bow-and-arrow sets.

"Of course, they want a train set . . . but I don't think so. Not this year," she added quietly.

Before Walter could reply, Joe let out a cry of excitement. "Whoa, did you see that?" He pointed at the train as it flew toward the station and the whistle sounded.

"It's coming through the tunnel. I want to watch." Kevin ran to the other side of the display, waiting for the train to come his way.

Their mother looked back at Walter. "I know they'd love some trains. And we have the perfect place for it, on the screened-in porch. My husband's very handy. He and the boys could make a little village like that one, too. It would be so much fun for them to work on it together. But I bet those sets are expensive. Way beyond our means," she said wistfully.

"Maybe not. We're giving a good discount on trains this year. We have a big inventory." That wasn't entirely true, but anyone could see how much the boys loved the trains. The whole family would love them, Walter was sure of that.

He named a price and saw her surprise. And

interest. She looked relieved and happier, and he felt happy, too.

"That is a bargain, Walter. I've seen them in other stores for much more. I'll talk to my husband and see what he thinks."

"Sure, talk it over at home. You can pay in installments if you like. We can work things out, I'm sure."

She looked even happier at that news, and Walter guessed he had made the sale. He wouldn't make much, but the Morgan boys would be thrilled on Christmas morning. Wasn't that the main reason he was in this business?

After Mrs. Morgan left, a few more customers came in, but never so many at one time that Walter had to call Frances for assistance. He could hear the sewing machine thrumming away upstairs. At least one of them was earning some money this morning. Most of the people who came in were just looking, and although he offered many good suggestions, he only made a few small sales.

Business will pick up. It's always this way at first, he reminded himself. Walter itched to get into his workshop. He felt productive there, even when the store wasn't selling much. Sitting at his workbench, his mind focused on making toys, his worries melted like cotton candy, and he lost all sense of time and place as whimsical creations came to life in his hands.

But it was too early for the workshop. Walter stepped behind the counter and took out a pad and pencil, then started sketching to pass the time until more customers showed up.

Walter wasn't sure how long he'd been sketching—long enough to fill a few pages. The bell on the shop door jingled, and he looked up as Oliver Warwick walked in.

"Hello there, Walter. How are you today? Did you have a good Thanksgiving?"

"It was swell. Franny's family came by and she made a big dinner. A tight fit in our apartment," he added with a grin. "But the more, the merrier, I always say. How was your holiday?"

"Quieter than yours, I'd bet. Just my parents and me," he added. "We had a pleasant day."

Walter smiled briefly. He wasn't sure what to say. He imagined a huge dining room at Lilac Hall, the Warwick estate, where three people sat in luxury at a long empty table, covered with fine china and silver as servants scurried around, serving a meal a cook had prepared.

Oliver's older brother had died in the war. Oliver had served, too, and returned a decorated hero. Walter had also been in the army, a soldier in the infantry. His company had been sent to fight in France, and though he hadn't come back with any medals, he always felt blessed to have survived. Those days were full of memories he rarely allowed himself to dwell upon.

"On to Christmas," Oliver said, a brighter note in his deep voice. "I have a feeling this is going to be a good one."

"I do, too," Walter agreed.

Oliver had a certain light in his eye that made Walter curious, but he didn't know the man well enough to ask more.

Nobody likes a nosy shopkeeper, he reminded himself, though he often found his customers confiding in him. People just liked to talk to him, to tell him their troubles. And their triumphs. "I just have that kind of face," he'd tell Frances. Then he'd mug and make her laugh.

Oliver's private life was widely known and thoroughly discussed around the village—though Walter wondered how well anyone really knew him. Tall and handsome, Oliver stood out from every crowd. Not because he was the only surviving son of the richest man in town, or because of all his medals and honors. Or even because of the gossip that swirled around him—his brief marriage and divorce, and his reputation as a playboy.

It was something about him. A unique combination of easy charm and self-assurance and genuine modesty that set him apart. He wore his social status and honors lightly. Gossip as they might, nobody would ever say he was a snob. Oliver Warwick was one of the most down-to-earth fellows Walter had ever met.

Dressed today in a finely tailored overcoat, a custom-made suit, and a silk tie, he looked like royalty as he examined a wooden sailboat Walter had made by hand.

"This is a fine little boat. I feel as if I could jump on and grab the rudder." Oliver grinned. "If someone shrank me down to fit."

"I haven't figured out that trick yet," Walter said. "I'll let you know when I do." Oliver was an excellent sailor who often won local races on his sailboat, *Kismet*. "But the boat is definitely seaworthy," Walter assured him. "Some folks around here do race miniature boats on ponds or lakes."

"So I've heard. Perhaps I'll take up the hobby someday. When I'm too old to sail a real boat." Oliver gently put the boat back on its stand, his eyes still admiring the lines and sails. "You're quite a craftsman, Walter. An artist, really."

Walter felt color rise in his face, though he was grateful for the compliment. "Thank you, Oliver."

"You have the most unique toys. I always love to look around in here. You know, every year, we hold a big Christmas party for the cannery workers. My father's secretary already arranged the gifts for that event."

Walter's hopes had jumped and now settled again. If only he had gotten that order. That would have settled every financial worry. *Maybe next year,* he consoled himself.

"But there are many people on our staff who don't work on the factory floor. I'd like to send gifts to their children, too. I thought maybe you could help me pick out some suitable toys?"

"I'd love to help you, Oliver. Did you have anything in particular in mind?"

It wasn't the huge sale that had been dangled for a moment. But it was going to be a large order, and Walter gave thanks for that.

Oliver pulled a scrap of paper from the vest pocket of his overcoat, probably made in New York, or even London, Walter guessed. Camel hair, with a silk scarf in a paisley pattern underneath. "Let me see . . . my secretary gave me a few notes. There are eight boys, ages three to ten. And six girls, from two years old to age nine."

Walter's brain—the shopkeeper's side—shifted into high gear. "Let's start with the girls," he suggested, steering Oliver over to the big display of dolls.

It took nearly an hour to choose enough gifts for Oliver's list. For once, Walter was relieved that no one else came into the shop and interrupted. He assembled the toys on the counter, near the cash register, then took his time tallying up the bill. He didn't trust himself to come up with the right total and decided to use his adding machine, which was dusty from neglect.

Oliver didn't seem to be in a hurry and made small talk as Walter worked. He seemed pleased by their choices of toys and looked as if he wanted to play with a few himself. "Some of these toys bring back memories, I must say. I can't wait to have some children and have an excuse to play with toys again."

Walter laughed. "Franny and I feel the same way. About children, I mean. Anyone special in your life right now, Oliver?"

Walter wondered if the question was too personal, but Oliver didn't seem to think so. Walter watched him smile, a soft look coming into his eyes. "There is, actually. She's very lovely. Stole my heart the first time I set eyes on her last summer. It's complicated," he added in a more serious tone. "But I do think it will all work out."

Walter met his eyes. He could see that Oliver was in love and felt happy for him. Was there anything in life more important than that? Walter didn't think so.

"That's wonderful news. I wish you good luck," Walter said sincerely.

"Thanks, Walter. It will take some luck to land this fish," Oliver said with a laugh.

Walter smiled and handed him the bill, feeling nervous a moment as Oliver glanced at the total. Would he decide he'd bought too much today and put a few things back? Walter wouldn't blame him. Even a portion of this sale would be plenty.

"You can give me a deposit if you like and I'll hold the items for you," Walter said quickly.

"Let's just settle up now. I think I have enough to cover it." Oliver took out his wallet and pulled out a stack of bills. "I was at the bank this morning." He counted out the bills and handed them over.

"Thanks, Oliver." Walter put the bills in the register and began to make change.

"Oh, don't bother with the change. I'm sure it will cost you more than that for the wrapping paper. I apologize for taking up so much of your day. I'm sure you have a lot to do."

"Apologize? This is the best order I've had in weeks," Walter replied honestly.

Nightingale's was the only toy store in Cape Light, but Walter knew that Oliver could have easily gone to a larger store in Newburyport or even Boston.

"Business dragging lately?" Oliver asked quietly.

Walter shrugged. "We're holding our own." *Just barely,* he nearly added. "I'm hoping we'll catch up with the holiday sales. In fact, I feel certain we will."

Oliver nodded but didn't reply. Walter felt there was something more he wanted to say. "I don't mean to interfere in your private affairs, Walter, but I think there's something I should tell you."

Oliver's tone sent off a silent alarm. Walter sensed that whatever Oliver was about to say was not good news. "What is this about, Oliver? Something about my shop?"

"More or less. I was at the bank this morning, and while I was waiting to talk to the bank manager, I overheard him discussing your account with some assistant manager in the loan department."

Walter felt his stomach drop, as if he were in an elevator that had suddenly skipped several floors. He felt a lump in his throat and swallowed hard. "What did he say?"

Oliver looked puzzled. "Your accounts are past due, Walter. The mortgage on this building and some loans you've taken out? You must have gotten letters. Maybe even phone calls?"

Walter sighed. It was too hard to admit how irresponsible he had been about his finances. Childish, actually.

He rubbed his cheek with his hand. "There have been letters. I did read one or two, a few weeks ago. But I didn't know what to do. I still don't," he admitted. "Once Christmas is over, I'll have enough cash to catch up and get back on track. I'm really counting on that."

"I can't say for sure, but it sounds to me like the bank wants their money now. Or they'll take action."

Was it really that bad? Maybe Oliver was exaggerating. "Do you really think so? What sort of action?"

"Legal action, Walter. They can call in the loans, and if you can't pay, close the shop, claim your property. I'm not saying this to scare you. I'm just trying to warn you, as a friend. I don't think you can ignore this any longer. Or wait for Christmas to straighten it all out. I don't think the bank will wait," he added quietly.

Walter felt stunned. The big order from Oliver had lifted him to the heights . . . and now, this dreadful news sent him crashing down.

"Can I talk to them about it? Can I get them to wait a little longer?"

Oliver didn't answer for the longest time. He stared down at the display of penknives, compasses, and field glasses. At last he said, "I'd be happy to help you, Walter. Whatever you need to stay afloat. Say the word, and I'll write you a check today."

Walter was tempted to just say, "Yes!" But he couldn't do that. He hardly knew Oliver. "That's very kind. But I think I need to sort this out myself. Maybe it's not as bad as you think?"

"Maybe not," Oliver said, though Walter could tell he didn't really believe that. "Here's what I would do if I were in your shoes. Open those letters and see what's what. You have to face it, my friend. No matter how awful this situation seems, God knows, we've both been through worse." Walter nodded, acknowledging their common experience as soldiers.

"Go to the bank on Monday, bright and early. Ask to see the manager, Richard Finley. Lay your cards on the table. Ask for more time. Tell him your plan to pay everything back from your holiday profits. He's a good man, honest and fair. We have a good rapport, and I'll put in a word for you."

Walter took a steadying breath. Oliver's advice was sound and made perfect sense. It was a hard prescription to carry out, but Walter knew he had no choice. He had to do his best to solve this problem and take some quick action—before the bank did.

He offered his hand to Oliver. "Thank you, Oliver. Thanks for warning me and for your good advice. That's exactly what I'm going to do."

Oliver gave Walter's hand a hearty shake. "Try your best, Walter. That's all we can do in this life, right?"

"Do our best and ask God to do the rest," Walter replied. He had already asked for heaven's help facing this emergency and knew he would offer many more prayers before Monday morning rolled around.

Oliver buttoned his coat and set his black fedora back on his head. "I'll be thinking of you, Walter. Let me know how it all turns out."

"Thank you, Oliver. I will."

Oliver wished Walter well again, and the shop door closed behind him. Walter heard the stops and starts of the sewing machine up above and felt relieved that Frances had not come downstairs in the midst of Oliver's visit.

He needed a few minutes alone to collect his thoughts. And his courage.

FRANCES HELPED IN THE STORE DURING THE afternoon, as she had promised, but when Walter returned to his workshop, he didn't finish the doll furniture, as he had planned. He pulled out the stack of letters from the bank. Frances rarely came back to his work space and would always announce herself, but he still stayed alert just in case. Perhaps it wasn't fair, but he wasn't ready to share this burden with her. Not just yet.

It was a painful process, but he opened each letter and read it through. The messages were all basically the same: polite but firmly worded reminders that he had fallen behind in his payments, requesting him to contact the bank and discuss the matter. The last few letters were more direct and to the point and were signed personally by the bank manager, Richard P. Finley, who had clearly lost his patience with the matter.

Walter knew he was in trouble. It was even worse than he had imagined. He was just about to stick the bundle of letters back in his desk when Frances poked her head through the curtain that separated his workshop from the store. He quickly slipped the pile under a sketchbook and turned to her, a pencil in hand.

"It's almost six, Walter. I think we can close, don't you?"

"Yes, dear. You go on up. I'll straighten things out for tomorrow." He set the pencil on the sketchbook and smiled at her.

"All right . . . Are you okay? You look . . . pale."

He shrugged and feigned surprise. "Never felt better. Just hungry for dinner."

He wasn't really; his stomach churned with nerves. But he didn't want her to guess that anything was wrong. His dear wife could read him like a book—a blessing usually. Though not tonight.

"Maybe you're just tired. You were up at the crack of dawn." She seemed about to ask him more questions but didn't. Walter was relieved. "Dinner will be ready in a minute. Don't fuss down here too long."

"I'll be right up." He watched her go and waited to hear her light step on the staircase. Then he lifted the sketchbook and stored the letters in the bottom drawer of the desk, as if stuffing an angry genie back in its bottle.

What would he tell the bank manager on Monday? Walter had no idea and tried to remember Oliver's advice. All the rational-sounding words had flown out of his head. *Don't panic,*

Walter. Ask God for help, for the right words to say to Mr. Finley. It will come to you. You'll see.

Upstairs with Frances, he tried to brush his worries aside as they sat together at the dinner table. "It's just leftovers from yesterday; nothing special," Frances said, bringing plates and bowls to the table.

"I'd take your leftovers any day, Franny. Besides, I think Thanksgiving food tastes even better the second day."

"Well, let's see how you feel by days three and four. Or five," she teased him. "It was a big bird. It's going to last awhile."

They had been economizing with their grocery shopping lately, and aside from that, Frances hated to waste food. Walter had no doubt that she would devise some tasty recipes, even if the turkey did last that long.

"I had a few customers while you were in the workshop," Frances reported. "I sold that cowgirl doll. The woman even asked if I could make some extra outfits and I took a nice order. I'm sure I can sew up a few things for her by Christmas."

Walter was impressed. "Good job, Franny. I knew that doll would sell right away. I hope you can make a replacement for her."

Frances smiled. "I can dress up another as a cowgirl, but she'll never be exactly the same. I know it sounds funny, but . . . I felt a bit attached to that one. I almost didn't want her to be

84

sold." When she met Walter's gaze, she seemed surprised by her own admission. "What a funny thing to say, right? We need to sell our toys. You're not mad at me for saying that, are you?"

Walter reached across the table to squeeze her hand. "Of course not. I must confess, I often feel the same. About the train sets mainly," he admitted. "I forgot to tell you, I may have sold one today. Adele Morgan's boys were mesmerized. She's going to talk to her husband. She said she'd be back tomorrow."

"That's wonderful, Walter. As long as you didn't give too big a discount?"

Walter didn't meet her glance but studied his dinner. "I may have shaved a bit off the price, to close the deal," he admitted. "Don't worry, we'll still make a good profit . . . Oh, and I nearly forgot. Better than *almost* selling something— Oliver Warwick came in and picked out about a dozen toys and paid cash on the spot. He needs the order gift wrapped and delivered to his office by next week."

Frances looked very pleased. "That's wonderful, Walter. Why didn't you tell me sooner?"

"Oh, I don't know. I was eager to get into the workshop, and it just slipped my mind. He's a good fellow, Oliver. I know people talk about him. They say he's a snob and spoiled by his father's money, but I don't think that's true at all."

"And you have a way of seeing only the good in people. You have to admit that." Walter could see that Frances was not convinced. She wasn't one to gossip, but she had doubtless heard enough about Oliver to have made up her mind. Unfairly, he thought.

"That's easy to say, Franny. But when it comes right down to it, I don't think many people in town really know him. They see him from a distance and make a lot of assumptions. He was very friendly today. Very down-to-earth. And very . . . kind," he added.

Frances looked curious at this description. "Because he bought all those toys for the children of his employees? Is that why you think he's kind?"

"Yes . . . and other things that he said," Walter added, recalling how Oliver even offered to loan him money. "He's not at all the way people make him out to be. That's all I'm saying. You can't believe everything you hear."

"Well, that's true enough."

It certainly was kind of Oliver to reveal what he had overheard at the bank, to warn Walter of the gathering storm and try to help him navigate through this rough weather.

"So, all in all, we had a good day," Frances concluded. "A very good day. You said that we would," she reminded him.

"Yes, I did," he recalled, knowing it had been

mostly wishful thinking that morning. But sometimes wishes do come true. He would have to remember that on Monday.

"It's just the start of the season. Things are looking up, Walter."

He didn't answer, feeling about to burst. He was so tempted to confide in her but again decided it wasn't time yet. Not until he had found a solution. She should not be burdened right now. It was his duty to protect her.

"You look worried, Walter. Is something wrong? Is there something you aren't telling me? It's all right if you gave Mrs. Morgan a discount. I was just teasing. You can give her the train set for free. I don't really care, dear. I know how happy it makes you to help people."

Walter finally found his smile again. "I didn't go that far. But good to know I have your blessings for the next time."

Frances rose and picked up the dirty plates from their dessert and set them in the sink. "I'm going to do a little sewing tonight. Lydia gave me a dress that needs to be taken in. She needs it back tomorrow."

Walter frowned, even though he planned on going back to his workshop again. "I wish you wouldn't take these rush jobs from Lydia. She'll have you sewing twenty-four hours a day."

"This is her busy time, too. It's hard to refuse the work. If I do, she'll find someone else.

But I did hear of another job. I know we're doing well with the store, Walter, but there's an opening at the Paris Boutique. I spoke to the owner, Nancy Trumbull. She needs someone to help with sales a few hours a week and she was happy to hear I could do alterations. The pay is much better than sewing for Lydia. I know it will be a lot for you to handle the shop on your own, but I thought I should try it and see how it goes."

Walter could see that she wanted to take the job, and probably would, no matter what he said. She was worried about their finances, too, he guessed, but didn't want to pressure him. She was trying to help without hurting his pride, and his heart was touched.

"Oh, I don't think that's necessary, Franny. We're doing fine," he insisted. "Remember what Dr. Elliot said? You shouldn't work so hard."

"I know, I know . . . but I'd like to try it. I think it would be fun, helping women pick out clothes. You know how I love fashion. Let's just think about it, okay?"

Leave it to Franny to make him feel as if he were keeping her from having fun. She was talking about a job where she would be on her feet all day.

"All right. Let's think about it," he agreed. "I need to go down into the workshop for a little while. I never finished the doll furniture."

"Yes, I noticed. What were you doing all afternoon, making sketches for new toys?"

Walter nodded. "Something like that."

He kissed her cheek and headed downstairs. He considered taking out the letters again but saw no point. There would be no new, more positive message on those pages. He took out a pad and jotted down a few notes for his talk with Mr. Finley, points he could bring up in his favor. Oliver had told him to lay his cards on the table and be sincere about his plan to repay the money after Christmas. Walter couldn't think of much more to say than that.

The fear and worry that had haunted him all day billowed all around, like a big, dark cloud. Walter closed his eyes and said a prayer. "This is all I can think of to say on Monday, Lord. Please let the right words come to me so that I can save my business. I know I've been careless and irresponsible, but I want to do better. Please help me straighten things out and get back on track."

Walter opened his eyes and took a breath. As so often happened after he opened his heart to God, he felt peace in his heart. A weight had lifted from his shoulders, and his mind was clear about what he needed to do. He felt much more hopeful that things could work out.

He set up his supplies and got to work on the dollhouse furniture. If he spent a little time tonight, it would all be dry by morning and he could set up the new house in the window. Selling a few dollhouses would go a long way toward repaying the bank, and working on toys always made him feel calmer.

He stretched and rubbed the tight muscles in his neck and checked the clock. It was close to midnight. Where had the time gone? He was sure Frances was fast asleep by now. He put his paints and other supplies in order. He always left his work space neat, with all the tiny bottles and tubes sealed tight and his brushes clean. He had brought down a mug of tea and some of Franny's special oatmeal cookies. The tea was cold, but he picked up a cookie and took a bite. Thick and chewy, with cranberries instead of raisins, just the way he liked them.

Just as he leaned over to turn off the brass lamp on his workbench, an earsplitting racket broke the silent night. It sounded like trash pails rolling around in the alley behind the shop. Had the raccoons tipped over the garbage again? Walter hoped not. The mischievous creatures made such a mess.

He walked to the back door and switched on the outside light, then stepped out and looked around the alley. A tin pail was on its side, the lid flipped off and the contents spilled all over. But instead of furry, masked bandits feasting on Thanksgiving-dinner leftovers, there was only a dog, gulping down whatever he could find without even chewing. Medium-sized, mostly brown with white and black spots, floppy ears, and a long muzzle. The hound was certainly a mutt, but with a lot of beagle in his family tree. Walter felt the frigid air seep through his thick sweater. The dog had no collar, he noticed. His thin coat showed the outline of his ribs and had the ragged look of a stray who had been on his own awhile. Walter felt so sorry for the little fellow. He crouched down and tried to coax him inside. "Here, boy . . . Come on, boy. Want to come inside with me? It's nice and warm."

The dog lifted his head and stared back with round, scared eyes. Walter tossed him the last bite of cookie, and the dog gobbled it up greedily.

"That's a good boy. More cookies inside. Come on, fella . . ."

Walter stood up and let out a low, soft whistle. The dog stared back with an alert look, but when Walter took a step closer, he hunched down and took off, his short legs churning.

Walter watched until he disappeared. Maybe the little guy had a home and his owners let him out at night. He didn't think that was the right way to treat a dog, but some people did.

The mess of trash could wait until the morning, he decided. Or what would be left of it, after the raccoons discovered the buffet. Walter turned and headed inside again, knowing he wouldn't sleep a wink. He would be thinking of the big job he faced on Monday.

CHAPTER FOUR

Sunday, November 25, 2018

MARTIN WALKED INTO VERA'S KITCHEN on Sunday morning, lured by the rich scent of hot coffee and freshly baked muffins. He had just walked Milo and bought a copy of the *Boston Globe* and quickly settled at the table for his breakfast and the newspaper.

Vera bustled around the room, packing cakes in cardboard boxes. "I'm running very late for church, Martin. Can you help me carry these boxes? I'm signed up for coffee hour and there's a lot to prepare. And I hate to miss the opening prayer . . ."

Martin could see she was frazzled—so much so, she had forgotten all about her campaign to have him attend church today. "Happy to help, Vera. Is this everything?" He quickly grabbed the boxes.

"Yes, all of those on the counter. Carry them carefully," she called, following him out the side door. "There's nothing worse than trying to patch together a broken coffee cake."

Martin could think of many problems far worse but didn't argue the point. He placed the boxes with care in the back seat of Vera's car, counting no less than three banana breads, a dozen carrot muffins, and two cinnamon-swirl coffee cakes. She had left a sampling of the bounty on a cake stand in the kitchen, and he was eager to return to it.

"I think the cakes will be fine on the seat," he said as she peered over his shoulder. "Unless you'd like me to put them in the trunk?"

"That won't be necessary. I'll drive extra slow." She slipped behind the wheel. Martin smiled. He doubted Vera drove any way but slowly.

He stepped away from the car as she clipped her seat belt and started the engine. The ignition made a dreadful whirring sound, but Vera let it run awhile. The engine failed to turn over, and Martin winced. This did not bode well.

"Oh dear . . . not that again. What a morning. I tell you . . ." Vera stared at the dashboard a second, then, with her mouth set in a firm line, tried to start the car again.

Martin heard the same sound, this time even louder, and the pitch even higher and more insistent. As if the car were saying it just wasn't going to budge.

"Come on now. Don't be like that." Vera spoke to the car in a kinder, more understanding tone.

"You can rest all afternoon if you like. We just have to get to church."

Martin bit his lip to keep from smiling. He was sure that he talked to his own car at times, but it was funny to overhear Vera's conversation. Funny and touching.

He stepped over and knocked on the window, which she quickly rolled down. "Doesn't sound good," he said simply. "Has this happened before?"

"From time to time. But if I wait a minute or two, and jiggle the key a little, it should come around. It's cold out this morning," she noted. "We had a frost last night."

"Does it happen because of the cold?"

"Not necessarily. But could be. You never know with cars. They can get finicky."

Old cars could, that was true. But Martin didn't want to say that.

"I'm going to give it another try. Stand back," she warned, as if the car might explode.

Martin took a step back, more to appease Vera than out of fear. She took a deep breath, and he heard the key ring jangling a moment— her secret method, he recalled as she turned the key.

The car whirred again, the sound extremely high-pitched, as black smoke billowed from the exhaust pipe.

Martin fanned the foul-smelling smoke away

with his hand. "Turn it off, Vera. I think you ought to give up."

Vera had already turned the engine off. She sat with her head bowed and sighed out loud. "I'm really running late now. I bet all my friends are already on their way. I suppose I can call a taxi—"

"Don't worry, I'll drive you," Martin cut in. He pulled open the back door and began taking out the boxes. "I'll put these in the hatch. They'll be safe and sound."

Vera's gray eyes grew wide and round as she came out of the car. For a moment, he thought she might hug him. Only the box he was holding prevented her.

"It's very good of you to go out of your way like this, Martin. I'm sorry to disturb your morning. I could see you were all set to read the newspaper."

"Not a problem, Vera. The newspaper will be there when I get back."

"I appreciate your help. Today, of all days, to have car trouble. Thank goodness you were here."

She took her purse from the front seat of her car, then went back to lock the back door. "What about Milo?" she asked.

"He'll be okay. He's already fed and had a little walk."

"Very good. He'll guard the house." Vera slipped into Martin's passenger seat.

Martin started the engine as Vera looked around like a curious bird. "My, my . . . isn't this nice. I like driving a little higher off the ground. You get the big picture, if you know what I mean."

"I do," he agreed.

"Maybe I should get a car like this. With all the driving I do to Connecticut, back and forth to see my grandchildren, a little SUV would be nice, especially in the winter. Does it run well?" Before he could reply, she said, "Art Hagen at Harbor Auto has an eye out for me. For a nice used car, something reliable but not too expensive. Gets to a point when it's not worth fixing an old car. That's what Art says, anyway."

"What's wrong, do you know?"

Vera shrugged. "Old age. Once you clock more than a hundred thousand miles, it's anybody's ball game. Happens to all of us sooner or later."

"I suppose so," Martin said. He glanced at her and smiled but didn't say more.

The parking lot at the church was nearly full when they arrived, but with Vera directing him, Martin found a spot near the door closest to the kitchen. As soon as they arrived, two women about Vera's age came outside to help carry in the boxes of cakes. Sophie, who walked with a cane, carried only one box.

"Sophie, Claire, this is Martin," Vera said, making the introductions. "My car was making the most awful sound, but Martin saved the day."

As Vera explained her emergency, her friends beamed, making him feel like a hero. He felt even more heroic helping them fill up several big percolators with water and then setting up long tables in the large room beyond the kitchen, which seemed to be an all-purpose gathering space for the congregation.

"I think we've got everything in order." Vera set out napkins and paper plates near the cakes, then surveyed the tables, looking satisfied.

"And in record time," Claire added as she took off her apron. "Thanks to Martin."

Vera and Sophie had taken off their aprons, too, he noticed, and were picking up their handbags.

"Two minutes to ten, time to spare. Though I did see the choir lining up already," Claire said. "I asked Tucker to save a few seats for us in the back so we wouldn't disturb anyone if we came in later."

Sophie nodded. "Good idea." She smiled at Martin. "I'm sure there's room for you, Martin. No worries."

Martin didn't understand for a moment, then realized she expected him to come to the service. "Oh . . . well . . . I . . . um . . ."

Vera met his glance. "You wanted to see the sanctuary, remember? The windows? Here you are. Perfect opportunity."

"Did I?" Had he said that? Martin didn't think so, but didn't want to argue with Vera about it in front of her friends. He'd been about to offer to pick her up after the service, and it did seem a waste of time to go all the way back to her house and return again in an hour.

Vera and her friends assumed his reply meant *Yes*.

"Let's get moving, everyone. We don't want to miss the Advent candle." Claire led the way, and Vera followed. She glanced back at Martin, who was dragging his feet, wondering if he could somehow slip out to the parking lot.

Sophie, using her cane, lagged behind as well. She came up beside him and took his arm. "Would you be so kind? Those two are running a footrace. I move slower these days, but I always get there. I'd just rather not interrupt the candle lighting, coming in late."

"Sure . . . I understand." He didn't understand entirely. All this talk about lighting candles. What was that about? It was a church service. Didn't they light candles every Sunday?

He slowed his step to keep pace with her, aware that her light touch on his arm was giving her some very necessary balance and support.

When they reached the sanctuary, Sophie steered him toward a back row in a side section where Vera and Claire were already seated. They slid in and made room. "I need to sit on the end, for my cane. You sit next to Vera," Sophie whispered.

Martin did as he was told. *No escape now,* he realized, flanked by Vera on one side and Sophie on the other. Both women glanced at him with small but satisfied smiles as they settled in place. He had been lassoed and pulled in, like the lost lamb in a Bible scripture. He nearly laughed out loud, feeling sure Vera and her friends thought of him that way.

"Do you have a bulletin?" Vera handed him one. Sophie and Claire were intently reading their own. Before he could reply, the organ sounded and everyone stood up. He heard voices lift in song and turned to watch the choir march in from the back of the church, down the center aisle, singing a lively hymn.

Reverend Ben marched at the very back of the line, singing in a low baritone. He wore a long white cassock with what looked like a blue scarf draped around his neck and hanging down over his chest. Martin knew there was another name for that piece of the clerical outfit but couldn't remember what it was. He wondered if the minister would notice him. The congregation was not large; he guessed that Reverend Ben would spot him sooner or later, even in the back row.

As the choir took their places, Martin noticed a family step up to the altar—six in all. The parents looked to be about midforties, and there were two teenage boys: identical twins with bright red hair. There was also a girl who looked a few years younger, and one that looked older. In her early twenties, he guessed. She stepped up last, and when she turned to face the congregation, his heart skipped a beat. Could it be? Was that really Officer Tulley up there with her family? Maybe his eyes were playing tricks on him.

Vera leaned closer and whispered, "The Tulley family. They've been asked to light the first candle of Advent. Part of the family anyway. They're a big clan. Mike Tulley is Tucker's first cousin." She glanced at the deacon who had showed them to their seats. "He's a lawyer, but practically all of the rest are law officers. Even Louisa, the oldest girl, is carrying on the family tradition."

Louisa . . . *that* was her name. Martin practically sighed aloud with relief. An old-fashioned name, but it suited her. In a good way, he thought.

He nodded at Vera, then turned his gaze back to Louisa Tulley and her family as they recited the day's special litany and lit the first candle on the display of four. Her long, dark red hair hung loose around her shoulders, and she wore a smart outfit, a soft, oatmeal-colored tunic sweater with black leggings and knee-high boots. She didn't look anything like a police officer today. No one would blame him for not recognizing her at first. He wondered if she still lived at home with her family. He didn't meet many girls who did once they started a career, but he wouldn't be surprised. She seemed the traditional type, but he didn't mind that. He kept hoping she would look his way, but she kept her gaze focused on the prayer they were reading.

The Tulleys returned to their pew, many rows ahead of him. There was no chance to catch her eye, even if he wanted to try. He was fairly certain she hadn't noticed him.

Martin had not been to church since the memorial for his grandfather, but his grandparents had brought him here on many Sundays, and as the service unfolded, he began to remember the various phases—the opening prayers and the reverend's Time with Children. He remembered being coaxed to run up and sit on that very rug and listen to the minister's words for the youngest congregants. Reverend Ben had a nice way with children, he recalled. Now he talked about their anticipation for Christmas, using an Advent calendar with little numbered doors to show the season's countdown.

Martin's attention was drawn back to the pulpit as Reverend Ben began his sermon, describing Advent as a journey, and a time of preparation and contemplation.

"Maybe some of you have noticed the blue stole I'm wearing today." He touched the edge of the fabric draped around his neck. "And the blue candles that are out on the altar. As many of you already know, blue is the color of Advent, the color of the night sky, the heavens above, where the Three Wise Men saw the star they followed to Bethlehem. To me it also symbolizes the heaven within each of us, where there is also a star we can follow. To many, it's the color associated with Mary and her time of waiting and preparing for her baby.

"When I was a boy, my mother began her plans and preparations for Christmas right after Thanksgiving. She soaked berries and fruit in a secret mixture for her famous fruitcake and began collecting gifts for our family, many made by hand.

"There is no true and deep experience of Christmas without preparation. Outward and deep within. Like the Wise Men who traveled so far, each of us can embark on our own journey, private and solitary, and not without challenges on the way. This Advent season, I encourage you to take time from your list-making and shopping and other tasks to journal, meditate, and pray, or simply be more mindful.

"Ask yourself these questions. Not just once, but many times in the weeks to come: 'What is the true meaning of Christmas for me?' 'What can I do to make this season more meaningful, for myself and my family?' You may have many insights, and you may start to notice moments that deepen your experience of the season, and moments that detract from it. I hope that you do," he added. "I also hope that this morning we can take the first step on this journey together, toward a richer, even mystical, Christmas."

To his surprise, Martin found himself wondering about the questions the minister had posed. How would he define the true meaning of Christmas? Martin had never thought much about it, but now the question engaged him. As Vera had told him, Reverend Ben didn't provide pat answers but left his congregation with plenty to think about.

After the sermon, there was time given to Joys and Concerns. Martin remembered, once it started, that it was a time for the minister to call on hands raised around the sanctuary. Members of the congregation rose and asked for prayers for people who were sick or facing other difficulties. Or they shared news of some fortunate event—a new job, a baby expected, a child who had been honored at school or on the playing field.

Martin's mind wandered as various people rose and spoke, most of them asking for prayers for health issues. But his attention suddenly focused as a woman about Vera's age asked for prayers for her brother, who had been disabled in a car accident and was now in need of a motorized wheelchair.

"Once he has that chair, he might be able to get his old job back. It would mean so much to him, to be out in the world again, earning his living. It would mean so much to his dignity and self-esteem," she added. She explained some complicated reason that had to do with insurance and government medical benefits why the chair remained financially out of reach.

Martin sat up straight. Reverend Ben had advised him to keep his eyes and ears open, and this was just the sort of situation he was on the lookout for. The cost of such a chair would hardly make a dent in the funds he needed to spend, but it would be a start. *My first gift,* he thought with satisfaction. All he needed to do was figure out who that woman was and where her brother lived.

"Vera, who was that woman who just spoke?" he whispered. "I didn't catch her name."

"Miriam Parker. She lives with her brother Ned, on Teapot Lanc." Martin nodded. Count on Vera to tell him all he needed to know.

Martin listened closely as others spoke, committing to memory the names of those he could help. He slipped out his phone and—making sure that Vera, who was paging through a hymnal, didn't notice—sent himself a text message so he wouldn't forget any names.

In the closing moments of the service, Vera touched his arm. "I'm slipping out now. Got to get back in the kitchen. Don't worry about driving me home. I'm sure I can find a lift."

After Vera left, he wondered about attending the coffee hour. He had skipped breakfast and felt his empty stomach growling. But as the closing hymn ended and Reverend Ben gave a final benediction, Martin decided on a prompt and swift exit.

Among the first out of the pews, he headed for a side door to the sanctuary, well ahead of the crowd and also to avoid having to speak to Reverend Ben, who had stationed himself at the big doors at the end of the center aisle. He would have enjoyed a word with the minister and even offered praise for his sermon, but the less he socialized, the better, he reminded himself.

On the way out, he noticed Louisa Tulley, following her family. Had she seen him? She didn't try to catch his eye or say hello. Just as well, he thought.

Outside on the green, Martin raised his collar against a chilly breeze and headed toward Main Street. He had to get back to Vera's house for Milo at some point, but decided he had time for a quick bite. The Clam Box Diner caught his eye. ESTABLISHED 1955—TRY OUR FAMOUS CLAM ROLLS, a sign in the window read. He wondered if it still looked the same inside. He couldn't get enough of the food there as a boy, though he doubted it would meet his standards now. Still, it would be fun to see the place. He pulled open the door and stepped inside.

· · ·

LOUISA HAD DRIVEN HER OWN CAR TO church. It was a tight fit with her family these days, even in her father's big SUV. Her brothers were so big, all legs and bony elbows. She decided to leave the car parked behind the church while she walked into town and did some errands.

She liked having the afternoon free but knew it would go by quickly. She decided to start at the end of the street and work her way back to the car. She wanted to browse in the Bramble Antique Shop for Christmas gifts. Her mother collected china cups, all different shapes and patterns. Louisa always gave her a new cup for Christmas. It was a fun gift to buy, and an easy one.

She needed to punch in at five for the night shift. Louisa didn't mind the late hours but could understand why coworkers with families wanted to trade when they pulled night work. Someday—when she was married and had children—she would probably gripe about it, too. She was a long way from that situation right now. A bit further than she expected to be. It was hard to face the holidays single, especially since her family and friends had expected Santa to bring her an engagement ring this year. Not Santa exactly: Brian Hammond. They had dated since high school and the next step seemed a logical progression. *But you were the one who broke it*

107

off, Louisa reminded herself. *No sense looking back. You know you did the right thing.*

Louisa had been sure, despite the puzzled reactions of her friends and family. She had loved Brian, which made the choice even harder. But she had come to see that it wasn't the type of love that could go the distance. Brian was a good person, kind and responsible. He hadn't been much of a student and had always planned to be a fisherman, like his father. He had worked on the same trawler for years, saving up to buy his own boat. He thought it was important to be his own boss before he asked Louisa to marry him. That was all that kept him from proposing, he often told her. Ironically, once he was ready, Louisa got cold feet.

She had been a bit frustrated with his plan over the years, but saw now that it had worked out for the best. She realized that she had stayed with him out of habit more than any deep passion, and that, she thought, was no way to start a marriage.

She and Brian parted in late summer, and Louisa had dated a few times since, but no one new had made an impression. "Give yourself time," her mother would remind her. "Go out, have fun. When you meet the right person, you'll just know."

Will I know? Louisa wasn't sure about that. For the longest time, she had felt that Brian was "the right one." When it came to men, Louisa often felt confused and ill-equipped. Some of her friends breezed around the social scene so nimbly. But Louisa had never felt that easy confidence.

Now that she felt ready for a new relationship, she wasn't sure how to go about finding one. It wasn't going to happen while she sat on the couch every Saturday night, streaming videos and eating popcorn with her little sister, as she had last night. She knew that much.

You have to move out of your comfort zone, step up your game. You can't keep doing the same thing and expect different results. She had learned that hard truth at the academy during her training, and it had stuck. If only her social life could be as easy and comfortable as her work.

You can face down home intruders and help panicked victims out of car wrecks. Surely you can figure out how to meet an eligible, likable guy.

She was just about to pass the Clam Box when she noticed Martin Nightingale in a booth near the window, staring at his phone. She had seen him in church that morning, sandwiched between Vera Plante and Sophie Potter. Vera had doubtlessly lured him to the service somehow. Louisa wasn't sure why she found that thought amusing, but she couldn't help smiling. Martin didn't seem like the churchgoing type.

Impulsively, she stepped up to the diner and

pulled open the door. She wasn't even hungry. Was she interested in Martin? He was attractive enough. She had liked his looks from the first time they met, and he seemed intelligent and clever. Though he was only here a short time, he'd told her, and he definitely wasn't her usual type. Which wasn't working for her lately, she knew. But a tax attorney? A far cry from a fisherman. Louisa thought the "right" type probably fell somewhere in between.

This is just practice. Like a training drill. Think of Martin as a crash test dummy. When the real thing comes along, you'll be better equipped to handle the situation.

Louisa glanced at Martin as she walked in, trying to catch his eye, but he was staring down at his phone and making notes on a slip of paper. He looked intent on the task, too.

She wasn't sure what to do. Sit at the counter? Stand on the take-out line?

"Oh, hello, dear. Don't you look nice," Trudy, a longtime waitress at the diner, greeted her. "Not to say you don't look nice in your uniform," she added. "Different, that's all."

"Thanks, Trudy. I know what you mean." Louisa felt embarrassed by the compliments and hoped Martin wasn't listening.

"All the tables are full. Care to wait? You can sit at the counter. All by yourself today, Louisa?"

"Yes, just me."

At the sound of her name, Martin lifted his head and caught her eye. "Oh . . . hi. It's you . . . I didn't see you there."

"Hello, Martin."

She didn't actually say "I didn't see you either" but tried to give that impression. She didn't want to seem too obvious.

"Would you like to sit here? With me?" He stood up and nearly knocked over his water glass, quickly reaching out to steady it.

"Sure . . . thank you." Was he really nervous talking to her? She found that sweet. His shyness gave her courage.

He politely helped her off with her coat, and she settled into the booth opposite him. "Was that you in church today, sitting in the back with Vera and Sophie and Claire?"

"Vera had car trouble and I drove her over. Before I knew what was happening, she and her friends herded me into the sanctuary."

Louisa laughed. "Never underestimate the power of church ladies."

"Lesson learned. I never will again." He shook his head, his expression solemn, then smiled and met her gaze again. He had very nice eyes. Dark brown with lashes thick enough to be the envy of any girl. "I saw you in church, too. Lighting the candle with your family. Does a different family do it every time?"

"Yes, each week of Advent. I'm not sure how

111

Reverend Ben decides who to ask. But it is sort of an honor."

"I can see that." Martin's expression was serious, but she wondered if he was being sarcastic. He probably thought she was hopelessly small town. *You can only be yourself. No point in trying to act more sophisticated. If he doesn't like the real you, so be it.*

"I thought it was a very nice way to start the service. Very personal," he said, putting her more at ease. His words hadn't been sarcastic after all, she realized.

She picked up her menu, though she knew it by heart. "How's your work going?"

He looked confused for a moment, then answered in a rush. "Oh, fine. The situation is moving along. Though not as quickly as I expected."

He looked disappointed by the delay, but Louisa was happy to hear that news. Maybe he would be in the village longer than he had expected. Trudy came by, and Louisa ordered a grilled cheese sandwich and a cup of tea. Martin already had his lunch: "the famous clam roll," which was the diner's specialty, and fries.

"What do you think of the clam roll?" she asked.

He looked over his plate and poked the sandwich with his fork. "It's still clammy. But not as good as I . . . as I've heard." He stumbled over his reply, she noticed. As if he had meant to say something else. And what did he mean by "still" clammy? As opposed to . . . when?

"So you've actually heard about it? I thought Charlie Bates just called it famous as a marketing ploy."

"My client who lives around here told me to try it," he replied. "I'll try the hamburger next time."

"It's not much better," she said quietly. "The fries aren't bad, though."

"Not bad at all. Would you like some?" He pushed the dish of french fries toward her, and she picked one up and ate it. She wanted to know more about him but wasn't sure what to ask. Work was usually a safe topic, but he seemed very vague and even discreet about that subject. That made sense. Attorneys needed to keep details about their clients confidential.

"How's Milo?" she said finally. "Has he caught up to any squirrels lately?"

Martin smiled. "Not yet, but he never gives up hope. He's at Vera's. I didn't expect to be gone this long. I should probably get back to him soon. If he had a cell phone, he'd be texting me every minute by now."

Louisa laughed. "Is that the only reason you don't get him one?"

Martin grinned. "Practically." He reached for a fry and frowned. "I think these fries could use a little salt."

She nodded. "I wouldn't mind that." She glanced around the table, but there was only a pepper shaker. Trudy was the only waitress serving all the tables, and there seemed no hope of getting her attention.

"I see some on the counter," he said, rising from his seat. "Be right back."

As Martin jumped up and set off for the counter, the scraps of paper he had been writing on flew off the table in his wake. Louisa leaned over and gathered them up, and she couldn't help reading his scribbled notes as she made a neat pile again.

It looked like a list of names—familiar names, of people who lived in the village. Why would he be making a list like that? He had given the impression that he was a stranger here, except for the anonymous client he sometimes mentioned. Was this something that had to do with his work? Possibly, she thought, though there was no way she could ask him. That would be admitting she had snooped and read his notes.

She tucked the papers beside his plate, where they had been, but couldn't help trying to read them upside down. Next to each name, he'd added a street address and notations she couldn't understand. Some sort of personal shorthand or code? And after that, for each name, he had written a sum of money. That part particularly piqued her curiosity.

Were these people doing business with him?

114

She doubted that. None seemed the type to need or even be able to afford a private tax attorney. Though, of course, it could be possible.

The scribbles made her uneasy, as if she had discovered that Martin was spying on these people for some reason. Was he a con man, preying on older, vulnerable people? Trying to get them to invest in some bogus product or scheme, perhaps? They were all seniors, she noticed, and all experiencing difficulty in their lives right now.

Slow down, Louisa. You're letting your suspicious law-enforcement brain run away with you. There's probably a very simple, innocent explanation. Though it would be awkward, if not impossible, to ask him and find out for sure.

Maybe you were enjoying yourself too much and have to find something wrong with Martin, is that it?

The question disturbed her. She knew very well that could also be a possibility. But so did his notes.

Martin returned. "Your saltshaker, madame." He offered it with a flourish.

Louisa had to laugh. "Gee, thanks."

He smiled as he handed it over. "You may do the honors."

She added a dash of salt to the fries. "That should do it."

He tasted one and nodded. "Perfect. So you're

a good cook as well as a law officer. Impressive."

She had to laugh at his crazy exaggeration. Their eyes met and locked a moment. She knew she was attracted to him. He wasn't just a crash test dummy. Her feelings were very real.

But was he for real as well? Or just trying to charm her?

She looked away, suddenly uncomfortable, remembering the notes. *Should I just ask what it means? I didn't mean to read his notes. It was all perfectly innocent.*

Her gaze wandered toward the slips of paper, but when he noticed that she was looking at them, he whisked the pile off the table and into his pocket.

"Making a Christmas list?"

He shrugged and smiled. A forced smile, she thought. "Something like that."

"I meant to get started today, on my list," she said, not wanting him to notice her suspicions. "At least do some window-shopping." Her phone buzzed with a text message and she took it out of her pocket. "Excuse me . . . it's my mom."

She quickly checked the screen: Can you drop the boys off at a basketball game on your way to work later?

Louisa would have to get an earlier start than planned but didn't mind helping out her parents when she could. No problem. I'll be home soon, she quickly typed back.

"Is everything okay?"

"My mom needs a little help driving my brothers around to their endless sports events. I'd better run."

She took some bills from her purse and set them next to her plate, but Martin reached over and touched her hand. "I'll get the check. You hardly ate a bite."

She was surprised at his offer. She had landed at his table and eaten half his lunch. Maybe he was trying to make a good impression? To seem like a totally nice guy, when he wasn't really?

Police paranoia taking over again. It's just a grilled cheese sandwich, for goodness' sake.

"Thanks, that's very nice of you," she said finally. "I owe you an order of french fries."

"I'll take you up on that sometime."

Louisa slipped on her coat and picked up her big leather bag. Martin's warm parting smile made her wish she could stay longer. It actually made her wish she had never read the slips of paper that had fallen to the floor.

"See you around," she said as she turned toward the door.

"Yes, see you, Louisa. Enjoy your shopping."

As Louisa pulled open the door to leave, she turned back to look at him again. He had taken out his pile of notes and was already working on them.

She headed down the street, feeling confused. Part of her felt attracted to Martin and wondered if she would see him again. She'd half expected him to ask for her phone number and was surprised when he didn't. Especially after buying her lunch.

But another part—her law-officer intuition, which she had learned was rarely wrong—insisted there was more to Martin Nightingale than he was letting on. There was something about him, about his explanation for being in town, that didn't ring true.

She was curious and wanted to know if her suspicions were valid. She considered searching his name on the Internet. If he was really a tax attorney, as he claimed, some posts might come up. She could search a criminal database, too, when she had time at work.

She still had time to browse the Bramble before she needed to get home. She headed farther down Main Street to the antiques shop. The building had once been a Victorian house. Set back from the street, it was surrounded by a picket fence and a border garden that bloomed wildly from spring through the fall. Right now, the shop was decorated for Christmas with pine roping looped around the porch rail and columns, tiny white lights intertwined with it. The window boxes were filled with pine branches, bows, and Christmas balls. A big wreath hung on the door, and the window display featured an antique Santa ringing a brass bell.

Louisa had always loved the shop, from the time she was a little girl. Her mother would take her in to browse but always made her promise before they entered the store, "Look but don't touch. Right, Lou-Lou?"

Louisa recalled nodding solemnly and only occasionally breaking her vow, when an antique doll or tiny tea set proved too tempting. Grace Hegman, who owned the shop, was a reserved woman. But she never spoke harshly to children. She just gently steered them away from the fragile items.

Just as Louisa was walking up to the porch, Vera Plante walked out, carrying two small bags.

"You had the same idea that I did, Vera. I hope you didn't buy up all the goodies in there."

"The best bargains do sell quickly. I found some pretty earrings for my granddaughters. Precious stones," she added. "Oh . . . I meant to thank you for sending me a guest last week. Martin Hanson? He said you recommended me."

"Hanson?" Louisa was confused. Had Vera made a mistake about Martin's last name? Was some other guest named Martin staying with her? "The man who was sitting next to you in church today? I didn't think his last name was Hanson."

"I'm sure I'm not mistaken. He's a tax attorney, in town on business," Vera added. "You must meet so many people, dear. It must be hard to keep all the names straight."

"Sometimes, yes, it is confusing," Louisa conceded. She didn't want to alarm Vera. But she had seen Martin's driver's license and car registration and was positive his last name was Nightingale. Obviously, he'd given Vera a different one. Which was not a crime, she reminded herself. But it tripled her suspicions about him.

"Is he a good guest? Nothing . . . unusual about his behavior or habits?"

Vera looked surprised at the questions. "Oh, he's a very good guest. Quiet and tidy, and has very nice manners. And his dog is nice, too. He jumped right in to help when I had car trouble this morning. Martin, I mean. Not the dog," she clarified. "Why do you ask?"

"No special reason. I guess I feel responsible, sending a stranger to you."

Vera's expression relaxed. "You know what they say: 'A stranger is just a friend you haven't met yet.'"

Louisa smiled at the quaint expression, though she knew very well that sometimes strangers did not turn out to be all that friendly, or full of good intent.

"Nice to see you, dear. I have to run." Vera waved and headed down the path.

Left alone in front of the shop, Louisa paused before going inside. There was even more reason now to suspect that Martin Nightingale, alias Hanson, was hiding something. And she was even more curious to find out exactly what it was.

She was due at the station for a shift today and decided she'd go in early. She would do a little digging around about Martin and see what she could find.

Chapter Five

Wednesday, November 28, 2018

"Hold it right there. Put your hands up over your head and turn around. Slowly."

The shouted command startled him. Martin had been fumbling behind the home of Paula Monroe with only the aid of a light from his cell phone but was suddenly bathed in a megawatt beam. He tried to shield his eyes as he turned, both arms raised as commanded.

"It's fine, Officer . . . I'm not doing anything wrong . . . honestly."

"Right. Which is why you're skulking around in the dark back here?"

Martin knew that voice. Louisa Tulley. Again. He was speechless with surprise as she walked closer, the searchlight slanted toward the ground. "Louisa . . . is that you?"

"Keep your arms up."

He followed her orders but couldn't believe she was treating him like a criminal.

"What's that in your hand?"

"Just my phone." He showed it to her and she

took it from him. "Hands on your head," she said again.

She patted his jacket and found a screwdriver in his pocket. She stepped back and held it out to show him. "I didn't take you for the handy type, Martin."

"I'm not. All thumbs, truth be told."

"But handy enough to pry open a door or a window? Anyone can do that."

"Pry open a window? . . . Wait a minute. I know this looks bad, but I can explain. Honestly."

"Okay, Martin. Tell me what you're doing prowling around back here at two in the morning."

"I'm not trying to break into this person's house. I was just l-leaving something for them." Completely flustered, his face felt flushed, and he was stammering. "A gift," he added in a quieter tone. "A surprise."

"A surprise, really?" She obviously didn't believe him. He didn't blame her. "What sort of surprise?"

"A sewing machine. Top-of-the-line, too. I heard the woman who lives here say that she needs one so she can keep working at home. Look on the back porch if you don't believe me. I just left it there . . . And yes, I did flip the lock on the door with the screwdriver, but it was only a hook and eye. Not exactly safecracking."

He could tell that she still doubted his story but

at least seemed willing to see for herself if it was true. "Okay, let's go see. You walk ahead of me."

She directed the light at the porch, and he started walking across the lawn. Was she really afraid he was going to make a run for it? It seemed so silly.

When they reached the screen door, he pulled it open. She whisked the beam inside and instantly caught the glossy wooden case of the new machine, which was topped by a big red bow.

She turned to him. She did not look convinced. "What are you up to, Martin Nightingale? Or Hanson . . . or whatever your name is?"

Martin cringed. She had found out he'd given a fake name to Vera. That was bound to happen in such a small town. He should have expected it.

A light went on in a window above. A woman's voice called down, sounding alarmed, "What's going on? Is that the police?"

"It's fine, Paula. It's me, Louisa Tulley. Everything is under control. I'm just helping this man . . . He's lost his dog."

Martin met her eye, relieved by her quick thinking. "Sorry to disturb you, ma'am," he added.

"Oh, for pity's sake . . . well, hope you find that dog, mister. Maybe he's wandered home on his own by now. You'd be surprised."

The shade dropped and the window slammed

shut. Louisa waved her light toward the driveway. "Come on, Martin. You have some explaining to do."

"Yes, I guess I do."

Standing across the street by the police car, Martin faced her. "It's a long story," he began. "I'll try to explain as simply as I can."

"Take your time. I have three more hours before I punch out." She stood with her arms crossed over her chest, daring him to convince her that his intentions were good.

As simply as he could, Martin explained his grandfather's will and the gifts he had to give out in order to fulfill his grandfather's wishes.

"—And it's all to be done anonymously," he added. "That's why I gave Vera the name 'Hanson.' That's my mother's maiden name. My grandfather was very well-known in his day, and it's important that people don't connect me with him." She didn't look convinced. "Look, I know this sounds implausible and far-fetched. I could hardly believe it myself when my grandfather's lawyer explained the situation."

"It does sound far-fetched. But actually, it's too strange to be made up." Martin let out a breath of relief. At least she believed him now. Or was trying to.

"I have to admit, when we were at the diner Sunday and you got up to find a saltshaker, your notes fell on the floor. I didn't mean to read them but couldn't help it. Then I saw Vera and she told me about the fake name, so of course I suspected that you were up to something."

"That makes sense." Martin had felt a sudden change in her attitude toward him at the diner and wondered what he had said or done to put her off. In a way it was good to know it was only because she'd misunderstood his scribbling and thought him a far cleverer character than he really was. "What did you think I was up to?"

She shrugged, looking embarrassed to tell him. "Oh, I don't know. Some sort of scam that involved fleecing seniors. I really wasn't sure. I ran your name through a few criminal databases, but you came up clean."

"Criminal databases?" he echoed. "I'm not even on dating sites." He wasn't sure why he'd admitted that, but he finally saw her smile.

"So, how's it going? Have you given out a lot of gifts yet?"

Martin felt a weight descend at the question. "This is my first. A motorized wheelchair is going to be delivered to someone named Ned Parker tomorrow. After that, I have no idea what to do," he admitted. "I spoke to Reverend Ben last week. I thought he could tell me about people who need help. But that plan didn't work out either."

"Really? That doesn't sound like him."

"He was very encouraging and had a lot of

good advice. But he didn't want to identify people in the community who need my gifts. He doesn't think my grandfather wanted me to solve the problem so easily. Reverend Ben thinks I have to be the one to find people who need help. That I need to be moved by their problems."

"That's probably true."

"It probably is, and I respect his opinion. But I'm still not making any progress."

She finally looked as if she believed him, and was even sympathetic. Before he could stop himself, Martin said, "You've lived here all your life, Louisa. I bet you know everybody. I'm a total stranger and not very good at making friends or getting to know a person's private problems. People just don't open up to me like that. Could you possibly help me spend this money? Would you? Please?"

She looked surprised by his request, and Martin held his breath, hoping she would say yes.

"Gee . . . I don't know what to say. It seems like an interesting project. Maybe even fun. But . . . I don't know, Martin . . ."

Was she about to turn him down? It seemed so. Martin felt himself panicking. In the few seconds since he asked her, he'd realized that Louisa was the solution to his problem. With her help, it would all be so easy. He would give out the money to the right people and meet his Christmas deadline. "I'm sure you're very busy, Louisa," he said, determined to convince her. "But I'd be happy to pay you for your time. Anything you ask."

He waited again, feeling a flicker of hope. But very quickly saw her expression change. His offer to pay her had tipped the scales, and not at all in his favor. "Wait . . . that was dumb. I didn't mean to insult you."

"I'm sure you didn't." Her clipped tone made him feel even more tactless and insensitive—as if she suddenly saw him as incredibly privileged and spoiled. "The thing is, I agree with Reverend Ben. I think you need to figure out this puzzle on your own."

"I hope I can." He saw a spark of sympathy in her eyes and hoped against hope that she would change her mind.

"I'd be overwhelmed in your shoes, too," she admitted. "It's a crazy assignment. Your grandfather sounds like a real character. But you said some of the money can go to groups and charities. Why not start there? Look around a little. There are lots of drives and fund-raisers going on right now. You could wallpaper your room at Vera's with all the flyers posted around town."

Martin smiled, despite his disappointment. "Good idea. I mean, looking for the fund-raisers. I doubt Vera would approve of any redecorating."

She returned his smile and caught his gaze a moment. Martin felt his heartbeat quicken.

"Good luck, Martin. Next time you're out playing Secret Santa, try not to sneak around like a burglar? My colleagues might not buy your story so easily." Her tone was warm and friendly now, and Martin hoped it was a sign she had forgiven him for his stupid slip.

He said good night and walked back to his car, then sat quietly, watching her drive off. He could think of a long list of reasons why it was not a good idea to get involved with Louisa Tulley and why it was actually a good thing that she hadn't agreed to help him.

You're in this town for just a few days, he reminded himself. *To do a job and get your inheritance. Not to start a romance with a local girl. The type of girl who wants a settled-down life out here in the country, marriage and children—the kind of life you don't plan on. Not right now, anyway. Maybe not for a long time. It would be wrong to get involved and end up disappointing her.*

Martin knew that was all true. But as he drove back to Vera's house, he couldn't help thinking about Louisa's bright blue eyes as she'd caught him "skulking" and her warm smile as they'd said good-bye. He couldn't help wondering when he would see her again.

"CAN I MAKE YOU AN ICE PACK, WALTER? OR is it a warm pack for a toothache? Did you take some aspirin, dear?"

Walter nodded, holding his hand over his jaw. "It's not so bad, Frances. Please don't worry. I just need to see the dentist. I'll go over this morning."

"Good idea." Frances filled her cup with coffee but didn't offer him any.

"I'd like some coffee," he said quickly, before she took the pot away.

"Do you think that's a good idea? It's so hot, it might make your pain worse."

He hadn't thought of that. He wasn't a very good actor, was he? "I'll wait till it's cooled off a bit."

She reluctantly filled his cup. When her back was turned, he took a quick sip then pretended to be blowing on it as she returned to the table.

"Must have come on suddenly. You didn't mention a thing about it yesterday," she mused.

Walter shrugged, yearning for more coffee but just eyeing the cup. He reached for a slice of toast instead but instantly read the alarm in his wife's expression.

"No toast, Walter. You'll hit the ceiling."

"Oh . . . right. It sort of comes and goes. I forgot . . . Teeth can be funny."

"It won't be so funny if you need that one pulled. You have a sweet tooth. I always tell you that."

He smiled. "Maybe that's the one that needs to come out."

She laughed but didn't reply. He wondered if she suspected anything, and he felt another pang about hiding his real destination this morning. It wasn't the dentist—though given the choice, he would have happily had a tooth removed instead of facing the bank manager.

FRANCES WAS ALREADY IN THE SHOP WHEN Walter came down. He wore an overcoat over his best suit and tie, though he wondered if his shined shoes and close shave would give him away. If Frances noticed, she didn't comment. He already had the papers he needed tucked in his vest pocket, and he gave her a quick kiss on the cheek on his way out the door.

"No telling how long this will take. I might need to wait awhile, barging in without an appointment." He wondered if the bank manager would see him at all without an appointment. He hoped so.

"I know. Good luck," she said with a sympathetic smile.

"Thanks, dear." *I need it,* he almost added. He tipped his hat and left the shop, a sick feeling in his stomach.

One foot in front of the other, Walter. You can circle the world that way, no less make it down Main Street, he thought, recalling advice from his infantry days.

It was only a few minutes past nine and the bank had just opened. Walter walked up the granite steps and through the brass-and-glass revolving door, which was flanked by marble columns. He saw the windows covered by thin brass bars where three tellers stood, helping early customers. Off to the left was a row of doors marked with nameplates; he guessed they were the offices for bank officials.

A woman sat at a desk in front of the doors, her speedy typing echoing in the space. Her hair was pinned up neatly and she wore glasses with stylish frames, the lenses shaped like cat eyes.

"May I help you, sir?" She looked up from her typewriter, and Walter noticed the name plaque on her desk: Mrs. Bowman.

"I'd like to see Mr. Finley. He's written to me several times and I thought it best if . . . if we could talk, face-to-face." He wondered how much he needed to say. Not too much, he hoped.

"Your name, sir?" She smiled at him politely, but he felt silly and awkward, forgetting to give his name.

"Nightingale. Walter Nightingale."

She glanced down at a large book on her desk,

following down a column with her finger. "Do you have an appointment, Mr. Nightingale? I'm sorry, I don't see your name."

"Uh . . . actually, I don't."

"I'm sorry, sir. But you really need an appointment to see Mr. Finley. He's a very busy man. I don't see a minute to spare in his schedule."

Walter's heart fell. But he was determined to get this over with today. "Sure, I understand. But this is sort of an emergency. Maybe he can fit me in somewhere? It shouldn't take long. I can wait. Or come back later," he offered.

She gave him a doubtful look. "I'm sorry, Mr. Nightingale. That isn't the way we do things here. You really need an appointment." She turned the pages of the book. "Let's see, I can find some time for you next week if you like. Next Thursday?"

"I can't wait till Thursday . . . A friend of mine, Oliver Warwick, told Mr. Finley I'd be coming by today. Could you ask him? Maybe he remembers."

Would it help to mention Oliver's name? Walter wasn't sure. Mrs. Bowman closed her book and met his glance. Then he heard her sigh and could tell it had helped.

She picked up the receiver on the intercom and hit a button. "Sorry to disturb you, Mr. Finley. There's a man out here, Walter Nightingale. He doesn't have an appointment but said that Oliver

Warwick may have arranged a meeting with you for today?"

Walter couldn't hear the bank manager's reply and waited anxiously. He rolled the rim of his hat along his fingers, a nervous habit he had at times.

Finally, Mrs. Bowman set the receiver back in place. "You're in luck. Mr. Finley doesn't have a lot of time but said that he can spare a few minutes for you. I'll walk you back to his office."

She rose from her seat, tucking a folder under her arm.

Walter jumped up from his chair and followed her. He didn't feel all that lucky—more like he was walking into the lion's den. *Buck up, Walter,* he coached himself. *Life can't be about playing with toys all the time. You need to face your responsibilities.*

The secretary opened a heavy wooden door and sailed through. Walter followed, but hung back a bit as she approached the desk and set the folder in front of her boss. "These letters need to be signed, sir. This is Mr. Nightingale," she added.

Richard Finley nodded at Walter. "Come in, Mr. Nightingale. Have a seat." He waved at the two leather chairs in front of his heavy wooden desk.

"Thank you, sir." Walter sat down and rested his hat on his knee. Mrs. Bowman walked out and closed the door. Mr. Finley leaned back in his large leather chair and picked up a silver cigarette box. "Cigarette?"

"No, thank you."

Mr. Finley took out a cigarette, lit it with a silver lighter, and inhaled. "How can I help you today, Mr. Nightingale?"

Walter took a breath. "I'm not sure where to begin." He took out the letters from his breast pocket. He hadn't brought all of them; only a few of the most recent. "I have some loans with your bank, sir. A business loan and a mortgage on the building where I live and have a store. Maybe you know it—Nightingale's Magical Toy Shop, on Main Street?"

Finley waved his hand. "Sure, I know that shop. My children can never walk past without dragging me inside." Walter wasn't sure whether he was amused by this, or annoyed.

"The problem is, sir . . . well, I've fallen behind with my payments. I didn't even realize how bad it was until I took a good look last week." Walter took out the letters from his pocket and offered them to Mr. Finley. The bank manager sat up, his expression more serious. And far less friendly.

"Let's see . . ." Walter watched as Finley quickly scanned the pages. He suddenly looked up. "This is serious, Mr. Nightingale. You have let this go a long time."

"Yes . . . I know. I'm very sorry. I'm usually much more responsible. If you look into my record at the bank, I think you'll see that I've always been much more responsible about these matters. I don't really know how it happened," he admitted. "But if the bank would just give me a little more time, sir. I'm certain I can catch up by Christmas. The shop is already very busy, and people have hardly started their holiday shopping."

Mr. Finley took a few more puffs on his cigarette and stubbed it out in a large ashtray. He sat back and Walter waited, balanced on the edge of his seat, holding his breath.

"How do you know Oliver Warwick . . . if I may ask? Is he a friend?"

Exaggerating his relationship with Oliver would probably help his case, Walter guessed. But he had to answer honestly. "I don't know if I'd go that far. I know Oliver a bit and like him very much. We attend the same church and I have known him for years."

"I ask because he's put in a word for you."

"He said he would," Walter replied.

"As much as I value Mr. Warwick's opinion, your situation is very serious. We have our policies. It's hard to be lenient for one customer and not for the next."

Walter's hopes fell. "I understand, sir. That's only fair."

Mr. Finley looked surprised, as if he had expected Walter to argue. "I don't mean to be harsh or hard-hearted. I know your shop. It's very unusual. Not the typical toy shop, not by a long shot. So many one-of-a-kind items; a real wonderland for children. Frankly, I'm surprised that your business isn't more profitable."

"I am, too," Walter said honestly.

"Have you tried advertising? How about raising your prices? Maybe you're not charging enough. Have you checked out the competition lately?"

"Those are all excellent ideas, sir. I appreciate the advice. We were planning to do more advertising this Christmas season. We just didn't get to it yet."

And now, probably never will, Walter thought, though he didn't say that aloud. Mr. Finley seemed to hear the unspoken words hanging in the air nonetheless.

"If only we had a little more time. Just a few weeks, until Christmas? I'll take your advice to heart and do everything I can to get these payments up to date. Honestly."

"Christmas, you say?" The bank manager picked up a small calendar and then looked over the letters. He made some notes on a yellow pad and tapped numbers into an adding machine that sat at the edge of his desk.

Walter waited and sent up a small prayer. *Please let all that tapping work out in my favor. Just a little breathing space, that's all I ask.*

Mr. Finley stretched the tape on the adding machine, scanning it and frowning. He made more notes, then finally sat back and looked up at Walter.

"Well, here's what I can do. If you can pay the bank half of the outstanding balance due on these loans by December fifteen, we'll wait until January for the rest."

He showed Walter the figures he'd worked out. "That amount down there, that's what you need to pay by the middle of the month. Do you think you can manage it?"

Walter wasn't sure. It still seemed like a lot of money to come up with in only two weeks. But this was his only chance, and he had to agree. *With God, all things are possible,* he reminded himself.

"Yes, I can manage it. I can definitely manage that, sir. And I appreciate you working things out."

"Don't mention it, Mr. Nightingale. We all hit some rough sledding now and again." Mr. Finley sat back, looking relieved and giving Walter the sense that he was a decent man who was happy to have found a compromise. "I'm glad this arrangement is amenable to you. I'll send you a letter to confirm the agreement," he added, catching Walter's eye.

"Of course. I'll look for it in the mail." Walter knew he would open this one, not just stuff it in a desk drawer. He stood up and smiled. "Thank you, sir. Thank you again."

Mr. Finley rose and shook his hand and Walter left the office, feeling suddenly so light from the burden that had lifted, he thought he might float up all the way to the ornately painted ceiling.

He sailed out of the bank and headed down Main Street, toward the shop. *Don't look too cheerful, Walter. Frances thinks you just had a tooth drilled, remember?*

He felt another pang of conscience and wondered if it was time to reveal their money problems to her. Maybe it was. She would understand their need to work doubly hard the next few weeks, and she might have some good ideas. And it was only fair. It was her shop, too, and her future hanging in the balance.

Frances was standing at the register when Walter walked into the shop. She had just finished a sale and she handed an older woman her package. "Hope to see you again very soon."

"Oh, I'll be back. I have a few more grandchildren to buy for."

Walter hoped so. He tipped his hat to the lady as she passed. "Was that a good sale, Frances?"

"Not bad. She bought that second cowgirl doll I made. And she asked if we had any mermaids. I think I'll make one and see how it goes over."

"That's a good idea. I bet a mermaid would sell in a minute."

Frances didn't reply. She didn't even smile, her mouth remained in a tight, straight line.

She smoothed a stack of paper bags and tissue paper. "How was the dentist, Walter? How's your toothache?"

Walter had forgotten all about it. He touched his cheek and shrugged. "The dentist took care of it. It wasn't as bad as I thought this morning."

"Really? That's funny, because this morning the bad tooth was on the right side of your mouth, and now you're rubbing the left."

Walter winced. He wasn't sure what to say.

"I was in the workshop, Walter. I needed some glue, and I found these letters in your desk drawer." Frances took a stack of bank letters from under the counter and set them on the glass. "You weren't really at the dentist, were you?"

Walter shook his head. He felt sad and embarrassed. "No . . . I went to the bank, to speak to the manager." He looked up and met his wife's gaze. "I'm sorry, Frances. I wanted to tell you the truth, but I didn't want to worry you. And . . . I was embarrassed," he admitted. "I've made a huge mess of things. I haven't been responsible. I haven't been taking care of you."

Frances still looked angry. "It wasn't right, Walter, keeping all this from me. When would I find out? When someone knocked on the door to throw us out?" She crossed her arms over her chest and tossed her head, the way she did when she was really angry and upset. Which happened only rarely.

"I intended to tell you all about it tonight, at supper. I really did." He paused and took a deep breath and tried to meet her gaze, though she kept looking away.

"I'm not sure if I believe you, Walter. I think you wanted to tell me but you would have found some excuse. Due to your good intentions, of course. But I'm not a child who needs to be protected from our problems. We have to share our troubles, Walter, as well as our blessings. Otherwise, it's not fair to either of us."

Walter nodded and pressed a hand to his heart. "I know, Frances. And you're perfectly right. It's just that . . . that I'm ashamed of how irresponsible I've been. How I've made such a mess of our finances. It's not fair to you. I've been a very poor husband that way, and you could have married anyone. I know you must be sorry now that you chose me," he said sadly.

Walter had known Frances since their school days. He had watched her from afar, never thinking she would be interested in a guy like him, a dreamer with no real direction in life, except for a love of drawing and a talent with his hands.

She'd had her pick of young men, all of them clearly primed to be far more successful and respected around town than he ever would. It pained him to think she might regret her choice, after all.

Her expression softened and she pressed a

finger against his lips. "Don't ever say that, Walter. I never once wanted to be married to anyone but you."

"Even today, when you found those letters?"

"Even today," she answered without a second's hesitation.

"I just love you so much, Franny. From the first time I saw you." He remembered the exact moment so clearly, even now. Junior year of high school, a bright day in early spring when the entire world seemed to be bursting into bloom. Frances had just moved to town and didn't know anyone in the school. He walked into history class, and there was the loveliest girl he had ever seen, sitting at the desk he always took. She was staring around nervously, as if she hoped someone would talk to her, though no one did. It took all his courage, more than he thought he had in him, but he walked straight over, sat down next to her, and introduced himself. One of his bravest moments—and one that had surely changed his life.

"—I've always dreamed I'd do so much better and give you a much easier life. Now I feel as if I've failed you. I've failed both of us."

"You haven't failed. You made a mistake, Walter. Everyone does from time to time. I don't expect you to be perfect. I wouldn't want you to be. And I wouldn't change a thing about you, or our life together."

Her words soothed him, though he didn't entirely agree. He smiled into her soft gaze, counting his blessings for her understanding. "Thanks for saying that. But I'm still sorry."

"Sorry for falling behind with our payments? Or for hiding it from me? That's what really upset me. Maybe I could have helped you work on this before it got to be such a tangle. Did you ever think of that?"

Walter sighed. "I know you could have. I know you're just as smart as me, Franny. Even smarter. It's not that at all . . . I was thinking about what the doctor told us," he admitted. "The less work and worry you have, the sooner you'll have a baby. I know how much you want one. How much we both do."

Frances looked moved by his admission, her eyes glassy for a moment. "Oh, Walter . . . I know you want to take care of me. But I'm not a china doll, to be set up on a shelf out of harm's way. We'll have a baby someday, heaven willing. In the meanwhile, I thought we were equal partners. All the time. Not just when there's good news to share. But you haven't treated me like one."

"I'll do better from now on, I promise. We're definitely partners. Good times and bad. I'm so lucky to have you." He took her hand and dropped a kiss in her palm.

Frances cupped his cheek with her hand. She

143

caught his gaze and held it. "So what happened at the bank, partner?"

Walter had to smile. "I managed to get some time with the bank manager, Mr. Finley, though his secretary nearly chased me away. He was very polite and respectful but didn't seem willing to bend the rules for us. Not at first. But we talked for a while and he finally offered an extension. He seems a good-hearted man, and he knows our shop and doesn't understand why we can't make a go of it. We have until December fifteenth to pay back half of the overdue amount. The bank wants the rest the first week in January."

Frances smiled. "Good work. That's something. That gives us some breathing room."

"A little." His first instinct was to sound more positive, but he remembered his promise not to shield her. "I'm not sure we can do it, Franny. Of course I agreed and thanked him ten times for the chance. But that's a lot of money to come up with in two short weeks. I just don't see how we can do it."

Walter was usually the ever-sunny optimist. Frances even teased him about it; and he saw a flash of surprise and concern on her lovely face as she took in his words. Then, just as quickly, her dark eyes shone with resolve.

"Don't say that, Walter. It's not like you." Her tone was low but as firm as he'd ever heard it. "Whenever I feel like giving up on something,

144

you always say, 'Whether you think you can or you think you can't, you're right.'"

Walter smiled. "You give me too much credit, honey. Henry Ford said that long before I ever did."

"Well . . . you're both right. The point is, we have to try. We have to put our shoulders to the wheel and give it our best shot. We've been given a chance, however slim, and I for one am not going down without a fight."

Her determination lifted his spirits. Wallowing in a defeated attitude never solved a problem. Walter knew that. He also knew that he was usually the one to take the lead in their business matters, especially at a moment like this one. *See where that's gotten us.*

Instead of assuring Frances that he would solve everything, he said, "I'm not going down without a fight either. But what do you think we should do?"

She looked surprised but glad to be asked. "Well, I told you that Nancy Trumbull is looking for a salesgirl, just for the Christmas season, right? I spoke to her on Saturday, to get the details. The pay is good and she'll give me a commission on a big sale, like a ball gown. I can work there a few hours a week and help in the shop, too. I'm the perfect fit for the Paris Boutique, don't you think?"

She smiled at her own joke, and Walter did,

too. Inside, he felt a little sad. "I'm sure you'd be great, honey. But I'm the one who should get an extra job. You do enough here, working in the shop and making all the dolls."

A woman with two little girls walked in. Frances gave Walter a look. They never talked over their personal business in front of customers. Walter reached over and patted her hand. "We'll talk about this later, dear. I'll take care of this lady."

Frances smiled and headed in the customer's direction. "I can take care of her, Walter. Why don't you make the sandwiches? I think you know where to find the lunch meat and mustard."

"So I do. I'll give a holler if I need any help."

Walter laughed as he climbed the stairs. Frances was feisty today, wasn't she? He couldn't blame her. He was lucky she was speaking to him at all.

Walter wished that he had told Frances about their situation sooner, but now that it was out in the open, he did feel relieved. She was right. Keeping that secret, no matter his good intentions, had not been right. But now, together, maybe they could find a path out. He could ask for no better partner to shoulder this burden and figure out a solution. That thought alone gave him hope.

The rest of the day passed quickly. After lunch, Walter took over in the shop and Frances worked on her sewing in their apartment. By dinnertime, they were both eager to talk over their ideas to save their business.

"I had a good idea today, Franny. A customer was saying what unique toys we have, compared to the other toy shops in the area—that big place in Newburyport and the one out in Hamilton. People always say that and I just thank them and brush off the compliment, but this time it got me thinking. Maybe those other stores would like to sell some handmade toys, too, in addition to all the mass-produced items on their shelves."

"That's a good idea, Walter. Why didn't we ever think of that before?" She set bowls of mashed potatoes and string beans on the table and then brought over a platter of meat loaf, one of his favorites. He knew that meant she wasn't mad at him anymore. "But how will you persuade them?"

"Good question. I'll have to be our traveling salesman, I guess. We can pick out some of our best toys tonight, and tomorrow I'll bring them around to the different shops. If the store owners like a toy, I'll take orders. It will be a lot of driving, but it could be worth it."

"It could work out very well. I can watch our shop tomorrow, and help you fill the orders, too, of course. I'm sure these other stores will want the toys quickly."

"I'm a little worried about that part. I never had to make toys for other people before, meeting a delivery date and all that." He took a bite of mashed potatoes, which were delicious. "One step at a time, I guess."

"Yes, one step at a time. Let's get some orders first before we fret. And do ask a fair price, dear? You know how long it takes to make our toys and the cost of the materials. People will pay for quality."

Walter smiled. "I won't give them away, Franny. Don't worry. Mr. Finley thinks we should raise our prices, but I don't want to go that far. Not yet."

"I agree," she replied. Walter was glad to hear that. "I just wish more people knew about our shop and what wonderful toys we sell. What about advertising in the newspaper or on the radio?"

"Mr. Finley said we should advertise, too. But it's so expensive. I don't think we can afford it. Not right now," he added, wanting to be more positive.

"That's too bad. Because I even thought of a slogan. Listen to this . . ." She sat up and dabbed her mouth with a napkin, then said, "'Where do you think Old St. Nick fills his Christmas list? At Nightingale's Magical Toy Shop! Santa is one of our best customers!'"

Walter laughed. "Very clever. Maybe we should make a sign like that and put it in the window."

"We can do better than that. How about making

handbills and posting them around town? We can give them out on Main Street on Saturday, when all the shoppers are out. We should offer something extra to draw people down to the store. Some extra reason to make them come here."

Walter sat up and stared at her. "You mean like a coupon or a sale? How about a raffle? Each flyer could have a number, and we could announce a door prize."

Frances laughed. "You always want to give away something, don't you, Walter? That's the first thing you think of."

Walter blushed, mainly because it was true.

Beforc he could reply, her eyes suddenly widened, and so did her smile. "I've got it! We can have Santa at our shop on Saturday. That will bring the parents with their children. And maybe we'll hold a raffle to give away a toy or two as well," she conceded. "We can definitely give out candy canes and cookies and hot cocoa. The kids will see our toys and ask Santa—and their parents—for a few?"

"Frances, that's brilliant!" Walter jumped up from his seat, ran around the table, and hugged her. "What a great idea. Santa will visit our shop on Saturday. We'll have a line around the block. But who can we ask to dress up?"

"You can be Santa, dear. I know you'd secretly love to ride around on Christmas night and give out all our toys for free."

Walter laughed. "You know me too well, Franny. I'd love to play Santa, even for a day. But I think we should find someone else. I'll be too busy handling sales. Maybe someday, when we're rich, I'll let the big guy know I'm ready to step in for him."

"Yes, someday. When we have bags of money. You never know," Frances agreed. "In the meantime, what about Digger Hegman? I don't think he's fishing or clamming much right now. I bet he needs the money."

Walter thought so, too. A fisherman and clammer, Digger lived outside of town in a little cottage near the marshes. He was younger than Walter, in his early twenties, but already had a wife and two little girls to support. His oldest daughter, Grace, was adorable and followed him everywhere. Digger was a wonderful, loving father and the best clammer for miles around. He was a bit eccentric; he claimed he could actually hear the clams communicating under the sand and that was how he found so many. But when Digger wasn't busy hunting down shellfish, he looked for odd jobs around town. Walter and Frances had hired him many times as a handyman and, in a pinch, as a salesclerk. A man of few words, Digger was not the best salesman they could have found. But he was very honest and hardworking, which counted for a lot in Walter's book. Still, Walter wasn't at all sure Digger was their best choice for this job.

"You know I would love to help Digger. But don't you think he's a bit young to play Santa? And a bit thin?" Walter never liked to talk about anyone's physical appearance, but it was true. Digger was a lanky fellow. Walter wasn't sure how he stayed aboard a ship in foul weather. Maybe he tied himself to the deck railing in a storm so he wouldn't blow overboard?

"A few pillows will fatten him up, and he has the most wonderful beard. All he needs is a little talcum powder and maybe some wire-frame glasses?"

"I can see you have all this worked out. All right. I'll ask him in the morning."

"Good. I'll work on the flyer tonight." She took her empty dish off the table and reached for his. He snatched up a bit of leftover meat loaf and wrapped it in a paper napkin. "There's a stray dog that comes to the alley. He looks like he hasn't had a real meal in weeks. I'm going to look for him tonight. I'll give him these scraps."

"It's so cold out, too. Poor dog. That's not enough for him. Why don't I put together a plate with some leftovers? You can give him a decent dinner."

Frances took a saucer and began assembling scraps for the dog. "He must be lost. I bet some family in town is looking for him. Did you see a collar or a tag?"

"He doesn't have a collar. I think he's been hurt or spooked by something. He won't let me get close. I'm trying to win him over, but it's slow going."

"Keep at it, Walter. Dogs love you." She set a saucer heaped with scraps from dinner on the table and touched Walter's shoulder as she walked by. "Dogs and children," she amended.

Walter laughed. "That counts for something, I guess."

"It counts for a lot. I think so, anyway."

Walter reached for the saucer. "Maybe he'll let me get closer tonight." He took an oatmeal cookie from the cookie jar, took a bite, then added a few bits to the dog's dish.

Frances looked puzzled. "What's that, dessert?"

Walter shrugged, his mouth full. "He loves your oatmeal cookies. I give him little bits every night. I'm sure he'll be looking for some."

"I'm flattered. I'll make extra for him next time I bake."

Walter didn't doubt she would.

"Do you think I can see him, too?"

"I don't know. He's very shy and he usually comes around later, but we can take a look. You need to come down to the shop for a while anyway to choose the toys I'm going to show to the other toy stores tomorrow. Remember?"

Frances smiled at him. "I didn't forget. I'm glad you didn't either."

Her tone made him laugh. With a wave of his hand, he stepped aside to let her go down the staircase first. It had done him good to hear her lighthearted laugh and toss around ideas together at their kitchen table. It gave him hope that everything could work out as they wanted. His wife was right. He should have asked her weeks ago to help him work out this problem.

How many times had he heard it said? *Heaven helps those who help themselves.* If he and Frances really pushed, heaven would surely lead them through this rough patch and help them keep their shop. He had faith that, somehow, it would all work out for the best.

CHAPTER SIX

Tuesday, November 29, 1955

WALTER LEFT CAPE LIGHT EARLY THE next morning and returned after eight o'clock that night. Frances was at the ironing board, but she had saved his dinner on a plate in the oven. She set it before him on the table, then sat in her usual spot to keep him company, sipping a cup of tea.

He was so hungry and tired, he didn't say a word for several minutes. "Sorry . . . I'm gobbling this stew like the stray dog in the alley." He set his fork down and wiped his mouth with a napkin.

Frances smiled over the edge of her cup. "Actually, I was thinking the same thing. Didn't you stop for lunch today?"

He shook his head. "No time. I had a lot of ground to cover. And a lot of talking to do. I yakked my head off until my throat got sore. Made me grateful I'm not a traveling salesman. I'd never make it."

"I'm sure it must have been difficult. You

154

were very brave to even try. Did the other store-keepers even want to meet with you? I've been wondering if they think of us as rivals."

"Most are decent guys and heard me out. And most ordered our toys, too, once they had a look. Compared to the toys in their shops, ours really stand out." He forked up another bite, but didn't bring it to his mouth. "I'd say the trip was definitely worthwhile."

Frances looked impressed and happy. "That's wonderful. Did they want any dolls?"

"Quite a few. I hope you can handle it, especially since we still need stock in our store," he said. "Maybe you shouldn't take that job at the dress shop after all. There's a lot more for you to do here now."

Even though he had promised Frances he wouldn't coddle her, he couldn't help it. He didn't want to see her work so hard.

"Too late. Nancy came in to buy some toys for her children. I told her I was interested in the job, and she hired me on the spot."

Walter could see his wife was very proud about her news. He couldn't spoil that for her. "That's wonderful, honey. When does it start?"

"Tomorrow. I was just pressing my red dress. And I set my hair. I hope it comes out okay." Frances's hair was covered with a scarf, and Walter noticed bobby pins underneath, a complicated process that involved hair spray and a restless night of sleep, reserved for weddings, holidays, and sometimes Sunday service. "I want to look smart my first day. It's a little different working there than in the toy store."

"I'm sure it will be. But you're an excellent saleswoman, and you look wonderful all the time. You don't need to worry." He wasn't sure how, but Frances always dressed well and looked so stylish, despite not spending much on her wardrobe. "I guess you won't be here on Saturday, for Santa Claus. Do you still think we should do it?"

"Don't worry. I told Nancy I needed to come in late on Saturday, and she agreed. I thought we could hold our event from nine to noon, so I'd be here to help. Digger agreed to be Santa, and I even made the flyer, so you can't back out now."

"You've thought of everything, haven't you?"

"I think so . . . But we have time, just in case I forgot something." She jumped up and walked to a desk in the foyer, then returned with a folder.

Walter removed a piece of drawing paper and looked over her efforts. The flyer was very striking, with bold letters that announced Santa's visit and the place, date, and time, along with a wonderful drawing. She'd found room to add details about the free refreshments and the giveaway, too.

"Very professional. You could get a job at the print shop if Nancy's boutique doesn't work out." Frances looked pleased at his compliment. Doubly pleased, because they both knew George Plante would never hire a woman. Everyone knew he was passing his business to his son, Lester, who was still in high school.

"I'll stick with dresses for now," she said with a smile. "But it's something to think about." She went back to the ironing board to resume pressing her good dress.

Walter slipped the flyer back into the folder. "I'll take this to George tomorrow and have a big pile made up. You've been very busy while I was out today, very productive. Any other news?"

Frances licked her finger and touched it quickly to the bottom of the iron. He heard a small sizzle. "That's it, for now. Just trying to do my part. While you were on the road, I covered the home front. We have to work together—we're a team."

"Yes, we are, honey. Truly." He smiled and met her warm gaze.

Out of their financial problem, he and Frances had grown even closer, their bond even stronger. He hadn't thought that could be possible, but it was true. His mother always said, "Some good always comes from some bad. You need to keep a lookout and find it. And try to focus on that." This time, it was easy to see the good that had emerged. He wouldn't easily forget it.

She was humming as she ironed. She finished the dress, draped it on a hanger, and carefully checked the flared skirt for hidden wrinkles. "What are you smiling at, mister?"

He shrugged and stood up, then stepped over and kissed her cheek. "Just thinking about how lucky I am."

It was true. Just when he thought he couldn't possibly love her more, he found that his love grew.

THE NEXT MORNING, WALTER SAT AT THE table alone, sipping coffee. Frances had made oatmeal for them earlier but then ran back to the bedroom to dress for work. She finally emerged in a cloud of cologne, looking very stylish in her red dress, high heels, curled hair, and lipstick.

"Well, what do you think?" She twirled on her heels.

"You look gorgeous, Franny. But I'm confused . . . I thought Nancy needed a saleslady. You look like a fashion model. Straight from the Paris runway," he added for good measure.

"Very funny, Walter." Frances gave him a look, but he could tell she was pleased. "I hope Nancy agrees. She said that we need to set a good example for the customers, so they'll buy more clothes."

"I can see the wisdom in that," he replied. "What time will you be home?"

"I'll work from ten to two o'clock today, then there's another girl who comes in from two to six. So I can watch the store in the afternoon if you need to get into the workshop."

"Good plan." Walter was itching to get into his workshop today, but he didn't want to pester her about it. He walked her to the door and gave her a good-luck hug. She set a saucy little black hat on her head and pulled on her dressy black gloves. "I'm off. See you later."

"Good luck, honey. Have fun."

Frances waved and sailed out the door. Walter ate his breakfast quickly and went down to the store. He turned the sign on the door to open, surveyed the stock, and then headed to his workshop.

You have work to do, he coached himself. *Frances will be back soon enough. It's all hands on deck and she's already doing more than her share.*

He pulled out the orders he had taken from other stores the day before and made a list of the toys he had to build and a schedule of how soon he had promised delivery. The workload was intimidating, even frightening. But Walter knew he just had to grit his teeth and get through it. There were no more second chances.

He had just set up his supplies and was about to start the first toy on the order list when the bell on the shop door rang, announcing a customer. Annoyance bubbled up, though he realized that reaction didn't make sense. But he couldn't help it. *If only Franny were here to take care of the shop.* Getting used to this new arrangement wasn't going to be easy.

He walked out to find Digger, who held a wooden boat very gently in his hands, carefully examining the sail with a fingertip. Digger liked to carve and work with wood and was very handy at repairing real boats when he wasn't fishing. Walter knew he appreciated craftsmanship, in any form, large or small.

"Digger, good to see you. How are you today?"

Digger looked up, his small blue eyes peering out from the edge of a black knit cap that was pulled over dark, wiry hair.

"Not bad, Walter. And yourself?" He smiled in greeting, though his beard obscured most of his thin face. A remarkable beard, as Frances had said. Long and full but very silky looking. He would be a wonderful Santa, and without too much trouble.

"Can't complain. I hear you've agreed to play Santa here on Saturday. That's very good of you."

Digger smiled and shrugged. He took a pipe from the pocket of his navy peacoat and tapped it on his hand. "Happy to help. I don't have anything better to do. Frances asked me to stop by. Something about a costume?"

Frances had mentioned putting together a Santa suit for Digger, making it herself or maybe borrowing one from the fire department. Walter wasn't sure of her plans, but however it worked out, the outfit would certainly need some major alterations for their Santa impersonator.

"Frances isn't here right now. She started a job today, at the Paris Boutique. She'll be back around two o'clock."

"I'll come then. No trouble. By the way, can my little girl, Grace, come with me on Saturday? She'll be a help with the young ones, and she'll never let on I'm her daddy."

Walter smiled at Digger's endorsement of his daughter. "Of course she can. In fact, in addition to your pay, we want you to pick out a few toys for your girls. I noticed Grace looking at the princess doll the other day. Has she mentioned it?"

Digger nodded, his expression suddenly serious. "She put it on her list for Santa Claus. But you can't give me that beautiful doll for free, Walter. I won't accept it."

"It's not for free. It's part of your wages, Digger. We won't feel right if you don't choose a few toys for Grace and the baby."

Digger lowered his head and sighed. "We'll see how it goes. I can pay you back over time. Maybe in lobsters and clams?"

"That's a deal," Walter said, his imagination quickly summoning an array of delicious dishes Franny could whip up with such a trade-off. "I'm going to hold you to it."

The shop bell rang and another customer walked in. Walter recognized her quickly: Mary Bates. Her husband, Otto, just opened up a diner across the street a few months ago, the Clam Box. Mary and Otto were also members of the church, though Walter didn't know them well. Otto seemed to be doing a good business so far. He claimed his clam roll was famous. Walter couldn't see how it could be, but he admired Otto's self-promotion. It wouldn't hurt to be more like that.

"Good morning, Mrs. Bates," Walter said. "Can I help you with anything?"

"Just browsing. I'll let you know if I have any questions."

"Please do." Walter watched her walk back toward the big dollhouse. He had learned that if a customer wanted to look around on their own, it was best to leave them be, at least for a while. There was a fine line between being helpful and annoying.

Walter turned back to Digger. "It's usually so quiet this time of day. I have a lot to take care of in my workshop."

"Oh, I can watch things out here for a while. I just came up from the harbor. No work for me there today."

Digger shrugged. Walter could see he was trying to hide his disappointment over his lack of work. But Walter thought the fisherman's free time was a stroke of luck. "If you really don't mind, I'll pay you for your time."

Digger looked surprised at the offer. "Oh, we'll see, Walter. Doesn't make much difference to me. Everybody's got to be someplace, and I'd just as soon sit here as down there, staring at the water. It's a heck of a lot warmer."

"Can't argue with that," Walter replied.

"You go make your toys. I'll talk to that lady about the dollhouse. Maybe I'll show her some boats, too."

Walter could have hugged the skinny fisherman but restrained himself. He headed back to his workshop, full of energy. He really did need to concentrate without interruption in order to work his magic. Digger seemed to understand. Maybe it was the same with fishing and clamming? Either way, Digger's help was a gift, and Walter settled down quickly at his workbench to make good use of it.

Frances didn't return until nearly three, though she did call to warn Walter that she would be late. Despite hours on her feet in the dress shop, she was full of energy as she unpinned her hat and shrugged off her coat.

"I'm sorry, Walter. There was so much to learn. Nancy Trumbull has her own ways, different from our shop. Writing up a sales slip, taking a special order, keeping track of the inventory. A big shipment of dresses came in, and she needed help getting them on the floor."

Walter had to smile at her enthusiasm. "You sound like a pro already."

"Were you very busy here today? I bet you didn't have any time in the workshop."

"We were busy, but I had lots of time at my bench, too. Digger stopped by. Something about fitting him up with a Santa suit? He offered to watch the shop while I worked on the orders, and it ended up just fine."

Frances looked relieved. "Maybe he can help here a bit when I'm out. I think it still works to our benefit. I'm getting a decent wage and commissions," she reminded him. "I almost forgot, I sold a formal gown today, to Mrs. Warwick," she said, mentioning Oliver's mother. "And Mrs. Detweiller came in. Her son just got engaged and she needs a mother-of-the-groom dress and her daughter Vera is going to be a bridesmaid. She'll need a formal dress, too. I'll get something extra in my pay envelope for that."

"Good for you . . . for us, I mean." Frances sat on a stool behind the counter, looking over the day's receipts, and Walter ruffled her hair as he passed by. She smiled but scolded him. "Walter . . . please. I didn't sleep a wink on those bobby pins. I can't go through that again."

He laughed and kissed her cheek. "I'll be in the workshop, Curly. Call me when dinner's ready."

Walter ate dinner at his workbench that night

and every night that week. He didn't want to be late on any of the orders for other stores and could see it would take working around the clock to make good on his promises.

Frances helped, painting the faces on dolls, adding hair and clothes to them and the finishing touches to dollhouse furniture. It was nice to have her in the workshop some nights, working side by side. But when she had to sew, she worked upstairs, where her machine and supplies were handy.

Left alone, Walter lost track of time and often worked until one or even two in the morning. But he never forgot to go out to the alley at some point of the evening to check for the stray dog, to offer a dish of scraps from dinner and fresh water—and crumbs of oatmeal cookies, the dog's favorite treat of all.

He would catch sight of the little guy cowering in the shadows, not far from the shop's back door, but just far enough away to be out of reach. It hurt to think the dog must have been treated badly, but Walter was determined to teach the little hound that people could be kind, too.

Walter would whistle and call to him. "Hey, pal, come and get it. Roast chicken tonight, with baked potato."

He would set down the dish in a spot about halfway between them, a distance the dog found acceptable. And each night, Walter would shift the dish an inch or two closer to the door, and stand by the dish a little longer, talking in soothing, friendly tones while the dog gobbled his food and slurped up the water.

In time, the dish would be at the back door and the dog would tolerate his proximity. That was Walter's plan. He looked forward to the night he could lead the dog inside to warmth and safety.

Oatmeal cookies were Walter's secret weapon. After the dog ate, he would sit by his dish and stare up at his benefactor, once or twice even wagging his tail in anticipation.

"Here you go. Is this what you're waiting for?" Walter would crouch down and toss a few bits of cookie in the dog's direction, every night dropping the pieces closer and closer to his shoes.

LATE FRIDAY NIGHT, WALTER'S SHOULDERS ached and his eyes were heavy with sleep. He had not only been working hard on the toy order, but he and Frances had been preparing for Santa's visit at their shop the next day. Practically asleep on his feet, Walter still ventured out to feed his timid friend.

The dog quickly ate his dinner and drank from his dish, then waited for his cookies. Walter didn't mean to drop the treat so close to his own feet, but he wasn't concentrating. Before he could make a better toss, the dog trotted up, snuffling the ground.

Walter, who was crouched down, stayed as still as he could, barely daring to breathe. He dropped more cookie pieces, and as the dog retrieved them, Walter slowly reached out and gently stroked the dog's head.

The dog glanced at him a moment, then continued searching for sweet crumbs. When the little hound was done, he took a few cautious steps back. But he didn't run away. Walter was surprised and felt encouraged.

The dog stared up at Walter and softly panted. He looked like he was smiling. *Saying thank you?* Walter wondered. He felt his heart melt.

"You're very welcome. I'd bring you inside if you'd let me. We're definitely making progress. I think you need a name. A real name. I can't keep calling you the stray dog. Or 'Here, Boy.' That won't do." Walter considered the possibilities. "Cookie is too girlie. Oatmeal is a mouthful. Scraps? No, that's not right. You're too dignified for a name like that. Wait, I've got it. How about Otis? Do you like that one?"

Walter was still crouched down and called to him, "Come here, Otis. Come here, boy . . ."

Otis stood and wagged his tail. He looked like he was smiling again. Walter thought for sure that he liked his new name.

The dog took a few steps toward Walter, but

when a car horn broke the silence, Otis grew rigid with fear. Then he turned and darted into the darkness.

Walter sighed. So close and yet so far. Well, they'd made some progress. That's what counted. He picked up the empty dish and left the bowl of water by the shop door, then headed to bed, tired but happy.

He could hardly wait to tell Frances that he had named the dog.

"COME ON UP, SONNY. DON'T BE AFRAID." Santa smiled and beckoned the boy forward. "I got your letter. But I wish you'd remind me of what you'd like me to bring you in my sleigh."

Digger, dressed as Santa, bent and cupped a hand over his ear so that the child could whisper to him. He listened attentively, nodding but not interrupting.

Finally the boy was done. Santa sat up and winked at him. "Sure . . . I know the kind you like. Don't worry. Leave it to me."

Walter marveled at Digger's acting skills. He would have never guessed the young man was such a natural with children. Then again, the devotion of his daughter, Grace, was a testament to it.

Wearing a dark blue jumper, white blouse, and red sweater, she stood by Santa's chair and handed a candy cane to each of the children after their turn. She took her job very seriously, but she was a quiet, solemn child most of the time. One of the only times Walter had seen her smile was when she was admiring the princess doll, touching the doll's hair and silky gown very gently. Walter was determined that she would have it, no matter Digger's refusals. He'd wrap it up and leave it on their doorstep Christmas Eve if he had to.

Frances had set up a cozy corner in the back of the shop for Santa's visitors. Santa sat in a huge armchair that Walter and Frances had dragged down from their apartment. Frances had worked nights during the week to paint a backdrop on brown paper that was set up behind the chair—a fireplace and mantel hung with stockings. On a nearby table, they'd set up a small Christmas tree strung with lights and placed a few gift-wrapped boxes underneath. The scene was set perfectly for their distinguished visitor.

Dressed in a red apron and a candy-striped blouse, Frances served hot chocolate and cookies to the children who waited patiently in line for their turn. Walter was shocked to see that the line stretched not only from the back to the front of the shop, but out the door and down the street, more than half a block long.

"Hold down the fort—we need more hot chocolate," Frances whispered as she ran past.

"I'll do my best." Walter took over and gave

out cookies. "It will be your turn soon, don't worry," he told the waiting children.

"So nice of you to do this, Walter. We couldn't get to visit Santa at the firehouse this year." Mrs. Morgan stood in line with her two sons.

"It's our pleasure," he replied, then, realizing the children were listening in on the conversation, he added, "When Santa wants to visit your shop, you can't refuse, right?"

"Of course not," Mrs. Morgan replied.

Frances soon returned with more paper cups of hot cocoa, and he ran over to the customers who were standing at the counter or browsing the shelves, waiting for his help. Most, if not all, were holding the flyer he had ordered at George Plante's print shop.

He darted from one customer to the other, like a bee in a garden. There was a knack for giving each one enough attention so that they didn't get frustrated and leave without making a purchase. Walter tried his best for that outcome.

The rest of Santa's visit passed in a busy blur. That afternoon, Frances left for her job at the dress shop, and Digger changed out of his costume and helped Walter. The toy store remained crowded for the entire day, and when Walter finally locked the door and shut off the lights, he headed upstairs feeling a strange mixture of exhaustion and elation.

"We should have Santa visit every day," he said

as he staggered to the dinner table. "Or at least every Saturday."

"He definitely bumped up our sales, but I understand now why he only comes once a year to other stores. I'm not sure we would survive any more than that."

He smiled at her, knowing she felt the same as he did: tired but happy. Today had been a good day. A very good day. Maybe things were finally turning around for them.

"WALTER? WAKE UP. WE OVERSLEPT." HE felt Frances shake his shoulder, and he opened his eyes. She stood over him, her robe hanging loose over her nightgown. She looked as if she had just gotten out of bed, though the room was filled with sunlight.

He sat up and yawned. "What time is it?"

"It's already nine. Better hurry or we won't make the service on time." She was already headed for the bathroom. "I made the coffee. I'll take the first shower."

"Okay. I'll be ready, don't worry." He sat on the edge of the bed and stretched, but it was hard to get moving. He had worked so hard the day before in the shop, and then in his workshop after dinner until well into the night. Frances had worked hard, too. *If she can get to church on time today, so can you.*

Less than an hour later, they sat side by side in

their usual pew, on the right side toward the back. Frances wore her red dress and black high heels, and Walter his blue suit and gray tie. He had missed his breakfast and his stomach rumbled. But otherwise, no one would guess how they'd slept past the alarm.

Up on the altar, the Potter family stood before the four blue candles and began to recite the litany for the first Sunday of Advent. Sophie held a baby in her arms, a daughter named Una, who was recently baptized—their newest arrival. Evelyn, only a few years older, held her father's hand and peered up with interest at the proceedings. Their oldest, a boy named Bart, peeked out from behind his father's leg. He looked a little scared to be up in front of everyone, Walter thought.

When it was time to light the candle, Gus lifted his son and settled him on one hip, then let him lean over and help them set the candle glowing. Bart looked thrilled with the job.

As they walked back to their seats, the baby fussed a moment and Sophie quickly soothed her. Frances sighed, her gaze fixed straight ahead. "Such a good baby," she murmured. "She didn't make a peep the whole time."

Walter could tell what she was really thinking. He put his arm around her and squeezed her shoulder. "Don't worry, my love, our turn will come."

Walter enjoyed the service and was glad they

had made the effort to be there. As he rose to sing the closing hymn, he felt renewed, spiritually and even physically.

At coffee hour after the service, Frances quickly left his side to admire Sophie's new baby. He stayed on the coffee line, where Oliver Warwick soon joined him.

"Walter, good to see you." Oliver greeted him with a smile. "Did you straighten out that business matter?" he asked in a quieter voice.

"I took your advice and met with Mr. Finley on Monday. He gave us an extension, and we're doing our best to catch up by the end of the month."

Oliver looked pleased. "Finley is a reasonable man. I knew he'd work something out with you."

"He was very reasonable," Walter said sincerely. "And I don't doubt mentioning your name helped, Oliver. Thanks for putting in a good word for us."

Oliver looked embarrassed. "It was nothing. You're the one doing the hard work. I saw all the flyers around town and a line of customers out the door of your shop on Saturday morning. Great idea to have Santa visit. That's the way, Walter. Once you get the word out, no one will be able to resist your toys."

"That was Franny's brainstorm," Walter said proudly.

"It was brilliant. And I bet you made good

sales yesterday, too. You'll catch up with your payments in no time."

"That's the plan. Though there isn't all that much time," Walter said honestly. But Oliver's encouragement buoyed his spirits. Oliver ran factories. He knew all about business.

Oliver poured a cup of coffee and handed it to Walter, then poured one for himself and added cream and sugar. "I did have a thought, about the church's toy collection." Walter knew he meant the annual collection at the church, which was distributed to children at orphanages and in hospitals, and to families who had no means to buy gifts. "I'm running the collection this year," Oliver continued, "and you're always the largest contributor by far—"

"—which only makes sense, all things considered," Walter cut in with a grin.

"That's true. But a lot of other people wouldn't be half as generous with their wares as you and Frances, even if they owned ten toy stores. The point is, there's no pressure to make your usual donation. I understand your business situation and can explain it, discreetly of course, to the others. Everyone will understand."

Oliver's words surprised him. Walter wasn't sure what to say. "I appreciate that. But we've never once considered skipping the donation. Or even making it smaller. As long as we have toys in our shop, we're happy to give them to children

174

who otherwise wouldn't find anything to unwrap on Christmas morning. I wouldn't feel right missing a chance to do that. It wouldn't feel like Christmas."

Oliver caught his gaze and held it. Then he rested a hand on Walter's shoulder. "I had a feeling you'd say that. Just think about it. Talk it over with Frances."

Walter already knew Frances felt the same way. But Oliver had a point; he had promised to include her in all the decisions about their business, and he would keep his word on that. "All right, I will. But I know what she'll say."

"Well, you have one over on me, then." Oliver smiled. "I can never predict what a woman thinks, or what she'll say. Especially the lady I'm seeing lately."

Walter doubted that. Oliver was the most eligible bachelor around, always seen with a beautiful young woman on his arm. But maybe he had finally met his match and one of those beauties was leading him a merry chase, for a change? From Oliver's wistful tone and expression, it seemed so.

"Good luck with the shop, Walter. I'm sure it will all work out," Oliver said finally. He offered his hand, and Walter gave it a firm shake.

"Thanks, Oliver. Hope so."

Oliver was called away by Pastor Whitaker, and Walter scanned the room, looking for Frances.

She was still talking to Sophie, who had passed baby Una into Frances's arms so she could sip a cup of coffee. His heart went out to his wife, who hid her secret yearning, and perhaps even envy, behind soft smiles and sincerest good wishes. Otto and Mary Bates stood with her, chatting as well. They didn't have children yet either, and Mary had told Frances they were also hoping to start a family. Maybe that made Frances feel better. Otto had served in the army during the war, alongside Oliver Warwick. He was focusing all his energy now on his new business, the Clam Box Diner, which seemed a success so far, Walter thought.

That's what I have to do, too. Focus on our business and steer us through this rough patch. Then we'll be ready for a baby. All good things come in the fullness of time. God's timing, not our own, he reminded himself.

A few minutes later, he helped Frances on with her coat and they walked out to the brisk, bright winter day. "I'm starved," Walter said. "I didn't eat a bite for breakfast, we were in such a rush."

"I can heat up some soup when we get home and make you a sandwich, too. Grilled cheese?" she offered, naming one of his favorites. He watched her pull on her dress-up gloves, black felt with pearl buttons on the wrists. Fine for church, but he wished he could buy her a pair made of leather, with soft fur inside. That would really keep her hands warm. Someday, he promised himself.

"We worked very hard yesterday, Franny. We deserve a treat. We haven't tried the Clam Box yet."

"You mean, to eat there?" Frances sounded surprised. *And why not?* he reflected. They rarely ate out at restaurants, and never on a whim.

"Yes, I mean to eat there. I think we can manage it. It's not the Ritz-Carlton, Franny."

On a rare visit to Boston, he and Frances had walked around the Public Garden and glided along in the swan boats. Then they had crossed the avenue for tea and finger sandwiches at the Ritz-Carlton hotel. It had been a grand summer day, a special day of their courting before they were even engaged to be married. They still had a joke about the famous hotel. "It's not the Ritz-Carlton," they would say to each other when faced with some mundane choice, "but it will do."

He glanced at her as they walked across the village green. She smiled and took his arm. "No, it's not the Ritz-Carlton. But I suppose it will do, Walter."

They huddled together for warmth, their laughter carried off by a sudden gust of wind off the harbor.

CHAPTER SEVEN

Saturday, December 1, 2018

H EY, MARTIN. HOW'S IT GOING?"
Martin looked up, startled by the greeting. He met Louisa Tulley's bold gaze and nearly tipped a paper cup of hot chocolate onto his laptop. He sat at a table in the little snack bar of the Cape Light Public Library, a quiet place to work on his gift list.

"It's coming along. A work in progress." He realized that it felt good to talk to someone who knew what he was up to. Except for Reverend Ben, she was the only one in town. "Did you make any big arrests this week? I hear there's a burglar roaming around." She smiled, dimples creasing her cheeks. *She really is so pretty, even in that stark outfit.* "You know me, always on the lookout."

"I'll bet you are." He raised his hands, as he had the night she cornered him, making her grin.

"I ran into Mrs. Monroe. She's very pleased with her new sewing machine. She's signed up enough orders to keep her busy for the next six months."

"Good for her. She must be a very good seam-stress to draw that much work."

"She is. But even the best craftsman can't get very far without tools. It must feel good to help someone that way. To give them back their liveli-hood."

Martin nodded. For some reason it was hard to admit that he did feel gratified by giving these gifts. He felt like a fraud, claiming that. He was just trying to fulfill the terms of the will, to make his way through the obstacle course his grandfather had set. But if he took a moment to get in touch with his deeper feelings, there was more to it, no matter how or why he gave the gifts. He did experience a rush of emotion, realizing he was easing the problems in someone else's life.

"It does feel good to know the sewing machine helped. Even if it was not my real intention. I don't think I'm entitled to any credit," he said honestly.

Louisa tilted her head to one side, her expres-sion suddenly thoughtful. "That is an interesting question. I wonder what Reverend Ben would say."

"Maybe I'll ask him sometime." Which wasn't a bad idea, Martin realized. The question did confuse him. "Are you on a break?"

"I just got off a shift and I came to pick up my brother, Ryan. He's here with a tutor. Calculus," she added, rolling her eyes. She glanced at her watch. "He should be done in a few minutes."

"Please . . . sit down. I didn't mean to be rude. I thought you had to get back to work." Martin jumped up from his seat and pulled out a chair for her.

Dressed in her uniform, she had three books tucked under her arm and set them on the table. He quickly scanned the titles—a biography of Winston Churchill, a mystery, and a book about finding the right relationship. Interesting selection.

"I loved calculus," he confessed. "I was sort of a math geek in high school."

"Really?" She sounded shocked, but then he realized she was teasing him.

"I'm sure it's hard to believe. I still have a tendency to turn everything into a spreadsheet."

"So I noticed." She glanced at his computer screen, where he had translated his notes of donations and recipients into just such a chart.

He felt embarrassed, then laughed. "It's just my way of organizing things." Though as soon as he said it, he realized that many things couldn't be organized or fit neatly into such an arrangement.

"I love history," Louisa confessed. "That was my major in college."

"I thought it was probably something like criminal psychology."

"I took courses in that, too. And then had a year at the police academy."

"How long have you been a police officer?"

"Two years in June."

Martin calculated her age to be around twenty-four. "You seem to like your work," he said.

"I do. I like helping people, keeping them safe. It's the right job for me right now," she added. "I may not do it my entire life, like my uncle Tucker."

"He's a police officer in town, too, right?"

"From before I was born. He'll probably retire soon." She was quiet a moment, straightening out her stack of books. "By the way, the strangest thing happened at the station today. Every winter we collect winter boots for children, and this morning, a huge truck from a big shoe store on the turnpike pulled up and delivered about a zillion pairs. There are so many boxes, we didn't know where to put them all. We stacked them to the ceiling, even in both jail cells. Luckily, they get very little use."

Martin feigned surprise, though his pleased smile was a total giveaway. "That is a lot of shoes. Where did they come from?"

She shook her head. "No idea at all. It was totally and completely anonymous. Everyone was amazed. Don't you think that's strange, *Mr. Hanson?*"

"It is," he said, pleased to see her so impressed

by his efforts. "Well, I have no idea who would do a crazy thing like that. I'm just a visitor here. I guess the word got around."

"To the right people," she added. "We did make an attractive flyer this year."

"Yes, I saw it in the bakery," he said with a sly smile. "There are a lot of notices like that around. I have them all listed right here, on my spreadsheet." He patted his computer.

Along with the boot drive, Martin had discovered a toy drive at the diner, and a collection at the firehouse for families who needed help furnishing their homes and replacing their belongings after fires. And at the library, funds were needed to expand the children's book collection.

"Glad I could help. So you've solved your problem, I guess."

Although she was smiling, she didn't sound that pleased.

"If only. I'm allowed to contribute *part* of the money to these worthy efforts. But most of it must be given to individuals, or families," he explained quietly.

He glanced around, hoping that their conversation wasn't being overheard. But the area was practically empty, with only a few people seated in nearby armchairs, reading newspapers or magazines.

"Did you tell me that? I must have forgotten."

She sat up, sounding brighter, while he felt suddenly deflated. Just talking about the stipulation made him feel as if he were facing Mount Everest. Wearing flip-flops.

"Maybe I left that part out. Mostly because it seems so impossible to me." He wondered if he should ask her again to help him. But he couldn't get the words out. What if she refused again? It had been hard enough the first time; he had just blurted it out on an uncharacteristic impulse. No, he couldn't ask again. If she really wanted to help, she would offer, wouldn't she?

He heard a text sound on her phone, and she pulled it out of her pocket and read the message. "My brother is done with the tutor. I have to go."

He watched her stand up and gather her books and felt his heart fall, mostly because he was enjoying talking to her so much. "Sure, I don't want to keep you." *Ask her out, idiot. At least ask for her phone number.*

Before Martin could figure out what to do, she looked down at him and said, "This is kind of short notice, but there's a party at church tomorrow night, an Advent party. We set up a tree and the kids have games. We sing carols. Why don't you come?"

Did she mean as her date? He hoped so but didn't dare ask.

"You'll be able to talk to people there, Martin. Maybe you'll get some ideas?"

"Right . . . I might," he replied. "Will you be there?"

"Yes, my whole family is going."

She didn't mean as her date, he decided. But at least she would be there. As for her suggestion, he doubted it would work out. He was very uncomfortable talking to strangers. And church suppers were not his first choice for an evening out either. But he would be able to spend more time with Louisa, and that was a selling point he could not resist.

"Of course I'll come," he added quickly. "Can I give you a ride?" He tried to sound casual about the offer.

"No thanks. I promised to help set up, and I have to be there early."

"I can help set up." Where had that come from? He was definitely not the "setup crew" type. This girl was getting to him, wasn't she?

Her smile quickly erased his reservations. "That would be great. We can use your help. Can you meet there at six? The party starts at six thirty."

"I'll be there," he promised.

Her phone buzzed again and she made a face at the phone, then looked up at him and grinned. "See you tomorrow, Martin."

He nodded and smiled. "Sure, see you."

He watched Louisa head off to meet her brother. Then he turned back to his computer but stared blindly at the screen. He knew he was still smiling. She just had that effect on him. He knew that he ought to be careful about letting her get under his skin. And about getting involved with her. But he didn't want to worry about that now. It felt too good knowing that it wouldn't be long before he saw her again—and he couldn't help feeling happy about *almost* having a date.

"YOU'RE GOING TO THE ADVENT PARTY tonight?" Vera seemed surprised, Martin noticed, but also pleased by the news. She was at the stove, cooking chili and baking pans of corn bread that filled the house with a sweet, buttery aroma that had drawn him from his room. She reached into the oven and set a pan of the golden bread on a rack to cool. "It's really such fun. I'm sure you'll enjoy yourself."

Martin wasn't nearly as sure, but any time he spent in Louisa's company was always interesting and, usually, enjoyable. "I can drive you over, if you like, Vera. I'll help you carry in the food."

"That would be a big help, thanks. My car isn't feeling one hundred percent today. I barely rolled up the driveway after church this morning. I'd better not push it."

Martin had to smile; Vera talked about the car like an aging pet. "I thought you were getting a new car. Didn't that mechanic you know say he found one for you?"

"False alarm." Vera shook more chili powder into the pot and stirred in the spice. "He thought he'd come across one, but the engine was burning oil. That's always a bad sign."

"It's a good thing you didn't take it only to find that out later."

"I was spared that trouble, but I trust Art. He'll come up with something that meets my needs."

Vera tasted a bit of rice, then put the lid back on the pot and lowered the flame. "What time do you want to leave for church, Martin?"

"I offered to help set up. Someone told me to come at six. Can you be ready by then?"

"Absolutely. I'll have all this food packed and ready to go."

"Very good. Let me know when you're ready."

He'd nearly told Vera, "Louisa Tulley told me to come at six," but caught himself just in time. Vera would get ideas and make more of the relationship than was really the case. *I may as well post my interest in Louisa on the Internet.* But his landlady was sharp and observant. He had a feeling she would come to her own conclusions, no matter how little information he offered.

He rose from the table and grabbed his coat and Milo's leash. Milo followed, wagging his big tail. He knew it was time for his quick break outside and then dinner.

Martin hated to leave Milo alone for the evening, but he knew his friend was tired from a very long walk they had taken earlier and would probably fall asleep as soon as Martin left.

BY THE TIME THEY REACHED THE CHURCH, it was a few minutes after six. Martin had been ready on time, but Vera had trouble removing the corn bread from the pans. It kept falling apart, and she fretted that she'd let it cool too long and now it was turning into a pile of crumbs.

Martin tried to offer what support he could, which included eating some of the crumbs and insisting it was delicious, maybe even better in its disintegrated state.

Vera glanced at him, covering the last pan with foil. "Sophie and Claire will disagree, but thank you for saying that. You're a nice young man, Martin Hanson."

Martin smiled but felt embarrassed by the compliment, mostly because she had used his assumed name.

There were already cars in the parking lot when they arrived, and he hoped Louisa wouldn't think he had gone back on his promise. Martin had never been to the church at night. At least, he could not recall if his grandparents had ever taken him there for an evening event. The windows glowed with warm golden light, and the stone walls seemed even more solid and imposing. The steeple seemed higher, too, starkly outlined against the clear night sky. The stained glass windows in the sanctuary, arch-shaped on top, glowed with jewellike colors.

Inside, the hallways and rooms were teeming with activity, with children giggling and chasing each other, members of the choir practicing in the sanctuary, and a group of people in the hallway sorting out branches of fresh greens. He followed Vera to the kitchen, which was filled with women and a few brave men, wearing long aprons and shouting directions at each other.

He noticed Vera's friends, Sophie Potter and Claire North, and hoped they wouldn't be too hard on Vera's corn bread. Vera was already explaining the problem as he dropped a covered pan on the counter. Claire checked the corn bread and declared it was fine. "People like it crumbly. They'll sprinkle some on top of the chili."

Martin wandered out to Fellowship Hall, feeling a sudden attack of nerves. It was even more raucous in there than in the kitchen; the voices and clattering sound of tables and chairs being set up echoed in the big room. Why had he volunteered to come here tonight? He suddenly couldn't remember.

But before he could retreat and consider an exit strategy, he spotted Louisa helping to push a large cart of folding chairs out from a storage area. He quickly headed over and came up behind her. "Sorry, I just got here," he explained. "Vera had a little crisis with her corn bread."

"That sounds serious." He could tell from her smile she meant just the opposite.

Two men stood at the opposite end of the cart. Martin recognized them from church. One was her uncle Tucker.

"Anytime tonight, Louisa." Louisa's uncle gave her a look.

"Sorry, we're ready." Louisa glanced at Martin, and he grabbed the metal bar at the back of the cart, his hands nearly touching hers. They fell into step and pushed the cart to the middle of the room. It wasn't all that heavy but was hard to steer.

As soon as it was parked, Louisa grabbed a chair and opened it, and then without a moment's hesitation, another. Her uncle and the other man were doing the same, and Martin quickly grabbed a chair to keep up.

But his chair was old or bent. Or needed oil? It was hard to push the seat down, and he felt foolish, finally getting it in place. Louisa glanced at him, but didn't say anything. She grabbed another chair and practically shook it open with one hand. "Pro tip, don't overthink it, Martin."

Her grin was infectious, even though he knew it was at his expense. He grabbed another chair and tried her "shaking it open" technique. He didn't quite succeed but was encouraged.

"Not bad for your first church event," she said.

There seemed a million chairs on the rack but

they were quickly opened, and just as quickly, others in the room had carried them away.

Louisa's Uncle Tucker stood with his hands on his hips a moment, catching his breath. He was not a very tall man, but looked fit for his age, with a stocky, square build, a fringe of reddish-brown hair tinged with silver, a large mustache, and friendly brown eyes.

"Thanks for your help," he said to Martin. "I don't think we've met, but I've seen you in church a few times."

Before Martin could introduce himself, Louisa said, "This is Martin Hanson, Uncle Tucker. Remember I mentioned he was coming?"

She introduced him next to her uncle's friend, Sam Morgan. In his late forties, Martin guessed, Sam was still a handsome man, with thick black hair touched with silver and a striking smile.

"Nice to meet you, Martin. I hope you don't have a bad impression of our church. I'm not sure what Louisa said, but you can have dinner whether or not you open the chairs and tables."

Louisa groaned. "Very funny, Sam."

Tucker had already started on the folding tables. He pulled one off the pile and laid it flat on the floor. The legs were up and locked into place a few seconds later, and Martin wished he had paid closer attention. Part of his brain was astounded that he was feeling so intimidated by these simple tasks. *You have two graduate school degrees,* that voice reminded him, *law and accounting. So what if you can't open a table?*

But another part didn't want to look like a clumsy dolt in front of Louisa—though anyone could see he was all thumbs when it came to mechanical things.

Sam grabbed one end, and the two men flipped the table over and set it in place. Then Sam pulled off another table and so did Tucker, and the process began again, this time in tandem.

"Here, help me grab one," Louisa suggested. He felt relieved at her suggestion, and together they pulled another table down. But instead of landing smoothly like the first two, it clattered to the floor with a deafening sound.

Sam winced. "Ouch . . . Easy does it, guys."

"My fault," Martin said quickly. "I didn't expect it to be so heavy."

Louisa was already working on the legs on her side. "Don't be silly. It's no big deal. They'll drop a few before the night is over, believe me."

Her words made him feel better as he struggled to get the legs on his side to lock in place. He pushed them up, just as he'd seen Sam and Tucker do, only to have them flop back down again. He felt clumsy but perplexed, and he glanced at Louisa to see if she was watching.

She had come to her feet and stood talking to a woman named Jessica—Sam's wife, Martin gathered. Jessica had a small brown puppy in her arms, and Louisa was practically swooning with delight.

"—Out of the way. We don't have all night." Carl Tulley, the church janitor and handyman, crouched down next to Martin. "You'll break the table like that. Then I'll get blamed."

Carl was Tucker's older brother. Vera had told him that in church, Martin recalled. The old man practically pushed Martin aside as he pulled up the table legs and snapped a bar in place that Martin had not noticed. The legs locked, finally stable. Carl turned the table over and pushed it a short distance to the side, where another group carried it away.

"Thanks. I didn't know how the legs locked," Martin mumbled.

Carl didn't seem to hear him. He pulled down another table and started working on it. Martin tried to help, but Carl gave him a look. "I've got this one. Stand aside. How many times should I say it?"

Martin backed off, surprised by his gruff tone. He knew that he shouldn't take it personally, but everyone else he'd met so far at the church was so friendly and went out of their way to make him feel welcome.

He watched Carl quickly set up the table and turn it over on his own. Then Carl started to push the table to the side, and Martin grabbed the other end. "I can help with this part," he offered.

Carl looked annoyed and about to deliver another rude remark when he was suddenly overtaken by coughing. He covered his mouth with one hand but needed the other for support as he fell toward the table.

Martin rushed up beside him. "Are you all right? Do you need some water or something?"

Carl stared at him, his bloodshot eyes bulging in their sockets, unable to speak. Louisa and Tucker appeared.

"Where's the inhaler?" Tucker asked. "Don't you have one with you?"

Carl couldn't answer but patted his shirt pocket. Tucker pulled out the device, opened it, and held it up to his brother's mouth. The older man took a deep breath, and then another. His body finally relaxed, and he began breathing normally again.

A few people had gathered around, looking on with concern, including Reverend Ben. "Dr. Harding is here. Do you want him to examine you?"

Carl shook his head. "No doctor. I know what's wrong. It's nothing. I'm fine now, see?"

Martin saw Louisa's eyes full of concern. "You look pale, Uncle Carl. Your hands are shaking. Let me take you home. I'll wrap up some dinner for you," she added.

In Martin's opinion, it was a thoughtful offer. He was about to offer his assistance, but Louisa's uncle seemed insulted, even angered, by her suggestion. "I just told you. Stop fussing . . . People don't want me here tonight, is that what you're saying?"

Louisa looked hurt by his gruff manner and sharp words. Martin wanted to defend her, but Tucker stepped forward. "No one is saying that, Carl. We're just worried about you. Let's go out and get some air. It's a little stuffy in here."

Carl nodded. His head hanging, he allowed Tucker to lead him out of the room.

Louisa looked on with a sad expression. "He's not always like that," she said.

Martin had never met the man, only seen him once from a distance. Still, he doubted Louisa's claim that her uncle was anything but cantankerous, but he didn't want to argue with her, and he certainly didn't want her to feel any worse. "Sure," he said. "He's not feeling well."

"My uncle has emphysema. It's getting worse and he doesn't take care of himself. We all wish he'd stop working, but he's very stubborn and . . . well, it's complicated."

"Hey, guys . . . is this tree straight?"

Sam Morgan had just stuck a tall Douglas fir in a tree stand and was holding on to the trunk with both hands, waiting for their response.

Louisa rushed over to help, and Martin followed. "It looks good, Sam. Can you hold it still? Martin and I will work on the stand."

She dove under the tree and started twisting the handles that secured the trunk. Martin crouched down and worked on the other side, conscious of how close they were, sheltered by the fragrant branches. But their task was quickly finished, and they emerged, then backed up a few steps to check their work with Sam.

"Perfect. The kids will decorate it later. We just need to put the lights on. I left them right here, in a big cardboard box." Sam glanced around the area, seeming perplexed.

"Left them in an infernal mess, you mean. I thought you'd know better than that, Sam." Martin turned and spotted an old man sitting nearby on a chair, long fingers deftly pulling apart the tangled strands of lights.

Martin had noticed him at Sunday service, too. His name was Digger, and most people in town treated him with respect if not downright awe. His long white beard was positively Biblical and the black knit cap on his head a classic touch. He wore a red and black plaid flannel shirt with red suspenders and yellow rubber boots up to the knees of his black corduroy pants.

"These lights look like a fishing net that's been through a hurricane. Might take all night to work out these knots."

Sam laughed and patted Digger's shoulder. "No rush, old friend. Christmas is only . . . twenty-three days away?"

Digger grinned but didn't reply then returned to his handiwork.

Reverend Ben walked over and admired the tree. "Nice job, everyone. Where are the lights?"

"Digger is trying to straighten them out," Sam replied.

Reverend Ben looked concerned. "The children will be in any minute with their decorations. I suppose we can distract them for a little while."

"I'll help with the lights." Louisa took a seat next to Digger and pulled another strand of gnarled lights from the carton.

"I can help, too," Martin offered. He took a seat on the other side of the old fisherman and also grabbed a set of lights from the box. *A ball of lights, you'd have to call it,* he realized.

"I don't think these can be salvaged," Martin said. "Why don't I run up to a store and buy some new ones?" He looked at Louisa and Digger to see what they thought.

Before Louisa could reply, an older woman stepped forward and touched his arm. "He didn't hear you," she said simply, glancing at Digger.

She wore a cardigan with a Christmas design and a long wool skirt. Her straight, chin-length hair was mostly gray, and her features bore a striking resemblance to the fisherman's. This had to be Grace Hegman, Digger's daughter. Vera often mentioned her.

"You need to talk into his other ear, the left one.

196

He lost the hearing aid for his right ear, and the other one is none too reliable," Grace explained.

Louisa looked concerned. "Lost it? When did that happen?"

"At least two weeks now. It costs a fortune to replace them. We'll see how the shop does over Christmas. Maybe we'll have enough extra to get him fixed up with new ones. I can pay over time, I suppose."

Louisa cast a meaningful look his way, but Martin had already made a mental note about Digger's need.

"So what do you think, Digger? Should I go buy more lights?" he nearly shouted into the old man's ear.

Digger heard him this time, he could tell. "Waste not, want not, young fella," he replied. "Most broke things can be mended. A little patience and some strategy is all you need. And maybe some glue and string."

Martin wondered if Digger's philosophy applied to things like cell phones and computers. "Okay, I'll try to show some patience. But what's our strategy here?"

Digger cupped his ear and frowned. He hadn't heard Martin.

"Our strategy?" Martin shouted.

"Simple, a knot is like any other problem in life. You can't yank it tighter. That only makes it worse. You can't fix a thing the same way you made the mess. Even Einstein knew that. You got to show it some understanding and get to the heart of the matter. Then it will loosen up easy, see? Like this . . ."

He took the string of lights he was working on and stretched it out with his fingers in all directions. The motion reminded Martin a little of the game cat's cradle, which he had played when he was a boy, lacing string around his fingers in different patterns.

"You make it all loose and open. Then you find the gist of it, what's causing the holdup. Right there, see?" He pointed to a particularly tight, tangled spot. "Once that part is persuaded, the rest will shake itself out like a wet dog."

Martin watched Digger focus on the spot he had identified, then gently thread the entire length of the lights through a single loop. As if by magic, the lights hung straight and knot-free.

"Amazing." Louisa looked awestruck.

"It's like a magic trick," Martin added.

Digger laughed. "I've done a few of them in my time, too. This is just common sense. Now you try it." He pointed to Martin's lights, which sat in a ball on his lap. "You were watching, weren't you?"

"Very carefully," he murmured, trying to remember the steps. "First loosen it, then stretch it as far as it will go."

"That's right."

Martin stretched out the wire in all directions with his fingers, as he had seen Digger do. Only his set looked like a larger ball of lights. "Let me see . . . hard to say where the sweet spot is on this one. I'll try this part," he decided. He pulled the length of the lights through a single knotted spot, but the trick didn't seem to work.

Digger reached over and flipped the lights around a bit, and the entire string was smooth and straight again. "You done it fine. Just needed a tweak," Digger praised him. "What did you say your name was?"

Martin leaned closer and spoke to Digger's good ear. "My name is Martin . . . Martin Night . . . Martin Hanson."

Digger looked confused. "Martin Hanson, is that what you said?"

"That's right." Martin nodded.

Digger shook his head and grinned. "For a moment there, I thought you said something else. Never mind me."

Reverend Ben walked toward them. "Any luck?" He sighed. "Maybe we'll do without lights this year."

"You can start with these." Martin handed over the two sets, and Reverend Ben's expression lit with gratitude and relief. "Thank you, Martin. Just in the nick of time," he murmured. Martin followed his nervous glance.

A crowd of excited children waited at the door,

herded by a few adults. They all wore paper crowns and carried ornaments and decorations made of construction paper and sparkles. Some of the ornaments were made of real cookies that hung on long ribbons, Martin noticed. And some of the cookies had been eaten a bit. Sam quickly draped the strands of lights on the pine boughs and Digger quickly produced one more, to fill the tree in completely. When the tiny white bulbs were turned on, Martin thought the tree looked perfect just as it was. He smiled with a Christmas feeling he had not known in a long time.

Chapter Eight

Sunday, December 2, 2018

THE CHILDREN COULD NOT BE HELD BACK any longer. They ran into the room and crowded around the tree. Louisa ran forward to help a few adults who had followed the little revelers.

Martin stepped back. He liked children, but the scene was intimidating, too chaotic for him. Louisa would have to brave this alone, he decided.

She seemed a natural with the little ones. They carefully handed over their ornaments and pointed to very specific branches. She took great care to follow their directions and hang each creation exactly where they wanted it. Her customers beamed with pride each time she was done.

While the tree was decorated, Vera and her friends brought out an assortment of foods, setting them on the long tables—hot dishes, salads, and baskets piled with fresh rolls and loaves of bread. Of course Martin would sit with

Louisa at dinner, but that probably meant sitting with her family, too. He had seen them come in a short time ago, but she'd been busy—too busy to introduce him. Was he ready for that? He couldn't remember the last time a young woman had introduced him to her parents.

He liked Louisa a lot; he would never deny that. But he wasn't here to start a relationship. He was here to take care of his business and leave town as soon as he possibly could. *You'd better remember that,* he reminded himself.

An older woman with blond hair and a charming smile took a seat at a piano that was tucked into the corner of the room. As she lifted the cover of the keys, Reverend Ben walked over and spoke quietly with her. From their attitude and gestures, Martin guessed the pianist was his wife. With his hand resting on her shoulder, she settled her glasses on the bridge of her nose and set up some sheet music, though she did not start to play.

"Welcome, everyone. May I have your attention for a few moments, please?" Reverend Ben stood near the piano and addressed the group. Except for some shuffling and whispers among the children, the room grew instantly quiet. "Thank you all for coming tonight. It's always a special pleasure to start the Christmas season with our annual Advent party. We have lots of fun planned for the evening, and a wonderful dinner to enjoy.

Before we sit down to break bread together, please join me in thanks for this meal and this wonderful evening of fellowship."

They all bowed their heads, and Reverend Ben said grace, but not as Martin had often heard it. The words were not memorized and repeated from some generic prayer book, but spoken from the heart, recognizing the simple but rich gifts in the room at that very moment—the gift of a child's wonder at the twinkling Christmas tree, and the skill and generosity of the many cooks who had made such a bountiful table.

The only person in his family who would offer grace before a meal had been his grandfather. Martin had not thought of that in a long time, but when Reverend Ben's prayer was over, he felt deeply moved, remembering. He looked up and realized Louisa had been watching him. She smiled, a small, soft smile that was different in some way than those that had come before, a smile that seemed to move them to new ground. Martin didn't even have time to question it or make a choice. It was just happening.

"Ready for dinner?" she asked.

"I'm starved. I promised Vera I'd try her chili, but everything looks good."

"There are some great cooks in this congregation. I don't think you'll be disappointed."

Balancing full plates, they looked around for empty seats.

"Louisa, we're over here," Louisa's mother called out, waving her hand. "You can just squeeze in on the end there. Grab some chairs."

Martin gave Louisa a doubtful look. There really didn't seem to be room for them. He followed her as she walked toward the table. "We'll find you for dessert, Mom. By the way, this is Martin," she added, introducing him. Everyone at the table waved and smiled, and Louisa's twin brothers called out in a teasing chorus, "Hello, Martin. We've heard *soooo* much about you." Martin could see Louisa was a little embarrassed, but all she said was, "There are just too many Tulleys in this town, that's the problem." She tilted her head toward another table. "There are two empty seats at Sam and Jessica's table. Let's sit with them."

She led Martin to a table nearby, where Sam Morgan sat with his family. "Sit down, sit down. The more, the merrier," Sam said as he saw them approach. He shifted his chair, making room for them.

"This is Louisa's friend Martin," Sam announced. To Martin he said, "This is my wife, Jessica, and our kids Tyler and Lily. Our older son, Darrell, is away at school," he added. "And this is my sister-in-law, Emily, and her husband, Dan . . . their daughter, Jane. And my in-laws, Lillian and Ezra."

Martin greeted everyone, feeling overwhelmed.

The man to his left, Ezra, leaned closer. "We'll test you on the names later, but don't worry, it's multiple choice."

"Pay no attention to my husband. He likes to tease," said Lillian, Sam's mother-in-law. Martin smiled at her in reply. She met his glance and looked away.

She didn't seem like the other women Martin had met so far at the church. Nothing like Vera and the kitchen crew. Not just in her manner but in her appearance, as well. Her white hair was swept up in a French twist that was becoming to her thin face and fine features, showing off large pearl earrings. She wore an elegant cream-colored silk blouse with a lavender cashmere shawl draped around her shoulders and many rings on her fingers, stiff with age.

He thought a moment and realized that she must be the formidable Lillian Warwick, now married to Dr. Elliot, though Oliver Warwick, long deceased, had been her first husband. Vera had told him a lot about these prominent village personalities.

Her husband, Ezra, still had most of his pure white hair, cut short and neatly combed to one side. He wore a tweed jacket with a green wool vest, a starched white shirt underneath, and a red bow tie imprinted with tiny Christmas trees.

A sharp, intelligent gaze peered out from wire-frame spectacles, and his expression was a playful smile. Vera had mentioned that he was a doctor, retired now.

Lillian and Ezra had to be in their eighties, Martin guessed. He wondered if they had known his grandparents. They seemed about the right age, but of course, he couldn't ask.

Jessica, Sam's wife, cast a friendly smile at him from across the table. "I hear that you're visiting the village on business, Martin. And staying with Vera Plante? How do you like our town?"

A very pretty woman, she seemed a good match for Sam, with dark curly hair gathered in a loose ponytail. A dark blue sweater brought out her blue eyes.

Before he could reply, Lillian said, "Visiting from where? Where are you from exactly?"

"I'm from Boston. Cambridge." *Exactly,* he added silently.

She nodded, seeming satisfied with the answer. "I was raised in Boston, in the Back Bay," she replied, mentioning the city's most exclusive neighborhood with quiet pride. "A long time ago," she added quietly.

"How do you like Cape Light?" Emily asked with a bright, easy smile. She seemed polished and self-assured but very friendly. She had been mayor of Cape Light for many years, he recalled, until the owner of the Clam Box, Charlie Bates, won the position. Vera didn't think Charlie was as good at the job as Emily had been and still hoped Emily would run again for the post, though everyone doubted she would. "It must seem very quiet compared to the city," she added.

Martin considered his reply carefully so that he wouldn't admit that he knew the town and had come there summers as a boy. "It's very charming. It's been a nice break. My dog Milo loves it."

"You brought your dog? That's wonderful. What sort of dog is he?" Jessica asked.

"He's a mutt, mostly border collie but mixed with something smaller."

"Those dogs are beautiful and so loyal. We had some puppies like that at the shelter. Their mother had been hit by a car, poor things. But they were adopted in a snap."

"A long snap," Sam corrected her, "which included staying up nights, bottle-feeding furry babies for a few weeks."

"Jessica runs an animal rescue shelter, Grateful Paws. She takes in all kinds of animals, not just cats and dogs," Louisa explained. "It's amazing."

"Amazing that my daughter, with an MBA from an Ivy League school and a long career in banking, would spend her days in such a way. Amazing to me, anyway," Lillian announced.

The table was quiet for a moment. Martin had never been one to break such an awkward silence or confront a person like Lillian. But the insight the old woman had offered into Jessica's history pushed buttons deep inside him. He, too, had degrees from Ivy League schools and worked in a "respectable" profession, but now he yearned for a change from a career he felt was sucking his soul.

"Is that why I saw you holding a puppy before?" he asked.

Jessica nodded. "He's comfy in his little crate now, stored in the choir room. Someone here has adopted him and is going to take him home. An early Christmas gift for the family."

"How nice," Martin said sincerely, thinking back to the puppy his parents had surprised him with one Christmas morning. "I think it's important to find work that's meaningful, that makes you happy to get up every day. It sounds to me like that's just what you've done, Jessica. I bet it wasn't easy."

Lillian sighed and adjusted the paper napkin on her lap. To Martin's relief, she didn't offer a rebuttal.

"Very true, young man. Very true," Ezra said. "What sort of work do you do, may I ask?"

"I'm a tax attorney . . . which I don't find very satisfying," he admitted. "That's why I admire someone like Jessica."

"I see." Ezra nodded with a thoughtful look.

"How is the shelter going, Jess?" Louisa asked.

"We're much better organized than last winter, when we started." She glanced at her husband,

and they shared a private smile. "But I wish I had more space to take in more animals. I just got a call this morning about twenty beautiful horses that will be put down if someone doesn't save them. I really want to take them, but I'd need to rent a big barn or a stable somewhere. I just don't have the space or the resources right now—and it would take me months, if not years, to adopt out that many."

"That's too bad," Louisa said. "I love horses. I used to ride a lot when I was young. I'd love to have a horse someday."

Martin was impressed. He had always been afraid of horses and never once tried to get in a saddle.

"How much time do you have? Maybe we can hold a fund-raiser," Emily suggested.

Jessica offered a weak smile. "I thought of that, too. But there's only a few days."

"Maybe someone will come forward, honey. You never know." Sam patted his wife's hand. "You're already doing all you can."

"Maybe. But I think it will take a miracle to save them. Or something very close."

Louisa and Martin shared a secret glance. Martin felt good that he could help someone like Jessica—who so clearly had her heart in her work—and help the animals she rescued, too.

Dessert was served and Martin got up with Louisa to survey the treats. He filled his plate with a selection of favorites—pecan pie, brownies, and fluffy macaroons—and tried to forget that it was time to meet Louisa's family.

But the table full of Tulleys had dispersed. Martin felt relief as he realized that Louisa's parents and siblings were in all different parts of the room, socializing. He and Louisa ate dessert quickly, then followed everyone into the sanctuary to sing carols.

Louisa had a wonderful voice, the notes she struck strong and bright. Martin thought she should have been up front with the choir, singing a solo.

After the carols, there were more games and stories for the children and projects for adults back in the hall. Martin made an ornament, though he had no idea what he would do with it. He never put up a tree, even a small one, in his apartment.

Louisa made ornaments, too. But mostly, she chatted with people she knew. And she seemed to know everyone, and everyone had a story. She would introduce him, and he'd mostly listen.

Just like Digger and Jessica, so many people spoke of some pressing need they faced—and very stoically, he thought as he learned of their situations.

A man named Tim O'Toole had been out of work for months and finally had a chance for a good job, but he needed a truck and had little means to get one. And a mother, Joyce Hoyt, spoke about her son, who had been a trouble-maker and dropped out of high school but was on a good track now. Louisa knew the boy very well and was pleased to hear he had broken from friends who were a bad influence and stepped away from risky behavior. The young man hoped for a job as an EMT or a fireman but couldn't pass the high school equivalency exam.

"If only we could afford a tutor," Mrs. Hoyt said. "Billy is smart. He just needs some coaching."

"Maybe I can find a teacher who would tutor Billy for free," Louisa said, but Martin knew what she really had in mind. And there was a younger woman, a single parent named Ellen Ebbinger, with several small children flocking around her. She told Louisa about her mother in California, too sick to travel east this year. Her mother longed to see her daughter and grand-children; this Christmas could be her last. But the young woman couldn't afford the airfare and didn't know what to do.

I can help her, Martin thought. *I can make a difference for this woman and her mother. I can help all of them.*

He felt a secret happiness bubbling up, a heady, almost giddy sensation, and one that surprised him.

The evening passed quickly, much faster than

Martin had expected. Families began to pack up and bid each other good night, but Louisa was staying to clean up, so he did, too. Vera told him that she would get a ride with Claire and her husband, Nolan, and not to worry about her.

Martin didn't really want to sling around tables and chairs again, but he did want more time with Louisa and hoped they could talk privately before the night was over.

"Watch out, Martin. Before you know it, we'll make you a deacon," Tucker teased as, together, they snapped tables closed.

Martin noticed it was easier to close them than open them, so that was a plus.

"Don't scare him off, Tucker. This one's a keeper," Sam added. "Louisa, did you hear that?"

Louisa glanced at Martin over her shoulder while she worked on the chairs but didn't comment. Martin kept his head down. He hoped he wasn't blushing, an annoying reaction he had never completely outgrown. The room was warm. The folding tables felt even heavier as he stacked them in a pile. He hoped Louisa chalked up his flushed cheeks to working hard.

After the tables and chairs were stored, a few other stragglers swept the floor. Finally, it was time to go. They found their jackets and headed out to the parking lot. The air was cold and crisp, the sky full of sparkling white stars that reminded him of the lights on the Christmas tree.

He wanted to take Louisa's hand, but something stopped him.

"Would you mind giving me a lift?" Louisa said. "I came with my folks and they left a while ago."

Martin could barely hide his happiness at hearing that. "No problem. My car is right this way."

As they stepped out to the church parking lot, Louisa stopped and grabbed his arm. "Look, a shooting star! Did you see it?"

Martin looked up at the night sky. "I'm not surprised. A meteor shower is due to pass through in the next few days. You can see a lot of them."

When he was young, he was very interested in the workings of the natural world, from ant colonies to distant galaxies. He still liked to watch science shows and even followed astronomy in the newspaper.

"That sounds like fun. Do you think we can see more tonight?" she asked eagerly.

"Probably. But we need to go someplace darker to watch."

"Let's walk out on the dock. There are hardly any lights, and there's a bench out there where we can sit down."

Before he could reply, Louisa tugged his hand. He loved the feeling of her small, soft hand in his and hardly minded being pulled along without ever agreeing to the plan. *Now I know how poor*

Milo feels on our walks sometimes, he thought.

This situation was far different, though, and he quickly fell into step with Louisa as they walked through the parking lot and onto a path in the village green that ran along to the waterfront.

"Are you warm enough?" he asked her.

It wasn't that cold for December, but he felt the lack of a scarf and flipped up the collar on his jacket. She glanced up at him and smiled, looking pleased at his concern. "I'm fine."

He wanted to put his arm around her but was too shy to be so forward. *Maybe later,* he thought.

They came to the dock and walked out on the weathered, gray planks. There was no wind. Martin was thankful for that. He smelled the salt water, and he heard gentle waves slap the pilings under their steps.

"Did you have a good time tonight, Martin? You can tell me the truth. I'm just curious," she said.

Martin was surprised at her question. "Didn't I look like I was enjoying myself?"

"I wasn't sure. I thought maybe you were just trying to be nice. You know, fit in."

"It was a different experience for me," he admitted. "I don't go to many church parties. Zero, actually."

Louisa laughed. "Maybe now you'll look for some."

Martin knew she was teasing him. "Maybe I

will," he countered. "But I won't know anyone. You seem to know everyone. You remember their names, the names of their children and their pets. I don't know how you do it."

"Oh, it's no big deal. I've lived here my whole life, and I'm a police officer now."

"I've lived in the same apartment five years and I don't know a soul. My neighbors aren't very friendly."

"Are you sure? Maybe they think the same thing about you."

Martin considered her point. "Maybe. The thing is, having fun was just a bonus. You know why I really came. For leads on people who need my help. And I got plenty, thanks to you. Thank you for inviting me tonight and introducing me to all your friends."

"I should be thanking you for helping them."

"I don't think so. You know why I'm doing it," he said quietly.

They had reached the end of the dock and sat on a bench, staring out at the inky water and tipping their heads back to look up at the sky. Across the harbor, small golden lights twinkled where houses were tucked into the trees along the shoreline. The dark water and the sky above were almost the same shade of deep blue, Martin noticed. The moon was just a silver slip, perfect for seeing any meteors streak by, though he hadn't spotted any more so far.

"Can I ask you a question? You don't have to answer if you don't want to," she said quietly.

"All right . . . I'll try to answer you."

"Do you feel any differently now? Putting names and faces to the gifts you have to give out?"

"I didn't really expect to, but yes, I do," he admitted. "Tonight, when all those people you know were explaining their concerns? I realized I could help them. Change their lives in a significant way. And they would feel happy and relieved, instead of so distressed. I'm not saying the gifts would solve everything, but at least one of their problems would be solved."

Louisa seemed pleased by his answer. "Good. That must make it easier for you to finish what you need to do."

Martin shook his head. "I wouldn't go that far. But I've made progress, thanks to you." He glanced down at his phone, where he had listed the names and needs of many of the people he had met at the party. "Now I need to figure out how to get their problems solved. Some are easy," he conceded. "Others, more complicated."

"I can help with your Santa Fund, Martin. If you still want me to?"

Martin turned to her, elated by her offer and half wondering if he had imagined it. "Of course I do. I'd be very grateful . . . Are you sure?"

"I'm sure. And I have a few ideas about the

gifts—how to find them and deliver them. Without breaking and entering. Most of the time," she added with a grin.

"If anyone could advise me on how to avoid breaking the law, you'd be the one," he replied.

Martin held out his phone, and they looked at his notes together. Once again, Louisa's connections in the town made it easy to solve the problems—such as finding a tutor. Or the best way to deliver a new truck to Tim O'Toole or plane tickets to Ellen Ebbinger.

"See, you're a natural at spending my inheritance," Martin teased her. "I knew you would be."

"Your Santa Fund, you mean," she corrected him.

"Yes, the Santa Fund," he agreed with a laugh. "That's the perfect name for it."

Caught up in strategizing about the Santa Fund, she had forgotten all about the meteorites, or shooting stars, as she called them.

A streak of light flashed above and Martin slipped his arm around her shoulder and pointed. "Look, there's one . . . and here come a few more."

Louisa stared in awe, her expression like that of a little girl who had never seen such a celestial display before. But she took great pleasure in simple things; he already knew that about her.

"Wow . . . that's awesome. Did you make a

wish, Martin?" She turned to him, her beautiful face and blue eyes still lit with excitement.

He met her gaze and held it. Had he made a wish? He couldn't remember. All he knew was that he needed to kiss her, long and slow, as if the moment could last forever. Maybe that was his wish, he thought vaguely as he pulled her closer.

Their lips met softly at first. Then the kiss deepened as she wound an arm around his shoulder and leaned her head back.

Martin felt lost in their embrace, the sensation of her sweet-tasting lips under his, the scent of her perfume and the silky softness of her skin as he cupped her cheek in his palm.

It was chilly at the end of the dock, and the bench they sat on was hard as stone. But he barely noticed and doubted Louisa did either; they were close and warm together.

Suddenly, she pulled away, glancing over his shoulder. He heard footsteps and turned to follow her gaze. A man walking a dog was coming their way. Louisa turned away from Martin but still remained in the circle of his arm around her shoulder. She stared out at the water and brushed her hair back with her hand. He needed a moment, too.

"Evening, folks. Did you see the shooting stars just now?" the man with the dog asked. "Just like fireworks."

"We did see fireworks," Louisa answered.

"At least I did," she added, glancing at Martin.

He laughed softly and kissed the side of her head. "I did, too. Better than the Fourth of July over Boston Harbor."

They soon walked back to the car and didn't speak much during the short drive to Louisa's house. They pulled up to a neat gray colonial with a long front lawn, not far from the village, and Martin parked in front.

"Can I see you this week? For some shopping or delivering?" He hoped there would be some eating dinner out and maybe even a movie mixed in with such a meeting, but still didn't feel sure enough to ask her on a real date.

"Sure. I have to check my schedule, but we need to get this gift list going," she replied in her usual can-do way.

"Exactly." He wanted to kiss her good night in the car—or maybe offer to walk her to the door and kiss her there?

Before he could decide, Louisa leaned over and dropped a quick, firm kiss on his cheek. "I can find my way from here. Good night, Martin."

"Good night, Louisa." He watched her slip out of the car and run up the walk to the front door. He waited until she was inside before pulling away and heading back to Vera's house.

The long list of reasons why he should not get involved with Louisa remained. Martin knew that. A few kisses, however wonderful they were, didn't erase it. But his time with Louisa tonight had left him in the mood to push aside his concerns and wonder if maybe something could actually come of this relationship.

Didn't everyone tell him he worried too much and tied himself in knots thinking things through? When maybe he should just take life one day at a time. One experience at a time. Most other guys in his situation wouldn't make a dilemma out of meeting a beautiful girl like Louisa, who made him happy with a smile or even a glance. *This is hardly a problem, Martin,* he reminded himself.

Louisa was an adult and knew her own mind. She knew why he was here and how long he planned to stay. Was it so bad to just enjoy her company for however long it lasted?

Martin gazed at the night sky above the road, a blue mosaic outlined by bare black branches. Maybe every question didn't have an answer. Maybe some stories had to reveal themselves, little by little, and you couldn't determine the right ending or guess it in advance.

The night he had arrived here, he would have never imagined that he would actually be fulfilling his task and enjoying it—almost—and with such an amazing and unexpected helper.

Who could predict what other surprises his return to Cape Light would bring? Martin knew he certainly could not, and probably should not, even try.

CHAPTER NINE

Monday, December 12, 1955

I'M SORRY, WALTER. I GET THE SAME sum." Frances had been working the adding machine, which was set up on the kitchen table. Bills, receipts, and Walter's scratched notes about toy orders and deliveries were piled all around. Not to mention the booklet from their savings account, which told most of the story.

"You included your pay from Friday and the check from the store in Newburyport? Oh . . . there's that deposit on the train set, from Mrs. Morgan. Maybe it's still in the cash register?"

Frances scanned the row of figures on the pad. "I tallied it all, Walter . . . I'm sorry."

"I just want to make sure. You're always better with numbers than I am." But even his wife's talent with figures couldn't make this equation come out right.

"It's not enough, is it?"

He dropped into a chair across from her and shook his head.

"How far off are we? Is it really that much of a difference?"

He showed her another list of numbers and pointed to the total at the bottom. "I'm not sure what Mr. Finley will say. But I'd say that's a pretty big gap between what we can pay and what we owe."

Frances stared at the pad, then looked back at him. She seemed deflated now, too. They had both been working so hard the last two weeks and had been so hopeful.

"We have three days. There must be something we can do."

Walter had been racking his brains over that question without coming up with any plausible answer. "I thought of selling the car. But it wouldn't bring in much. Not enough to make a difference."

"I thought of that, too." She sighed and sat back. "Maybe the bank will give us more time. Can you ask them?"

"Of course I will," Walter promised. Though he doubted there would be a third chance. The bank had already given them a second, and this payment was not even all they owed. More was due in a little over two weeks. If they couldn't keep this part of the bargain, he assumed Mr. Finley would just give up on them.

But Walter didn't want his wife to worry any more than she was already. He reached over and took her hand. "We did our level best, Frances. I know we did. We went the limit and then some. You especially, working at the dress shop and in our store and sewing all hours of the night."

"You did the same, Walter. It wasn't just me." Frances looked like she might cry but was trying not to.

"I'm just trying to say, we have nothing to regret or be ashamed of." He took a breath, gathering his thoughts. "I've been thinking a lot about this. And praying a lot, too. We've done all we can to keep the shop—and things might still work out," he added, despite his doubts. "But eventually, we have to accept whatever God wants for us. It could be something we can't even imagine now."

"Oh, Walter . . . I wish I had your faith." Frances was crying now and brushed away tears. "How long do you think it will be before we have to leave? Will we need to close the store right away, before Christmas? Will we need to move out of our home, too?"

"I don't know, Franny. I'm not sure how these things work," Walter said honestly. Would the bank be that heartless? Mr. Finley seemed a decent man, but maybe the decision wouldn't be up to him. "Let's not worry about that. We have until Thursday. We can't give up yet."

"You're right. We can't give up." She rose from her chair and offered a small smile. "I'm so tired. I'd better go to bed. Doesn't seem there's anything more we can do about this tonight. Maybe things will look better in the morning."

"Maybe," he echoed.

She leaned over and kissed him on the cheek, then headed for the bedroom. Walter wished there were something more he could say or do to comfort her. She was right to head to bed early. He should do the same. Problems loomed so large at night and looked so overwhelming. A new day didn't solve everything, but it gave you a fresh perspective. A better perspective, he hoped.

Walter filled the kettle for tea and set it on the stove to boil. He gathered the papers and stuffed them in a folder, then carried the adding machine back to its spot on the little desk in the hallway.

Balancing a mug of tea, a plate of cookies, and the scraps he had saved for Otis, he headed downstairs. Working until the small hours of the night again seemed futile, but he couldn't admit that yet. Not even to himself.

Stay the course, Walter. Hold fast to your faith. Even if it looks hopeless right now. You never know what's going to happen, for better or worse. Isn't that the beauty and mystery of life? You never really know.

He tied on his shop apron and gathered supplies, but he couldn't concentrate. A breath of fresh air would help, he decided. Besides, he needed to feed Otis. He carried out water and the dog's dinner and set the dishes down near the door. He whistled, short but shrill. "Otis? Suppertime. Come and get it, pal."

Moments later, he heard the scratchy sound of the dog's paws. Otis appeared, looking happy to see him. Walter sat down on a wooden crate near the dishes and waited.

"That's a boy. Beef stew, your favorite."

Otis trotted up and ate heartily. Walter watched for a moment, then reached down and stroked the dog's soft head. It took him a moment to realize that Otis was finally tolerating his touch, and his proximity.

When Otis finished eating, he sat at Walter's side. He leaned on Walter's leg and looked up. Walter felt the warmth of his small body and stared down into his soulful eyes. Eyes that told a story of all the little dog had been through. Walter could not resist giving him a piece of the oatmeal cookie he had saved in his shirt pocket. "Here you go. I didn't forget your dessert, don't worry."

Otis crunched the cookie, eating it in one bite. Walter gave him another piece, then continued to pet him and even scratch behind his long, floppy ears. Otis gave a contented *whuff* and pressed his head into Walter's hand.

"That's a boy, Otis. I'd never hurt you, you know that now, right? Franny and I have some troubles, my friend. We might even lose the shop, but I won't forget you. Maybe you can come with us if we have to go. Though I'm not sure where."

Would they end up in a place where they could have a dog? Another worry to add to his list.

"If you can't come, I'll be back every night with your supper. You can count on that."

As he gave the dog's head one last pat, Otis leaned forward and licked Walter's hand. Walter was astounded. Maybe it was just a speck of gravy on his fingers? But Walter decided to believe that Otis really liked him and trusted him, finally.

Encouraged, Walter pulled open the shop door and held it wide for Otis to see inside. "Would you like to come inside? It's nice and warm. More cookies in there, too. Plenty, pal," he promised.

Otis leaned forward and sniffed, stretching out his neck. He looked up at Walter, tail wagging. But he still seemed confused by the invitation. Perhaps he'd tried to get indoors from time to time and people had chased him out?

Walter considered carrying the dog in. He wasn't very big, about thirty pounds or so? But maybe that would be going too far. He didn't want to frighten Otis again. It seemed better if the dog came in by his own choice.

Before he could coax any more, they both heard a sound. Another creature stirred behind a pile of boxes, just a few feet away. Otis turned, his posture instantly defensive. His back stiffened, and the hair on the back of his neck bristled as he growled low in his throat.

Walter stood perfectly still, waiting to see what would emerge. The boxes tipped and a bushy, bottom-heavy raccoon stared back with bright, beady eyes. Hand-like paws clutched a half-eaten apple.

Otis tossed his head back and let out a long, throaty howl. A haunting sound that seemed far too big to come from such a small dog.

Walter had to laugh, just listening to it. Seconds later, the dog sprang at his prey. The raccoon froze for a second, then nimbly hopped over a fence, and Otis followed and disappeared from sight.

Walter sighed. "Good night, my friend. Have fun. But I certainly hope you don't catch up with that masked bandit."

Walter didn't sleep much that night and woke up on Tuesday with a heavy heart. But he opened the store early and kept a sharp lookout for customers while he made toys in his workshop.

At the end of the day, despite their hopes and prayers, the balance in their bank account was very much the same as it had been the night before. Walter had called the bank earlier and made an appointment for ten o'clock Thursday morning, though he had no idea what he would say.

While he waited for Frances to return from

the dress shop, he chose toys for the church collection. He planned to bring the donation over after the shop closed.

He was packing the items in cartons when Frances came in. She smiled and slipped off her coat. "You stayed open late. That was a good idea. Did you make many sales today?"

"A few," he said vaguely. Was it past six already? He hadn't even noticed. There had only been three customers all day. All he had sold was a box of Lincoln Logs and a yo-yo. But he knew that scant report would be far too gloomy.

Frances pulled an envelope from her purse and handed it to him. "I asked Nancy to pay me early this week. She was very nice about it. It's a little bit better than usual, with the overtime from Saturday. Every little bit helps, right?"

"Definitely, dear." He peeked in the envelope and forced a smile. It was full of bills, but it still wouldn't save them.

"I was wondering, Walter, do you want me to go to the bank with you? Maybe I should." He could tell she was nervous but trying to hide it. "Maybe if we both talk to Mr. Finley, it would work out better."

"Oh, I'll be okay. I appreciate your offer, Franny. But, if you don't mind, I'll go on my own."

"I don't mind. I just thought I'd offer." She sounded relieved, and Walter realized he had given the right answer.

"Have you thought of anything else you could say?"

Walter had been thinking of only that all day, rehearsing his speech to the bank manager in his head for hours. But he still felt at a loss for the words that would win a reprieve.

"I'll offer him the money we have and hope he'll go easy on us."

"You'll ask for more time, won't you?"

"Yes, of course I will," he promised. The first time Walter had met with the banker, he had felt so sure that all they needed was a little more time to catch up. But he wasn't sure at all now and wondered if he could make that promise again.

"I know you'll say the right thing." Frances touched his shoulder as she passed, heading for the stairs. "I'll get dinner ready. Just soup and sandwiches tonight. I hope that's okay."

"I'm not hungry, dear. I had a late lunch," he said, though he hadn't eaten much all day, since his stomach was churning with nerves. "Why don't you grab a bite and put your feet up? I'll bring our toy donation over to the church."

"All right. I'll save you something. Don't be too late. I heard it's going to snow tonight."

"I won't be long. I'll be home well before the bad weather."

Walter turned the sign on the shop door to closed and finished packing the toys, several boxes filled with their finest creations. As he loaded the bounty into the back of his car, he realized he was happier giving away his stock to a good cause than imagining it sold for pennies on the dollar to the highest bidder in an auction . . . which was what would happen if the bank seized his property.

Don't think like that. Mr. Finley might give you another chance. You can't give up without even asking. You promised Frances.

There were cars in the church parking lot and lights on inside when Walter pulled up. As he unloaded the boxes, a few church members came out the back door.

Dr. Elliot saw him and walked over to his car. "Need any help, Walter?"

"Thanks, Ezra. It looks like a lot, but the boxes are light. It's just some toys for the collection."

"Gee whiz, you gave us half your shop. You need to leave a few for Santa to give out on Christmas Day, my friend."

"That's what I'm always telling him." Oliver had come out of the church and stood next to Ezra. Walter hadn't noticed him approach.

Wearing a long overcoat, a white silk muffler, and a black homburg, he looked as if he might be headed to the opera or dinner at his club. Or wherever wealthy men like him spent Tuesday evenings.

"Don't worry, gentlemen," Walter said. "There

are plenty left for Santa. And he has his own workshop, full of helpful elves."

Ezra laughed and slapped Walter's shoulder. "You're a good fellow. We appreciate your generosity. Above and beyond the call. Say hello to Frances for me. Give her my best wishes."

"I will, Ezra." Walter was not surprised to see Ezra Elliot make himself scarce once Oliver had appeared. Walter wasn't sure of the details, but the two men had a complicated relationship. Friends and rivals since childhood, even they didn't seem to understand their feelings for each other.

Frances had heard the two men were both in love with the same girl these days. Walter wasn't sure the gossip was true, but if it was, he predicted Oliver would win the hand of the young lady in question. That "difficult but prize catch" Oliver was trying to reel in, Walter recalled. Frances thought so, too. Ezra was intelligent and kind, but Oliver was dashing and charming, with matinee-idol looks. Few women could resist that combination.

As Ezra walked off, Oliver took a cigarette from a slim case and lit it with a heavy silver lighter. "You have outdone yourself this time, Walter. Ezra wasn't kidding. Doing well at the shop? I hope the situation has improved."

Walter intended to reply in some vague way but found that he couldn't put forward an upbeat, false front. Not to Oliver. "Not much, Oliver. Not as much as we'd hoped."

Oliver looked surprised. He blew out a puff of smoke. "But you've been advertising. I saw flyers all over town and a line out your door last Saturday. And you told me there are orders from other stores. That still didn't help you meet your obligations?"

"It helped some. But not enough. I'm due at the bank on Thursday, and I'm afraid that the payment will be short. Even though we've pooled every cent. Even money for heat and groceries," he confessed. "I'm just praying that Mr. Finley will give us more time. Though I don't know why he would—and frankly, I'm not even sure that will help."

Oliver looked concerned, even distressed, by the news. He dropped his cigarette and ground it out with his shoe. "How short are you, Walter? Do you know the exact amount?"

"Of course I do. I see it in my sleep." He told Oliver how much he had to give the bank and how much was missing, his words stumbling.

"I see," Oliver replied. "The difference is considerable."

Walter's heart sank. Oliver knew about these things. If he said the difference was "considerable," what he really meant was that the bank manager was not likely to grant another extension.

"I don't know what to say. I feel like a failure,

but Franny and I have tried our best. We've given it our full effort these last two weeks. We just couldn't catch up. I've been trying to keep up a brave face for her sake, but I'm afraid Thursday's meeting won't go very well." Walter glanced at the boxes. "I was happy to pack up all these toys today, knowing they'll be given to kids who really need them. It seems a better fate for my creations than being sold at a bank auction."

Walter couldn't help it; the confession had come out in a rush. He had been under so much pressure, and he knew Oliver understood.

Oliver rested his hand on Walter's shoulder. "Walter, don't despair. I can easily loan you the money you need, and more."

"Oh, no. You can't do that. I wasn't asking for help. I never expected—"

"I know you weren't and never would. You're the type who goes down with the ship, for better or worse." His charming smile and humorous tone made Walter smile, despite himself. "I know how hard you and Frances work. Everyone needs a helping hand once in a while. You never turn away from a chance to help others. Everyone knows that. Now it's your turn. Let me help you, please. I'd be happy to."

Walter was overcome with so many feelings: surprise, gratitude, relief. Also pride—foolish, perhaps?—telling him he shouldn't accept the offer.

"That's incredibly generous. I appreciate your offer very much. But I'm already in debt to the bank. I'm not sure I should be in debt to you, too, Oliver. Maybe it's a sign that I just shouldn't be in business. Maybe—"

"—Don't even say it, Walter. You can't quit now. I won't let you." Oliver's tone was stern, the look in his eye commanding, reminding Walter that Oliver had led men into combat and risked his own life to save other soldiers. Otto Bates was one and couldn't say enough about Oliver's courage. Walter could see that side of Oliver now. Under the cashmere and silk, there was a steely will, just as persuasive as his smooth charm.

"You're not thinking straight," Oliver said in a softer tone. "Maybe meeting me tonight by chance is a sign that you should stay in business, that you should continue. Did you think of that?"

Walter actually had not. Oliver had him there.

"Consider it a gift," Oliver added. "And if you won't accept a gift, then pay me back whenever you're able."

Before Walter could sort out his thoughts, Oliver picked up a carton and carried it toward the church. "I think it's going to start snowing soon. Let's get these boxes inside, and we'll figure out the details."

Walter nodded, his throat too tight to speak. "Thank you, Oliver. From the bottom of my heart. I feel as if . . . as if an angel just swooped down and saved us."

"I wouldn't go that far." Oliver laughed. "If I'm an angel, St. Peter must be opening the pearly gates for a lot of riffraff these days."

By the time Walter returned home, snow had started to fall—small, frosty flakes drifting, captured in the beams of the streetlights.

He thought about going back to the alley to look for Otis, but knew he had to see Frances first. She met him at the door, already in her nightgown and robe.

"What took you so long? I was worried. Did you have trouble with the car?"

"I'm sorry. I should have called." Walter hung his hat and coat by the door. He felt a smile break out on his face, and when he turned to Frances, she gave him a curious look.

"Walter . . . are you all right? If you stopped at the pub, I understand—"

"I didn't go to a pub, Franny. Although I wish we had a bottle of champagne handy right now. I went out to the cannery with Oliver Warwick. The most amazing thing happened. Oliver gave us enough money to make our payment on Thursday."

He slipped his hand under his sweater, into the breast pocket of his shirt, and took out the check that Oliver had written out to him. He handed it to Frances, to prove he wasn't imagining the story.

"I didn't want to take it, but he kept insisting."

Frances looked down at the check and then back up at him. Her face went white as paper and she dropped down into a chair. "I can't believe it, Walter. Why would Oliver Warwick loan us so much money? He's practically a stranger."

"He might be a stranger, but he's a very kind stranger. That's for certain."

Walter sat down next to her and related the conversation, as much as he could recall. "—I was too shocked to answer at first. And I had my doubts about accepting the favor. But Oliver was so well-intentioned and insistent, I couldn't say no."

"Thank goodness you didn't. Why would you?"

Walter had to be honest with her. "I did wonder if we're just postponing the inevitable. We have to make another payment after Christmas, and that sum is even larger. We were saved by a miracle tonight, but if we come up short next time, I won't let Oliver bail us out again. That wouldn't be right."

Frances leaned over and took his hand. "Let's not worry about the next time right now. I think God wants us to keep the shop open or He wouldn't have sent Oliver's help. I think we just need to keep working hard and hope for the best. Isn't that what you always tell me?"

"Exactly." Walter smiled to hear his sunny philosophy tossed back at him. "Maybe this is our last Christmas in the Magical Toy Shop. Maybe God has something different and even better planned for us. We'll have to accept whatever comes. All we can do now is make the next two weeks the best Christmas ever. We've been working so hard, Franny, maybe losing touch with the joy we always feel making and selling toys. That's how I'm going to spend the next two weeks, with a lighter heart, enjoying the season."

"I'm glad to hear that, Walter. We'll get through this, one way or another. We'll always have each other."

"Thank goodness for that." Walter leaned over and kissed her, cupping her face in his hand. "You're the greatest blessing in my life. I could lose everything and it wouldn't matter at all, if I still had you."

He leaned forward and their lips met in a tender kiss. He loved the flowery smell of her perfume and the way her hair felt like silk against his fingers. But he'd barely put his arms around her when a loud, echoing howl broke the silence. It seemed to be coming from the alley behind the shop.

Frances looked alarmed. "That sounds like a wolf . . . though I know it can't possibly be."

"It's not a wolf, it's Otis. I'd better go down and see what's going on." He jumped up from his chair as the clatter of trash pails and a high-pitched chattering filled the air. "Raccoons. They can be vicious." Walter grabbed a flashlight from a kitchen cupboard and flew out the door.

"I'm coming, too." Frances followed, slipping on her shoes before they ran down the wooden steps to the store and then through the workshop.

Walter opened the door cautiously, not sure what he would find. The snow was still falling lightly, though he barely noticed. He stood still and listened, then heard a whimpering sound. He quickly spotted Otis, lying on the ground, panting. Walter ran to him and called out to his wife. "Otis is hurt. He's bleeding. Get some towels or sheets."

Frances ran into the shop as he kneeled down by the dog and gently stroked his head. "I'm here, Otis. I'm going to help you. You'll be all right, don't worry. Frances and I are going to take care of you."

A short time later, he and Frances had Otis in their kitchen and were tending to his wounds with soft rags and warm water. Otis liked the attention and didn't fuss or try to pull away.

"Maybe it's not as bad as it first looked." Frances softly dabbed cuts on the dog's leg and paw. "He was bleeding a lot, but this cut isn't very deep. And his ear and muzzle are just scratched."

"It's not too serious, but it must be painful." Walter hated to think of his little friend in discomfort. "He must have had a fight with another animal. The other night I saw him chase a raccoon that was three times his size. He's a brave little chap."

Frances smiled at Walter. "Maybe he was defending our trash pail," she teased.

"I think so," Walter replied in a serious tone. He had pulled out a phone book and looked up the number for a veterinarian. "The office is closed—no one is answering," he said after a moment. He hung up the phone. "I'll bring him there tomorrow. He might need shots or some medicine on those lacerations."

"Good idea. He should be checked by a vet anyway. Since we're going to keep him," she added. "A stray dog needs all sorts of care. Starting with a bath, I think."

"Very true." Walter glanced at her but didn't say more. Frances had never been a real dog lover. Walter was glad to see that Otis had won her over so easily.

He was a charming little hound. There was just something about him that was so touching; he was vulnerable and still so spunky. Walter realized Otis had missed his supper and checked the fridge for leftovers. He saw a dish covered with wax paper and pulled it out.

"That's your sandwich. I left it for you," Frances said. "Ham and cheese."

"I forgot all about supper. I'll share it with Otis. He must be hungry, too."

He broke half the sandwich into small pieces and set them down by the dog. Otis staggered to his feet and gobbled the offering. Frances filled a bowl with water and gave that to him, too. "We need to get some dog food tomorrow. He needs proper meals. Twice a day?"

"That sounds right. I'll ask the vet. Where should he sleep? It's not very warm in here at night." Walter looked around the kitchen, trying to determine the coziest corner.

Frances smiled and headed to the hallway. "I'll make him a bed in our room. Would that be all right?"

"That would be better. We don't want him to get scared out here all alone on his first night with us." He realized how silly that sounded. Otis was used to sleeping out in the cold, under a car or behind a pile of boxes.

Frances opened the linen closet and pulled out an old blanket. "Don't forget to sing him a lullaby before you tuck him in. I've heard dogs really like that."

Walter smiled and looked down at Otis, who had curled up on the towel again. "Good idea. Maybe I will."

Walter fell asleep moments after his head hit the pillow, his last thoughts a short prayer of heartfelt thanks for Oliver's gift. They were saved, for now. It was still hard to believe.

Late in the night, Walter woke up, not sure why.

He heard Otis softly snoring and realized the dog had left the bed in the corner that Frances had made for him. Walter reached down and patted his head. Otis had made himself comfortable on the rug, right next to their bed. Walter closed his eyes and smiled. Heaven had sent two gifts to him yesterday.

WALTER PEEKED OUT THE WINDOW AS SOON as he got out of bed. The world was covered with a soft, white blanket of snow. Main Street was barely plowed, a few determined cars bouncing along with chains on their tires. Some shopkeepers were out early, shoveling the sidewalk in front of their stores. Walter knew he had to get out there, too. Though he doubted many shoppers would brave the weather, and Wednesdays were notoriously slow anyway, even during the holiday season.

Just as well, he thought. He would relish the time in his workshop and take care of Otis, too. The dog stood by his side, wagging his tail, and Walter was glad to see that his injuries were bothering him so little. He guessed that the dog wanted to go out. Otis found a shoe and picked it up in his mouth, then brought it to Walter, lest there be any doubt.

"I got the message, buddy. Give me just a minute." There would be some changes in his day for sure now that Otis had come along. But

Walter didn't mind taking care of him, not one bit.

The streets were too snowy for a trip to the vet, and even Nancy's shop was closed for the day. While Frances sewed upstairs, Walter headed down to the store. He thought Otis would stay in the apartment, but the dog followed him everywhere.

When Walter went into his workshop, Otis was right behind him. Walter fixed another bed downstairs and the dog quickly settled there, content to watch Walter work.

Walter was grateful for the quiet. The snow seemed to make the world more peaceful. It certainly made Main Street serene, with few people or cars out and the usual noises muffled. Feeling clear of any worries about his meeting at the bank the next day, Walter picked up his drawing pad and charcoal, ready to concentrate. He had a special project to start today, an order for stuffed toys. He didn't usually make stuffed toys, but a store nearby was willing to pay an attractive sum. Walter thought he would try his hand at some designs.

He considered the classic teddy bear or a floppy-eared rabbit. But once his gaze fell on Otis, it seemed obvious to start with a simple dog. He had the perfect model sitting right in front of him. He lifted the charcoal and began to fill pages of his sketchbook with loose, quick drawings.

Exhausted from his hard life in the alleyways and his injuries, or just deeply grateful to be in a clean, warm place, Otis hardly moved a muscle all day. Walter found he didn't need to exaggerate the dog's features one bit to end up with an incredibly cute, endearing design.

Using graph paper, he carefully broke down the drawing into pattern pieces, figuring out the most efficient way to cut fabric and sew it together to make the toy's body. It was important the seams didn't show much, or at all, and that the body could be easily filled with stuffing. The tail, ears, nose, and other details would be sewn and glued on later. He had some good ideas on how to make those little details really enhance the dog's personality.

He pinned the paper patterns on white muslin, cut the pieces out, and checked how they fit together. He corrected a few glitches, then found some brown, fuzzy fabric in a bag of remnants Frances had left for him. He pinned the pattern pieces to the fuzzy fabric and snipped again, following the outline carefully. Then he began to sew it all together. He couldn't wait to stuff the body and show Frances.

"I think we've got something here," he told Otis. "It's turning out very well."

Otis lifted his sleepy head and panted a moment, then rested his nose on his paws, his warm brown gaze fixed on Walter.

Walter heard Frances on the stairs, and she soon stood in the doorway, wearing her hat and coat. There were big black boots on her feet, and she carried her high heels in a paper bag.

"Nancy called. She's opening the store after all. I'm going to walk up there."

"I can drive you, Franny. Just give me a minute," Walter murmured without looking up from his work. He really didn't want to leave his workbench but knew he had to offer.

"That's all right. It will be a bother to clean the snow off the car. I don't mind walking. Nancy said most of Main Street is shoveled. Did you do the sidewalk in front of our store yet?"

Walter finally looked up. He felt as if he had been awakened from a dream. "What, dear? . . . Uh, no. Not yet. I meant to, but I got distracted."

"You've been quiet as a mouse down here all morning. What are you working on?"

"A stuffed dog." Walter wished he had more of it completed. He had stuffed the body, but had only put the tail and ears on. It was still missing all the other cute details. "It's not finished, but here are the sketches. You can get a better idea of what I'm aiming for. What do you think?"

Frances took the dog and held it out at arm's length. Then she looked over the drawings. He couldn't read her reaction from her expression and got nervous. Had he wasted the whole morning?

"Walter, it's adorable. I love it. He's so sweet. He looks just like Otis."

Walter smiled. "I did use Otis as the model."

"You captured his sweet hound dog personality perfectly. And it will be even cuter when you add the trimmings." She glanced at the sketch pad again. "I have some thread upstairs that would be perfect for whiskers and eyebrows. It might be nice to sew a black nose from thick thread, too, instead of gluing on some hard, plastic piece, don't you think?"

"That's a good idea. I didn't know what to use." He had known Frances would have good suggestions. She always did.

"I can do that part . . . if you want me to."

"Of course I do. I'll make the body and you can add the finishing touches tonight. I want to put him in the window, sitting on the sleigh next to Santa. I want the window to be extra spectacular this year." *Because it might be our last in the shop,* he nearly added.

But he didn't want to dampen the mood. It had been such a happy, productive morning. A new day, as fresh as the snowfall.

ON THURSDAY MORNING, WALTER MADE sure to give himself an extra-close shave and to shine his shoes and choose a spotless tie from his meager collection. "I'm headed to the bank for a little while this morning," he told Otis as he fed the dog his breakfast. "I won't be very long. Don't worry."

He had gone to bed early, weary from a long day in the workshop and wanting extra rest to face Mr. Finley. It was Frances who stayed up late working, and he found the results on the kitchen table. The stuffed dog was complete and even more wonderful than he had ever imagined.

Along with adorable features, which mirrored those of the real Otis, Frances had added an outfit, a red felt vest, a green hat, and curled-toe boots, the sort that elves wore.

Looking very sleepy, she walked into the kitchen just as he was admiring it.

"Frances, you've outdone yourself. This is the cutest toy I've ever seen. I'm going to put him in the window this morning, before I go to the bank."

Frances laughed and poured a cup of coffee. "I didn't realize Santa had a dog, but that makes perfect sense. I think we should call him Otis, in honor of your inspiration."

"Of course. I'd never name him anything else."

"Are you all set for the bank, dear?" Frances poured some cornflakes into a bowl and added a dash of cream.

"I have everything right here." Walter patted a manila envelope on the table.

"Good luck," she said sincerely.

"Thanks, but I'm not sure I need it now. Not with Oliver's help."

Walter was placing the stuffed toy in the shop window when Digger arrived. He was going to watch the store while Walter was at the bank and Frances went to work at the dress shop. Walter placed the toy dog in the perfect spot, right next to his jolly master. The Otis dog was not large but was very eye-catching and made all the difference in the display, Walter thought.

Digger was already in the store when Walter climbed out of the window. Digger gave him a hand jumping down. "That's a cute toy you set up in there, Walter. Is that a new one?"

"I made it yesterday. Frances made the clothes. I hope you don't mind real dogs. We just took this one in the other night. He was living in the alley behind the shop," Walter explained.

Otis had been waiting for Walter to come out of the window and greeted Digger, wagging his tail.

"He's a nice little hound. They're smart and loyal." Digger patted the dog's head. "I think we'll get along just fine."

"I won't be long," Walter promised. Otis wanted to follow him, but Walter persuaded the dog to stay in the shop, though part of him wished he could bring Otis along, if only to calm his nerves for the meeting.

It will definitely be easier than the last time, he reminded himself as he walked up to the bank.

You can give Mr. Finley the payment due today. It's just the next time that will be difficult. Walter hoped the banker wouldn't ask about that. *Don't worry about the next time now. Just get this over with.*

DESPITE HAVING AN APPOINTMENT, WALTER waited a long time to see the bank manager. Finally, Mrs. Bowman led him to Mr. Finley's office.

The meeting went by very quickly. Finley seemed relieved that Walter had the payment and had kept his side of their bargain. Which supported Walter's impression that Richard Finley was a good-hearted man who didn't want to cause hardship for others, even when they had gotten into trouble with his bank.

As Walter left, the bank manager stood up and offered his hand. "A pleasure doing business with you, Mr. Nightingale. I'll see you around the first of the year. Have a merry Christmas."

"Same to you, sir." Walter smiled as he shook Mr. Finley's hand, knowing the days would pass quickly.

As he left the bank, Walter checked his watch. He had been gone far longer than he had expected. He hoped Digger was not overwhelmed. Main Street was crowded with shoppers eager to catch up after the snow had kept most of them inside the day before.

As Walter entered the shop, Otis ran up to greet him. He took off his hat and gave the dog a pat. There were several customers wandering the aisles. *A good sign,* he thought.

Digger was showing a woman a pogo stick when he noticed Walter come in. "Be right back, ma'am." He ran over to Walter.

"Sorry I was gone so long, Digger. I had to wait awhile for my appointment."

"That's all right. These folks have kept me hopping. You know that stuffed dog in the window? I couldn't sell it. You forgot to put on the price tag."

Walter touched his hand to his forehead. "You're right. I was so eager to show it off. Did someone want to buy it?"

"A lot of folks. I had to make a list." Digger handed Walter a long list of names and phone numbers.

"That many people asked about it?" Walter started to count the names. There were nearly thirty. He wondered if Digger had made some mistake. "All these people wanted the dog?"

"That's right. You ought to pull a number from a hat and raffle it off," Digger suggested.

"Or make a lot more dogs," Walter replied.

Digger thought for a moment and scratched his cheek. "Hey, now you're talking. Can you and Franny make all those dogs in time for Christmas?"

"Sure we can. We can make dozens—more if we need to." Walter left the list on the counter and headed for the stairway. "I'm going to change my clothes. This tie is strangling me."

"You do that, Walter. Ties are dangerous. I bet they're unhealthy," Digger agreed. "You get rid of that monkey suit. I can stay awhile longer."

"That would be great, Digger. I want to get into the workshop and get started on these dogs."

"That's a good plan, Walter. Strike while the iron is hot. You only have ten days till Christmas."

"Yes, I know." Walter headed up the stairs, two at a time. Ten days to make good on his promise to the bank. Without any help from Oliver this time.

CHAPTER TEN

Saturday, December 8, 2018

MARTIN ROLLED THE NEW BIKES OUT OF the shop, then studied the back of his car. They were small bikes, for two young children, but he was worried they wouldn't fit. The back of the Subaru already looked packed to capacity.

It had been tricky to keep the boxes and packages out of Vera's sight. He was lucky that many of the gifts he had given out were the kind that didn't come in a box—like picking up the bill for a new furnace or dental work. Or Digger's hearing aids. But others were bulky and boxed.

It took a while to rearrange the packages, but he finally got everything in. Could he see anything out the rearview mirror? He didn't think so, and he hoped Louisa didn't whip out her book and give him a ticket for that. The side-view mirrors and her help would have to do.

Finally, he unfolded a large blue plastic tarp and covered the bounty. That had been Louisa's idea, too. Not because she feared someone would break into his car, but "Because everyone is so snoopy in this town, they'll find out where all the gifts are coming from." He tucked the plastic around the edges, satisfied the pile was snoop-proof. And there was still room for Louisa in the front passenger seat.

It wouldn't be any fun without her, he thought, as he started the car and headed for his next stop. He honestly didn't know what he would have done the last few days if she had not been helping him. Given up, probably. With her advice and inside knowledge, he had made real progress. Not only did she know everyone in town, some-times he felt as if she wore special glasses that helped her see when a person had a problem or a need, even when that person was trying to hide it and act as if things were fine. People trusted her and opened up easily, confiding their prob-lems and worries. And Louisa had a talent for figuring out how to make their lives better.

Martin wondered if that was a gift a person was born with. He had come to rely on her, and some-times felt he was taking advantage of her good nature. But he could see she greatly enjoyed figuring out the gifts and working on the Santa Fund. He was going to pick her up at five o'clock, and just after sunset, they would drive around the village and make their stealthy deliveries. He had offered to take her out to dinner afterward and felt relieved when she accepted. He'd thought she might make some excuse or have other plans.

He knew he liked her, very much, but he wasn't at all sure how she felt about him. Sometimes he thought she was just being helpful, being a "nice" person, by advising him. And that for her, the Santa Fund was mostly something different and fun to do, especially in her sleepy, quiet town.

He thought about her all the time and could hardly wait to see her again when they parted. But, as usual, Martin held his cards close. He was slow to show his feelings, especially with a girl like Louisa, who he was sure had her pick of guys who wanted to date her. Even if she liked him, what could come of a relationship? He didn't know; his future was so unclear. That didn't seem fair to her. But he couldn't help being happy that he would see her tonight.

It was only three, and he still had time to get a haircut, change his clothes, take care of Milo, and make one more important stop on the Beach Road before he picked up Louisa.

He drove down Main Street and had just caught sight of the barbershop's red and white striped pole when his cell phone rang. The screen said *Dad,* and he picked it up.

"Martin? Glad I caught you," his father greeted him.

"Hi, Dad, what's up? Is everything all right?" Martin saw a space and quickly parked. His father didn't call very often. Martin wondered if there was something wrong in Arizona.

"Everything's fine, Martin. I've been thinking about you. Did you ever go to Cape Light?" Martin's father knew about the terms of the will, and though he agreed with Martin that the stipulation was eccentric and frustrating, he could offer no advice on how to satisfy it. Or maybe he just wouldn't. Martin knew his father didn't even like to think about Cape Light; it was a topic largely off-limits.

"I'm here right now, Dad. I've been here since Thanksgiving night."

"Really? So you're trying to carry out Granddad's wishes after all?" His father sounded surprised. Probably because Martin had complained so much about the terms and had even fought in court to nullify the clause. "How's it working out? Have you been able to spend the money?"

"Not all of it. But I'm making progress." Martin glanced at the back of his car, wondering if he should take a photo and send it to his father.

"Good for you. I wouldn't have even known where to start."

"Someone is helping me, a girl I met who's lived here her whole life. She knows everyone and has a huge family. Her last name is Tulley," he added, wondering if his father would remember Louisa's family.

"Tulley? Sounds familiar, but it's not an unusual name," his father mused. He was quiet for a long moment, and Martin thought he'd lost the connection.

"Dad . . . are you still there?"

"Yes, I'm here . . . I was just wondering, Martin. Did you see the house?"

The house his father had grown up in, Martin knew he meant; the house Martin was about to inherit. It had been held in trust since his grandfather's death, and Martin had the key.

"I was going to stop there later today, before it gets dark. My attorney said it's empty. The family that was renting moved out about a week ago."

Martin had been surprised that the house had gone to him, and not his father. He would never know for sure, but he sometimes thought his grandfather had done that to send his son a message. Martin's father had visited so rarely, and Martin knew that slight had hurt his grand-parents, who had doted on their only son.

But Martin's father didn't seem to resent the decision. He'd once told Martin, "You needn't feel guilty about getting the property, son. Your grandfather gave me plenty. Maybe he wanted to be sure that you would inherit something of value, even if you weren't able to fulfill his request about the charity money."

"Let me know how it's holding up. I'd be inter-ested to hear. When do you think you'll be done with all this rigmarole?"

"I'm not sure. It's already taking much

longer than I expected. I have to be finished by Christmas."

"That's right. I almost forgot. I hope it works out, Martin. Maybe you can spend the holidays with us. Suzanne was asking about you. I know she'd love to see you. We all would."

"Thanks, Dad, I'll think about it." Martin knew his father and stepmother, Suzanne, meant well and were trying, as they always did, to make Martin feel he was part of their family. But Martin would rather spend Christmas alone than in sunny Scottsdale with his stepsiblings, tearing open gifts by a swimming pool and having a barbeque for Christmas dinner.

"I'll see how it goes," he said finally. He ended the call and headed into the barbershop. He had been avoiding a visit to the house and decided he didn't have time today, after all. He would go there another day, when his mind was clearer.

First things first, he decided, putting aside his real reason for delaying the visit. He knew there were so many memories there, it wouldn't be easy.

LOUISA STARED INTO HER CLOSET, wondering what to wear. She always drew a lot of compliments when she wore blue. It brought out her eyes—her best feature, she thought. But her uniform was blue, and she got so tired of the color. On her days off, when she didn't have to wear the bulky, stark outfit, she alternated between pure comfort, with leggings and hoodies, or chose flowery blouses and openwork sweaters over jeans, the total opposite of her mannish suit and heavy black shoes.

She pulled out two sweaters and then a peasant blouse and held each up in the mirror, but still had no clue. Were they going on a date? She wasn't even sure.

She had been helping Martin this week with his Santa Fund. They'd made plans to drop off some presents around town this evening, and "Maybe we can have a bite to eat after somewhere?"

Of course she had agreed. They'd had fun this week, shopping and arranging for anonymous deliveries. But some of the gifts could not be dropped off by a store, and she was happy to help Martin, if only to make sure some other police officer did not find him skulking around a backyard again.

She wasn't quite sure yet what to make of Martin. He was an interesting guy, different from most that she knew and still a mystery to her. She wasn't sure why, but from the moment they'd met, there was something about him she found very touching. He always tried to act so in control, but most of the time, he didn't have a clue. He could seem reserved and distant, but he was really just shy, she'd realized. Not the type of guy to swagger around thinking every girl was falling for him. Just the opposite, which was another thing she liked about him. She was sure a lot of women found him as attractive as she did. He never mentioned a girlfriend in Boston, but that didn't mean there wasn't one. She had to remember that. Or maybe just ask? But that might seem too pushy. Too presumptuous. She wasn't sure if they were at that stage yet.

Maybe tonight, she'd find out more. She hoped so.

She finally dressed in a thick, Aran-knit sweater over brown leggings and boots. She left her hair loose and skipped makeup entirely; she rarely wore it, except for some lip gloss. She pulled on a bunch of silver bangle bracelets, then pulled them off again. She wanted to look good, but not as if she had thought about it too much or tried too hard. *Less is more,* she reminded herself.

She heard noise downstairs. Her siblings had scattered in the morning for basketball practice and piano lessons, but everyone was home now and her parents were trying to decide when to go out for the Christmas tree, she gathered from the conversation.

She worried about Martin feeling overwhelmed by her family. He had narrowly avoided the full treatment at the Advent party, but he'd have to meet them sooner or later. They were definitely "an adult portion." There were pluses and minuses in being the oldest. She often considered finding her own place, now that she was launched in her career, but she hadn't made any plans yet. She earned a good salary, but keeping up with college loans definitely made a dent. Louisa thought it was probably best to save awhile before she took on her own apartment, even if it meant putting up with her younger brothers and sister.

"Someday you'll look back on these times fondly," her mother would say when she could tell that Louisa was losing her patience with the younger ones. Louisa knew that might be true, but it didn't always help her hold on to her patience.

As she came downstairs, her brothers were laughing and pushing at each other, rough-housing around the living room like two wild bear cubs.

"Knock it off, you two." Louisa caught a lamp just before it crashed to the floor. "Can you at least try to act housebroken?"

Neil glanced at her. He had his brother's arms pinned behind his back, though both were still laughing. He offered her a goofy smile. "Yes, Officer. Absolutely. Whatever you say."

Ryan saw his chance, wriggled loose, and punched Neil in the arm. "I think the officer's boyfriend is coming. Better chill or she'll lock us up."

Louisa put the lamp back on the table. "Awww,

my little bros? I'd never do that to you guys. I'll just call animal control. The tranquilizer darts don't hurt a bit, honest."

She hoped her sarcasm masked her embarrassment. Martin was certainly not her boyfriend, and she shuddered to think one of them might say that in front of him. How did those two goofballs even know he was coming? Her mother must have said something. Louisa left them before they resumed their wrestling match. Maybe her mother could devise some strategy to get them out of the way before Martin arrived? She hoped so.

At the doorway to the kitchen, her little sister flew out. Louisa jumped to the side to let her pass. She was very upset, holding on to the edges of a knit ski cap that was pulled down over her ears, as low as it would stretch.

"What's the matter, Carly?" Louisa called to her. "What's going on?" A tiff with their folks? A snub by one of her friends? Gossip that some boy she liked had a crush on someone else? There were so many dramas lately in Carly's life.

"My hair! It's horrible! I look like an alien."

"Awww, honey . . ." Louisa sympathized. A bad haircut could be traumatic, especially at that age. Louisa followed her to the staircase. "I'm sure it's not that bad."

"It's pathetic. I can't leave the house like this."

"Can you show me? Maybe I can do something

with it." Louisa wasn't sure what. A blow-dryer or flat iron might help?

Carly shook her head. "Nothing will help. Ever. Maybe a wig," she called over her shoulder before running into her room and slamming the door.

Louisa's mother had followed Carly from the kitchen. "She's so upset about her hair. Did you talk to her?"

"I tried to, but she wouldn't even let me see it."

"I don't think it's that bad, but they did cut more than she expected, and her bangs are a little short."

"No wonder she's freaked out. Good bangs are crucial for survival in middle school, Mom. Everyone knows that."

"Really?" Her mother hadn't really heard her. The boys were acting out again and drew her attention. "Neil, Ryan, what did I tell you about wrestling in the house? Get in the shower, ASAP. We're going out soon for the tree."

The action figures suddenly went slack and headed meekly for the stairs, though Louisa did notice Neil poke Ryan in the back.

"Where's your date? Is he late?" her mother asked.

"He should be here soon, and it's not a date, Mom. I told you. He's just a friend. And his name is Martin."

"Yes, your friend Martin. That's what I meant."

261

Louisa could tell her mother didn't believe her. "He's visiting on business, right?"

"That's right." Louisa knew she couldn't really explain. "You met him at the Advent party, remember?"

"Just to say hello. But he seemed nice. A little quiet. But maybe he opens up more with you. Now that you're getting to know him?"

Louisa could tell her mother didn't think Martin was her type. Brian, her most recent boyfriend, had been very outgoing, barreling through life like a big, friendly Labrador. Martin was more like a skittish greyhound.

"How long will he be in town?" her mother asked.

"I'm not sure. At least until Christmas, I think."

"Oh . . . that's good." Louisa wasn't sure what her mother meant by that. Good for Louisa? If she liked Martin, it would be better if he didn't leave quickly? Louisa did wonder what would happen if things progressed. Boston wasn't that far, but far enough to test the frail bonds of a new relationship.

"Maybe he'd like to come over tomorrow night when we trim the tree? He can have dinner with us," her mother suggested.

"Uh . . . maybe." Louisa really wasn't ready to ask Martin to meet her family. She didn't even know if they were going on a date tonight or just hanging out as friends, working on his Santa

Fund. He didn't seem the type of guy who would take that sort of invitation casually. Louisa had a feeling it would terrify him.

The doorbell rang. Was that Martin? He was a little early, she noticed. She hoped that her mother wouldn't blurt out the dinner invite as soon as he walked in the door.

"I'll get it." Louisa trotted over to the door, took a breath to settle her nerves, and fluffed out her hair. She pulled the door open and smiled.

"Hey, Lou, how's it going, honey?" her uncle Tucker greeted her. He was dressed in his uniform and didn't seem to notice Louisa's surprise at seeing him there. "I hope I'm not interrupting anything."

"Not at all, Tucker," her mother said. "Mike is in the family room. I'll let him know you're here. Can I get you something? A cup of coffee?"

"No thanks. I can't stay long. Just taking a quick break." Louisa already knew he was on duty, with the radio clipped to his belt making crackling sounds.

"Mike, Tucker is here," her mother called as they headed toward the back of the house. Louisa followed, curious about why her uncle had come. He didn't often drop by like this out of the clear blue, especially while on duty. It had to be something serious.

Her father got up from his leather armchair and put aside the newspaper. "Tucker, good to see you." He reached out and shook his cousin's hand. "How is everyone? How's the grandpa business going?"

Tucker had two grown children, a son and a daughter. Both were married, and his son had a little boy, about two years old.

"Going great, Mike. I might go into that business full-time, if I can manage to retire. Fran and the kids are fine . . . But Carl isn't doing very well. You told me to keep you posted, so here I am."

"Of course we want to know." Her father leaned forward, looking concerned. "What's happened, Tucker? What's going on?"

"Another bout of emphysema. A bad one. Luckily, I was at church with Reverend Ben, and we called nine-one-one."

"I'm so sorry," her mother said. "He didn't look well on Sunday night. We were worried about him."

"Is he in the hospital? Should we visit him?"

"He was in the ER awhile. They watched him a few hours, made sure his heart was fine and he could breathe on his own again. They didn't keep him overnight, thank goodness. You know how he gets."

Her mother looked concerned. "I know he hates hospitals, but I'm afraid for him when he's on his own. He doesn't follow the doctors' directions and doesn't take all his medications."

"Never mind medication, cigarettes don't help," her father said. "I saw him outside the church during the party, having a smoke in the parking lot. He told us that he quit."

Her father was a kind man but plainspoken. He had been a detective for Essex County for fifteen years, then earned a law degree at night, which wasn't easy with four little children at home. He was in the county district attorney's office now and didn't go out of his way to sweeten a difficult situation.

"Maybe he did quit, Mike, but fell back into it. Most people don't succeed on the first try," her mother said, her tone more sympathetic.

"More like the fiftieth. At least he keeps trying," Tucker said, sounding weary. "I guess what I came to say is, I don't know how much longer Carl can go on like this . . . and I don't know what to do. He won't stop working at the church, even though his doctors say he should. Mainly because he doesn't have anyplace to go. That apartment of his is like a tiny, dark box. He's never liked being there. I've asked him to live with me again, but we tried that a long time ago. It didn't work out well," he admitted.

"No fault of yours. We all know how difficult he can be," her mother said. "Carl likes his independence. We've offered him our spare room, too. I doubt he wants to live with any of us."

"He's a proud man," her father said. "To his credit. And a stubborn man, too."

"He's stubborn, all right. You should have seen him in the ER. I thought he was going to march out of there with the IV in his arm, still wearing that skimpy gown they make you put on." Tucker shook his head. "We have to figure something out. This can't go on. I'd like to find someplace where he could have his privacy and dignity—but get the help and care he needs. Some assisted-living place."

"There are plenty around here. But those communities are expensive," her father said. "We know Carl has no savings. There might be a small pension from the church, but he'd only get a small payment from Social Security. He lost a lot of time in the workforce while he was away."

Louisa knew that by "away," her father meant when Carl had been in prison, serving a sentence for manslaughter. An argument with a stranger in a bar had escalated into a fistfight, and Carl had landed what turned out to be a fatal punch. Carl always claimed he had been acting in self-defense. But an inexperienced, court-appointed lawyer, along with a damning record of bad behavior and no help from eyewitnesses, had landed Carl in jail.

The two brothers were complete opposites, Louisa always thought. Tucker was not only a police officer but such an upstanding citizen, active in many charities and a deacon in their church. He was also Carl's greatest advocate and unflinching support, never once turning his back on his wayward, difficult older brother.

"All true, Mike. All true. I did find a place in Peabody. It's not a country club, but it has plenty of services, everything he needs. The apartments are very comfortable. It's a far sight better than the place he's living now."

"That sounds promising. How much does a year cost?" her mother asked.

"Around sixty thousand," Tucker replied quietly. Louisa heard her father's soft whistle, but before he could say anything, her uncle added, "I know it sounds like a lot. Well . . . it is. But relative to the other communities I looked at, it's on the low side. And the thing is, all he has to do is pay the first six months, then his benefits from the government will take over, and he's home free."

"Well, that's better news," Louisa's father admitted. "But it's still thirty thousand. That's not pocket change."

"It is a considerable amount," her mother agreed. "And maybe if the families get together, we can figure out some way to cover it."

Tucker didn't look convinced. "Maybe, though as his brother, I feel the most responsible. I could borrow against my house. Or my retire-ment fund. I can keep working awhile. If the force will keep me," he added in a joking tone.

"I'm sure you can stay as long as you want, Tucker. But you just mentioned wanting to retire. It would be very hard after taking on that kind of debt. I think we should get the families together and talk about this," her father said.

"I do, too, Tucker. This isn't just your problem. We should all help," her mother agreed.

"That's good of you two. I'm not sure everyone else will see it that way, and I don't blame them. Everyone's got their own responsibilities. You have three more kids to get through college."

Her father rolled his eyes. "I didn't forget, don't worry."

Louisa had been listening to the conversation like a fly on the wall. But she suddenly felt about to burst with what could be the perfect solution. Martin might be able to pay for Carl's care. He would probably be happy to. For one thing, it was so expensive, it would use up a good portion of the money he was required to spend. And of course, he would be happy to help an old, sick man live out the rest of his days in a safe, peaceful place. Maybe he would even be happy that he was helping a member of her family?

But how to explain it? They would ask a lot of questions, and Martin's identity had to remain anonymous. All she could do was jump right in and find out if they were even willing.

"I know of someone who might help Uncle

Carl. Someone who would donate the money." Her parents and her uncle Tucker looked over at her. "I can't say for sure, but it really could work out."

Their curious expressions made her nervous. As if she were a little girl again and had just made some silly statement, like "I bet the moon has a big lightbulb inside. That's why it's so bright at night."

"Really, I do," she insisted.

"Give us a private loan, you mean?" Her uncle seemed wary of the suggestion.

"Not a loan. A gift. He wouldn't need to be paid back. He wouldn't want to be. Of course, I'd have to check with him first, but I'm pretty sure it could work out."

Her parents and Tucker looked totally confused. And suspicious. "Who is this mysterious bene-factor, Louisa?" her father asked.

Louisa wasn't sure how to answer. She felt her face flush, and her mouth went dry. "I'm sorry. I know it sounds odd, but I can't tell you that. He's not from around here. You don't really know him," she said, which was mostly true.

Would they connect the gifts that people in town had been receiving the past week or so with her offer? Paula Monroe had announced in church last week that she'd found a sewing machine on her sunporch, and Charlie Bates talked about the huge donations the diner had received for their toy drive, and Louisa's boss had given thanks for the amazing number of children's shoes that had arrived at the police department.

Martin had not been at church, but Louisa was going to tell him about these little speeches later. Her parents and uncle had been there, and she waited, wondering if they would connect the dots.

Finally her father said, "Why would a total stranger do something like that for Carl?"

"I guess you'd say he's sort of a philanthropist." *Who was forced into the role, just until Christmas,* but she didn't add that. "He just wants to help people."

"I appreciate the suggestion, Louisa, but our family doesn't need charity," Tucker said firmly. She could see his pride was hurt.

"It's not like that at all, Uncle Tucker. We wouldn't be taking charity . . . It's hard to explain," she admitted.

Her father looked doubtful, too. "I think Tucker's right. Carl has a family. He's not a charity case."

"We know you mean well, honey," her mother added, "but we'll figure it out. This mysterious philanthropist sounds a bit suspicious. There are always strings attached."

Not this time, Louisa wanted to argue. But she could see she had not made any headway and wasn't going to convince them she had a solution.

There's time, she reminded herself. *Uncle Carl can't make any big changes in his life overnight. Certainly not before Christmas.*

The doorbell rang again, and this time, she was certain it was Martin. "I'll get it." She jumped off the couch and ran to the door before any of her siblings could.

CHAPTER ELEVEN

Saturday, December 8, 2018

MARTIN STOOD ON THE PORCH, HIS HANDS in the pockets of a dark green jacket. She could tell that he'd just had a haircut, and his beard was neatly trimmed. Under the jacket, he wore a slate-blue shirt and black wool vest. He was handsome; she'd thought that from the first time they met. But she could see he had taken extra care tonight. Still, she didn't want to assume anything.

"Come in, Martin. I'll just grab my things." She opened the door, and he stepped inside as she took her jacket and shoulder bag from the coat tree in the foyer.

Back in the family room, she could hear her parents and uncle still deep in conversation about Carl. She called back to them, "I'm leaving. See you later."

"Good-bye, dear. Have a good time." Her mother suddenly popped out of the family room. "You must be Martin."

Louisa froze, feeling awkward. She had hoped

to avoid this scene tonight. "Martin, this is my mother. Mom, this is Martin Hanson."

"Nice to meet you, Mrs. Tulley."

"Nice to meet you, Martin. Finally. Did you enjoy the party last week? I'm sorry we didn't get a chance to talk."

"Oh, yes, I enjoyed it very much." Martin nodded, his expression grave, as if her mother had asked about a documentary on global warming. Louisa could tell he felt put on the spot. "Lots of Christmas spirit," he added.

"It's a great way to start the season. We haven't decorated one bit around here yet. We're going to put up our tree tomorrow." Her mother looked at Louisa. "Maybe Martin would like to have dinner with us tomorrow night, Lou?" She looked back at him. "I'm making pot roast. I just throw it in the oven before we put the tree up, and it practically cooks itself."

"That sounds easy. And good." Martin glanced at Louisa. She silently groaned. She hoped her mother wouldn't recite the recipe, as she sometimes did, given the least encouragement.

"Martin probably has plans, Mom. It's such short notice." Martin seemed about to speak, but Louisa kept talking. "We'll figure it out," she promised, taking charge of the situation. "We'd better go. See you later."

Martin politely stepped aside and held the door

for her, then turned to her mother. "Good night, Mrs. Tulley."

"Good night, Martin. Hope to see you soon."

"Good night, Mom." Louisa tried to hide her irritation. She hated it when her mother extended invitations to friends—especially male friends—without checking with her first. Now Martin felt pressured to come for dinner, and she doubted that he wanted to.

They got into his car, and Martin started the engine. "I hope that seat isn't too cramped for you. I had to push it up to get the bikes in the back."

Though the Outback was loaded with gifts, Louisa had barely noticed. "It's fine . . . and you really don't have to come for dinner tomorrow night. My mom just . . . just says things without thinking sometimes."

He glanced at her, looking puzzled. "You mean, she doesn't really want me to come to dinner?"

"No, I mean, yes. Yes, she wants you to come. But you don't have to, if you don't want to. She should have asked me about it first."

Martin didn't reply, his gaze fixed on the road. He turned at the end of her street and headed for the village. "So . . . *you* don't want me to come?"

"No, that's not what I meant at all." Now she'd done it, made him think she didn't like him or want him to meet her family. "It's fine with me, but only if you really *want* to come. I don't want you to feel cornered into it."

"I don't feel cornered," he said quickly. "I think your mom is nice." They were stopped at a light, and he turned to face her. "Do you want me to come? I won't come if you don't want me to. It's okay. I get it."

Louisa's head was spinning. "Martin, there's nothing to get. I'd really like you to come to my house and meet my crazy family. But I didn't want to ask. I wasn't sure. I mean . . . I don't even know if tonight is a date or not."

Had she made a mistake being so blunt? You do get an answer that way, she'd learned. *But not always the one you want to hear,* she thought.

Martin looked surprised. He glanced at her and then back at the road. "I want it to be. But I wasn't sure you wanted it to be. I thought maybe you just liked doing Santa Fund stuff."

Now it was her turn to be surprised. "Don't be silly. Of course I'd like to be on a date with you."

Had he really just admitted that he liked her, as more than a helper or even a friend? And she'd admitted the same to him?

"Great. Here we are. Bona fide date." Martin smiled at her, then glanced over his shoulder. "But now we have all these presents to give out."

"Yes, we do." She glanced at the back of the car again. There was a lot of stuff back there. She sighed and faced forward again. "Most guys just take you to the movies. At least you're original."

"That's one way of putting it. The faster we get this done, the sooner we can go out to dinner."

"Do these packages have tags or anything?" She peered into the back seat again but couldn't see much beneath the tarp.

"Everything is labeled, and I made a list of all the names and addresses." He reached into the pocket on his door and handed it to her. "It's not in any particular order. Maybe you can plan the fastest route."

Martin said she was sharper than Google Maps when it came to finding the best routes around town. She could drive around the town blindfolded and knew all the shortcuts. She quickly read the list, ordering the names so that they could drive in a big circle to give out the gifts.

"Make a left at the next corner. We can drop off the travel packet for David McCoy on Ivy Street."

Through a friend who taught at the high school, Louisa had learned about a boy who was a music prodigy and longed to study violin at a conservatory. He was a finalist for a scholarship at a famous school in Chicago, but his family couldn't afford to send him there for the audition.

While Martin waited in the car, Louisa snuck up to the mailbox and slipped in a large envelope addressed to David that held round-trip airline tickets, a paid hotel reservation, and a generous prepaid credit card for his expenses.

"I can't wait to hear from Kate if he gets the scholarship," she said as she slipped back in the car.

"I hope he wins it. I won't be around to help with tuition if he doesn't get a good scholarship." Martin sounded concerned about the boy, and she could see that he was getting more involved with the personal stories of the people he was helping. But his comment was also a sobering reminder that Martin would not be in the village forever. The more she helped him, the faster he would return to Boston. Louisa glanced at him, watching the road as he drove to their next stop. She hoped by then he'd find some reason to stay longer, at least until Christmas.

Since it was Saturday night, many houses were dark, and the worst they had to put up with were a few barking dogs. Most of the gifts were compact, but some were heavy and needed a combined effort to be delivered, like a piano keyboard, an amplifier, and a microphone for a musician who'd been in a car accident.

Louisa had been on duty and had raced to the call. The driver had emerged without a scratch and managed to stumble clear of the dented hatchback before it caught on fire. But her instruments, sheet music, and amplifiers had been destroyed—along with her livelihood, and during her busiest time of the year.

"Are you sure this box isn't too heavy for you?" Martin whispered as they crept up the driveway, each holding a side of the carton that contained the amplifier.

"Martin, I'm fine. I work out with weights all the time."

"I'm impressed." She could tell he was struggling to hold up his end. "I should do that, too," he muttered. "Been meaning to get back to the gym."

"All this loading and lifting is better than a gym," she assured him. "And more fun."

"Way more fun," he agreed as they carefully set down the amp beside the other gifts. "Though I doubt it would be fun without you."

Louisa felt her face flush and was glad for the cover of darkness. "One more to go," she said as they returned to the car. "On Main Street. The Baldwins."

"Right, the bicycles."

Judy Baldwin was a single mom who strung together several jobs to make ends meet. Martin had told Louisa how he'd overheard Judy talking to a friend over coffee in Willoughby's Café. While he pretended to read a newspaper at the next table, Judy told her friend how downhearted and stressed she felt about Christmas, admitting that she could only buy her kids a few items that they really needed—warm jackets and hats—and one small toy each. They had their hearts set on bikes, but she just couldn't swing it this year.

She'd even told her friend the exact kind of bike her daughter, Nicole, and son, Noah, each wanted, and Martin had jotted quick notes on a napkin as she spoke. Martin's only problem had been finding out her name and where she lived, but Louisa had helped with that part. They made a good team, she thought, working on the Santa Fund—and in other ways, too.

Taking care not to ruin the big red bows, they took the bikes from the hatch and rolled them up to Judy's apartment building, then into a small lobby with brass mailboxes and buzzers.

"Ready?" Louisa whispered.

Martin nodded. "Whenever you are."

Louisa gave the buzzer for the Baldwin apartment a long, hard push. A woman's voice came on the intercom. "Who is it?"

"It's Santa," Louisa said in a deep voice. "Early delivery for Nicole and Noah."

"Excuse me, what did you say?"

"Go . . . go. Hurry!" Louisa gave Martin a push and he finally started for the door. Louisa ran after him. They burst through the entrance and ran down the street.

Louisa was laughing so hard, she had to stop and catch her breath. Martin was laughing hard, too. Each time he'd stop, their eyes met and they started all over again.

Finally, they both caught their breath and stood smiling at each other. "I think we saved the best for last," Louisa said.

"Perfect way to end the present run. For tonight," he added, hinting there would be more of them. She hoped so. It was the most fun she'd had in a long time, and it certainly beat sitting through a movie and an awkward dinner conversation.

"That family was a find, Martin. Good job," Louisa said as they walked down the street toward his car.

"Not bad, for an amateur. You're the pro. You found practically everyone else," he pointed out. "Not that I'm complaining."

It was true, but Louisa wasn't trying to gloat. "You figured out Digger Hegman's hearing aids. I didn't say a word."

Louisa hadn't realized it, but they were steps away from the Bramble. It was beautifully decorated, with boughs of pine draped on the porch railing and a big, fresh wreath on the door, wound with gold and white ribbons.

Small white tapers glowed in all the windows, upstairs and down, and Louisa noticed that lights on the lower floor, where the store was, were still on. It looked like Grace had kept the store open late for Christmas shoppers.

"That's their shop. It looks like they're still open. Why don't we go inside and say hello? I'd love to see how Digger is doing, now that he can hear again."

"Sure. Let's go in," Martin agreed.

Martin could vaguely recall a visit to the Bramble Antique Shop. His grandmother had taken him here while doing errands on a hot summer day. The place hadn't registered much on a little boy. Mostly, he recalled waiting for her on the porch. If he'd met Digger, or even Grace, he did not remember.

He gazed around as they walked in. Grace Hegman stood behind a glass counter where lovely pieces of antique jewelry were displayed. Martin saw Digger in the back of the store, polishing a table with smooth, round strokes, a chamois cloth in one hand, a can of lemony-smelling wax in the other. Grace was busy helping a customer but soon walked over to them.

"Hello, Louisa. Looking for anything special?"

"I noticed you were open and just wanted to browse. This is my friend Martin. Maybe you've met at church?"

"Yes, I think so. Maybe at the Advent party?"

"That's right," Martin said, remembering Grace with her father as they untangled the lights. "Nice to see you again. This is a pretty shop. You have some nice pieces of furniture."

His gaze fell on a vintage rolltop desk in

excellent condition. The golden oak had been polished by Digger's patient hand, he had no doubt, and showed little wear. He had always wanted one but didn't have enough room in his Boston apartment.

You'll have plenty of room in the old house. If you don't sell it off right away.

"I like that desk," he told Grace. "Is it very expensive?"

She named a price he thought surprisingly low and very fair.

Much less than he'd seen for similar pieces in the city.

"The wood is in fine condition. Not a scratch. But the rolltop does get stuck here and there," she admitted with surprising honesty. "If you're really interested, my father might be able to fix it. So many of these pieces come in needing repair, and he has a knack for brightening them up."

"I can see that. Maybe he can take a look." Martin was eager to speak to Digger and was glad when Grace called to him.

"Hold your horses, Gracie. I'm coming." Digger made his way to the front of the shop, armed with his rag and polish. "I'm not done with that table. The legs need a good going-over."

"This man is interested in the rolltop desk, Dad. You know how the cover sticks. Did you ever take a look at it?"

Digger eyed Martin. "Hey, I know you. Martin, from the party. The tree lights, remember?"

"I do. And now I'll always know how to untangle knots, thanks to you."

Digger nodded, looking gratified. "No thanks necessary, son."

"How are you doing?" Martin asked.

"Couldn't be better. Got some new hearing aids." He pointed to his ears with a wide smile. "Clear as a bell. I can hear a spider creeping down the wall two rooms away."

"Oh, Dad . . ." Grace shook her head and laughed. "He's exaggerating, as usual. But these are much better than the old ones. It's amazing how God provides," she added with a more serious expression.

"And when he sends a surprise package, he sure don't skimp. Top-shelf, all the way."

Martin noticed Louisa biting her lip to keep from laughing.

He felt the same and could hardly respond.

"It was the strangest thing," Grace continued. "I went out to the mailbox Monday morning, and I found an envelope. No stamp or return address. It had my name and Dad's on it, and inside, all the money we needed for the new hearing aids and a simple, handwritten note. I was shocked to tears. And so was Dad," she added quietly.

"I wish I could thank whoever done it. People

are good-hearted in this town. But that's above and beyond." Digger shook his head, his eyes misty.

Martin didn't expect that the old man would be so moved. And he didn't expect his own reaction either. He swallowed a lump in his throat, barely able to speak.

"Who do you think it was?" Louisa asked.

Grace shrugged a thin shoulder. "We thought it might be Dr. Elliot. He's a quiet man but doesn't miss much. And he's very kind and generous. Dad was his patient for years."

"I saw Ezra at the post office this morning and asked him," Digger put in. "He said he wished he had thought of it, but he couldn't take the credit. I believe him, too."

"I'll speak up tomorrow in church, during Joys and Concerns. I hope, whoever and wherever they are, the message gets through," Grace added.

"I hope so, too. But I still wish I could thank that person face-to-face someday," Digger added. He met Martin's gaze. "Life is funny. You never know what's going to happen, one minute to the next."

"Very true," Martin agreed.

"Why don't you take a look at the desk, Dad?" Grace reminded him. "We got off track."

"That's all right. We're not in a hurry," Louisa assured her. "What time do you close?"

"When the customers stop coming," Digger

replied as he wiggled the rolltop down out of its hiding place above the hutch and row of pigeon-holes. "Track is sticky. I can work on it. Can you come back, Martin?"

"I will," Martin promised. He wanted to talk more with Digger and searched for the right questions to ask. "How long have you had this shop?"

Digger laughed. "Feels like forever. Let's see . . . must have been about nineteen sixty or so we opened. My wife and I, rest her soul. I was out clamming and fishing mainly, but I'd work on the furniture in between. I was always fixing up pieces and selling them here and there, but never had enough extra to make a business of it. A friend gave me the money to open the Bramble. Walter, his name was. Walter Nightingale." Digger smiled, remembering the kindness of his benefactor, and Martin felt his heartbeat quicken. "He was a good man, Walter. Heart of gold. He ran a toy store, just up the street. People came from all around to visit Nightingale's Magical Toy Shop."

Martin didn't know what to say. He had portrayed himself as a stranger, so now it was hard to ask more pointed questions.

"I've heard of that place," Louisa said. "My grandparents still talk about it. What was it like inside? I've always wondered."

"Hard to describe, exactly." Digger looked at

his daughter. "Ask Grace. She'd remember. I'd watch the store for Walter and she'd tag along with me. Walter never minded if she played with the toys. Remember, Grace?"

"I do." Grace nodded and smiled. "One time you dressed up as Santa, and I gave out candy canes. What a day that was! The shop was a magical place," she told Louisa, "just like the sign said. Walter and Frances made most of the toys by hand. Wait, I have the book we made at church. I think there's a picture of them in here . . ."

Grace searched a bookshelf near the counter and quickly found the book she had been looking for. She pulled it out and thumbed through the pages, then set it down on the counter near Martin and Louisa.

"Here they are, the Nightingales, standing in front of their shop. If you look close, you can see all the toys they made, the dollhouse and miniature sailboats."

"Those little boats were plenty seaworthy," Digger said. "Folks would race them on the pond near Potter Orchard."

Martin knew that pond. His grandparents' property stretched to the shore, and he recalled how his grandfather had made him a boat just like the one in the shop window and shown him how to sail it. Martin wished now that he had saved that little boat.

Louisa moved closer to see the picture. They were standing shoulder to shoulder, and Martin's head filled with the scent of her perfume. He stole a glance at her lovely profile, and she turned to him. Their eyes met and she smiled, and he suddenly felt as if they were the only two in the room.

She was the only one who knew what looking at this photograph meant to him. He had not seen a picture of his grandparents at this stage of their lives in a long time. They looked about his age, maybe a little older, so young and hopeful. It was hard to hide his reaction. It was hard not to admit that this vital, happy couple, whom everyone in the town admired, were his grandparents.

"I still miss my good friends," Digger said wistfully. "Walter done well for himself, no question. But there was a time when they had nothing, or pretty close to it. But he was still happy as a lark 'cause he had Frances, the light of his life. They had a real love between them, and when their boy, Tom, finally come along, the picture was complete. A loving marriage and a family, that's what really counts, don't you think?"

Digger met Martin's gaze, and Martin nodded, his throat too tight to speak. He had witnessed the enduring bond between his grandparents firsthand. Would he ever find a love like that in his lifetime? He guessed the chances were one in a million.

"I know it's hard to see, but right there, in the corner of the window? That's the princess doll Santa brought me," Grace explained. "I'd stand and look at her for hours when Dad took me to the store. Walter always told me I could play with her, but I wouldn't dare. She seemed too special. That was the best Christmas ever, when Santa left that doll under the tree. Of course I realized later that Walter had given the doll to Dad for me."

"Walter would give you the shirt off his back then run home for a sweater," Digger added. "Don't you still have that doll somewhere upstairs, Grace?"

"Of course I do. In my collection. I have one of Walter's stuffed dogs, too. Santa dog, remember?"

"How could I forget?" Digger asked with a chuckle. "Walter made this dog once. It was so cute, you couldn't look at it and not start smiling. There was this little hound he'd taken in, a stray he called Otis. He made a toy that looked just like him."

"That sounds adorable. Is there one in this picture?" Louisa picked up the book and scanned the photograph.

Grace looked over her shoulder. "Let's see . . . no, I don't think so."

"Why don't you go get 'em—the doll and the dog? Show Martin and Louisa," Digger urged her.

Martin felt his breath catch, his heart beating like a drum. He glanced at Louisa, wondering if she could hear it, too. He knew the toy Digger spoke of, and he knew the story of the real Otis, too, beloved by the whole family. There had been a stuffed dog like that in his bedroom at his grandparents' house. He wondered now what had become of it. Had his father saved it when the house had been cleared of their belongings? He hoped so. Martin made a mental note to ask the next time they spoke.

Part of him wanted to see the treasured toys, and another part worried it would be too much. The photograph had been hard enough. He wasn't sure he could keep up the charade without exposing his true identity and his reason for visiting Cape Light.

Before he could decide, Grace headed for the stairs that led to the second floor. "Oh, it's no trouble. I won't be a moment."

Martin glanced at Louisa. He didn't know what to say, but she obviously sensed his unease. She offered a reassuring look and squeezed his hand.

Grace had just climbed the first few steps when a woman bustled in. Several large shopping bags hung over her arm, and a list was clutched in her free hand. She flagged down Grace as if hailing a cab. "I'm so glad you're still open. Do you remember me? I was in last week, looking at a tea set. White Wedgwood with a blue border. I hope you still have it."

Grace didn't seem to remember the customer but definitely recalled the set. "I know the one. It's in the china closet in the next room. I'll be right in to help you." She turned to Louisa and Martin. "Can you wait a few minutes until I help this lady? It shouldn't take very long."

"Oh, we don't want to bother you, Grace. You seem busy," Martin said. "I'll come back another time about the desk," he said to Digger.

"I'll have it shipshape for you, Martin," Digger promised. "Don't be a stranger. You know the way now."

Martin smiled at the turn of phrase. He so often felt just that—awkward and out of place, even among people he knew. But for some reason, he didn't feel that way in this town, even with people he'd just met, like the Hegmans.

"I'll be back, Digger," Martin promised. "I'd love to hear more about . . . about the village. The way it was when you were my age."

Digger smiled and nodded. "I got stories for you, son. Plenty of stories. You come back any-time. I'll be here."

Martin smiled and waved good-bye. He didn't doubt that was true.

"Where should we have dinner?" Martin asked as he and Louisa walked back to his car. "Is there anyplace special you'd like to go?"

It wasn't very good date etiquette not to plan out a restaurant in advance. Especially for a first official date. But he didn't know the area or the type of food she liked.

"There aren't many places open at night in the village. Maybe we should go up to Newburyport. There's Thai, Japanese, Indian—"

"No lack of exotic cuisine around here," Martin replied. He glanced at her and smiled. "I remember a restaurant in an old warehouse in Spoon Harbor. You had to walk out on a pier to go inside. They made the most amazing popovers."

"Oh, I know the one you mean. Bailey's Wharf. The same family has run it for years." She turned to him. "They have the best lobster, too. I love that place."

"Enough said. That's where we'll go." She looked delighted by the choice, and Martin was happy to please her.

SPOON HARBOR WAS A SHORT DRIVE FROM Cape Light Village. With Louisa's help, he found the way to Bailey's Wharf. The restaurant had not changed at all, except for a modern sign and brighter lights. It was crowded inside, but they were quickly shown to a table in a quiet corner.

"It's nicer here than I remember," Martin said. There were linen tablecloths and small candles on each table, casting a warm glow. Large windows along one wall framed a view of the harbor and night sky.

They did not need long with their menus and quickly ordered two lobster dinners, with clam chowder to start.

"I haven't been here in a long time," Louisa said.

"I bet I have you beat."

"I bet you do. When was the last time you remember?"

"I was about ten. I think it was my mother's birthday. July twenty-second. My father surprised her with a trip to Paris."

"Wow, what a great gift."

"It would have been. She died in a car accident a few days later, driving out to Rockport to visit the art galleries. Someone ran a red light and hit her car."

Martin knew his voice sounded flat and matter-of-fact, but that was because it was still hard to relay the story.

Louisa's gaze was full of sympathy. "You were so young, Martin. That must have been a nightmare for you."

"It was hard for everyone. My father blamed himself. He was supposed to drive her there but decided to stay back at the last minute to catch up on some office work. There was nothing he could have done to prevent it, but he still blamed himself." Martin took a deep breath, staring out at the water. It was hard to relate this part of his life to her, but he felt he had to. It was part of him and in a large way had shaped his personality. "We used to come to Cape Light, the three of us, and stay the whole summer with my grandparents. But after we lost my mother, my father didn't want to come back anymore."

"That's too bad. But I guess I can understand why."

"My grandparents understood, too. They never took offense. But it still made them sad. They came to see us in Boston pretty often," Martin offered. "Until my father remarried and moved to Arizona."

"So you've lived in Arizona, too?"

"No, I went to boarding school, in New Hampshire. I only went out West for school vacations."

"That must have been lonely," she said. "My brothers and sister drive me crazy sometimes, but I can't imagine living apart from my family at that age."

"I was an only child, so it was different for me. I was used to being alone and amusing myself." The very reason he'd become an insatiable reader. "And my grandparents were still living here and close enough to visit on weekends."

And he might not have made it through school without those visits, Martin could have added. He had been lonely at times, but he didn't want to admit that either. "I still don't get out to Arizona much, though my dad is always inviting me. I'm not a desert sort of guy. I prefer pine trees to cacti."

Louisa laughed. "I can't really see you in a Stetson and cowboy boots, I have to say."

"I'll take that as a compliment." He grinned and finished his clam chowder. "What about you, Louisa? Have you ever thought about living somewhere else?"

Louisa gave the question a few moments' thought. Her face looked so lovely in the flickering candlelight.

"I was dating someone for a long time. His name was Brian. We never got engaged but we did talk about marriage," she added. "He was a fisherman and wanted to move to North Carolina. He thought he could make a better living there, buy his own boat and all that. I was willing to go, though I would have lost some time with my career."

Martin put his spoon down and dabbed his mouth with a napkin, trying not to look as interested as he felt in her disclosure. "What happened? Do you still see him?"

"We broke up last summer." She shrugged. "It just didn't feel right anymore. We'd been dating since high school, and I guess I'd outgrown the relationship."

"I understand," he said, a sympathetic expression masking his relief.

"How about you, Martin?" she asked, catching him off guard.

"Well . . . let's see . . ." Martin paused, wondering how to reply. "I've never asked anyone to move to North Carolina, if that's what you'd like to know."

Louisa smiled but wouldn't let him off the hook that easily. "You know what I mean."

A waitress came by, carrying a basket filled with golden, freshly baked popovers that looked and smelled delicious. She set one on each plate, and Martin was glad for the momentary distraction. He and Louisa quickly tore them open, adding pats of butter that melted into the golden pastry.

"These are so good." He closed his eyes, savoring the taste. "Even better than I remember."

"They are," she agreed. "But you never answered my question."

He stopped himself from taking a second bite. She had been open with him, and he owed her the same.

"I was seeing someone recently, another attorney. I liked her very much, and things felt serious. To me, anyway. But she was very focused on her career and took a job in New York. We thought we could manage a long-distance relationship, but it didn't work out. Maybe it was just bad timing," he added. "I think that matters a lot—where people are in their lives with careers and all that."

"Sometimes. But I think that if you meet the right person, the other parts of the puzzle will fall into place."

She took a romantic view, he thought, but he didn't totally disagree. Once he and his former girlfriend were living at a distance, he realized that their bond wasn't really very deep and she probably wasn't the one for him.

The waiter arrived with their lobsters, and Martin was relieved to have a break from such personal conversation. He felt torn between the habit of clinging to his privacy and feeling that he wanted Louisa to know him better, and wanting to know her better, too.

Louisa clearly knew her way around a lobster and quickly cracked open a claw. "How are you enjoying Cape Light, Martin? Or are you not enjoying it at all?"

"It was hard to come back," he admitted. "It's . . . loaded for me. So many memories. But now I'm glad I did, and at least tried to accomplish what my grandfather asked. When Digger was talking about him, I started to see the Santa Fund a little differently."

"What do you mean?"

"Just that Granddad wasn't trying to make me jump through hoops or run an obstacle course for my inheritance. Maybe he just wanted me to honor his memory by doing some good in the world; by doing what he did all the time. Maybe it never occurred to him that it would be hard for me," he added.

Louisa grinned. "I guess a man who would give you the shirt off his back and then run home to get you a sweater would expect that kind of generosity comes naturally."

Martin laughed. "That's exactly what I mean. I guess what I'm trying to say is, I've stopped thinking of it as such a burden and more of a way to honor him."

"I think the Santa Fund is fun," she said.

"I wouldn't go that far," he answered honestly, then added, "My grandfather also left me his house. It's an old Victorian, with all these peaky roofs and a turret, just off the Beach Road. Scudder Lane, not far from the orchard. I was looking for that turn when you stopped me for speeding," he confessed.

"If you weren't going so fast, you might have found it."

"As you pointed out to me at the time," he conceded.

"I think I know that house. What's it like inside?"

Martin wasn't sure he could describe it, though he wandered the rooms often enough in his dreams. Happy dreams, mostly, though once in a while, he dreamed he was looking for his mother and couldn't find her.

"I haven't been back inside yet. A family was

renting it, but they moved out a week or so ago. I remember large rooms and long windows, and a back staircase that led from the kitchen to the second floor and fascinated me. The property was on the big pond near the orchard, and there was a dock where we'd tie up our rowboats and a big, wooden swing that hung from a tree right next to the shore. It was painted bright red. At high tide, you could be dangling your feet over the water. Sometimes I'd swing back and forth and jump right in."

"That sounds fun." Louisa took another bite of her lobster.

"It was. I wonder if it's still there."

"You ought to check on the house if it's vacant. There's very little crime here, but anything can happen to an empty house in such a secluded spot."

"Very true. I should go see it soon."

"What will you do with it?" Louisa asked curiously.

"I'm not sure. I might keep it, as a sort of landing spot when I travel," he added. "A lot depends on what shape it's in. I have to see it first, I guess."

Martin wondered if she would like to come with him but couldn't muster up the words to ask her. It seemed a favor you'd ask of someone you were more seriously involved with—or ready to be. Still, it would help to have someone there who could give their opinion, and Louisa had a lot of common sense.

Who are you fooling, Martin? You'd like her there for company and support. You know that visit will be bittersweet, at best.

As Martin brushed aside his internal debate, their dinners were cleared and they ordered dessert. Martin had apple pie, and Louisa a chocolate tart.

"Do you like being a police officer?" He wasn't sure why that had popped into his head. Her caution about the empty house, perhaps?

"Most of the time. I think it's a good job for me. For now. I like helping people, and that's our main purpose, helping and protecting."

"I know that you're very good at it. I've seen you in action." He feigned a "caught in the act" look and raised his hands, still holding a fork in one.

She laughed and used her low, hard officer voice. "Drop the fork, Martin, and no one will get hurt."

"You'll have to fight me for it. This pie is too good to abandon now," he replied, taking another bite. "I don't think I'd like having emergencies and unexpected situations thrown at me all day. You just have to jump in your car and race to the rescue. Aren't you nervous or frightened sometimes?"

"Wearing a uniform doesn't make you Superwoman. But you learn to put your feelings aside and move to higher ground. You learn to trust your training and experience."

She was usually so cheerful, with a fun-loving sparkle in her eyes he'd come to treasure. This side of her was different. Beyond her sunny, friendly nature, Martin saw a strong, serious side and an impressive confidence he admired.

"I've been wondering something about you, Martin," she said, the playful lilt returning to her tone.

"What is that?" He was charmed but also alarmed, half afraid of what she might come out with.

"Are you really a tax attorney? Or is that another part of your cover story, Mr. Hanson?"

Martin laughed. "That part is true, unfortunately."

She looked curious. "Why do you say that? You don't enjoy your work?"

He shook his head. "The ever-changing labyrinth of tax law fascinates some people, but it's not for me and has never really been a strong interest, or even a talent. I was unsure about what to do with my life after college," he continued, "and my father persuaded me to go to law school."

"I see," Louisa said thoughtfully. "You're still very young. I'm sure you can find a more fulfilling career."

"That's my plan. When I get my inheritance, I'll leave this job and figure out something else to do with my life . . . Right after I take a very long trip."

"Sounds like you have it all figured out." Louisa smiled, but she didn't look quite as relaxed as before. "Where are you going on this trip?"

"I'm not sure about that either," he admitted. "I guess I'd like to be like a character in a book, roaming around the world and reinventing myself."

"That sounds exciting." She sat back, studying him. "But when you come back to Cape Light, I might not recognize you."

I may never come back, he almost replied. But he stopped himself. For one thing, he might keep the house. For another, if Louisa was here, that would be reason enough. He thought so right now, anyway.

"Don't worry. I'll make sure you remember me . . . Maybe you'll like me even better."

"I like you fine right now, Martin. I don't see any big improvements needed. Except for your driving," she teased.

She met his gaze and held it, then looked out at the water and lights framed by the window. Her words surprised him and made his heart hopeful. He was glad the shadowy light hid his reaction.

They drove from Spoon Harbor to Louisa's

house without saying much. Martin didn't mind. It wasn't the tense silence he had often felt with other girls. It was fine to be quiet with her. He felt content and comfortable and thought she felt that way, too.

When they reached her house, he took her hand and walked her to the door. "Thanks for a great time, Martin. I'm not sure what I liked better, giving out the gifts or the lobster and popovers."

"That means we need to do it all over again, so you can decide."

Before she could answer, he pulled her close and kissed her. He had been wanting to kiss her all night. She was so beautiful and smart and sweet. Her lips felt so soft under his own, and he pulled her closer, their embrace lingering.

A dog barked, then a dark brown head popped up at the bay window next to the front door. The dog stared at them a moment, then threw back his head and howled.

Martin laughed, but Louisa groaned and rolled her eyes. "The joys of living at home. I have a chocolate Lab guarding my virtue."

"You'd better go in. Your father might sic the dog on me," Martin said, though he found it hard to let her go.

"I know you're joking, but it's happened." She took out her key. "By the way, you really don't have to come to dinner tomorrow. Don't worry, I'll figure out some excuse."

302

Martin had forgotten Mrs. Tulley's invitation. He could tell that Louisa was still embarrassed but realized she might be more embarrassed if he backed out. He guessed she really did want him to come but didn't want him to feel obligated.

"Of course I'll come. Let's talk tomorrow. You can let me know the time."

"Okay, Martin. Good night."

When she opened the door and turned to look back at him, he knew he had done the right thing. The warmth in her smile took his breath away.

CHAPTER TWELVE

Sunday, December 9, 2018

MARTIN RETURNED TO LOUISA'S HOUSE at four, right on time for the family's Sunday dinner. He wasn't sure whether to bring flowers or cake as a house gift, so he had bought both and was carrying a big bouquet for her mother in one arm and a chocolate cake from Willoughby's, decorated for Christmas, in the other.

If you're not really serious about this girl, it's hard to tell, pal.

The truth was, he did have feelings for Louisa, feelings that were getting stronger and deeper every day. Their time together last night had made that very clear.

But this morning, he had wondered if it was a mistake to come here today. He wondered if getting more involved with her was the right thing to do. She was committed to Cape Light, to her career here, her family ties and friendships. No matter what she said about moving, he couldn't imagine it. And he didn't see himself settling down here—settling anywhere—for a long time.

Before he even rang the bell, the front door flew open. A tall, gangly teenage boy with red hair even brighter than Louisa's stood there. He wore a striped rugby shirt, jeans, and basketball sneakers that looked twice the size of Martin's shoes. He held back the barking Labrador with one hand and waved to Martin with the other. "Come on in, Barkley doesn't bite. Much." He turned and shouted up the staircase, "Louisa, that guy is here for you."

Martin had seen the boy before—he was one of Louisa's twin brothers. "You must be Ryan or Neil," he said, stepping inside.

"Ryan, the good-looking one," her brother replied with a goofy grin.

Christmas music filled the house. Martin had to strain to hear his answer. He wished Louisa would come down. He wasn't sure what to do with the flowers and feared for the fate of the cake. Barkley had stopped sniffing his jacket and was now very interested in the bakery box.

Mrs. Tulley ran out of the living room. "Neil, why didn't you tell us that Martin is here?"

Neil? Martin knew the boy had said his name was Ryan. He caught the mischievous glint in the twin's eye and realized he'd been pulling a prank. More to come, Martin guessed. He would have to be on his toes in this household.

"Martin, let me help you." Mrs. Tulley took the

flowers and cake box and shooed the dog aside. "We're running a bit behind today, just finishing the tree. But dinner's almost ready."

"That's all right. It smells delicious . . . Those flowers are for you," he added.

"For me? Oh my goodness, they're beautiful." Mrs. Tulley took a closer look at the bouquet. "How thoughtful. Thank you."

"And the box is for dessert. Chocolate cake."

"From Willoughby's," she said, noticing the label. "I'd better hide this. The boys will want to eat it right now."

Louisa came downstairs just as her mother disappeared back into the kitchen. Her long hair hung in loose waves, and she wore a big turtle-neck sweater made of fuzzy, white yarn, with jeans and high brown boots. She looked so pretty, his breath caught in his throat.

"She isn't kidding about the cake." Louisa took his jacket and scarf and hung them on a coat tree. "My brothers could devour it in five seconds flat. Come inside. I think they're almost done with the tree."

Martin followed Louisa into a spacious living room, where a fire crackled in a large stone hearth. The mantle was decorated with pine boughs and red candles in brass holders, and holiday tunes filled the room with music.

A large Christmas tree stood in the corner, covered with lights and ornaments. Martin saw

Louisa's father on a ladder, adjusting the star on top. A girl, about twelve or so, kneeled at the coffee table, threading a hook through the top of an ornament in the shape of a penguin. Martin saw several more in an open box; it seemed to be part of a penguin-ornament flock.

"Carly, Dad, this is Martin," Louisa shouted over "Jingle Bell Rock."

Louisa's father glanced down from his perch and waved. "Hello, Martin. Nice to meet you." Then he turned back to his task. His dark brown hair was touched with silver, Martin noticed. He had a strong jaw and the same blue eyes as Louisa. He looked fit for his age, in a plaid flannel shirt and khakis—more like a high school sports coach than a lawyer, Martin thought.

Carly looked up at him curiously. She wore a pink hoodie with matching workout pants and a knitted hat that draped down to a long point. It was white with green stripes and a red pompom on the tip, like the kind an elf might wear.

"I like your hat," he said.

"That's good, because I can never take it off," she confided in a solemn tone. She pressed her hands to the edges and pulled it farther down on her forehead, as if a stiff wind might blow it off any minute. Amused, Martin wondered why but didn't dare ask.

"Louisa, can you help Carly get the rest of the ornaments on the tree? I don't know what happened to your brothers," her father said. "I can't seem to get this star to light. Maybe we need a new one."

"Sure . . . let's see." Louisa sat down by the table, and Martin kneeled beside her. "Want help?" he asked Carly.

Carly handed him a penguin. "These are my favorite, but you can hang one."

"I'm honored," he said sincerely. While he checked the tree for a good spot, Louisa hovered nearby and hung up a polar bear.

"I'd better be careful. Polar bears snack on these little guys."

Louisa laughed. "Right, but not on our Christmas tree. Everyone gets along just fine."

Martin looked over the tree as they worked. He saw special ornaments for each person in the family. A football for her father and an apple for her mother, a basketball for Neil and a trumpet for Ryan. There were ice skates for her sister and a soccer ball for Louisa. She must have played when she was in school, he realized. Did she still play? He had to ask her.

When he was young, his family had put up a Christmas tree every year. Martin had loved the smell of pine needles and gazing at it once it was decorated, drifting to sleep as the colored lights swam in front of his eyes.

But the tradition had faded after his mother died. His father's family in Arizona put up an artificial tree that was made of white, feathery-looking stuff with the lights already stuck on. Martin's father thought it was a terrific invention. "I just plug it in," he always said. Martin would rather have nothing than a tree like that.

A few minutes later, the ornaments were all in place. Louisa's father had worked on the star and stuck it on top a second time. "I think that will work," he said, climbing down. He started to fold up the ladder, and Martin noticed him wince and touch his back.

"I'll get that, Dad," Louisa said before Martin could offer to help. The ladder was light, and she quickly put it away.

Her father offered a small smile but still seemed uncomfortable as he straightened up to his full height. One hand rubbing his back, he called out, "Come on in, everyone, the tree is done."

Louisa's mother and her brothers appeared, coming from different points in the house. Barkley had been snoozing by the fire, but got up and walked over to see what the excitement was about.

"Did you fix the star, Mike?" Mrs. Tulley asked.

"I think so. Let's see. Ryan, plug it in," he told the twin who Martin had not yet met. Ryan looked identical to Neil, though his neat V-neck sweater and shirt suggested a more subdued personality.

Ryan leaned over and held the plug near a

socket on the wall behind the Christmas tree. "On the count of three, everyone. One, two, three . . ."

He stuck the plug in the socket, and the tree lit up. The group let out an audible sigh, even Louisa's sarcastic brothers.

"The star looks fine. Glad I didn't give up on it." Mr. Tulley stepped back to admire his handiwork.

"Perfect, top to bottom. It's the nicest tree we ever had," Mrs. Tulley replied.

Louisa laughed. "You say that every year, Mom."

Her mother shrugged. "Maybe I do, but they just get better and better."

"It's a very pretty tree, and beautifully decorated," Martin agreed. Mostly because it was done by a family, with lots of care and love, he thought.

"Thank you, Martin," Mrs. Tulley said. She turned to her husband. "How's your back holding up, Mike? You're walking funny."

Her husband gave her a look. "I'll be fine. I just need to lie on the floor with an ice pack later. You know how it goes." He turned to Martin. "Pulled something out of whack moving the boxes from the attic. These two lugs should have helped me more," he said to his sons, but in a good-natured way.

"Sorry, Dad. We'll put the boxes back," Neil promised.

"Good idea. After dinner you two can clean up," Mrs. Tulley told her sons. "Let's sit down, everything's ready. Louisa, can you help me in the kitchen?"

As Louisa followed her mother, Martin followed the family to the dining room, where the table was set. The bouquet he had given Mrs. Tulley stood in a china vase as the centerpiece. He wasn't sure where to sit, but Carly directed him.

"So, Louisa says you live in Boston, Martin," her father began soon after they sat down. "You're in town on business?"

Martin nodded. "I have a client here. I'm a tax attorney," he explained, hoping her father wouldn't ask many more questions.

"Your client must have a big problem if you need to stay so long." Mr. Tulley wasn't accusing him of anything, but Martin sensed he didn't quite buy the story.

It was not uncommon for someone in his profession to visit a client. But most tax situations could be solved with relatively brief meetings or after a day or so in the office. Records were all on computers these days, and there was rarely a need to search through file cabinets and ledger books.

"Yes, it's a very big challenge," Martin answered, thinking of the Santa Fund. "But I think we're working through it."

Before Louisa's father could question him further, Louisa and her mother swept into the room carrying platters and bowls. A huge dish of pot roast was set before him, along with at least half a dozen side dishes. The smell was so delicious, Martin felt light-headed. "This looks amazing, Mrs. Tulley."

She seemed pleased by his compliment. "It's nothing, just pot roast. Louisa helped. She's a very good cook."

Louisa looked embarrassed. "I may have chopped some carrots," she said to Martin. "Nothing more."

Martin smiled. "I'll be sure to try some of those."

Her father led the family in a prayer of thanks, and the food was passed around the table. Martin served himself with a generous hand, but Louisa's brothers both heaped their plates.

"Neil, can you leave some noodles for the rest of us?" Mr. Tulley said.

"Sorry . . ." He passed the dish to Martin. "Here, Martin. I left you . . . two noodles. Go for it, man."

There were more in the dish than that, but Martin played along. "I'm fine with one, thanks. Maybe Louisa would like the other?"

He passed the dish to Louisa, who grinned. "You're not doing too badly with the twin monsters," she whispered.

"What do you do for the holidays, Martin?" Mrs. Tulley asked. "Do you have family in the area?"

He knew she was just trying to be friendly, but the question set him off balance. *Not anymore,* he almost answered.

"My father used to live in Boston, but he moved to Arizona about fifteen years ago. He remarried after my mother passed away. I don't go out there often. It's hard to get the time off from work," he added, though that wasn't entirely true. The real reason was too personal.

"That's too bad. I'm sorry to hear of your loss. You must have been very young." She glanced at Louisa for confirmation, but Louisa didn't respond. "It's hard to be away from family on the holidays."

"Oh . . . I manage. I always get plenty of invitations from friends." That much was true, though he usually declined them.

He didn't blame her, but Mrs. Tulley didn't seem to realize that there were many people in the world who just hunkered down and ignored Christmas. Or tried to, whether for lack of family or estrangement from close connections or other reasons, none of them good. He was a longtime member of that club.

"Hey, what about all those people at church who got anonymous presents again?" Louisa looked around the table. "Who do you think is doing that?"

Martin appreciated the change of subject. But he wondered if she was asking the question to prevent anyone ever suspecting her—and him. He would have to ask her about that later.

"Those reports are amazing," her father replied. "But I have no idea who it could be. Who do you think it is?" he asked her.

Louisa shrugged. "I have no idea."

"It must be someone rich," her mother said. "Lillian Warwick and Dr. Elliot?"

"I doubt it's Lillian Warwick," her father replied with a small laugh. "That *would* be a surprise."

"Digger thought it was Dr. Elliot," Louisa said. "But he asked him, and Dr. Elliot swears he's not the one."

"What surprises me is how this person has figured out all the people who need help, and how he or she gets the gifts to them without being caught." Her father looked as if he'd been puzzling over this question. Martin recalled that Mike Tulley was once a detective and wondered if he would figure it out.

"It has to be someone who knows everyone. And the only people I can think of with that many connections are Charlie Bates and Reverend Ben," he added. "And I doubt either of them are behind it. They just don't have the means to buy all that stuff."

"Maybe it's Emily Warwick," Carly said.

"Emily was mayor of Cape Light for, like, a zillion years, so she knows everyone's business. And her family is rich. Or used to be. Maybe she has some secret pile of money or something. And she's definitely nice enough to do it. Everyone knows that."

Mr. Tulley looked impressed by the theory. "I didn't even think of her, Carly. She *is* a possibility."

"I guess it could be Emily." Louisa shrugged, feigning a baffled look that nearly made Martin laugh out loud. "Maybe we don't need to know. Maybe this generous person doesn't want credit or attention for their good deeds. Isn't that what Christmas is about?"

"In part," her father conceded. He frowned a bit; he was clearly a man who liked answers and felt frustrated by the mystery.

A cell phone rang, and Mr. Tulley pulled one from his pocket. "No phones at the table, Dad," Carly reminded him.

"I know . . ." He checked the screen and looked at his wife. "It's Tucker. I'd better take it." He put the phone to his ear and got up then walked into the living room.

"Hey, Tucker. What's up?" Martin heard him say. The family resumed eating, but everyone could hear the conversation.

"—That's too bad. Sounds like he has to go into the hospital again. Did you call an ambulance?"

Louisa and her mother exchanged concerned looks. "It must be Carl," her mother said. "He must be sick again."

Martin heard Mr. Tulley say, "I see . . . yes, I understand. Don't worry, I'll go right now," he promised. "I'll call you as soon as I see him. Don't worry."

He ended the call and returned to the table. "Carl had another attack but won't call an ambulance. Tucker is at work and can't help him. He's afraid if he calls an ambulance, Carl won't let them in, so I'm going over there now."

"I'll come with you, Mike. You can't drive with your back like that," Louisa's mother said.

"I can handle it. He's just in town."

"What if you need to take him to the hospital? You'll be ten times worse after driving to Southport," her mother warned.

"I'll go," Louisa said. She glanced at Martin. "Martin can come with me. He can help me with Uncle Carl. Right, Martin?"

"Uh, sure. Of course I will."

Martin could not think of anything he wanted to do less at that moment. He had met Carl only briefly and found him to be extremely disagreeable and unpleasant. But he could not refuse Louisa's request.

"You can't go, Louisa. I'll go," her father insisted.

"Your daughter is trained to handle situations

316

just like this, Mike. You seem to forget that," his wife reminded him.

Louisa's father didn't answer. He started toward the kitchen, then suddenly gripped his back with an unexpected spasm. He winced and gave a quiet moan.

Louisa's mother jumped up from her chair. "That settles it. You go inside and lie down. I'll bring you some ice and ibuprofen." She turned to Louisa. "Sorry, honey, but you have to check on your uncle. Thank you, Martin, for helping her. We appreciate it."

"That's all right. I hope you feel better soon, Mr. Tulley."

Mr. Tulley managed a small wave as his wife led him away. Martin followed Louisa to the front door and helped her with her jacket.

"I'm sorry, Martin. Thanks for coming with me. I don't think this will take too long. All we need to do is call an ambulance."

Martin nodded as he shrugged on his peacoat. He hoped that calling an ambulance really would be the long and short of it.

IT DID NOT GO AS LOUISA HAD PREDICTED. It did not go well at all, Martin thought. Carl wouldn't open the door. They could hear him coughing and wheezing on the other side.

"I'm going to get the super, Uncle Carl," Louisa said finally. "I'll show him my badge, and he'll open this door in two seconds flat. You're being silly now," she added.

They waited a moment, then heard the sound of the locks turn. Carl opened the door but did not greet them. He walked to a chair at a small wooden table and sat down heavily, his breathing too labored for him to speak. He pulled up the mask from a small tank of oxygen that sat in front of him and took a deep, desperate-sounding breath.

Martin could see the whole apartment from where he stood, just inside the door. Two small rooms, one that held a table with two chairs and had a compact kitchen in one corner, and one with a single bed and a dresser. The space was neat and clean but very spare, the furniture shabby and second- or even thirdhand. It was a grim, joyless place, Martin thought, the home of an old, sick man. He could barely wait to leave.

He stood back and waited while Louisa sat at the table across from her uncle and tried every tactic to persuade him to go to an emergency room. Speaking in a firm, commonsense tone, cajoling him, and finally even losing her temper.

"That's it, Uncle Carl. I'm not going to argue with you anymore. I'm calling an ambulance. I'm not going to sit here and watch you have a heart attack or something even worse."

"Leave me alone, why don't you? You're giving me a splitting headache, never mind a heart attack. You and the family, with your badges and billy sticks. I've been bossed around by people in uniforms all my life. Nobody cares about me. You all just feel guilty. That's all it is."

"That's not true. We're worried about you. You're sick. You need a doctor."

"I don't want any doctors. What part of that don't you understand? Now get out of here, you busybody, poking your nose in my life. Who asked you to come here? I didn't." He raved at her, waving his arm, unable to catch his breath for a moment. "I got rights, you know. I can say what goes in my own house—"

"Uncle Carl, please . . ."

Louisa was upset. Martin went to her and put his hand on her shoulder. "You can't talk to her like that," he said angrily. "She's trying to help you, you stubborn fool. You're sick. You need to go to the hospital."

Carl pushed himself to his feet and thrust his face close to Martin's. "Who do you think you are, coming in here and talking to me like that? I'll knock you into next week and back, buddy. Total stranger, comes in here and starts shouting orders? You think you're better than me, huh? Is that it?"

Martin shook his head, not sure what to say. "Of course I don't. Please, calm down . . . Louisa is upset."

"Don't tell me to calm down, you spoiled little

so-and-so. I bet you grew up on third base and think you hit a triple. I know your type."

"Uncle Carl, please. Martin is my friend. He's—"

"He's no friend of mine. Why does he have to see me like this? He's not even family. Get out, you. Get out of my house right now, before I throw you out . . ." He turned to Martin again, wild-eyed. He held himself up on the table with one hand, looking as if he planned to throw a punch with the other.

Louisa had come to her feet. She gently touched her uncle's arm. He tried to shake off her hold but was seized by another coughing fit. This time, it was worse. Louisa stuck the mask back on his face, and Martin helped her get him back in the chair.

"Long, slow breaths, Uncle Carl. Calm down a little. Please?" With his big head bowed, he finally did as he was told, and the coughing subsided. "If you won't go in an ambulance, we'll take you to the hospital and wait with you. They just need to look you over. They'll probably let you go, like the last time," she reminded him.

He glared at her but finally nodded.

MARTIN DROVE TO SOUTHPORT WITH CARL in the front seat, the oxygen tank on the floor by Carl's legs. Louisa sat in the back but kept leaning over the seat as Carl complained and fussed the entire ride, almost as badly as he had in the apartment. Louisa tried her best to keep him calm and Martin did his best to ignore him, but it wasn't easy.

Martin had expected a long wait in the emergency room, but the triage nurse asked Carl a few questions, checked his vital signs, and led him straight back to a curtained cubicle, where she told him to lie on the bed. She attached oxygen and opened his shirt, then hooked him up to a monitor with a clip on one finger and a blood pressure cuff on the other arm.

"When did you start feeling sick, Mr. Tulley?" she asked, holding her chart.

Carl was already annoyed. "When am I going to see a doctor? You're no doctor. What do you know?" he grumbled.

Louisa tried her best to smooth things over and fill in the blanks with his medical history. Another nurse arrived and asked more questions, and Carl lost his temper again.

"I didn't want to come here. They forced me. That guy." Carl jabbed a stubby finger at Martin. "He's the one. I don't want him here. He's no friend of mine. What is he doing back here, spying on me? I can't stand the sight of him."

Carl glared at Martin as if Martin were the source of a lifetime of troubles. Then his fury dissolved into another fit of coughing.

Martin looked at Louisa; he didn't know what

to do. He didn't want to leave her alone, but it seemed his presence was doing more harm than good.

"Just settle down, Mr. Tulley. Don't pull out the oxygen, please." The nurse had set Carl up with small tubes that fit in his nose, releasing oxygen, but he kept pulling them out.

While the nurse made sure the tubes were in place, Martin turned to Louisa. "I really don't want to leave you alone here with him. But he gets so upset just looking at me. Maybe it would be easier if I leave."

Louisa nodded. "Sure . . . I understand. You're right. You'd better go. My uncle Tucker will come when his shift is over. He'll give me a ride back. Listen, Martin, please don't take it personally. Carl can barely stand family looking after him."

Martin had not been sure if he meant he would leave the hospital, or just leave the triage area and wait outside. But she seemed embarrassed. He wondered if she would feel more comfortable, too, having only family deal with Carl.

Still, Martin felt bad leaving her there alone. It was certainly not the gallant choice from the boyfriend playbook. Was he her boyfriend? It was hardly the time to figure that out.

Before he could decide what to do, a doctor swept through the curtains and stepped up to the bed, a stethoscope in hand.

"All right, Mr. Tulley. I'm Dr. Singh. I'm going to examine you, and we'll probably need an EKG. Can you sit up a bit, please?"

Carl glared at Martin. "No exam. Not with him in here."

Martin and Louisa exchanged a look. "I'd better go. I'll speak to you later?" he said quietly.

"Sure." Louisa nodded. He couldn't tell if she felt relieved—or abandoned—to see him go. He slipped out into the triage area, dodging gurneys and rushing medical staff as he headed for the exit.

Martin reached the waiting area and stood in front of the big glass exit doors, watching them automatically slide open and closed as people walked out.

He couldn't go. He couldn't leave Louisa here, even if she didn't even know he was waiting. He checked the time and decided to wait for her. Or maybe just until Tucker Tulley arrived. He chose a seat in the waiting area with a clear view of the path Louisa had to take to leave the hospital. There was plenty to read on his phone. *I can sit here awhile,* he thought. *What else do I have to do? I just need to know that she's okay.*

It was two hours later when Martin finally spotted Louisa walking his way. She looked weary and distracted.

He stood up and she finally saw him. Her eyes

widened in surprise. "What are you doing here? I thought you left."

"I was going to," he admitted. "But I wanted to make sure you were all right."

She stared up at him and didn't answer for a long moment.

"I'm okay. Could be worse, I guess. They're going to keep Carl overnight. Tucker is with him now. I was going to wait in the coffee shop."

Martin had not seen Tucker Tulley come in but perhaps had missed him, he thought, or maybe Tucker had come in through another entrance. It didn't seem to matter now.

"I'll take you home. Why don't you send him a text and let him know?"

"Okay." Louisa took out her phone and quickly sent her uncle a message. She looked back up at him and offered a small, tired, but very gratifying smile. "Thanks for waiting for me, Martin. Really, thank you."

It was hard for him to answer. He really just wanted to hold her. But he resisted the temptation. "It's all right. It's been a long night, Louisa. You look tired. Let's go."

He put his arm around her shoulder and led her to the exit. She slipped her arm around his waist and rested her head on his shoulder. She was a very strong person, of that he was sure. But even a strong woman like Louisa needed support at times, and it felt good to be there for her.

He knew the night had drawn them closer, though he didn't know what was to come for them, and wasn't even sure what he wanted. But as he held Louisa close, their steps falling into time, Martin was very glad that he had waited for her.

Chapter Thirteen

Saturday, December 17, 1955

WALTER WAS IN HIS WORKSHOP, carefully cutting the pattern for the new stuffed dog, focusing to keep his hand steady in order to get it just right. He had already cut scores of these patterns and would cut scores more before the day was done, but he couldn't think about that right now. Rushing would only ruin it. He had to concentrate.

He heard the bell on the door and then the sound of someone walking into the shop. Otis jumped up from his bed and growled low in the back of his throat. It was late, well after closing time. Had he forgotten to turn the sign and lock the door? That was possible. He wasn't himself the last few days.

Walter stepped out into the store and looked around. "Sorry, we're closed. Please come back on Monday."

"Walter, it's me." Oliver stepped forward. He took off his hat. "I saw the lights on, so I came in. Sorry to bother you."

Otis ran forward and sniffed Oliver's leg, then wagged his tail. Walter had already discovered that his dog was an infallible judge of character. He immediately sensed who was nice and who was not and, especially, who liked dogs.

Oliver bent down and petted the dog's head. "What a fine little fellow. Looks like a real sporting hound. Where did you get him?"

"More like he got me," Walter said with a smile. "He'd been living in the alley for weeks and finally let us take him in."

"You've made a friend for life, I can see that. I bet he's great company while you work."

"He is . . . More than that, he's been an absolute inspiration." Walter couldn't help bragging about Otis. "I got a request for some stuffed toys and used Otis as a model." He picked up a Santa Dog from a display on the counter. "I made this dog and Frances dressed it up. I put it in the window, and we've been swamped with orders ever since."

Oliver held up the stuffed dog and examined it. He grinned from ear to ear. "Bravo, Walter. Well done." He slapped Walter on the back. "This one is a winner, no question. No wonder you're working all hours. Just the surge of sales you need. You'll be in the black by Christmas morning, I'd say."

"I hope so, Oliver." Walter wished he could sound as encouraged. "I did think at first the toy had saved us. People have been coming in and calling all hours. They see Otis in the window, and they're wild to have him. And other toy shops have been calling us every day, from as far away as Worcester. I was dancing a jig. But now, I'm not so sure. We've worked ourselves ragged the last few days. Me, Franny, and even Digger and his wife. But we're just not keeping up with the orders," he admitted.

He riffled a pile of pages near the cash register. "I'll have to call a lot of these people on Monday and tell them we just can't make the dogs fast enough to deliver in time for Christmas shopping."

Oliver looked shocked, then slammed his hand down on Walter's orders. "No, you won't. You'll do nothing of the kind. This is a gift, Walter. You can't turn it down. I won't let you."

Oliver was so adamant, Walter didn't know how to react. "I'd rather do that than go back on my word," he said. "We can't make all those toys in time, Oliver. It's not possible."

"Of course it is." Oliver checked his watch, then shrugged off his coat. "Grab your paperwork, the orders, and any lists you have for purchasing supplies, that sort of thing. Let's go somewhere we can talk."

Walter was doubtful, but did as Oliver instructed. He already knew that when Oliver got an idea in his head, it was impossible to talk him out of it.

Walter led Oliver upstairs, where Franny was also working on the stuffed toys. She jumped up from her chair in the living room, surprised to see Oliver at this time on a Saturday night.

While Frances made coffee, Walter and Oliver spread the toy orders and other paperwork out on the table. Oliver spent a long time going over every page and making notes on a pad.

Finally, he looked up. "Walter, do you know why Henry Ford was so successful?"

"Of course I do. He invented the automobile."

"Not exactly, though he often gets the credit. But he did figure out how to make them cheaper and faster," Oliver explained. "He didn't invent the production line either, but he figured out how to apply it, and he ran rings around his competition. That's what you need, too. People sewing, stuffing, putting on the finishing touches. Packing the toys and delivering them. It couldn't be more obvious."

Walter's heart sank. He had been surprised by the way Oliver had barged in and taken over, but he expected that his advice would really help. Deciding that they needed a production line did not help at all.

"That would probably solve my dilemma, Oliver. But how am I going to do that? It's impossible! I know you mean well, but it's not very helpful," he said, perhaps a bit louder than he intended.

Oliver looked unfazed. He picked up an oatmeal cookie from the plate Frances had served along with their coffee. "These are delicious cookies, Frances. Very chewy."

"Thank you, Oliver. I'll send some home with you . . . Walter? Are you going to apologize?" Frances gave him a look.

"I'm sorry. I didn't mean to snap at you. I'm very tired. You've done so much for us, and I appreciate your advice, honestly. But even if I could find a factory where we could do this work, who would we hire? How would I pay everyone and buy all the materials?"

"Those are all excellent questions, Walter. And I'm not upset at all that you're asking them. These are questions a good business has to ask. And answer," he added.

Oliver wasn't going to drop the subject, was he? Walter felt cornered into taking it seriously. "Okay, let's say I can use some of our savings and I ask for a deposit on the orders from the other stores. I might have most of the money I need to get started," he mused.

"You might," Oliver agreed. "And I'm happy to loan you any more that you'll need. As an investment," he clarified. "I'd be a fool not to get in on the ground floor with the Santa Dog. I mean that, sincerely."

"I know plenty of women who can do this work and would like to make extra money before

Christmas," Frances offered. "If they could find someone to watch their children."

Now he had to find babysitters, too? It was late, and Walter felt far too tired for this pie-in-the-sky conversation.

"Wait a minute . . . I know just the place." Oliver smiled, looking like the cat that ate the canary. *Or two,* Walter thought.

"A place for the women to drop off their children?" he asked.

"And set up the factory," Oliver replied. "The children could come with their mothers, and the women could take turns watching them. There's a carriage house on our estate that's empty right now. It's spacious and comfortable. There are a few pieces of furniture left, but nothing too cumbersome to get in your way. You can set up cutting tables and sewing machines without a lot of rearranging. You can use different rooms for the different stages of building the dog—cutting fabric, machine sewing, hand sewing, stuffing, adding the trimmings, et cetera. If women need to bring their children, they can play on one floor, or even outside, if it's not too cold, while their mothers are working."

"That's brilliant, Oliver!" Frances was so excited she jumped up from her chair. "All we would need are sewing machines and worktables. I bet most women would prefer to work on their own machines, if the machines could be moved there. I do my best and fastest sewing on my own machine."

"We have a truck on the estate. I'll ask the groundskeeper and his men to move sewing machines if need be. For the cutting tables, what about big sheets of plywood on sawhorses? Would that work, Walter?"

Walter was stunned. He could actually see this homespun factory taking shape. "Plywood will work out fine. We can throw those tables together in no time." He met Oliver's gaze, his heart full of gratitude once again.

He felt ashamed now for resisting the idea, but he could see Oliver had taken no offense. If anything, the debate had amused his worldly friend. "If I ever say the word 'impossible' again, you have permission to sew my mouth shut," Walter told him.

Oliver laughed and slapped him on the shoulder. "I'm not very handy with a needle and thread. I'll leave that job to Frances." He glanced at her and winked. "The Bible says God made the whole world in six days, Walter. Surely we can make a few stuffed dogs?"

Walter found himself grinning. Oliver made it sound so easy. Walter doubted it would be quite that simple, but Oliver's confidence was contagious. Walter decided that, once again, heaven was sending him a message not to give up.

They talked over a few more details of the

carriage-house factory and made plans for the next day, to get everything there ready for Monday.

When Walter went to sleep that night, he said a prayer of thanks for Oliver Warwick's guidance and support—and the amazing solution Oliver had figured out for them.

THE NEXT DAY AT CHURCH, FRANCES SPOKE to a number of women she thought might want to work on the toys, and she and Walter hired a large group, including a few husbands. Many of them were eager to make some extra income so close to Christmas and happy to help turn the Warwick estate carriage house into a work space.

On Monday morning, Walter and Frances set off very early, with extra supplies in the back of their car. While an icy fog rose from the Beach Road, they drove toward the Warwick estate. The high wrought iron gates were open, and they drove up to the carriage house. Lilac Hall, the big stone mansion where Oliver lived with his family, was off in the distance, on a hill that overlooked the water.

"There it is, Walter. Our factory. Or soon it will be. I can hardly believe it." Frances jumped out of the car first. She was so excited. "It came together in the blink of an eye. I feel as if I'm in a happy dream."

"It did fall into place in a magical way," Walter agreed. "But faith can work miracles. Some people think seeing *is* believing. But I think you have to believe in it before you see it."

Frances pulled a big picnic basket and coffeepot from the back seat. "Let's get in there. I want to have coffee ready for everyone, and I made a few loaves of cinnamon bread. Oh, and I brought the radio from the kitchen. It will be nice to have music playing while we work, don't you think? I want to make the first morning very welcoming. Some of the women have never worked outside their homes before."

Walter had been thinking so much about the equipment and supplies they needed, he hadn't given a thought to the atmosphere. But just because their employees were organized in a production line didn't mean their little factory had to be a cold, impersonal place. He had never managed employees before, aside from Digger, who was more of a friend. But he felt intuitively that people would do much better and even faster work if they felt happy and comfortable. Frances clearly knew that, too.

"You brought coffee, cinnamon bread, and music to keep everyone happy. And I brought Otis," he said, opening the back door so the dog could jump out. Otis was well trained and could have been left alone without any problem. But Walter had never even considered it. He wasn't

334

even sure he could work well anymore without Otis looking on.

Frances smiled at their loyal companion, who had happily run ahead, wagging his tail. "I can't forget Otis. He'll be our factory mascot. He's the reason we're able to do this at all."

Their workers arrived and settled down to their jobs with greater ease than Walter had expected. The little carriage house was soon a beehive of activity. Pattern cutters carefully clipped, sewing machines hummed, and stuffers and trimmers chatted happily as they finished each dog with care. One by one, a collection of Santa's Dogs were wrapped and packed and made ready for delivery.

In the kitchen, toy makers shared meals and snacks. Hot cocoa, coffee, tea, and cookies were readily at hand. Cheerful music played along with the sound of the sewing machines' hum, and just as Frances had hoped, mothers took turns watching the children, who played on the second floor and outdoors. By midday, someone had made a sign that read santa's workshop and hung it on the outside door.

"Santa's Workshop—just perfect. I bet the real one in the North Pole isn't half as lively and cheerful," Oliver said as he walked in late that afternoon.

His handsome face wore a grin from ear to ear as he surveyed the scene. Dressed in a three-piece navy pin-striped suit and puffing on a thin cigar, he looked every inch the dapper prince of industry that he was. *The perfect business mentor and guardian angel wrapped into one,* Walter thought.

"What do you think now, Walter? Will you fill the orders by Christmas?"

Walter still wasn't positive, but he had learned a lesson about not voicing the least bit of doubt. In Oliver's earshot, anyway. "We're going to do our level best . . . and let God do the rest."

Oliver picked up one of the finished dogs. He noticed a little illustrated booklet attached to the dog's collar by a thin red ribbon and examined it curiously. "What's this, Walter? I didn't see this touch before."

"That's just a little story Frances made up to go with the dog. It's about how Santa takes in a stray and, one Christmas night, lets him ride on the sleigh, never expecting him to help. But Santa gets caught in a storm and his list flies away. He doesn't know where to deliver his presents. But the little dog sniffs out the cookies all the children have left for Santa and guides the sleigh to every house on the list."

Oliver laughed. "That's terrific. Your wife is a very clever woman . . . as well as beautiful," he added. "But who did these drawings? They're wonderful."

"That was my contribution. George Plante

printed up a pile of the booklets last week, but now it seems we need more," Walter said.

"I'm headed to the village right now. I'll take care of it for you," Oliver offered. Walter walked him to the back door, which was in the kitchen. Oliver couldn't resist one of Frances's oatmeal cookies.

"I may not drop by for a few days. I have a lot on my plate. But if you need help, don't hesitate to call," Oliver reminded him. "Take good care of my investment. I'm counting on you."

"Will do," Walter promised.

Oliver waved good-bye as he slipped into his British sports car. Walter waved back, amazed that he had made such an unlikely friend. It was just as he had heard: There really was no one like Oliver Warwick. He was one in a million.

AS PEOPLE IN TOWN LEARNED OF THE HAPPY little factory on the Warwick estate, many stopped by to ask if they could be hired, too. Walter and Frances realized that with extra workers coming in and out almost around the clock, they would surely meet their deadline. Walter opened the carriage house before dawn each day and stayed past midnight. The hours were grueling, but when he grew weary, he coached himself to hang on for a few more days. Or regret it the rest of his life.

The week passed in a blur. Walter didn't see Oliver again until Friday, the day before Christmas Eve, and hardly realized how close it was to their deadline.

"Walter, for pity's sake. You look like you've been up all night," Oliver greeted him as he got out of his car.

"Practically," Walter admitted. He had only been able to grab a few hours' sleep the last few nights, and even when he'd had a chance to rest, he'd been too excited and restless to take advantage of it. "I can sleep plenty when we're all through. It's time for working now."

"I bet that's what Santa says about this time of year, too," Oliver teased him. "So tell me, Walter. What's the verdict? Have you filled all those orders? Will you be ready to see Mr. Finley in January?"

"We're filling all the orders you saw at my shop last week, and then some. I shouldn't have any trouble at the bank."

It was hard to tamp down the note of pride in his voice. Walter did feel he had the right to be proud of the effort he and Frances had made, but he knew they would have never succeeded without help—Oliver's help and help from heaven above.

Before Oliver could reply, Walter said, "I could have never done this without you, Oliver. We're endlessly grateful. I can't see how someone like me could ever help you. But if a time comes, I hope you'll call on me. For any reason at all."

Oliver seemed moved by the offer. "Thank you, Walter. I knew you could do it. My reward is seeing you succeed. That's more than enough compensation." Oliver reached into the back seat of his car. "I've brought you something. A gift for you and Frances." He handed Walter a bottle of champagne, topped by an elegant white bow. "You need this to celebrate."

Walter didn't know much about champagne, but the bottle looked expensive, with a fancy French name on the label. "That's very kind of you. If all goes well, we'll pop the cork tomorrow night. Will you come by at the end of the day and join us?"

"I'd love to, Walter, but I'll be in Boston. On some special business," he added. "If all goes well, I'll see you on Christmas Day. It could be a very special one for me."

The look in his eye and the tone of his voice made Walter curious. He had a feeling that the special business involved the young lady Oliver had been seeing for the past few months. Lillian, Walter thought her name was. Walter had heard she was from a prominent Boston family who objected to the match, but he doubted that would stop Oliver if he was determined to win the girl's heart and hand.

"Good luck, Oliver," Walter said sincerely. "I

hope you have the best Christmas ever." *May God bless you and Lillian,* he added in his heart.

THE NEXT DAY, CHRISTMAS EVE, WALTER and Frances watched as the last stuffed dog was packed and went out for delivery, just in time to be snatched up by last-minute shoppers who would be roaming stores until they closed that night. It was only noon, but Walter didn't want to keep his hardworking employees at the carriage house any longer. Everyone had families waiting at home, and they were all eager to get ready for Christmas.

Walter and Frances gathered their crew in the large room on the first floor of the carriage house. Christmas music played as they all enjoyed one last lunch together. Walter gave out pay envelopes with extra in each and gave out toys to all the children. Soon it was time to go, and the Nightingales bid each of their employees a merry Christmas. Walter felt as if he was saying good-bye to friends or even family, not merely folks who had worked for him.

When the carriage house was finally empty, the sudden silence and stillness seemed shocking. Even the radio had been turned off. Walter stood with Frances in the parlor. "We did it, Franny. We really did it."

Frances smiled, blinking away tears. "I can hardly believe it, Walter. But yes . . . we really did." She stepped into his arms for a long, tight embrace. He wasn't sure where the energy came from, but he suddenly lifted her up and spun her around the room with joy.

Frances shrieked with surprise. "Walter, what in the world! Let me down . . . are you crazy?" he heard her protest, but she was laughing, too. Otis circled them, barking and then letting loose one of his now-famous howls, which made them both laugh.

Finally, Walter set his wife on her feet again but still could not release her. "Frances, we're going to have the most wonderful Christmas ever. We have so much to be thankful for. And so much to look forward to."

"Yes, Walter. By the grace of God, we truly do." Frances didn't say more. In her dark eyes, brimming with happy tears, he could see she was too overwhelmed to say more.

Saturday, December 15, 2018

MARTIN HAD PLANS WITH LOUISA TO GIVE out a few gifts on Saturday afternoon and, afterward, go out to dinner. This time there was enough room in the car for Milo, which made Martin happy. He hated to leave his friend alone at Vera's for long stretches, though Milo and Vera had developed a very nice friendship, and she liked having the dog with her in the kitchen while she cooked. But he knew Louisa would be happy to see Milo, too.

He picked up Louisa at three o'clock and explained his plan. As they drove away, she said, "I don't know, Martin. I'm having the strangest feeling of déjà vu. Isn't this the same date we had last weekend?"

Martin grinned. "Okay, you caught me. But you know what Digger says, 'If it ain't broke, don't fix it.'" Louisa laughed, and he added, "Actually, I wanted to take a little detour. Do you mind if we stop at my grandparents' house and look around? I haven't had a chance to go there yet, and I need to figure this out."

"I don't mind at all. I love to look around old houses. It will be fun, Milo, don't you think?" She turned and patted Milo's head, and he leaned forward and licked her cheek. They both seemed happy and excited, and Martin wished he felt the same.

He had decided that morning that he couldn't put it off any longer. He knew that he could have gone on his own anytime. But it would be easier with someone else there. Especially if that someone was Louisa.

With Louisa's help he found the turn, even though the sign was hidden by branches. His car bounced on the rough road, and finally, the house and the pond just beyond came into view.

Martin pulled up and parked on the gravel

drive. "There it is. Looks almost the same from the outside, except for some wear and tear."

The big Victorian was still the same color he recalled, a sunny shade of yellow with white trim. Never at a loss for whimsical touches, his grandparents had painted the front door lavender-blue and the shutters a dark shade of pink, which his grandmother had called "peony." She had been as creative and artistic as his grandfather and had a wonderful eye for color.

"It could use some fresh paint, but I'd never change the colors," Louisa said as they got out of the car and Milo bounded out from the back seat.

"When I was a little boy, I never noticed anything unusual about the combination. I guess I wouldn't change the colors either. If only for old times' sake."

Martin had gotten the keys from the attorney who held the house in trust for him. They walked up onto the porch, and he searched the ring for the front door key. The porch was empty except for a few pieces of wicker furniture covered with a green tarp and tied with rope. He remembered how his grandmother would have the entire porch filled with flowers in the summer—window boxes and potted plants and colorful blooms in hanging baskets that trailed long vines.

Louisa touched his sleeve. "Look at the view. Isn't that perfect? I bet you sat for hours out here, reading a book or just watching the sunset."

The large pond at the edge of the property was in full view of the wide, wraparound porch. Late-day sunshine glittered off the blue water, and tall, straw-colored reeds waved in the wind.

Martin watched Milo lift his head and sniff the air. He knew what was coming after that. "Not now, Milo. Stay with us. We'll let you run around later."

The dog looked up at him, and when Martin was sure he'd minded, he turned back to Louisa. "I did sit and read out here, and also in my secret places."

"That sounds fun. Can you show me where they were?"

"If I can find them," he promised. He opened the door, hoping Louisa didn't notice how his hand trembled with nerves as the key found the lock. He felt as if he were about to open a door in his own heart, where he'd kept so many memories locked away in the dark.

Martin opened the door and stepped aside for Louisa and the dog to enter first. Milo trotted inside, as if they had just gotten back to their apartment in Cambridge. He sniffed the air and walked into a room off the large foyer.

Louisa took a few steps forward, her head tilted back as she studied the ornate ceiling. "The ceilings are so high. Look at all this molding. And the tile floor . . ."

Large rooms opened on the left and right, a

sitting room and library on one side, and on the other, a formal parlor that adjoined a dining room with pocket doors in between. They walked into the library first, the walls lined with floor-to-ceiling bookcases.

Louisa walked over to a shelf and pulled out one of the old books that had been left there. "These bookcases are amazing. Were they always here, or did your grandparents have them built?"

"My grandfather built them. He loved to read, especially after he gave up his store. He'd never had a chance to go to college, but he was self-taught and read very widely. He could never buy enough books, and to me, this room seemed like paradise."

Louisa smiled. "What happened to his library? There must have been hundreds."

"My father took a few, and we donated some. But I have most of them. My apartment looks like a library," he joked, though it was true. There had been so many books that he couldn't part with that he'd put many of them in storage.

"These shelves held books just for me," he recalled, showing Louisa the special section near a window. "My grandparents would find books they thought I'd like and save them for me here. Classic children's novels, books about insects and Egypt. Even when I was away at school and couldn't visit them much, they never stopped. I saved those, of course. I haven't even read them all yet."

When he turned to Louisa, she was wearing a thoughtful look. "Maybe your own children will read them someday."

"Maybe." He met her clear blue gaze a moment, then quickly looked away.

They continued through the house, room by room, Milo sometimes padding after them and sometimes exploring on his own. They parted on the second floor; there were so many rooms and doors to open, most of them on a center hall. But there was also a side hallway with more rooms, smaller than the large bedrooms that circled the main staircase.

Martin found the room that had been his as a boy. It was still painted the same color, and even though it was empty of furniture, he could picture it exactly as it had been. He opened the closet and saw his scrawled handwriting on a wall. He used the light on his cell phone to make out the scribbled letters. *If you find this note, you will probably know all about the famous astronaut Martin Thomas Nightingale, who is me.*

His childish bravado made him smile, feeling affection for his younger self, brimming with fantasy and ambition. Never doubting he could reach any heights he set his eye on, do anything he dreamed of.

Where did that boy go? Martin didn't know. He felt like a stranger to his younger self and knew he would be ashamed to meet that younger

Martin face-to-face. Somewhere along the way, he had lost that spark; he had let that little boy down.

Maybe with this inheritance, he could make a new start; he could find that optimistic, confident spirit again. It wouldn't be easy. But he hoped so.

"There you are; I've been looking all over." Louisa appeared in the doorway. Milo trailed after her and looked at Martin, matching Louisa's questioning expression. "Did you find something in the closet?"

Martin shook his head. "Not really. This was my room when I used to visit in the summer. The bed was there, under the window. And all these shelves were filled with toys—some that my grandfather had made. Sometimes at night I thought they would come alive, but not in a scary way."

He turned to another wall. "These shelves held shells and rocks and all sort of things I'd find. And this one held a row of jars, filled with little creatures. I only kept them for a short time. Then I turned them loose," he quickly added. "My mother made me."

"She sounds like a smart woman," Louisa said quietly.

"She was smart. She went to Brown University on a scholarship. That's where my parents met. She was an orphan, raised by an aunt. She didn't have much family. She loved my grandparents as if they were her own parents, and they loved her, too. Very much." He stared out the window, wondering if he was confiding too much. But being in the house was hard; the memories came flooding back. "We were here together a lot, me and her. My father came, too. But he had his work in the city, always pulling him back. My mother was fun. We never ran out of things to do. On rainy days, she played the piano and read to me. Those are some of my best memories of her."

"I'm sorry, Martin. It must be so hard for you, coming here." Louisa seemed to suddenly understand the gravity of this visit for him.

"No need to apologize. But it is difficult," he admitted. "More than I thought it would be."

"You still miss her very much."

"I do. She was such an easy person to be around, a sunny personality, and so open with her feelings. Everyone liked her, automatically. She and my father balanced each other out."

Martin felt that he was more like his father, who was just the opposite. His mother had been the glue that had held his family together; he could see that now. When she died, their family was fractured; his grandparents included. His grandparents had tried, but they never really got along with their new daughter-in-law. Martin had been caught in between, and his father had thought the best solution was to send him away to school, where he had learned to shut the memories away and distance himself from the heartbreaking loss.

"It does hurt less, over time. But it never goes away," he confided.

Louisa touched his shoulder, her eyes full of sympathy. He took her hand in his and twined his fingers with hers. "The sun is going down. It would be nice to walk outside awhile, before it gets dark."

They headed downstairs and Milo followed. As Martin locked the door, he saw the dog jump off the porch and head for the pond.

"Good idea, Milo," Louisa said. "Let's walk to the pond and watch the sunset." She had already started to follow Milo. "The swing is still there, just as you described it," she called back.

Martin walked to the swing and looked it over. "So it is. Except for the rope, which looks brand-new. Thank goodness."

Louisa had a playful look in her eye. "Should we test it out?"

He glanced at the swing, then at the water, and shook his head. "I don't think so. If we fall off in this weather, it won't be much fun."

She still looked tempted but didn't argue. Milo was investigating at the edge of the gently lapping water. "It's so pretty here," she said. "I bet this part hasn't changed at all."

"No, it hasn't," he agreed.

"You know Sam and Jessica Morgan live just on the other side of the water, over there." She pointed. "Restoring old houses like this is his specialty. He does beautiful work. I'm sure he'd be happy to give you some advice."

Martin felt she was jumping ahead a bit for him. He still had no idea if he should keep the house or not. "I'll keep him in mind. If I need help," he added. "I thought coming here would help me decide, but I still don't know what to do. The house is beautiful, or can be again with some work. But I'm not sure if repairing this place is a project I want to take on right now. I don't know if I want to keep renting it either. It will just get more run-down."

Louisa listened with a thoughtful expression, and he sensed his confession had made her uncomfortable. Still, he had to be honest with her; he owed her that much.

"What will you do, sell it?"

"Maybe," he replied.

"I'm surprised you would give it up so easily. It has so many memories for you. The other night, you seemed to think you might keep it. What did you say—'as a landing spot'?"

"I was just thinking out loud. And I hadn't come back here yet," he pointed out. "It's hard to have the past staring back at you, every place you turn. Even if the memories are happy ones. Today, it seems those good memories make it even harder."

"I understand." Louisa sounded sad, even disappointed, and he didn't like the direction their conversation was taking.

You can stop right here. You don't have to talk about this anymore, a voice in his head warned. *Do you really need to put your cards on the table right now? She's special. You know that. You haven't felt this way about anyone in such a long time. Think about this.*

But wouldn't that be stringing her along? Louisa didn't need a boyfriend who wasn't there for her. Who wasn't giving her all the attention and affection she deserved.

This was not at all what he had expected to happen tonight. He wasn't even sure how it had started. But he felt something pushing him forward and couldn't stop himself.

"I'm sorry, Louisa. But I can't mislead you. The time we've spent together the last few weeks has meant a lot to me. But I think you should know . . . well, what I mean to say is . . ."

Why was he so terrible at talking about his feelings? He took a breath and started again. "I'm almost done with the task I came here to do, and in a few weeks, I don't know where I'll be. I can't make any sort of commitment, to anyone, right now. Especially the kind a girl like you deserves."

Louisa looked stung. "'Commitment' is a serious word, Martin. We've only known each other a few weeks. How could I expect that?"

"I guess I have serious feelings for you. Or I know they could be," he confessed. "Which makes this so much harder. You should be with a guy who knows what he wants and where he's going. You told me the other night you don't believe in bad timing. But I do. Maybe if we'd met some other time, when I felt ready to put my whole heart into a relationship, things would be different. We haven't known each other very long," he agreed. "But I know that's the least you deserve, Louisa. I hope you never settle for anything less."

"You sound like you're saying good-bye, Martin. Are you leaving already? Is that what you're trying to say?" Her beautiful blue eyes were glassy, but she wouldn't let herself cry.

"I didn't mean to sound that way, but yes . . . I'm leaving soon. There's hardly any money left to give away. I'll probably be done by the end of next week."

Christmas was a week from Tuesday. Martin expected to be done with his gift-giving by Friday, Saturday at the latest. He'd considered staying in town for the holiday but didn't see the point. Especially now. It would only make it harder to leave. It was hard enough already.

"I see. Thank you for letting me know your plans." Louisa turned and started walking toward the car. Martin knew he had hurt her and felt sick about it. That was the last thing he wanted. But he had no idea what to say to make things better.

Should they talk it out more? Would she settle for what he had to give right now? Maybe he shouldn't worry about the future so much and just see where their relationship led.

He turned and whistled for Milo, who had wandered out of sight. Luckily, the dog came running without playing hide-and-seek. "Come on, Milo. Time to go," Martin murmured as he led the dog to the car, where Louisa stood waiting for them.

He was about to ask if she wanted to go somewhere and talk more when her phone rang. She pulled it from her jacket pocket. He could tell it was a call from the police station.

"Yes, I can do it. It's not a problem," he heard her say. "All right. See you then."

They got in the car and he started the engine. "That was the desk sergeant. He's had a few sick calls. I'm going in to work tonight to cover for someone."

"All right. I'll take you home." Martin had the feeling that if their evening had been going better, Louisa would have said she was unavailable for the extra shift. But it was a convenient way out for her—and maybe for him, too.

Why drag this out with a long, heart-wrenching conversation? he asked himself. *I think you already know what the conclusion would be.*

CHAPTER FOURTEEN

Saturday, December 22, 2018

I T'S A SHAME YOU WON'T BE HERE FOR Christmas, Martin." Vera sounded disappointed, but was not too distracted to flip a row of pancakes on the griddle and set a stack of three on his plate. Warmed maple syrup, creamy butter, and dishes of baked apple slices and crisp, hot bacon were already on the table. He would miss Vera's cooking, that was for sure.

She set her own plate on the table and sat down across from him. "Are you sure you can't stay? This Sunday is 'The Twelve Gifts of Christmas'—stories and poems and all special music. And the services on Christmas Eve and Christmas Day are wonderful, too. The choir has been rehearsing for weeks. They're going to sing the 'Hallelujah' chorus. The famous part," she clarified. "And Jessica Morgan is bringing live animals for the pageant. Newborn lambs and a goat—"

"No camel?" Martin asked. She took him seriously for a moment, then grinned at his teasing.

"No dromedaries of any kind. But she might find a donkey in time. Did you hear about her horses? She rescued a whole herd headed for the slaughterhouse. She and Sam had nowhere to keep them warm, then that Secret Santa found an empty stable and rented it for Grateful Paws for the whole winter. Isn't that something?"

Martin was relieved that Vera had gotten off the subject of his departure, but the topic she had landed on was still a slippery slope.

"I think I did hear something about that," he replied between bites.

Milo had been waiting patiently for some bacon and now rested his head on Martin's knee, just in case he had been forgotten. Martin took the dog's chew toy, stuffed in a slice, then slipped it to him. The dog took the prize gently in his mouth and crept to a small, round rug by the stove, where he worked hard to get the treat loose.

"It's all very mysterious, if you ask me." Vera paused to sip her coffee. "All these gifts popping up everywhere. Who could it be? There are very few people in this town well off enough to afford it, for one thing. Charlie Bates at the diner says it has to do with Oliver Warwick. That was Lillian's first husband. He was the richest man in town for a very long time. He owned a cannery and a mill and a big estate on the water that's been turned into a museum. He died a long time ago, and in disgrace," she added in a sad tone. "He lost his whole fortune. But some people think he socked a bit away and put some special clause in his will, asking that at a certain time, all the hidden money be given out."

"That's quite a story. How does Charlie know that?"

Vera shrugged. "Didn't say. But he knows a lot of people who know a lot of people. If you know what I mean."

Martin took a breath, surprised at how close to the truth this theory came, even though it was concocted out of thin air. It was definitely time for him to get out of town. If he stayed any longer, he might be found out.

"Did you see the article in the *Cape Light Messenger*? They made a list of all the gifts the Secret Santa gave out. Some people didn't want their names announced, but most didn't care." Vera had a copy of the village newspaper on the table and opened it up for him to see.

He took the paper and pretended to read it. *Secret Santa spreads joy*, the headline read. He smiled at the thought that it was him. Him and Louisa. He had already read the article and was sure that Louisa had probably read it by now, too. It would have been so much fun to share it with her.

He had seen her coming out of the diner the other day when he was walking Milo. He stopped and stared straight at her, hoping she would meet his glance and say hello, and maybe they could talk for a moment or two. But she pretended to not see him and jumped in her car and drove away.

Later that night, he sent her a text, asking if she would meet to say good-bye. She never answered, though that was two days ago, and he still checked his phone every minute, hoping that she might.

"That's a long list. Almost as long as the real Santa's," he said, handing the paper back.

"It is indeed. God bless that person, whoever they are. There's not enough kindness and good-will in the world. It makes you feel so good to see someone who really believes in it."

Martin nodded, at a loss for a reply. *It's not like that,* he wanted to say. *I don't deserve your praise or your blessing.* Instead, he finished his pancakes and cleared the dishes from the table.

"Are you all packed?" she asked.

"Almost. I didn't bring much."

"Well . . . I'm going to miss you. And I don't say that to all my guests. The house will seem very quiet without you and Milo."

Martin knew he would miss Vera, too. He'd become so accustomed to her rambling chatter and stories about her everyday adventures. Vera could go to the store for a quart of milk and return with an hour-long tale.

"We'll keep in touch. Who knows, I may come back someday."

He didn't think he would but didn't know what else to say.

"For your business, you mean? That would be nice. You let me know. I'll have your room all ready."

Martin smiled, wishing it were true. "What are you going to do for Christmas, Vera?" he asked, trying to change the subject. "Are you going to Sophie's house?"

"No, I'm going to be with my own family. I've made train reservations for Christmas Day. I'll head down right after the service. There are a few connections, and carrying my packages won't be any picnic. But I have to see my grandchildren. It won't feel like Christmas otherwise."

There had been some confusion in Vera's plans. She wanted to be with her family in Connecticut but didn't trust her old car to get there. The last Martin had heard, she was going to stay in Cape Light and have Christmas with Sophie Potter's family.

He wondered if she could get a refund on her train ticket. She wouldn't need it when her new car was delivered. A new car for Vera was the last gift he had picked out. It had used up the last of the Santa Fund and a little extra, which he had paid for himself. He wasn't sure why he hadn't realized sooner that it was the most perfect idea, and the most enjoyable to arrange, too.

A brand-new Subaru, just like his, which she

admired each time she rode in it. It was certainly far more reliable and safer in bad weather than the used compact she had been looking for. It would be delivered to her doorstep on Christmas morning. He wished he could be there to see the look on Vera's face. But he knew that would not be possible.

"I'm going over to church in a little while. The poinsettias were delivered, and we need to set them up in the sanctuary with the manger figures. Will you be here when I get back?"

"I don't think so. I guess we ought to say good-bye now." He paused, searching for the right words of farewell. "Thank you for opening your home to me, Vera. I've rarely felt so welcome or so comfortable anywhere."

"It was my pleasure, Martin. You're a fine young man, and I wish you every happiness. And Milo, too."

Martin leaned over and gave Vera a hug. He really would miss her and was sorry he had to go.

He went upstairs to pack a few more belongings, then checked the closet, dresser, and bathroom to make sure he hadn't left anything. He had heard Vera leave the house a few minutes after he'd gone to his room, but just as he was closing his suitcase, she came inside again and called to him.

"Martin? Sorry to bother. Can you give me one more ride to church? I'm sure you can guess why." The frustration and resignation in her voice made knowing about her surprise even sweeter.

"Sure. I'll be right down," he called back. He closed his bag and grabbed his jacket. Then he walked down the back staircase and met her in the kitchen.

"Can you believe it?" She shook her head. "And you thought you were rid of me. I'm like gum, stuck to your shoe."

"I'd never say that." Martin smiled and clipped Milo's leash. "It's no trouble. I should have thought of it."

As usual, the trunk of her car was filled with boxes she needed to bring to church. Ribbon and baskets for the plants, and cakes for the Fellowship Hour on Sunday. They quickly transferred everything to his car—Martin was careful to place all of Vera's baked goods beyond Milo's reach—and set off for the village.

He parked behind the church and helped Vera carry in the boxes. He knew Milo would be fine waiting in the car a little while. As they came through the glass doors near Fellowship Hall, Sophie and Grace Hegman hurried to meet them. Martin knew immediately something was wrong—though for Vera's friends, a few crushed poinsettia plants might inspire alarm.

But Vera was not their focus. He was, which surprised him. Grace tugged his arm. "Martin, thank goodness. Come quickly . . . you have to help."

"What's the matter? What's wrong?" He allowed himself to be pulled down the hallway, flanked by Sophie and Vera.

"What's going on?" Vera asked, trotting behind him.

Claire North bustled out of Reverend Ben's office to join them. "A pipe burst in the basement and Carl can't stop the water. He's down there alone and needs help bad."

Martin backed up a few steps from the stairway. "I'm sorry . . . I don't know a thing about plumbing. I'd just be in the way. Have you called anyone?"

"Claire called Reverend Ben, and he's calling the plumber. But Carl needs help now," Grace insisted. "He's in a fit of temper. Claire went down there and he nearly bit her head off."

"And he was coughing something awful," Claire added.

Martin knew that Carl would take one look at him and both his temper and cough would get even worse. But the women had lined up behind him, blocking his path. He had no choice but to turn and head down the stairs.

He glanced out the big glass windows in the hall but saw no sign of Reverend Ben. Carl would rant and rave, but he could at least try.

"I'll see what I can do, but you'd better try

Reverend Ben again." Then he turned and headed down the steps to the church basement. The light was dim, coming from a few small, high windows on ground level. It was an unfinished space, damp and dusty with a cement floor, rough cement walls, and old wooden beams above.

Even before he reached the bottom of the steps, Martin heard the sounds of gushing water and Carl coughing. Then he noticed a thin but steady stream of water coming his way. The basement was starting to flood.

He saw Carl in the shadows a short distance away, twisting a faucet on a thick pipe near the ceiling. Carl gripped it with a huge wrench, his face contorted with effort as he tried to turn it, but it didn't budge. He turned and stared at Martin, his eyes wide with shock. "You? What are you doing here?"

"Does it matter?" Martin shouted over the noise. "What should I do to help? How can we stop the water?"

Carl grumbled something under his breath that Martin was glad he couldn't actually hear. Then he said more clearly, "The valve on the main line is stuck. The faucet must be rusted. This one might work. Reach up here, help me turn it."

Martin could see that Carl was too weak to turn the wrench but wouldn't admit it. Martin ran through a puddle and grabbed the tool. Carl sank back in a coughing fit, doubled over. Martin turned, afraid the older man would collapse on the floor.

Carl waved at him with a desperate expression. "Do as I said! Shut off that blasted water!"

Martin looked back at the pipe and gripped the wrench. It didn't turn at first, but finally, he put his weight into the effort and felt it move a bit, then a little more. He twisted with all his might, and the water gushing from a split pipe on the ceiling, a few feet away, trickled and stopped.

Martin stepped back, sagging with relief. But when he turned, Carl was on the basement floor, gasping for breath. He ran to his side, crouched down, and cradled the old man in his arms.

Carl stared up, looking suddenly weak and gentle. He was trying to say something, and Martin leaned very close so he could understand the murmured words. "Tank . . . get it. Choir room . . ."

The oxygen tank. He should have remembered. He pulled Carl to a dry space and stuffed a canvas drop cloth under his head. Then he ran to the bottom of the stairs.

Claire was coming down to see what was happening, and he shouted to her, "Carl needs his oxygen tank. I think it's in the choir room. Call nine-one-one. He needs an ambulance."

"Right away," Claire called back, and disappeared.

Martin ran back to Carl, who lay with his eyes

closed, struggling for breath. The sound of his wheezing was agonizing. Carl's eyes suddenly opened and he gripped Martin's hand. He tried to sit up, his wordless distress beyond anything Martin had ever seen. Then he sank back, looking as if he had gone unconscious.

Martin felt for a pulse and a heartbeat. He didn't know much first aid, but he realized Carl wasn't breathing. He pulled away the canvas pillow and started CPR, breathing into Carl's mouth for a steady count and watching to see if his chest rose and fell on its own.

"Come on, Carl. Please. Hang in there . . ." Finally, he saw Carl start to breathe again, but he continued to work on him, not daring to stop, waiting for the oxygen tank or the ambulance. Waiting for help of any kind at all.

Finally, he felt a hand on his shoulder. "Martin, I have the oxygen. And the ambulance is here. They'll be right down."

Martin looked up. It was Reverend Ben. He knelt down on the other side of Carl and fitted on the oxygen mask. Carl's eyes slowly opened. He stared around, looking dazed, then his gaze fixed on Martin's and held it.

Martin leaned back on his heels. His pants were soaked from kneeling in the water. He hadn't even realized.

"We couldn't find the oxygen tank. It wasn't where he usually keeps it. He'd left it in the cloak closet," Reverend Ben explained. "I think you saved his life."

Martin sighed, too overwhelmed to speak. "I hope so," he said finally.

An EMT ran down the steps and came over to examine Carl. Martin quickly explained what had happened.

"He has emphysema," Reverend Ben added. "He's had frequent episodes like this lately."

Martin could attest to that. He wondered if there had been any more trips to the ER since he had taken Carl there with Louisa almost two weeks earlier.

Two more medical technicians carried a stretcher down the steps. Carl's face was covered by a larger oxygen mask, and he was carefully lifted onto the stretcher and strapped down.

"Let's go up now," Reverend Ben said. "We'd better get out of their way."

Martin followed the minister up to the top of the stairs, where Vera and her friends were waiting. Louisa's uncle Tucker was just coming into the church. He looked distressed and ran up to them. "Where's my brother? Is he okay?"

"The emergency technicians are about to bring him up, Tucker. He needed oxygen, but I think he'll be okay," Reverend Ben told him. "Martin gave him CPR."

Tucker met Martin's glance and touched his arm. "Thank you, Martin. Thank God you were able to help him." Then he headed downstairs, unable to wait.

Vera came to stand beside Martin and patted his arm. "Martin, thank goodness you were here. What would have happened if you hadn't driven me to church today?"

"Lucky for Carl. More than luck," Sophie said. "Someone was watching over Carl Tulley today, that's for sure."

Martin couldn't answer, knowing he was the least likely guardian angel for the old man. The EMTs finally appeared at the top of the stairs, bearing their patient on a stretcher, with Tucker following behind them.

Martin ran to open the door and saw a police car pull up.

Louisa climbed out and looked straight at him, her expression pure surprise.

Then she stood at her car and watched as Carl was loaded into the ambulance. She spoke briefly with her uncle just before he climbed in the back. Seconds later, the ambulance was gone, the siren quickly fading in the distance. Martin waited by the church door, wondering if Louisa would leave, too. She gave him a long, considering look. Then she walked toward him, her chin held high. He took a breath and waited.

"Thank you for helping Carl. Uncle Tucker said you may have saved his life."

"I just did what I could. He was lucky. Reverend

Ben found his oxygen, and the ambulance came in time."

"From what I heard, you should take more credit than that," she said quietly. She met his gaze a moment and looked away. "I don't even know why Uncle Carl is still working. Everyone in the family has asked him to quit. Even Reverend Ben has spoken to him about it."

Martin had wondered about that, too. "What will happen now? Surely he can't keep going like this. Didn't you tell me that your family is working something out for him?"

"They're trying to. Uncle Tucker found a place in Peabody where Carl can live, where he can have his independence and get the care he needs. It's much nicer than the place he lives now."

Most anyplace would be, Martin thought. "What's the holdup? Is there a waiting list or something?"

"They have room. Carl would have to pay the first six months, then it would be free. But six months costs a little over thirty thousand dollars. Of course, he has no savings. My family is trying to figure out how to cover it, but everyone has their own responsibilities."

Martin felt upset and confused. "Louisa . . . why didn't you tell me this sooner? I could have helped him. I could have easily covered that for him."

She sighed. "I know . . . I tried to explain that I knew of someone who could help Carl, no strings attached. But my family is too proud. Uncle Tucker said we don't take charity." Her gaze met his, her blue eyes piercing his soul. "That night we took Carl to the hospital, I thought you would see for yourself that he needed help. But he didn't make it easy for you."

"He didn't," Martin agreed. "But I should have thought of it anyway. I shouldn't have taken anything he did or said personally. He was hurting and frightened."

He had finally seen that today, and had felt real sympathy for Louisa's uncle—a sick, scared, lonely man. Why was life so filled with "If only . . ." lately? It didn't seem right.

"Is it too late? Did you spend all the money?"

"I bought Vera a new car. That was the last of it, and then some."

Louisa didn't answer for a moment, just gazed out at the village green. "All right. I guess that's that, then. We'll figure something out. Tulleys are a resourceful bunch." From what he'd seen, he would never doubt that.

She looked back at Martin, squaring her shoulders. "I thought you left for Boston."

"I was on my way. But Vera needed a lift to church." He paused and tried to catch her gaze, but she kept looking away. "I wanted to say good-bye. I sent you a text. Maybe you didn't see it? I understand if you didn't want to answer," he quickly added.

"I saw it. I didn't know what to do." She finally met his glance, and the proud, hurt, hopeful look on her face nearly broke his heart.

Her radio signaled and she grabbed it off her belt. He heard a garbled voice, a street name, and some numbers, describing an incident, he guessed.

"Copy that. On my way," she replied. She sighed and looked up at him. "Have a safe trip. No speeding now, right?"

He nodded, all the sweet words he really wanted to say flying out of his head in all directions. Like the butterflies he used to chase and capture and then let loose into the summer sky all at once.

She ran off to the police car. "Say good-bye to Milo for me," she called over her shoulder.

"I will," he said. *And Milo will want some explanation for how I ever let you get away from us, Louisa Tulley.*

CHAPTER FIFTEEN

Christmas Day, Sunday, December 25, 1955

STILL WEARY FROM ALL THEIR HARD WORK, Walter and Frances had overslept Christmas morning and were nearly late for church. When they returned home, Walter headed straight for the Christmas tree, eager to open their presents.

"Walter, wait for me. You're like a little boy," Frances said, laughing at him. She carried a tray of eggnog and Christmas cookies and set it on the side table. Walter wasn't even thinking of his own gifts, though he saw several there, wrapped with care. He could hardly wait for Frances to open the gifts he had found for her.

"Let's see . . ." He reached under the tree and handed her a slim box, a cheerful candy cane pattern on the wrapping paper. "Open this one first, I think . . . then this big one."

While Frances stared down at the first box, he pulled out a second box that was much larger. Then a very small one, wrapped in gold paper.

"When did you go shopping? You must have

hidden these from me very well," she said, in awe at the pile.

"I can't tell you all my tricks." He sat back and watched her, waiting to see what she thought of his gifts.

The first box contained a pair of leather gloves, soft as silk and lined with fur. Her eyes widened as she took them out and tried them on. "Walter . . . these are beautiful. The leather is so soft." She stared at him. "They must have cost a fortune."

He could see she was thinking the gift was too expensive and had to go back. "Please don't worry about that. It's fine, Frances. Really. I promise."

He wasn't just humoring her. His gifts had been purchased at the last minute, after he had calculated the profits from the sales they had made over the last week or so. Even deducting the bank payment, the luxuries were well within their means—an experience Walter had known very rarely.

"Open the next one, hurry," he urged her.

She gave him a curious look, then tore the bright paper on the big package. She opened the box and lifted out a beautiful suit of camel-colored wool, a short jacket with a nipped-in waist and a long, slim skirt. Frances would look stunning in it, he was very sure.

"Walter . . . this is too much. I was eyeing this suit in Nancy's shop," she admitted.

"I know, I asked her to help me. She even knew that you had tried it on."

Frances blushed. "I guess I did. I was hoping that after the winter, she might mark it down. If it was still there. I hope she gave you a discount."

"We figured it out," he said vaguely. "You're a businesswoman now, Frances. A partner in an up-and-coming toy company. You need a good suit."

"When you put it like that, I guess it's okay. I do love it. It's so smart, and the tailoring is excellent," she said, fingering the smooth shawl lapel.

"You deserve it, dear, and much more, for all your hard work. I got us into some hot water," he admitted. "But you never lost your cool head."

"We're a team, Walter. You said it yourself." She looked down at the last gift. "What's in here?"

"Open it. Let's find out." He turned to Otis, who sat right by his side, watching intently. "What do you think that one is, Otis?" He leaned over and listened. "No, it's not biscuits. That's what *you* like," he said to the dog, making Frances laugh.

She had unwrapped the small box and clicked open the lid.

"Oh my goodness . . . this is so beautiful, Martin." She held up a black velvet box where a gold locket nestled against white satin. "Where did you find it?"

"In my travels," he said. "Let me help you put it on."

He rose and Frances pushed her hair aside. Walter took the locket and closed the clasp. Then he gently turned her around to see how it looked.

Frances touched it and smiled. "I love it, Walter. I'll put your picture inside and wear it every day."

He smiled. "I made sure to get one that has room for more than one photo," he said quietly. They both knew he meant the photo of a baby. But he was too happy today to dwell on any lack in their life.

With her fingertips still on the locket, she said, "We'll have a family, in time. One way or the other. If I've learned anything this week at all, it's that God works in mysterious ways. And on His own timetable."

"That is for sure," Walter agreed.

Frances had several gifts for him and for Otis. She gave Walter a fancy argyle sweater, a set of fine drawing pens and a leather-bound sketch-book, and a box full of history books, *The Story of Civilization* by Will Durant. Walter had been borrowing copies from the library, but Frances knew how much he wished that he owned them.

"Frances, these are beautiful. The whole set?" He dug through the box and pulled out four thick volumes.

"What there is of it so far. The saleswoman

at the bookstore said the author plans to write seven more. I thought it was a good place to start building your library. We can fit a new bookcase right there, next to the fireplace."

"Good idea. These books deserve a special spot. And more to come," he added cheerfully.

Otis stuck his head in the box of books and sniffed. Walter laughed at him. "New books smell good, don't they, Otis? But that's my present. Don't worry, you've got a few presents of your own."

Otis got a stocking full of treats and chew toys, and a sweater that Frances had made for him, just like the sweater worn by the stuffed dog that carried his name. He didn't seem to mind wearing it, once they got it on.

"He looks very dignified," Walter said. "Maybe you could make him a little hat, too?" One of the stuffed dogs had been left under the tree, and Walter held it up, comparing the copy to the life-size original.

"That would be a sight," Frances said.

"I think we need to take a family photo. I can't remember a better Christmas. Not even when I was a boy. I never expected we would be so happy today," he admitted. "We're able to repay the bank every penny next week. Thanks to Santa's Dog." He stared down at the stuffed toy in his hand. "That has to be a miracle, don't you think?"

"Maybe, but you had the idea, Walter. And the talent to make it turn out so adorable. You have to give yourself some credit."

"Yes, I created it. But I really feel it was an inspiration from above. And it wouldn't have come to much if Oliver hadn't helped us. He's got to be our guardian angel. In his hand-tailored suits and British sports car."

Frances smiled. He could tell she agreed with him. "He looked very happy today with his new wife on his arm. Lillian? Is that her name?"

"Yes, it's Lillian. I heard that she's from Boston. Leave it to Oliver to elope with a girl on Christmas Eve."

"She is beautiful. I hope they're well suited to each other. She seemed a bit overwhelmed by all the attention in church today. I can understand that."

The girl had seemed a bit aloof, Walter thought, but he didn't want to judge so hastily. "She was probably nervous, meeting so many people at once. Maybe she's shy. Any girl who marries Oliver should be prepared to be a celebrity. Around here, anyway." He smiled, thinking about his friend. "Oliver was distracted all week. I knew he was planning something. But he wasn't too distracted to think of us, too."

Otis was up on the couch, and his head rested in Frances's lap. She stroked his fur, half listening. "What do you mean?"

"Today in church he told me about a toy company in New York. He's told the owner about Santa's Dog, and they want to meet with us. Oliver said they want to make a deal to manufacture Otis and sell him all over the country next Christmas. This company is sure the toy will be a huge hit, just from the way it sold around here the last few weeks."

Frances sat up, jarring their snoozing pet. "Walter, is that really true? Are we really going to meet with this man?"

"All I have to do is call tomorrow," he replied. "I have his name and number right here." He patted his vest pocket. "Oliver may come with us, for advice. I have no idea how to make a big business deal like this."

"We'll figure it out, dear. Just like we've figured out everything else." She sighed. "I can hardly take this all in. Do you realize our worries are over? All because of a silly little dog." She looked down at Otis, her words full of affection.

Walter sat down next to her and took her in his arms. "We have so much to be thankful for. We'll have our family, Franny. In due time."

"I know." She touched the locket again. She had tears in her eyes, but she smiled. "Let's just enjoy our peace and good fortune, and share our blessings wherever we can. That will be our family tradition."

Walter smiled at her suggestion. He would never be one to argue with that.

Sunday, December 23, 2018

WHEN MARTIN WOKE UP ON SUNDAY morning, it took a moment for him to remember he was back in his own apartment in Cambridge, and no longer at Vera's house. He sat on the edge of his bed, collecting his thoughts. Milo stared at him hopefully, and his tail beat the floor when Martin looked his way.

"Right, pal. I'll take care of you. It's getting late."

He dressed quickly and took Milo for a walk around the neighborhood, returning with thick Sunday editions of both the *Boston Globe* and the *New York Times* under his arm and a bag that held a large coffee and a muffin. A far cry from one of Vera's sumptuous breakfasts. He already missed her cooking, and even her cheerful chatter.

For weeks now, he'd been pulled away from his Sunday ritual of reading the newspapers front to back. Finally, he could go at it uninterrupted all day. But the pile of papers on the kitchen table didn't look as enticing as he remembered. Catching up on the news would hardly occupy his day. His apartment was in order, just as he had left it, and there was no cleaning up to do, save emptying his suitcase. The rooms looked a bit bare, and even sterile, compared to Vera's cozy house, decorated for Christmas. He wondered if he should pick up a little tabletop tree, but quickly dismissed the idea. He never did that. Why start this year?

A patch of gray sky, framed by the window, promised snow, or at the very least, a cold, raw day. Still, the last-minute shoppers would brave the weather, he guessed. He had sent a few gift cards to Arizona, and had no other Christmas obligations. Unless he visited friends. A few had been in touch by text, inviting him to holiday gatherings, large and small. Martin had his choice and scanned his messages, knowing he should reply. Though he wasn't sure if he felt like taking part in Christmas parties this year.

His father had also called last night while he was driving, and he had been too tired to call back after he came in. It was still early in Arizona, but Martin knew his father would be up and out on a golf course while the sun was still low in the desert skies. Martin did not expect his father to interrupt the game and pick up the call, but thought he would try anyway and leave a message.

To his surprise, Tom Nightingale answered on the second ring. "Martin, hello. How are you doing? Are you back in Boston yet?"

"I just got back last night. I'm doing fine. A little tired," he admitted, though he wasn't really physically tired, he thought; more weary of spirit. As if he'd been on a roller-coaster ride and had come crashing down.

"You don't quite sound yourself. But I expect your trip was draining. Did you manage to fulfill the terms of the will? Last we spoke, you weren't sure you'd make it."

"It wasn't easy, but yes, I think I did it. I'll squeak in just under the wire. The last gift will be delivered Christmas morning," he added, thinking of the new car Vera would find at her doorstep as she left for the church service on Christmas Day.

Which reminded him that he also had to call the dealer in Beverly, to make sure the delivery was on track.

"Well done, Martin. I'm impressed . . . and very proud of you."

Martin's father did not praise him often, and rarely so extravagantly.

"Thanks, Dad. It wasn't easy, but I had a lot of help. A girl named Louisa Tulley. She's lived there her whole life and knows everyone in town." *She made it seem fun, almost . . . magical,* Martin nearly added. But he thought that would sound silly, especially to his father.

"I think you mentioned a local girl helping the last time we spoke. Will you see her again?"

Martin was surprised at the question. His father rarely inquired about his social life. He paused before answering. "No, I don't think so."

"Well, you were fortunate to meet someone willing to get involved. I don't think I could have done it, with or without help. I think your grandfather knew that. That's why he set the task for you and skipped right over yours truly."

Martin had never thought of the request that way, and he needed time to consider the idea. "I'm sure you could have done it, Dad. If you needed to."

"I'm not so sure, but I won't debate. The point is, I know it wasn't an easy assignment. You should give yourself a lot of credit. You carried out your grandfather's wishes, and that means a lot. To me, anyway. If he's looking down at us now, I'm sure he's very pleased. I can practically see that mischievous little grin."

Martin could, too, and was once more surprised by his father's candor. He didn't talk about his parents much, though Martin was certain his father had enjoyed a happy childhood. But maybe that was why it was so hard looking back—feeling the loss of his close, loving family?

"Tell me, did you see the house?" The house he'd grown up in, Martin knew he meant.

"I went there a few days before I left." He pushed aside thoughts of Louisa and the painful scene that had played out that day. "It needs some work, but it's in pretty good shape, all things considered. I think I might sell it," he added, though he was still not entirely sure.

"Really? I thought you'd keep it. If you sell, it will probably be knocked down."

His father's tone was matter-of-fact, but his words still felt like a warning.

"Yes, I've thought of that. I guess I'm still not sure."

If he did keep the house, he would have to go back, and it would be hard to know Louisa was close, yet still out of reach.

"Was it hard for you? Going back, Martin?"

"It was. More than I expected," Martin admitted.

"You were brave to face it, son. I'm not sure I could have done that either."

Martin didn't argue with him there. Visiting the old house may have even been more challenging for his father. There were even more memories there for him.

He heard voices in the background and then heard his father say, "You guys go on, I'll catch up. It's my son, in Boston."

"Are you playing golf, Dad? We can talk later."

"That's all right. I'm bogeying every hole. I might pack up my clubs and go home."

Martin laughed at his father's golfer's angst. He was actually a very good golfer but rarely satisfied with his score.

"I'm glad you called, Martin. I've been

thinking about you. I'm glad that girl was able to help . . . but I should have been there. I should have come East and gone to Cape Light with you. You shouldn't have been left to handle that all alone."

His father's heartfelt words touched Martin's heart and thoroughly surprised him. "Don't be silly. I never expected you to go with me. It never occurred to me to ask you."

"I know it didn't. That's part of the problem. I love you, Martin. More than you'll ever know. But I'm afraid I haven't shown you that. Not when it counted most," he quickly added. "I haven't been a very good father. Not since we lost your mother," he said quietly.

"Don't say that, Dad. It's not true," Martin insisted. "You've been a great father. Sure, you've gone on with your life. Mom would have never wanted you to be alone and unhappy. I don't either," he insisted. "I know that you've tried to include me with Suzanne and the kids. I haven't made it easy for you."

"All right, we both can do better. But the real blame falls on me. I'm your father and should know better. That's the way I see it, anyway. The point is, we've been too long apart, Martin. At a great distance, and not just on a map. One that's been slowly stretching, wider and wider," his father explained. "I can see that now and I'm not getting any younger. It troubles me."

While most of his father's points rang true, Martin didn't want his father to be so distressed. "I'm an adult now, Dad. You don't have to hover, or even worry about me."

"Of course, you are a very self-sufficient young man. I'm proud of that. But it does a person good, at any age, to know someone who loves them is always in their corner. That's what my parents did for me. But I don't believe you think of me that way. That's my fault entirely. Not yours, son."

Martin sighed. He wanted to reassure his father that he'd never felt any lack of attention or support, but the truth was, over the years, he had learned not to expect much in that department. He'd learned to be independent and self-sufficient and had been praised for those qualities.

"You did the best you could, Dad. I know it was hard after we lost Mom. I don't blame you for anything, believe me."

His father didn't answer for a moment. Martin wondered if the connection was lost. Then his father said, "You let me off the hook too easily. It was hard for all of us. I can't make up for the years we've lost, but we can have a better relationship. A closer relationship. You know you're always welcome here, especially on the holidays. But I want to come East and visit, just you and me."

"That would be great, Dad. I'd like that very much," Martin said honestly.

"You've set a good example. I think I should go back and see the house before you sell it. There are so many good memories there. Some of the best days of my life. I can't shut the door on all that. It isn't right."

And memories there to put to rest as well, Martin finished silently. "I understand. We should do that. Together," he added.

"Good. I'll make plans very soon," his father promised. "What are you doing for Christmas? You can still jump on a flight to Arizona. We'd love to see you."

The heart-to-heart with his father made the invitation tempting, but Martin decided to decline. "Thanks, but I'll stick around here. A few friends have invited me for Christmas parties. I won't be alone."

"All right. I'm glad you have somewhere to go. We'll call you on Christmas, and we can talk more about my visit."

"That's great, Dad. I'll talk to you then." Martin wanted to thank his father for his honesty and reassurances. But he couldn't quite find the words. *I'll tell him when he comes. It will be better face-to-face anyway.*

His father was right; they had been living at a distance in more ways than one. Martin had just accepted it. Now he was hopeful the gap would slowly close and the wounds of the past would heal, for both of them.

"Before I forget," Martin said, "do you know what happened to those toys Grandpa made that were in my room at the house? I was thinking about that little sailboat and the Santa Dog."

"I packed them up when we emptied the place. I thought you might want them someday. The box is here, up in the attic."

"Thanks, Dad. I do want them." The toys had been on his mind after talking with Digger and Grace, and visiting the house. Martin was happy to hear the precious mementos had not been lost. "And, Dad? Don't stress about your golf game," he added. "You're a very good golfer. You could have been a pro." That part was perhaps a small exaggeration, but who could really say?

Martin's father laughed. "Thanks, son. And you don't need to send me a Christmas gift now, after that package of baloney."

It was good to end the call on a cheerful note. Martin was left with a lot to think about, questions and issues he would ponder later— maybe when he took Milo to the dog park.

But first he needed to call the car salesman about Vera's Christmas surprise and make sure the delivery was going as scheduled. That was the last of the gifts from the Santa Fund. He could close the file and send all the information to the estate attorneys. He was well and done with the assignment, and very soon the terms of the will would be satisfied.

If only he could close a file on his feelings for Louisa. Since she left him standing in front of the church yesterday, he had barely stopped thinking of her. Or second-guessing his decision to break off their relationship and leave Cape Light before Christmas. Had he made a huge mistake—one he would spend the rest of his life regretting? He already regretted it. As he'd stood there with her in front of the church, all the words he had imagined saying if he saw her one last time had flown right out of his head. There would be no second chances. He knew the moment to fix their awful rift had passed. If it was even fixable.

He looked at Milo, sitting nearby. "Maybe I should write her a letter, Milo. What do you think?"

The dog gazed back at him and suddenly stretched and yawned, making a growling sound.

"Yeah, you're right. Pretty lame. What would I say? *Sorry, I acted like good boyfriend material, then totally flipped out and completely let you down.* Why would she ever trust me again?"

He had not only disappointed her, but after all the help she'd so freely given, he had failed to help her family. He could have easily solved the crisis with her uncle Carl. Which she'd hidden from him? No . . . not at all. He could never blame her for that. It was staring him in the face his entire time in Cape Light, a situation he had simply failed to see.

Because you were always thinking about yourself when you were with Carl. How he spoke so gruffly to you and acted out at the hospital. You took it all too personally, worrying about your own feelings instead of seeing that he was hurt and ashamed.

And a very sick man. You could have done a lot for him. But you missed that moment, too.

Technically, once the last gift was given to Vera, his grandfather's request would be completed. But Martin felt now that he had actually failed at his task. Contrary to his father's praise, he didn't believe his granddad would be proud. Not entirely. And, whether or not he had ever met Louisa, he would still regret not helping Carl Tulley.

Martin had not told his father that part of the story. Maybe when his father visited, they could talk it over. Maybe his father would have some advice for him.

His phone rang, and Martin recognized the name of the salesman who had sold him Vera's car.

"Mr. Nightingale? It's Frank Fowler," the salesman said. "Glad I caught you, sir. It's about the delivery of your new car."

"Great, thanks. So, we're all set for Christmas morning, right?"

"That's just it. I just found out that we're short on staff this weekend and not able to deliver it by Christmas, after all. It won't be ready until the day after, but we'll be happy to get it there then. My manager said I can drop the prep and delivery charges from your bill, too. How does the twenty-sixth sound to you?"

Martin felt a sudden pressure in his head. This couldn't be happening. Why now, after everything had gone so smoothly? And of all the presents he'd arranged, why did it have to be Vera's car? This couldn't be happening.

"Terrible, that's how it sounds," Martin blurted out. He rarely lost his temper with salespeople, but he just couldn't help it. "This gift is a surprise. I explained it to you. For an older woman who has no transportation to her daughter's house on Christmas Day. You promised the car would be ready, Mr. Fowler. You promised me it would be delivered on time."

"I know I did, and I'm very sorry. Soon as I heard, I talked to my manager, but there's nothing we can do. But I'll tell you what, I'll throw in a free cargo cover and weatherproof mats. That's a pretty good value."

Martin took a breath to get a grip on his temper. "It's not the cost, Mr. Fowler. I'd pay extra for you to just get the car there on time. Can I speak to the manager?"

"Uh . . . sure. That would be Mr. Schmidt. I'll put him right on . . . And Mr. Nightingale, thanks for your business. Have a very happy holiday."

"Same to you," Martin grumbled. No sense in killing the messenger. Though he sure felt annoyed at him.

Mr. Schmidt came on the line next, sounding harried and annoyed to be pulled into the mess. He heard Martin out for a few moments, then, in a polite but firm way, explained there was no possible way Vera's car could be ready and delivered to Cape Light by Christmas. He was sorry his salesman had promised, but if Martin checked the fine print on the receipt, he would see these matters were ultimately up to the dealer's discretion.

Martin felt frustrated and backed into a corner. He was sure that the estate attorneys would give him a pass if the last gift was not received by the deadline. It was bought and paid for, and the delay was certainly not Martin's fault.

But what really upset him was that Vera wouldn't have her new car in time for her trip to Connecticut. Sure, she could take the train, as she had planned. But that would be so difficult for her, with all her packages and luggage. Not to mention the plastic containers of cookies and cakes, a given for all her trips. It was not what Martin had planned for her.

"I'm sorry, Mr. Nightingale. I'd like to help you, but there's really nothing we can do," Mr. Schmidt said finally.

Martin hated to give in but finally assented and

ended the call. He took a deep breath, fuming inside. He wasn't sure what to do to fix this, but he knew there had to be some way to get Vera her car on Christmas morning.

Louisa would know what to do, he thought, almost tempted to call her. She was the Secret Santa Queen. But no, he had to figure this one out on his own. The final, highest—and unexpected—hurdle in the course he had to run.

CHAPTER SIXTEEN

Christmas Day, Tuesday, December 25, 2018

L OUISA AND HER FAMILY WERE LATE TO church. Her family had lingered happily by the tree, opening gifts and enjoying their traditional Christmas Day breakfast of her mother's baked French toast with apples.

The choir was already leading the congregation in the first hymn, "Joy to the World," when Louisa followed her parents, brothers, and sister into the sanctuary. Luckily, the singing and organ music provided ample cover for their noisy entrance.

Tucker spotted them and helped them find seats in the rear pews. There were five empty seats in one row, and behind that, two more on the aisle. Louisa let the rest of her family sit together and took a seat next to Vera Plante. There was one more seat empty beside her, right on the aisle, where her uncle would sit when he could steal a minute or two from his deacon's duties.

Vera stood straight as an arrow, reading glasses in place, as she sang loud and clear. She glanced at Louisa and offered her hymnal, and Louisa quickly joined in.

The carol was Louisa's favorite, but it was hard to catch up. She felt distracted and out of sync. She had felt out of sync with Christmas altogether this year, ever since Martin had broken off their relationship at the old house on the pond.

Louisa tried not to think about that. Or about the expression on Martin's face when they had said good-bye the other day, after he had helped Uncle Carl. As much as she had wanted to see him one last time before he left town, she knew it would hurt and wouldn't change a thing. And that was exactly how it had worked out.

"Merry Christmas, everyone. Behold, the child is born. Let us give thanks for this blessed day," Reverend Ben greeted the congregation, then led the opening prayers.

Louisa read along, mumbling mostly. The sanctuary looked beautiful decorated for Christmas, the altar filled with red and white poinsettias, glowing candles, and the crèche on the altar, complete with the swaddled baby in its rough wooden crib.

Louisa tried to focus on Reverend Ben's words, but her mind wandered. She wondered if Vera missed Martin, too. Or if she had heard from him the last few days. Maybe she would ask her later.

Maybe not. No sense encouraging the situation. It wouldn't do any good.

She settled back and stared down at the liturgy, knowing she had lost her place again. She felt her uncle sit down next to her but didn't look up. He leaned close and whispered in her ear, "Merry Christmas, Louisa."

Her head spun around to face him. It wasn't her uncle Tucker. It was Martin. She sat there in shock, unable to believe her own eyes. Then Vera turned, wide-eyed, and sent Martin a secret little wave. She looked surprised as well, but not nearly as stunned as Louisa felt. She noticed Vera glance at the two of them, then settle back with a pleased, knowing smile.

Louisa turned to look at him, and he met her gaze, looking very satisfied that he had caught her by surprise. He leaned over and whispered, "I'll explain everything later." Then he sat back in his seat and gave his attention to Reverend Ben.

But when he reached over to take her hand, she didn't resist. She twined her fingers with his and felt suddenly and deeply settled inside. As if she had been shaken like a snow globe the past few days and the white, whirling storm within had gracefully settled to reveal a beautiful landscape.

The service passed quickly. Tim O'Toole, the man who had received a truck for his new job from the Santa Fund, came up to the pulpit to read the day's Scripture.

Martin gently poked her with his elbow, and

they shared a secret smile. Louisa almost didn't recognize Tim in a suit and tie today, with a fresh haircut and beard trim. He looked bright and cheerful as he read the first Bible passage from the Old Testament aloud. She had the sense that he and his family were having a wonderful Christmas. Better than he'd ever expected.

Reverend Ben took the pulpit next and read from the New Testament, the Book of Luke, a passage about the angels visiting the shepherds and telling them the good news.

" 'And it came to pass, as the angels were gone away from them into heaven, the shepherds said one to another, Let us now go even unto Bethlehem, and see this thing which is come to pass, which the Lord hath made known unto us.' " The reverend lifted his head a moment and smiled, then added, " 'And they came with haste and found Mary, and Joseph, and the babe lying in a manger . . .' "

When the Scripture reading was concluded, Reverend Ben looked up at the congregation.

"For once, I took my own advice—the advice I gave everyone the first Sunday of Advent—and this year I started preparing my sermon for today well in advance. But I became distracted and pulled off track by the mystery in our own congregation, and our community—the Secret Santa, who has gifted so many of you here today."

Reverend Ben's words drew smiles and even some soft laughter from his audience. This time, it was Louisa's turn to give Martin a gentle nudge. While they both sat poker-faced, staring straight ahead, she could sense him struggling to control his expression, just as she was.

"I must put my original words aside and speak to this mystery, which isn't so far off the track of my first theme—a mystical Christmas—after all, is it?

"Today, instead of talking about the angels or the shepherds, or the Wise Men, or even the blessed family, I'm going to talk about Santa, who looms so large over Christmas, casting a big red secular shadow, if you'll permit me that notion.

"Along with sacred teaching, we're raised to believe in him, too. Most of us, anyway. And to believe in his power to know our heart's desire and deliver that longed-for gift without fail. That's what he does, what he is, his very reason for existence. By all accounts, Santa loves to do this. It's not a nine-to-five job he hopes to retire from someday. Or a burden in any way. He never complains about it. To the contrary, this responsibility fills his heart with joy.

"Children may dutifully leave plates of cookies and glasses of milk by the tree as compensation, but we know Santa will happily carry on with or without these offerings. And though some children might be coached by thoughtful parents to write Santa a thank-you note, I have a feeling he receives very few. In fact, practically none. He doesn't expect, or even want, them.

"This Advent season, I've encouraged everyone to explore the true meaning of Christmas, what it means to you and your family. I'd have to say, thinking about it now, Santa embodies most of what Christmas means to me. I don't mean to sound irreverent, or flip."

Reverend Ben paused and looked out at the congregation, gauging their reaction to his confession, Louisa guessed. Everyone was listening closely. Louisa, too, was curious to hear what their minister thought about the Secret Santa, not just the way the gifts had helped people, but the higher, spiritual meaning of the effort as well.

"The Santa who gives so generously for the sheer joy of it, with no expectation of receiving anything in return; that, in a chestnut shell, is my idea of Christmas." The reverend's voice rose on a happy and animated note.

"That's why I've put aside my carefully worded sermon to speak to you now about the Secret Santa who's given so much to so many these past few weeks. We don't know who you are, or even if you're here today among us." Reverend Ben gazed across the pews, his eyes narrowing behind his round spectacles.

Louisa glanced at Martin and saw him squirm.

He looked down at his hymnal, and for a moment, Louisa did, too, just to keep from smiling too widely.

"Let me thank you, Santa, from the bottom of my heart," Reverend Ben said sincerely. "Not just for bringing ease and joy to so many in our church family with your generous and perfectly devised gifts. But for providing us with a stunning example of God's own love and generosity in action. The love personified in His greatest gift of all, the swaddled baby in the manger. The love that we can all feel and express and act upon if we open our hearts to each other.

"Though some of us, myself included, complain about the commercialism of Christmas, it would be a sad, hollow day without gifts given and received. Not for their material value, of course. But for their spiritual essence and energy—the love and care expressed that flow through us, from God above."

Reverend Ben paused and seemed to be searching the congregation. Louisa saw a playful spark in his blue eyes, even from her distant spot at the back of the church.

"If you ask me who I think the Secret Santa might be, I have a few guesses. But first, I'd ask you, does it really matter? All that is good comes, first, from God. He is the source of all of our blessings, and certainly of all the love we experience in this brief, earthly dance. The secret benefactor is only a channel. As we all are from time to time. Or can strive to be."

He let that point settle a moment. Louisa thought it was a good one.

"Our Secret Santa—he or she—sets a high bar," he continued. "A remarkable example for us to carry forward, to live by. Not just on Christmas, but every day. An example of giving sincerely and truly from the heart, as God so gave the world His beloved Son this very day.

"So now, I'd like to ask that we all say a quiet prayer of thanks for this very special individual in our midst and the good work they've done. I'm sure it was not easy. We ask God to bless them now and in all their future efforts."

He bowed his head a moment, and everyone else did as well. When he lifted it again, he added, "May God bless you all on this day, and always. And may we all enjoy a very merry Christmas."

As Reverend Ben left the pulpit, the choir began another favorite carol, "O Come, All Ye Faithful." Louisa and Martin stood and shared a hymnal. Louisa noticed Martin's hand shaking a bit, and when she glanced up, she saw his eyes glossy with unshed tears.

Vera leaned over and whispered to her, "Wonderful sermon. But if the reverend knows who it is, I wish he would have told us. So many people here want to thank that person."

Louisa smiled but didn't answer. She doubted

that Martin wanted to be thanked, even if the terms of his grandfather's will had made that possible. Maybe the unexpected spotlight Reverend Ben had just put on Martin's efforts had been enough.

Finally the service was over. Reverend Ben gave his blessing to the congregation and the choir sang the "Hallelujah" chorus from Handel's *Messiah*. Louisa always loved that part of the Christmas Day service but could hardly wait for the last hallelujah to ring out so that she and Martin could talk somewhere privately.

But that was not going to happen as fast or as easily as she had hoped. As soon as they filed out of their pew, Martin leaned over and whispered to her, "I want to talk to you, Louisa. But first, we need to get Vera out to the parking lot."

Louisa wondered if it had something to do with Vera's gift. She knew Vera was due to get her new car today, and maybe that had not happened yet?

Before she could ask, Vera leaned over and quickly hugged Martin. "Martin, I'm so happy to see you. You came back for Christmas, after all."

She glanced at Louisa, then back to him. "I had a feeling you'd left too soon."

"I think you're right," Martin agreed easily. "I had to come back for a few reasons, it turned out. Partly to give you a ride to the train station this morning. You're still going to Connecticut, aren't you?"

"My train leaves in half an hour. But I called a cab, you needn't bother."

"I want to Vera, honestly. Milo's in the car; he's waiting to see you."

Vera laughed. "All right then. I'm just going to wish Reverend Ben a merry Christmas and I'll be right out. I'll meet you in the parking lot in two shakes. My bags and things are in Fellowship Hall. I can't miss this train. I'll never get there today otherwise."

"I understand. We'll wait for you out back."

Then Martin took Louisa's hand and pulled her out of the sanctuary and through the crowd that had gathered just outside the big doors, spilling out to the corridor. But instead of going out the back door of the church, he led her out the side. Luckily, she had grabbed her coat off the back of her seat and slipped it on in time to meet the chilly but bright day.

"But we're supposed to meet her in the lot, Martin," Louisa said.

"I know. But we're going to wait here, out of sight. And watch her reaction."

He led Louisa down the side of the church, where they could see the parking lot but were still out of view.

He stepped aside, and she saw a brand-new Subaru Outback with a big red bow on top, parked right in front of the exit from Fellowship Hall. A hand-lettered sign across the windshield read: *For Vera Plante. Love, Santa.*

"It's beautiful, Martin. She'll be so surprised. But I thought the car was going to be delivered to her house this morning."

"That got messed up . . . but turns out, it was a good thing. It made me realize I had to come back." He looked down and met her gaze and held it. "For a few reasons. As I told Vera."

Before he could say more, they saw Vera emerge from church, carrying a suitcase. Her friends Claire and Nolan followed close behind with several shopping bags. How Vera had ever expected to carry all that on her train ride was anybody's guess. But now she didn't have to, Louisa realized.

"Let's get out of sight. I don't want her to suspect."

Before the seniors could spot them, they stepped back to watch, shielded by the shrubbery.

"Vera . . . what's this?" Claire was the first to see the car. She turned to Vera and her husband, Nolan. "It looks like the Secret Santa struck again!"

Vera dropped her bag and trotted the rest of the way down the path. She stared at the car and took a few steps around it, then pulled off the sign.

"Heaven help me! I can't believe it!" She

pressed a hand to her chest, looking as if she might faint.

Nolan stepped up beside her and grabbed her arm. "Steady, Vera. Would you like to sit down and get your breath?"

Vera didn't answer. An envelope was taped to the sign, and she pulled it open. She quickly read the note and removed a set of shiny keys.

"I'll have a seat in my new car, thank you, Nolan. I might as well get used to it."

She pressed the remote, unlocked the door, and slipped inside. With the widest grin Louisa had ever seen, Vera sat back and beeped the horn.

Louisa and Martin heard her whoop with joy, and they burst out with laughter. Martin turned to Louisa and grabbed her shoulders. "Time for some serious acting. Are you with me?"

She nodded her head in agreement and gathered her composure.

Then she followed Martin to the parking lot.

"Vera! What is this? A new car?" Martin walked around the car, feigning his delighted surprise in a very convincing way, Louisa thought.

"What an awesome car, Vera!" Louisa chimed in. "You just found it here? Waiting for you?"

Vera nodded, smiling from ear to ear. "It had this sign stuck on the windshield, and this letter with the keys in it. And a full tank of gas, too," she added, peering at the dashboard.

"More than enough to get you to where you

need to go," Martin remarked. "That car gets good mileage."

"I'll bet. Not like my old gas-guzzler, that's for sure. I'd better get going. There will be some traffic, but I'll be driving on a cloud. This has to be the best Christmas ever!"

Vera came out of the car and supervised the loading of her luggage, shopping bags of gifts, and containers of Christmas treats. Then she hugged everyone good-bye.

"Safe travels, Vera," Martin said.

"Thank you, dear. Merry Christmas, everyone. God is good. Don't ever forget it."

She climbed back into the car and, with a delighted smile, started the engine and slowly drove out of the parking lot.

Louisa stood next to Martin and watched Vera drive out of view. Then he turned to her and took her hand. "Let's walk to the harbor, where we can talk."

Louisa nodded. Her thoughts exactly.

THEY HEADED ALONG A PATH THROUGH THE green that led to the Harbor—and the dock where they had sat outside one night and looked up at the stars. Martin thought that place would be a good one for his apology. Although he was encouraged by Louisa's reaction to his appearance at church, he knew he still had some explaining to do.

He wasn't sure where to start and didn't say anything as they fell into step.

"You must feel relieved, seeing the last gift from the Santa Fund delivered," Louisa said.

He glanced at her, distracted by the sight of her right beside him, her beautiful red hair touched by the bright sun and lifted by the breeze.

"I'm happy to see Vera in her new car. There was a moment or two when I didn't think I could get it here in time."

Louisa looked curious, and he quickly explained the distressing phone call he'd had two days earlier with the dealership, and how he'd finally solved the problem by canceling that sale and calling every dealer within one hundred miles in order to find a car that could be readied by Christmas Eve that he could pick up and drive to Cape Light that morning.

"So where's Milo?" Louisa asked. "I hope you didn't forget him in Vera's new car?"

Martin laughed. "Of course not, though I'm sure he wouldn't have minded spending Christmas with Vera's family. He's back in Boston, with a friend. Well taken care of, I'm sure."

"You even left your dog to make Vera's gift work out," Louisa marveled. "That's sweet, Martin. You really closed the book with a bang."

"It was a bang, but the book isn't closed yet. There's still at least one more gift that was delivered this morning—and still to be found."

They had come to the end of the dock, and Martin looked out over the bay. A trio of gulls sat atop the worn pilings, preening their feathers.

"What is it? Can you tell me?" She looked up at him, her eyes as blue as the sky above.

"A check to cover the expenses for Carl's first six months at that assisted-living community Tucker found. I left an envelope and a note at Tucker's house. It was on my way, and I get the sense he handles these matters for his brother."

"Yes, he does. That was a good way to do it," Louisa replied evenly, though she looked dumbfounded. She blinked and didn't say more. Then she turned and stared up at him. "I thought you said the Santa Fund was gone. Used up with Vera's car and then some."

"It was gone. But I decided that didn't matter. I used my own money. I wanted to do this for Carl. I needed to. Not just for you," he added, glancing at her, "though I'd be lying if I said my feelings for you had no part in it. But mainly because it was the right thing to do. The only thing to do if I really want to fulfill my grandfather's wishes. Not just technically, but the real spirit of what he wanted me to do. What he wanted me to learn."

He stared out at the water, struggling to put his feelings into words. "When I dropped off that gift, I felt as if I'd finally learned the lesson my grandfather set out for me, Louisa. It made me very happy to help Carl. It's what I really *wanted* to do. That's what my grandfather was trying to show me. It's really very simple. I just kept making it so complicated."

"I think you're right," she said quietly. "But still, there aren't many people who would take that step, not after all you've done for everyone else. I know my family will be very grateful. And impressed," she added.

"That's good to know." He met her gaze, his expression hopeful. "As long as you're pleased? That's enough for me."

She held his glance and tilted her head to the side. "Really? Is that your story now, Mr. Hanson? You didn't seem very concerned about my feelings last weekend at your grandparents' house."

He had expected this but was relieved to hear the teasing note in her words.

"I plead . . . totally confused and completely idiotic." Then in a more serious voice he said, "Honestly, I don't know how I could have been so stupid to say the things I did, Louisa. So confused to push you away. I guess I was scared. But that's no excuse. If you give me just one more chance, I'll never let you down again. I promise."

She sighed, and he wondered what the verdict would be. She rested her hands on his shoulders and stared into his eyes. "Okay, Martin. I'll let you off this time. With a warning."

"I'll take that deal in a heartbeat." Then he

dipped his head toward hers, unable to wait a moment longer to kiss her.

Their lips met in a sweet, warm kiss as her arms wound around his neck and his arm circled her waist and nearly lifted her off the ground.

Martin wasn't sure how long they stood there. He was lost in the sensations of their embrace and never wanted it to end.

Noisy gulls swooped overhead, breaking the silence. He tilted his head back, feeling he might jump for joy.

"I had to come back. I could never let things end with you the way they did," he said quietly.

"It's good to hear you say it. I wasn't so sure," she confessed, her head tucked under his chin.

"I've thought about the house, too. I've decided to keep it. It's as good a place as any to decide what I want to do next. Maybe the best place."

"It could be." She pulled back and met his gaze. "What about all that traveling you planned . . . to reinvent yourself?"

She recalled his words too accurately, and he felt a bit embarrassed by that plan now. "Running off to reinvent myself seems a bit childish. I think I've outgrown that fantasy."

"I think so, too. You seem different than when you came here, Martin. In a good way."

He smiled at the compliment. "That's mostly because of you, Louisa. You make me want to be a better man."

She laughed. "I won't take all the credit. But I think I am a good influence."

"An influence I won't mind more of," he said, hugging her close.

"We'd better get back," she said. "My family will be wondering what happened to me. Do you want to have Christmas dinner with us?" She paused, her expression suddenly nervous. "No pressure, Martin. It's fine either way. I just thought I'd offer."

"Of course I want to come. I thought you'd never ask."

She laughed and squeezed his hand as they started back down the dock. "Not so fast," he said. "I have one more gift to give. It won't take long."

She stared at him. "Right here, you mean? A gift for me?"

"That's right. It's not part of the Santa Fund, but related, in a way." He pulled a slim package from the inside pocket of his jacket, a rectangular box wrapped with gold paper and a white bow. "Merry Christmas, Louisa."

She took the box and stared at it, looking very surprised. "Martin, you shouldn't have. I don't have anything for you."

"That doesn't matter. Read the card first, please."

She opened the small envelope, and as she read the words to herself, he silently recited them. He had worded it so carefully, he knew the message by heart.

"Dearest Louisa, if you're reading this card, then you've forgiven me for my foolishness and my heart is full of joy. This gift belonged to my grandmother. I never met anyone I wanted to give it to, though I've often imagined who that woman might be. You are more wonderful than I could have ever expected or imagined, and now you know my heart belongs to you."

"Oh, Martin . . ." Louisa's eyes looked glassy as she put the card aside and gazed up at him.

"Go ahead, open it," he urged her, touched by her reaction to his heartfelt words.

She quickly tore open the paper and snapped up the lid of the dark blue velvet jewelry box. Nestled on the satin lining, she found a gold locket, heart shaped, on a long gold chain.

Louisa looked awestruck, and his heart did a happy flip. "Martin . . . this is exquisite. It belonged to your grandmother?"

"My grandfather gave it to her for Christmas, before my father was born."

"It's so beautiful . . . I love it. Will you help me put it on?"

He stepped behind her and lifted her hair, then carefully fastened the clasp. When she turned to face him, she was smiling, touching the gold heart that hung just a few inches down her neck. It sparkled in the sun.

"It has a place for pictures," he said. "I'll show you how to open it later."

"Good. I'm going to put your picture inside and wear it every day."

Martin's heart felt so full, he couldn't reply. "That makes me very happy, Louisa . . . because I love you."

He hadn't meant to tell her. It was too soon, he worried. He hadn't even been entirely sure himself—or didn't want to face it. But once he got back to Boston, he knew. Fat lot of good it did him there.

Martin waited, wondering what she would say. Was it too much? Had he scared her away?

She took his hands in hers and lifted her face to his. "I love you, too, Martin. Very much. I don't know how or when it happened. But I'd never deny it. Seeing you in church today was the answer to a prayer. And hearing you say that you love me makes this the best Christmas of my entire life. I couldn't be any happier."

Martin swept her up again in his arms and buried his face in her flower-scented hair. "I don't think I could be happier either, Louisa. But if you stay with me forever, I'll sure try."

Epilogue

~~~

Wednesday, December 19, 1956

"You picked the perfect spot for the tree, Franny. It looks perfect framed by the windows." Walter added the last ornament and stepped back to admire their work.

"There were so many places we could have put it. We didn't have many choices in the apartment."

He laughed. "Very true. Maybe we should put a tree in every room. That would be fun."

And they could afford it, though Frances knew he was only teasing. Even though they were well-off now by anyone's standards, his thrifty habits lingered. "Our first Christmas tree in our new home. We should take a picture," he said.

"Yes, we should. But Otis looks so comfortable. Let's not wake him right now. Let's just sit awhile and enjoy the fire. This is such a comfortable room."

"It is," he agreed. He leaned over a moment and patted the snoozing dog, who was stretched out on a fluffy bed near the fire. Then he sat down beside Frances on their new couch.

There was another, smaller and more formal, parlor off the dining room, but they had decided to use this room as a study and a library.

"I'm going to build some bookcases in here, floor to ceiling, on every wall. Then I'm going to fill them all with books."

Frances twined her arm in his and rested her head on his shoulder. "I hope you do, Walter. You have a few boxes to start with," she added, glancing at the boxes in the corner that still needed unpacking.

"I'll start right after Christmas. When the business is slow. Though these days, there's rarely a dull moment."

"And thank heaven for that," Frances murmured.

"Yes, thank heaven. And Oliver," he replied.

Through Oliver's connections and with his advice, Walter had struck a deal with a toy manufacturer, and the Santa Dog had hit the stores all over the country, just in time for Christmas. Their business was booming, and their lives had changed overnight.

They had found a beautiful Victorian house on the pond, not far from their good friends Sophie and Gus Potter. With Frances's good taste and artful touch, Walter was sure their home would be a showplace in no time. She'd already had it painted a beautiful shade of yellow, with whimsical touches on the door and shutters.

"I'd like to get Oliver something special for Christmas," Walter said. "I don't think we even gave him a present last year."

"Yes, we definitely should, though he's going to be a hard one to buy for. I had a thought, Walter," she added. "Would it be all right if I bought Lydia Bauer a new sewing machine? I stopped by to say hello to her the other day when I was in town, and her old Singer is on the blink, past the point of repair now, I think. You know how she relies on it for her income, and she helped us so much last year when we ran that little factory in the carriage house. She was our best seamstress."

"Yes, of course. That's a great idea, Frances. Let's get her the machine and give it to her as a surprise. She doesn't even have to know who it's from."

"That's perfect, Walter. You know how proud she is. The last thing I want to do is embarrass her."

"Of course not, Franny. Now that we're comfortable, we should share our good fortune with our friends, don't you think?"

"I do, Walter. Otherwise, what's the point of it? I bet if we think about it a bit and maybe even ask a few discreet questions, we can find a lot of other folks in town that we can help this Christmas."

Walter nodded and squeezed his wife's shoulder. "That's a wonderful idea, Franny. That's exactly what we should do." He sighed, happy to be so in sync with his wife. They were so often of one mind and heart, especially when it really mattered.

"It will be fun to do the shopping this year," he said. "We'll have to make a list. Otherwise, it's only you buying for me and me buying for you."

"True," she said, drawing out the word. She turned her head to meet his gaze. "I already have a surprise for you. I don't think I can wait for Christmas morning."

"Oh, I can wait. You don't need to ruin the surprise, honey."

"But I don't want to wait. Not a minute longer. Walter . . . I'm going to have a baby."

The words hit him like a thunderbolt. He could barely believe his own ears. He sat up straight and gripped her shoulders. "Really? A baby? . . . Are you sure, Frances?"

She nodded, tears spilling from the corners of her dark eyes. "I took the test last week, and Dr. Elliot called this morning. I've been waiting all day to tell you. I couldn't find the right time . . ."

"Any time is the right time for this news. I'm glad you didn't wait until Christmas, darling." He pulled her close, feeling as if he would never let her go. "I'm so happy, Franny . . . I could cry.

Wait, I think I am crying," he admitted, rubbing the back of his hand across his eyes.

"I am, too," she said, between happy sniffs. "Our prayers have been answered, Walter. I never thought they would be, though I kept hoping."

"We're truly blessed, dear. We'll finally have a family, and I don't think I could be any happier, Franny . . . But I'll sure try."

Frances laughed. "I know you will, Walter. I know you surely will."

Books are produced in the United States using U.S.-based materials	Books are printed using a revolutionary new process called THINKtech™ that lowers energy usage by 70% and increases overall quality	Books are durable and flexible because of Smyth-sewing	Paper is sourced using environmentally responsible foresting methods and the paper is acid-free

Center Point Large Print

600 Brooks Road / PO Box 1
Thorndike, ME 04986-0001 USA

(207) 568-3717

US & Canada:
1 800 929-9108
www.centerpointlargeprint.com